A SPOOKY LEGACY

THE SPECTRAL FILES
BOOK 5

S.E. HARMON

This is a work of fiction. Names, characters, places, and incidents either are the product of the author's imagination or are used fictitiously. Any resemblance to actual persons, living or dead, events, or locales is entirely coincidental.

A Spooky Legacy © 2024 by S.E. Harmon.

Cover Art © 2024 by S.E. Harmon.
Cover content is for illustrative purposes only and any person depicted on the cover is a model.

All rights reserved. This book is licensed to the original purchaser only. Duplication or distribution via any means is illegal and a violation of international copyright law, subject to criminal prosecution and upon conviction, fines, and/or imprisonment.

Any eBook format cannot be legally loaned or given to others. No part of this publication may be used or reproduced in any manner whatsoever, including but not limited to being stored in a retrieval system or transmitted in any form by any means, electronic, mechanical, photocopying, recording or otherwise, without the written permission of the author.

For Angel

When I wake up and see you lying next to me, I can't help but smile. It will be a good day simply because I started it with you.

— ANONYMOUS

FOREWORD

Before you dive in, I'd just like to mention this book contains topics that may be sensitive for some. Don't worry, there's also love and laughs and two of your favorite guys doing what they do. But there's also murder, violence, domestic abuse, the death of a child, and a brief mention of suicide. So if topics of this nature make you uncomfortable, I would give this one a skip.

I hope you enjoy this one.

Happy reading,

SEH

1

Even with its proclivity for all things spooky, this Halloween was outdoing itself.

I usually had a lot of different ways I liked to spend the holiday. There was candy involved, pilfered from Danny's hopeful stockpile for trick-or-treaters. Horror-movie marathons went well with all that candy. The movies were usually more amusing than anything...while I was watching them. They were less so when I got up to pee at three in the morning, and it not only seemed possible but *highly probable* that there was something nefarious behind the shower curtain.

Some Halloweens, I tapped into my social side and made an appearance at a party or some such. Since I'm old, that usually resulted in me haunting the refreshments table and having a few kitschy hors d'oeuvres shaped like Halloween things. I might do a stiff dance or two where I moved my arms a lot and my body very little, and then it was homeward bound for me.

When I was feeling like a particularly good uncle, I took my nieces trick-or-treating. My favorite part of the evening was candy sorting time, when I removed the "questionable" pieces from their haul. And ate them. You know, just to be safe or whatever.

Danny usually carved a jack-o'-lantern, and my mother roasted the seeds. I always did my part and licked the salt off them. This year, I decided to carve one, too, and it came out pretty well, if I do say so myself. I mean...I have to say so myself. My family wasn't exactly encouraging about it.

Danny, my husband and supposedly the love of my life, offered a vague *mmpgf* noise when I proudly showed him my work. Then he hesitantly asked if that was my practice pumpkin when he damn well knew it wasn't. The abuse didn't stop there. When left unsupervised, our geriatric German shepherd, Watson, took a bite out of the back of it. I only noticed when I came back to put the flameless candle inside. My mother assured me that it looked *much* better. The teeth marks indicated the pumpkin had been attacked, which provided an explanation for why it was so very ugly.

Ingrates.

Last on my Halloween "must do" list was singing "Thriller" while doing the dance—the parts I knew, anyway. Yes, I did the entire speaking part at the end. And the maniacal laugh, my hands upraised in claws, while my husband talked about divorce statistics loudly.

Anyway, I certainly never expected to end up in the Everglades, fresh from discovering two trash bags full of body parts. The black bags had been tucked away in a tangle of mangroves and cypress trees, the bottoms soggy with a mixture of blood and swamp water. The bags were already attracting a lot of insect activity that made my skin crawl. It was hard to keep my candy down, but I managed. Somehow.

I also managed to eat some more. Somehow.

As I watched the crime scene techs do their thing, I unwrapped yet another miniature and popped it in my mouth. I'd nicked a handful at work from our receptionist's skull-shaped candy bowl before we left...then rounded back for another handful while she was busy on the phone. Some of the smell shifted my way as someone jostled one of the bags, and my stomach lurched. I carefully avoided looking that way until I had it under control.

So. Yeah. It was pretty obvious that this day sucked, but it needed to be said. So, I did. Loudly.

Standing to my left, my husband snorted without turning my way. His big arms were crossed, legs akimbo as he surveyed the scene. Even before those perfectly shaped lips moved, I knew what he was going to say. Something about this being my fault or his name wasn't Daniel Christiansen-McKenna.

"You're the one who found them, Rainstorm," he said. Predictably. "*I* wanted to pass out candy to trick-or-treaters and watch a *Halloween* marathon."

"Those movies are terrible," I informed him, and not for the first time. "And technically, I didn't find the bodies. Franklin did."

"Explain to me who this Franklin person is, again?"

Well, first and foremost, he was a ghost. Now, I'm fully aware that seeing ghosts isn't something a detective would normally cop to. But after years of fighting the paranormal part of me—and ignoring it—I finally accepted that it wasn't going away any time soon. More importantly, I discovered how very important being a medium could be. The dead had unfinished business, and it was my business to help them set things right.

Admittedly, there had been a bit of trial and error. And by a bit, I mean avalanche, trouble rushing down behind me as I scrambled for safety. But I'm learning. Honing my unusual set of skills. My mind, previously mired in the concrete, had opened and expanded to accept the strange and downright impossible.

I wasn't sure why I could see and communicate with them. My spiritual advisor, Dakota Daydream, seemed to think I had a better connection to the earth than most. And maybe that was true. Or maybe someone up in heaven got bored and decided to put a little something extra in my Build-A-Bear kit. Whatever the case, I'd made my peace with it.

Most of the time, anyway.

I looked over at the ghost in question, dressed like an actor from a period piece. I had a feeling his outfit was real and not a costume. I was probably seeing the version of Franklin that he liked the best, the one in fawn-colored breeches and a shirt with ruffles, his brown curly hair reminiscent of Lord Byron. He looked like he would be right at home prowling some moors with a cape while he pondered lost love.

"I don't know who Franklin is, exactly," I finally said. "He hasn't been very chatty about himself. He just told me that he was having a devil of a time sleeping, and I was just the guy to help. And because he told me it was rude to ask for a favor without something in return, he decided to give me a gift that only a detective could appreciate."

As if by unspoken agreement, Danny and I both looked at the blood-soaked bags. "If ever there was a need for a gift receipt," he murmured.

"At least they're neatly bagged this time," I said with a sniff. "The way I see it, a thank-you is in order."

"Yes," he said dryly. "I'll make sure to get right on that."

A guy dressed like a domino called out something to one of the techs as she passed. She didn't pause as she hustled back to the road, which was now lined with several police cars and a CSI van. I was pretty sure the annoying domino was Detective Joss from homicide. He said something to a steampunk detective that required a lot of angry arm movement. If I had to guess, he was hoping and praying the double homicide would be kicked over to our department.

Fat chance. I might have found 'em, but fresh bodies weren't in our purview...unless they were connected through our investigation to *not* so fresh bodies. So Joss could uncross his fucking fingers.

Because Brickell Bay PD had a trick-or-treat event earlier, it was strongly suggested by the higher ups that we wear something seasonal. Suggested, commanded, whatever. So our crime scene was a bit more interesting than usual.

Danny's idea of a costume was a black *The Nightmare Before Christmas* t-shirt and some black ripped jeans. So... pretty much his usual attire plus Tim Burton. I probably didn't have any room to talk. I'd decided a tie with a jack-o'-lantern pattern was festive enough. Macy, our department receptionist, had taken one look at me and shaken her head with despair. Then she took off her cat ears headband and plopped it on my head. I'd felt more than a bit silly. Now? I was feeling right at home.

My lips twitched as I watched while Wonder Woman and a red M&M roped off the crime scene with yellow tape. My—*Franklin's*—discovery had interrupted a party in homicide. So needless to say, the mood could be described as *not very pleased with Rain Christiansen McKenna*.

But this wasn't my fault. Going quid pro quo with a ghost could be dicey business, yes, but Franklin had seemed like a perfectly lovely man. His biggest offense—since I'd known him at least—was spouting poetry at random and recounting the story of how he died.

Apparently, he'd been thrown by his darling horse, Barclay. The feisty palomino had managed to even step on him twice before she thundered off. I mean, animals would be animals, but there was a ghost horse who wouldn't be getting a fucking apple from me. But Franklin? He still *loved the horse.* So how was I to know that such a soft soul would gift me a dumping ground?

"I'm waiting," I said after it was clear Danny wasn't going to give any gratitude.

"For what?"

"My thank-you, of course."

He snorted. "Thank you, sweetheart. Thank you for delivering me bags full of body parts. Thank you for them being headless—why not, after all—which should make our victims exceptionally difficult to identify. Thank you for making sure it was in the Everglades, because it's no fun standing around a crime scene unless you're—" He smacked his arm and then continued grimly. "A one-man buffet for mosquitos."

"They do love you for some reason," I murmured. And more than anyone else, at that.

He wasn't quite done. "And lastly, I'd like to extend a huge thank-you for discovering what is probably another serial killer, operating freely right under our collective noses."

I stuffed another miniature in my mouth. "Took you long enough," I mumbled around a mouthful of chocolate and nougat. "Also, this isn't going to be ours. They'll kick it out to homicide, just you wait and see."

He didn't look convinced in the least. He also seemed extremely interested in my candy consumption. "Do you have any more of those?"

"No," I said quickly. The four in my pockets were certainly melty by now, and I wouldn't give substandard candy to the love of my life. I couldn't possibly.

At the sound of Danny's phone buzzing, my shoulders tensed. I didn't relax until he answered and mouthed *Tate* at me. I blew out a quiet breath. So...not The Call, then. If I was going to do that every time his phone rang, I was going to need medication. Maybe we could just go natural and have someone follow me around, spritzing me in the face with lavender.

I'd been a bit of a wreck since he'd told me that Harper Scott, our adoption case worker, told him that we passed the vetting process. I'd been hard pressed not to demand, *But how?* I'd planned to present the best version of Rain to her. Interview Rain. Upfront, well-adjusted, and calm Rain. Fully capable of raising a little human into a full-grown adult Rain. But in my nervousness, I'd wound up presenting the *real* Rain instead.

That really should've been enough to send us to the bottom of the pile. Real Rain was a little bit neurotic, a whole bunch sarcastic, and more likely than not to say exactly the wrong thing at exactly the wrong time.

But then there was Danny.

The bastard was so stable and dependable that he'd fucking canceled out my neuroses! Upon hearing the good news—also known as the holy fuck news—he'd immediately busied himself with sending his mother a text. Predictably, Paula answered within seconds. She was already up our asses and around the corner about her future grandchild.

I'd busied myself with glaring at his stupid handsome face.

He hadn't even noticed. He just kissed the top of my head and told me that now it was just a matter of time. We just had to wait for The Call. I'd done my best to contain my asthma attack until I was in my office with the door closed. As if that wasn't enough, living with the knowledge that any day The Call could change our lives, there were the fucking bicycles in the shed.

Yes. Bicycles.

I'd found them by accident of course, as most great secrets are revealed. It's never satisfying for someone to come clean with a heavy sigh and say, "Okay, so here's the deal." No, it's much better to stumble upon treachery. To open up the door to a room, have a moment of obligatory shock, and then demand, "The fuck is this?"

It all started with a squeaky door. After digging through all of our supplies, I trudged out to Danny's shed, otherwise known as the last stop on my *where the hell did I put that WD-40* tour. And there they were, two kids' bikes sandwiched between ours. Just... *sitting* there.

Even though our bikes were identical, they were easy to tell apart. Danny's had flakes of mud in the tires and a couple scratches on the paint. Mine was almost as pristine as the day he showed up with that instrument of torture. I might not use it often, but I was pretty sure the last time I parked the damned thing, those miniature versions weren't there.

I mean, yes, we'd talked about it. And yes, we agreed to do it. But my plan had used words like *soon* and *at some point*. I'd married someone with no concept of the Hollywood-esque, "we absolutely must get together sometime." Like the time he said we should clean the garage on the weekend and actually woke me up on Sunday with gloves and garbage bags. I mean, *really*.

We'd had the house renovated, expanding a two bedroom with a massive yard into a four bedroom with a good-sized yard. I'd gotten my pool six months ago—a nice long rectangle and not that kidney-bean-shaped business. Danny thought I wanted to do laps. I'd just wanted enough room for a good-sized floaty, and now I had several.

But I'd rather forgotten the reason we'd shelled out extra dough for all that lovely space. Hell, maybe I hadn't so much forgotten as put a pin in it and stuck it to the corkboard of life. Then I moved some Post-its over the top. Really layered that bitch up like fifteen Post-its deep. And then?

Bicycles!

Christ on a pogo stick. I dug a finger in between my collar and my neck, wondering why it was so hot all of a sudden. Hopefully, he'd confer with me before he brought the little bastards home. Our kids, I mean. Shit, I should probably start cleaning up my language. If such a thing is even possible. Maybe it would be better to get a swear jar the size of our garage. That ought to put the rugra—*our kids* through college at least.

My sister, Skylar, had done some shit-stirring herself on our last anniversary.

"Rick and I talked about it at length, and I'd like to offer my uterus to the two of you," she'd said grandly. *"As a gift."*

"Well, you can stuff it right back in your body where it belongs," I informed my troublemaking twin. *"We like cash."*

Then I dodged her hand as she tried to wallop me good.

Entirely too used to our antics, Danny ignored our roughhousing. He'd looked touched, his cheeks and ears slightly pink. He reached out and pulled her into a one-armed hug, dropping a kiss on the top of her head. *"That's a nice offer, Sky,"* *he said with a smile.* *"But we're going to adopt a few. There are so many kids out there who need a home, you know?"*

I stopped joking and hugged her, too. It wasn't just a nice offer. It was amazingly generous, and I told her so. Mid-hug, something Danny had said filtered in, and my eyes bulged. *"A few?"*

He shrugged. *"Why not?"*

"One. One," *I said with emphasis.* *"We agreed on one."*

"Yes, to start with," *he said reasonably. As my eyes got even bigger, he hid a smile.* *"Whatever you want, sweetheart."*

And that was good. 'Cause we sure as hell weren't doing what *he* wanted, which apparently required the purchase of a passenger van for the Christiansen-McKenna bunch.

I jerked at the sound of Danny's soft whistle as he hung up the phone. It was a moment before I could shelve all things family-expansion related and get focused. "How's our esteemed leader?"

"Pissed." He kept swearing Lieutenant Lindsey Tate's bark was worse than her bite. He usually said that after I was nursing the sizable chunk she'd taken out of my ass, so the jury was still out on that. "She also wants to see you first thing."

"Tell her I'm dead."

"Too late." His voice was a damn sight too cheery, especially considering he'd just signed my death warrant with all caps. "I told her you'd see her at eight, sharp."

Which just goes to show you, things can always get worse.

Someone dressed as Spider-Man waved and Danny waved back before recrossing his arms. Spider-Man waved again, more vigorously this time, and Danny sighed. "I'll be back. Either Kevin found another freaking dead body, or he's got to use the bathroom."

"Either way, wash your hands," I advised, much to his amusement.

"Wow," Franklin murmured. "I...just, wow."

I turned to find his eyes trained on Danny as he strode away. Yes, I was aware of exactly how nice his ass looked in those dark wash jeans that were worn and torn in all the right places. And yes, that shirt showed off his defined biceps. That didn't mean I was putting up with all the fucking ogling, ghost or no.

I narrowed my eyes. "Would you like to see if it's scientifically possible to die twice?"

He held up his hands. "Nothing wrong with looking, is there?"

"When it comes to my husband? Yep."

"Your husband?" He hummed, his face filled with something akin to wonder and this time his *wow* was a lot less pervy and more filled with wonder. "Things...have certainly changed. Yessir, I think I'll stick around for a little while."

Okay, maybe I liked him a bit more. Didn't mean I wasn't going to try to get him to cross over. I'd learned the hard way that it wasn't good for spirits to just wander until they lost all sense of themselves. But while he was here....

I turned to Franklin, now picking flowers that verged on weed territory. "I don't suppose you can tell me anything else about these body parts," I said. "Like, I don't know, how you found them?"

He didn't bother to look my way. "I hear things."

"Okay," I said slowly. "So where are the heads?"

"Not those sorts of things."

I sighed. "Of course."

A few hours later, I spotted our ME making his way to the coroner's van. He had a trash bag in each hand and was carrying them like they were filled with unicorn dust. I saw Joss heading that way to intercept him and startled into action, hustling through the mushy sawgrass. Dammit, I had questions, too. Like how long it would be before we could turn this shitshow over to homicide.

I beat him by a couple seconds, probably because his long legs were slightly hampered by his boxy-shaped domino costume. Deckland, his partner, was only a few steps behind, his steampunk hat slightly askew. And then there was me, hands on my hips and cat ears perked. We all regarded Saunders questioningly, looking like the strangest superhero team ever assembled.

We knew better than to rush him as he polished his glasses. "Two bags, two bodies," he finally said. "Looks like we're missing more parts than just the heads, but I'll have to play a little match game in my office to be sure."

I grimaced. I preferred Monopoly, but to each his own. I had a feeling that building a Frankenbody was not a bad way to pass Halloween for a ghoul like Saunders. I couldn't help but notice he still hadn't answered the question we were all waiting for with bated breath.

I felt a presence behind me. I knew it was Danny before he even said a word. Considering how quietly he moved, that should be quite a feat. But we were connected in every possible way. Simple as that. I'd know him anywhere, even in pitch-black darkness.

Sure enough, I heard his baritone a second later. "Cut the bullshit suspense, Saunders. How long?"

I swallowed an inappropriate laugh. Hey, I never said he was a people-person. He was *my* person, and that would always be more than enough.

A whisper of a smile that Saunders would never admit to made his mustache twitch. "Well. I certainly can't give you an exact answer without proper analysis of the remains in my office," he said, drawing things out as long as possible. I had a feeling he was the type to open gifts by carefully peeling up each piece of tape. "I *can* tell you this, though. The body parts appear to have been frozen at some point."

I groaned.

Homicide 1, Cold Case Squad 0.

Joss punched the air with a quiet whoop, then fist-bumped his partner. "*Yes,*" he said with feeling just as Danny swore. "And just like that, I'm back to the party. See ya, boys. Have a good murder."

Joss and Deckland ambled back to the side of the road. Once a long, lonely stretch of highway with swampland on either side, it was now lined with vehicles. Joss turned and saluted us both, right before he got in his Ford Explorer. I wistfully watched as the taillights illuminated and he drove off.

"Fucker," Danny muttered.

I concurred thoroughly.

2

We didn't leave until after midnight.

I drove with the radio on low and the windows down so I could stay alert. My mind was usually buzzing after leaving a crime scene, but I'd passed that stage hours ago. Now I was just trying my damnedest to keep my eyes open.

As if to agree, there was a huff and a sigh from the passenger seat. I glanced over fondly at the Danny-shaped lump using his hoodie as a pillow against the window. He swore he'd help keep me awake but abandoned the plan five minutes into the drive. I wasn't mad about it. We'd caught a case where our main clue was assorted body parts in a few Hefty bags. We were going to need all the rest we could get.

Lost in thought, I saw movement in my rearview mirror and glanced up only to find my backseat fully occupied. A woman was sitting in the seat behind Danny, and oh joy, Franklin was back, too.

I sighed because it was too damn late at night to be dealing with these bloody single-minded ghosts. "That had better not be another gift. Your last one wasn't exactly a crowd pleaser."

"I didn't bring her," he protested. "She came on her own."

I glanced up in the mirror again. The woman was dressed casually in an oversized t-shirt covered in sunflowers, and black yoga pants. She was small but curvy, and short, probably no more than five two. Her wavy dark hair fell to her shoulders in a style that bordered on tousled and messy, and her face was rounded and sweet. She had whiskey-brown eyes.

Anxious brown eyes.

"Have you found my daughters?" She asked.

"Erm." I cleared my throat. "This may seem particularly redundant, seeing as how you seem to think we're in the middle of a conversation and this is the first time I'm seeing your face, but who are you again?"

"Quinn Parker," she said impatiently. "We haven't spoken?"

"Can't say I've had the pleasure, no."

"Oh." She briefly looked flummoxed. "Well, that's strange. But things *have* been a tad fuzzy since…"

She waved vaguely at herself. I couldn't see anything that would've led to her demise. Thankfully. It was rather hard to talk to someone with a gruesome injury. Unfortunately, I knew that from experience.

"I can imagine," I finally said.

"But you'll help find them, right?"

"It's kind of what I do." Unfortunately. I looked between her and Franklin and took a wistful shot in the dark. There was nothing I loved more than knocking out two birds with one stone. "I don't suppose you two know each other?"

She glanced back at Franklin as if startled to find him there, and then gave an *oh, him* kind of wave. "I'm here about my daughters. I don't know who he is and to be perfectly honest, I'm not all that bothered to know."

"I'm not all that bothered, either, in fact," Franklin said in his faintly lilting accent.

"Okay, in the competition of who's the most fucking bothered, I win, hands down," I said. That shit was undebatable. "Quinn, do you know who did this to you?"

"Well, they seem to think we left on our own," she said with a frown. "But that just can't be right."

"But you don't know for sure."

"Well...no," she admitted. "But if we left on our own, then why am I dead? Shouldn't I be living under an assumed identity someplace?"

Well, she certainly had me there.

"What do you remember about your last day?" I asked.

"I'd been fighting off a bug all weekend, and by Monday, I could tell resistance was futile," she said. "So I called in sick and worked remotely."

"Where did you work?"

"The Hope House. It's a women's center in Aventura." She smiled a little wistfully. "I got a delivery of flowers and a mini cake from Nate, which was a nice surprise. Sunflowers, my favorite."

"And Nate is your...husband?" I guessed.

"Yes. I picked up the girls after school and we settled into our normal routine. Homework, dinner, baths...the usual. Just a day like any other." When I glanced up in the rearview mirror, she was frowning. "Seems so wrong that such a day would be our last."

"What happened after dinner?" I asked quietly.

"We watched a movie, I think. I don't even remember what it was now. The girls fell asleep halfway through, so Nate and I put them to bed." Another wistful smile. "We went back downstairs to clean up and fell asleep on the couch."

I waited a few moments until I realized that was it. "That's the last thing you remember?"

"Sorry. I know that probably wasn't all that helpful." She bit her lip. "Please...just find my girls. I need to know they're okay."

"I will," I assured her. "Ferreting out the truth is kind of what I do."

I just wasn't sure she'd like the result.

I glanced up in the rearview again, wondering if there was something else I could do to help her find peace in the meantime. Dakota had helped me figure out a way to send a spirit on to the next plane—

willing or not. Of course, things went a lot smoother if they were willing, but either way, I could help them move on.

Hesitantly, I lifted my hand. Little sparkles of gold danced from my fingertips that only we could see—bridge and spirit. She reared back as if I'd thrown a live fish in her face. "Easy," I said gently. "I just thought I could help you—"

"Find my daughters." She narrowed her eyes at me. "I already told you how you can help me."

She wasn't the only one perturbed. Judging by the nervous looks he was sending me, Franklin wasn't too keen on my particular brand of help, either. "They said you'd try to do that," he said anxiously.

"Who's they?" I demanded.

Neither ghost deigned to answer what was a very clear question.

Guess it was only appropriate that I'd be gossiped about in the ghost world, too. My colleagues certainly did enough of that. Even without confirmation that I saw ghosts, they made a meal of the rumors. The general consensus seemed to be that I was nice enough but a little creepy. And our solve rate was also a touch too high for a cold case department. The higher ups seemed to concur, but with the added caveat that I was too good at my job to let go. I was certain there was a compliment in there if I squinted hard enough.

"I debated whether I should even come to you," Quinn muttered to herself. "I mean, I could've waited for the new star, but that will take far too long. I need experience. Not innocence."

"What?" I frowned. "And more importantly...what?"

"I'd like to stick around for now, so none of that if you mind." She pantomimed my fingers with the sparkles. "When you find them, my girls will be needing their mother."

"Up to you," I said. "Just trying to help."

I felt her impatient gaze on the back of my head as I continued to drive.

"So...when do we start?" She finally blurted.

"Not at freaking midnight, that's for sure," I said dryly. "Also, if I need your help doing my damn job, I'll let you know."

She huffed. "They said you'd be like this."

"Who?" I demanded again as she disappeared like a figment of my imagination. I turned my stare to Franklin, who just shrugged. "I'd rather not get involved."

Yeah, well. Too bad some of us didn't have that option.

"Pity," I murmured.

3

I hadn't planned to dive into the Parker case until Monday. But on Sunday, my father needed Danny's help in the garden. I suddenly found myself with a lot of free time. So what's a guy to do? Twiddle his thumbs? Watch TV? Tackle any one of the dozen household chores building up? All of those options—especially the last one—went under the category of *Nah*. And a subheading of *Get Real*. The Parker mystery had me in its grasp. Mundane chores would just have to wait.

I worked in the waning daylight coming through my office window. I'd probably need the lamp soon, but I wanted to enjoy natural light as long as I could. I'd also sneaked to the foyer and snagged the plastic Halloween pumpkin by the door. Danny hopefully filled it with candy, year after year. We never got any trick-or-treaters, but the candy managed to, erm, disappear anyway.

It was a good thing the only witness to my thievery was spectral. Franklin was curled up in my armchair by the window. He had a blanket pulled around his shoulders as he looked out at the backyard. The lights were on in the pool, and the surface glistened like blue glass. My mother had hung fairy lights on her back porch, giving it an almost fairy-tale quality. So I could see why he was enjoying the view.

I just didn't know why he had to enjoy the view from *my* favorite chair.

When I asked him rather tartly if there was some place else he needed to be, he'd just smiled beatifically. *No, but thank you kindly. All I need is a quiet place to rest and think. The soil is talking and I'm tired of listening.* He also asked if he could trouble me for a cup of tea, a request that I thought was kinder to just ignore. I blinked away images of him drinking a carefully prepared cup of tea, the hot liquid running through his ghostly form and seeping into my upholstery.

It wasn't like I could kick him out. I mean, I *could*, but I wouldn't. That just wouldn't be fair. My office was the only room in the house we allowed ghosts to enter, after all. At first, it had been good enough to keep the bedroom and bathrooms ghost-free, which we did with the help of a salt/rice ritual recommended by my mother. But after some particularly nasty encounters with ghosts and finding out some of the frightening things they could do, we'd salted and riced the entire damn house.

That didn't help me beyond that space, though. Everywhere else was fair game, like work. The grocery store. The park. My car. It was a rare occasion that I didn't have a ghostly passenger on the highway, chattering over my music and making me regret...well, all my choices in life.

Usually.

There had been a lot less of them lately. While I was happy about that, I couldn't help but wonder why. There was always a *why*. And always a chance that the *why* could get me very dead. But for now? I was going to enjoy the dearth of ghosts around me. They didn't need me, and I certainly didn't need them. Or something less bitter.

I heard the murmur of voices outside and peeked out the blinds, only to find Danny and my father still in the garden. Danny had changed into basketball shorts, a tank top, and beat-up sneakers—his version of gardening wear—and was wielding a shovel. If I had to guess, it was probably to dig a hole for the row of large leafy plants near my father's foot.

My father shook his head and made a couple of hand gestures. I could almost feel Danny's sigh as he moved a few inches to the left. *Not that much!* I could read my father's lips as he shook his head again.

Oh my. I bit back a laugh. I wasn't aware that digging a hole required so much supervision. Clearly, my father had decided to measure the length of Danny's patience and see when it intersected the fuse for his temper.

With a long-suffering sigh, Danny moved back to the original spot. My father made the hurry-up motion with his hands, which made Danny look down at the shovel. Calculatingly. As if remembering the possibility of witnesses, his gaze shifted to my office window. His face looked very, very grim.

I snapped the blinds shut.

I wasn't worried. Danny was well acquainted with what family *wasn't* supposed to look like. His father was in prison for homicide and had been for most of Danny's life. He didn't even know where his drug-addicted birth mother was, or if she was even still alive. And while he'd been lucky to get adopted by Paula, her love had always come with strings—my words, not his.

So the love he had for my parents was a tangible thing. He loved my family down to their kooky bones and they loved him right back.

Satisfied that I wouldn't have to arrest my husband for beaning my father in the noggin with a shovel, I got back to work. I quickly logged in to a database I no longer had the right to use. I knew I wouldn't have long, so I printed out the most interesting bits as I found them.

The Parker family had gone missing nearly ten years ago. Quinn, Nate, and her two daughters—twins, Regan and Ryan. Quinn's brother Caleb had sounded the alarm, spurring a nationwide search that lasted six weeks. No one could say law enforcement didn't put everything they had into finding the girls. The FBI had led the charge, coordinating with local law enforcement and a platoon of volunteers.

But then life happened.

That was just the way of things. News ebbed and flowed, and

there would always be something more pressing to cover. More murder, more missing people, more natural disasters, more thoughts and prayers. Rinse and repeat.

In this case, the Parker family got bumped by a storm that swept up the East Coast. Hurricane Nina made sure that the authorities had plenty of other things to worry about and lots of missing people to account for. The hunt for the Parkers was put on ice, swept away in the current of more pressing news.

It didn't help that their financial situation wasn't the best at the time. Nate had invested in some risky stocks and lost the majority of their retirement fund. They'd borrowed money from friends and family alike, money they had no chance of repaying. Their car payments were late, and the mortgage was behind as well. I could certainly understand why the original detectives assigned to the case felt like the Parker disappearances had been all too convenient.

Only I now knew that wasn't the case.

Something had happened in that household that fateful night. And whatever happened had led to the four occupants of that house disappearing like mist. But who would have had it in for the Parkers? And how had our killer pulled off their macabre magic trick and made an entire family disappear without a trace?

My phone rang, jarring me out of my thoughts. I checked the name on the display, letting out a quiet laugh even as I slid a finger across the screen to accept. "What?"

"Really?" Chevy demanded.

I grinned even as I hit the Speaker button. "Certainly took you long enough. You're slipping."

"I'm not *slipping*," she said peevishly. "I was curious. I had to see what was important enough for you to risk my wrath for hacking me yet again."

Chevrolet Sullivan had been my go-to office contact when I worked in the field at the FBI in the BAU-3 department. Our history together had convinced me that there wasn't a detail she couldn't find or a database she couldn't hack. She'd even once made the top of my Christmas list by recovering information from a tablet a suspect had submerged in mud. In a pigpen. So it went without saying that she was clutch in any professional capacity. Somewhere along the way, we'd also become friends.

I still wasn't sure how that shit happened.

"It wasn't all that hard to do," I said with a shrug. "Just so you know, my dear Swifty, *areyoureadyforit21* is not a good password."

"I'm trying to figure out why you're pestering me for help, and on a weekend at that," she said with a sniff. "Aren't you a cop? Last time I checked, you had a database and a team of your very own."

She still sounded a little put out by that. But I wasn't coming back to the FBI, and they'd just have to get used to it.

"My team is fantastic," I confirmed. "But the FBI's database is and will always be infinitely better than the archaic system at BBPD. I'd also like to point out that I have not, in fact, asked you for any help."

"But you will."

"Negative," I said as my connection winked out.

The screen dissolved into the FBI logo, the credential and password boxes empty. I grabbed another couple pieces of candy from the container neatly tucked under my desk. I made sure to crinkle them near the phone as I opened them, and she made an irritated noise.

"So." I popped them in my mouth, leaning back in my chair. "How are things? And Kurt? How's Kurt?"

"Things are just fine," she said suspiciously. "Kurt and I are thinking about moving in together."

"That's wonderful," I said with feeling—marveled, really. "I still can't believe you found someone who tolerates you and your ways."

"You did," she said pertly. "That gave me hope. I had all but given up on finding love when you got back together with Danny and put a ring on it. I looked in the mirror and said Self, if that prickly little ghost whisperer can find a guy to love him like that—"

"Hey—"

"A guy like Danny no less, who is walking, talking hotness—"

"I swear to God if one more person hits on my husband today, I'm gonna—"

"Then there's hope for us all," she went on. "The day you finally locked that down, I reactivated my dating profile."

Despite my sudden urge to drop her off in the Everglades, I was amused. "You're such a witch."

"Hey, when God is handing out miracles, you get your ass in line."

I glared at Franklin. He hadn't made a sound, but his shoulders had started to shake suspiciously. *Hmph.* The next time he asked me for a cup of ghost tea, I was going to remind him that he was, in fact, quite dead.

"Let's get down to the nitty gritty, Christiansen," she said. "It's late, and I have better things to do."

"Doubtful. And it's not like I actually called you," I said with a huff. She was silent because we both knew that me poking around in the database with her credentials was as good as flicking on a Gotham searchlight, but with her initials instead of a bat silhouette. "Okay, fine. What do you know about the Parker murders?"

"The Parker disappearances," she said promptly. "Unless you know something the rest of the world doesn't."

"For the sake of argument, let's assume that I do."

"And just how would you...ah," she said awkwardly. Ghosts and anything related to something she couldn't see, touch, or taste made her downright uncomfortable. I could relate. "Right."

"I can only speak for Quinn," I said. "But I think it's pretty safe to assume that if the mother is dead, the kids probably are as well."

"You're all heart, Christiansen," she said dryly. "Hopefully, you'll be a touch more sensitive when you have a kid of your very own."

Jesus Christ. That was one way to send my heart thumping into overdrive.

Franklin let out a relieved sigh. "Oh, good, you don't have children. I wondered when I saw those bicycles in the shed. I like them, but they are noisy little buggers, aren't they?"

Chevy hummed. "I can only assume from your silence that you are having a patented Christiansen freak-out. Now you see why I wrote *Godspeed, Daniel McKenna* on your wedding gift."

I sent my phone a squinty-eyed look. "I do *so* love it when we catch up. Let's do this again as soon as we're both free. Pencil me in fifty years from now, yes?"

She snickered. "Don't get your boxers in a twist."

"They would make a great soft pretzel right about now," I warned.

"Alright, alright. Jeez, you used to be a lot more fun."

"No, I wasn't."

"No, you weren't," she agreed. "I was just being nice. And as far as the Parkers...look, I don't have to tell you that bad things happen to vulnerable people. The primary FBI concern was that they'd run afoul of a predator of some sort. A serial killer. Sexual offender. Kidnapping and trafficking. The usual."

"The usual," I echoed dryly. Her tone had been hopelessly matter-of-fact. Sad topics, all, but shit, we'd been doing this a long time. "Anything else?"

"Well, of course, they considered the fact that their disappearance could've been purposeful. Honestly, that was best case scenario. In that same vein, her dear ex-husband could've been trying to get away with a quadruple." She paused. "I'd imagine it would be a simple matter to make someone 'disappear' if she was already, in fact, trying to disappear."

She wasn't saying anything I hadn't already acknowledged.

I chewed on the inside of my cheek, thinking. My next step should probably be to take a deep dive through Joshua Keller's life. I'd love to know what he'd been up to in the days before his ex-wife's family disappeared. I'd said I wouldn't need Chevy's help, but while I had her on the horn....

"I need that FBI file and I'm allergic to red tape," I said bluntly. "You think you could do something about that?"

"My dear, the list of what I can't do is damn near microscopic," she informed me with a sniff. "But you know Graycie will find out."

I expected nothing less. I might not be psychic, but I saw some consulting I didn't have time for in the near future. Alford Grayce, my former boss at the FBI, would make sure of it. He was a man who would stare blankly at the word *boundaries* and ask, "What are those and how do I get some?"

I didn't know how many times I had to tell him I was a cold case detective now, not a profiler in his BAU-3 unit. Maybe it would help if I stopped using FBI resources. But old habits were hard to break, and these damn near had me in a chokehold.

"Put it on my tab," I said before I hung up.

A few hours later, I finished the last dregs of coffee in my cup. It was cold but I was enough of a caffeine addict that I still enjoyed every drop. Danny had made it for me earlier, presenting it to me in my planet-sized mug. I took it from him carefully, barely managing not to clap for joy like a seal who'd earned extra fish.

I took a good sniff and sighed. It was hot and steamy and exactly the right color, which meant he hadn't skimped on the cream. I'd smiled up at him as he raced to the top of the best husband list. "Thanks."

"You're welcome, sweetheart," he said, reaching over to turn on my lamp. I squinted in the glare, but let it be. He had a thing about reading with perfect light, and I didn't want yet another lecture on eyestrain. "One nice big cup of decaf."

Decaf? I'd looked at him in dismay as he fell from the best husband list faster than a shooting star. "Now that's just uncalled for."

He chuckled softly, dropping a kiss in my hair. "Not too long, yeah?"

Despite feeling like a kid who'd been granted extra TV time, I nodded. He and I both knew that I could get lost in my research for hours. And while I sometimes still worked until my eyes were gritty and dry and stumbled to bed a few hours before the sun came up, I liked knowing there was someone who cared.

Turns out I didn't really need the warning.

It was impossible to concentrate when he was in the house doing something else. I could tell from the ambient noises exactly how he was spending his time. He'd taken a shower and shaved. Then he buzzed around in the kitchen, loading the dishwasher and making something in the microwave. He was on the phone for a bit, and I could tell it was work from the tone of his voice.

An hour later, I heard the clink of stainless-steel bowls as he fed Watson. Then the jingle of his leash before Danny took him outside. I had exactly a half-hour of concentration before the front door opened and the security system beeped. My ears started straining again, desperate for any bit of Danny we could hear. All I had at the moment was the paltry murmur of the TV in the living room.

It wasn't enough.

I wanted to know what he was watching. I wanted to know what he'd made when I'd heard the microwave humming. A hot drink? A snack? I wanted to see his face and hear his laugh. How the hell could I miss his company when he was right fucking there? With all the time we spent together, that should be fucking impossible. And yet here we were.

I shook my head with a rueful smile. I supposed there were worse things than missing one's own husband. As long as he didn't find out how very pitiful I was without him, I could deal.

I shut down my laptop and turned off the lamp. Remembering belatedly that my office was occupied, I turned it back on and glanced at Franklin, still curled up in my favorite chair. At least, I think it was still my favorite. How long would my carefully cultivated ass dent last with an interloper parking his spectral fanny it? Only time would tell.

"On or off?" I asked.

He didn't look my way. "Off."

Guess he was staying a spell, then. As long as he understood the rules of this Airbnb, we wouldn't have a problem. Don't set foot anywhere else in the house. Don't turn the A/C below seventy-two—we already had to contend with that damned ghostly chill. Don't touch my cookie stash. And don't try to inhabit anyone else's body.

You know. The usual.

I clicked the lamp off again and left, closing the door quietly behind me. Outside of the cocoon of my office, I could finally discern what Danny was watching—a baseball game. I found him on the couch in a wrinkled Star Wars t-shirt and his softest, most worn pair of gray sweats.

With his bare feet propped up on the coffee table and a beer in one hand, he was the very epitome of relaxation. Watson, his faithful companion, was posted up on the other couch, sprawled out and snoring hard. I still wasn't sure why we'd bothered to spend a hundred bucks on an orthopedic pet bed, and it didn't look like that riddle would be solved any time soon.

Danny looked over at me lurking in the doorway and raised an eyebrow. "You need an engraved invitation or what?"

Or what. I wasted no time crossing the room. I flopped on the couch, relishing his curse as he steadied his drink. Then I proceeded to lay lengthwise, moving his phone off his thigh and settling my head in his lap.

I looked up into an amused pair of blue eyes. "Nice."

"It is, isn't it?" I held up his phone and he plucked it from my fingers, placing it on the side table. "So who were you talking to earlier?"

"Saunders."

"Did he find out anything else about the bags of body parts?"

"The art of bedtime conversation is truly lost." He brushed my hair back from my forehead as I nestled in farther. "I'm all relaxed and shit, and you come in here talking about dead people."

"I find murder very relaxing," I said with a yawn. "And two bodies with missing heads? Name a better bedtime story than that."

"Any of them," he said dryly. "All of them."

When it was clear he wasn't going to tell me about the bodies, I gave his flat abdomen a poke. He sucked in a breath on a laugh even as he caught my questing hand. "Alright, alright. No need to get violent."

"Apparently, there is." I readied my index finger again—no quarter given for his stomach. And this time, I intended to find the soft, ticklish part.

"The two victims are male. I can only guess that whoever dismembered them did so for easy storage, so he could keep them on ice until the heat died down. Then he could dispose of the parts at his leisure. Burn them. Toss them in different trash cans. Maybe even dump them in the swamp and hope the alligators do what alligators do."

Those long fingers playing in my hair made it extremely difficult to focus. "That would certainly explain why they were in the Everglades."

He hummed. "We found tire tracks. Looks like a car went off the road and got mired in the muck."

"Flat tire?" I raised an eyebrow. "So they could've been transporting the bodies and had to call for a tow. Then stashed them before the tow truck driver arrived, to pick up later. Only, there was no later because we turned their temporary dumping ground into a crime scene."

"Maybe," he agreed. "Saunders said that the cuts are neat and precise. Our killer would have to be someone extremely familiar with human anatomy."

I made a derisive noise. "That could be anyone from doctor to sports therapist to a *Grey's Anatomy* enthusiast. Not to mention, they could be familiar with anatomy now because they've had plenty of practice."

"I wasn't aware I had to use the phrase *preliminary findings*," he said mildly.

I huffed. I knew that. But let's just say there was a reason I usually ejected my Pop-Tart out of the toaster before it popped up on its own. Patience wasn't exactly my strong suit. We were at the part of the investigation I disliked the most, when the killer could be any-fucking-where or any-fucking-one for any number of fucking reasons.

"I wonder why the killer kept the heads?" I mused.

"Well, if you can tell me that, I can mark *closed* on several bags of body parts, toss them in an incinerator, and make our lieutenant a very happy woman."

"Tate? Happy?" I raised a skeptical eyebrow. "How you *do* go on."

"It's possible," he insisted with exactly zero proof.

"The heads were probably trophies," I murmured, closing my

eyes. "Or maybe the killer took them so we wouldn't be able to identify the victims through dental if they were ever found and—*mmph!*"

I wasn't expecting his mouth on mine, and it took me a minute to get with the program. But get with the program I did. With him leaning above me and me arching up at an odd angle, it was some weird ass Spider-Man kissing. I certainly wasn't about to complain... not until he pulled away, that is.

He bent down to give me one last peck. "You taste like a chocolate factory."

"Well, I did have a piece of candy."

"Just the one? Because I can't find the jack-o-lantern I had by the door."

I gave him a squinty-eyed look. "Are you accusing me of something, McKenna?"

"Yes," he said bluntly.

To my credit, I gave up the ghost fairly quickly. I'd done nothing wrong, after all. After the holiday passed, holiday-shaped candy could be confiscated. The fuck else was he gonna do with a crapload of Reese's in the shape of a pumpkin? I was doing him a favor. It was the same reason I helped him out by eating all that white chocolate peppermint bark after Christmas. Further bylaws could be found under the clause of *Stop Riding My Ass Unless You're Gonna Do It Properly.*

"Halloween is over," I informed him. "And if you wanted trick-or-treaters, perhaps you shouldn't have bought property where your only neighbors are gators."

"My only neighbors are your parents. And let's be real, that's one hundred percent your fault."

He kissed me again before I could defend myself—or at least point out that they belonged to us now, not just me.

"Okay, look," I said, pulling back breathlessly. "If you keep doing that, I'm going to assume you're open for business."

He chuckled and gave me one last peck, which didn't answer my question at all. His next words didn't bode well for getting freaky. "We have a long day tomorrow. I'm going to bed."

I blinked at him, trying to shift gears instead of staring at his full lips and begging for a repeat of those last steamy minutes. "Okay?"

He dangled a gray rectangle in my face. It took me a second to realize it was the remote, and I plucked it from his hand. Then he was up off the couch, and my head bounced on the cushions. I lay there, sprawled, á la dead raccoon. *Le sigh.*

He stopped at the doorway and turned, giving me an upraised eyebrow. "You coming to bed?"

Dead raccoon is suspicious but interested. "That depends."

"On?"

"On whether you're talking about brushing our teeth, setting the alarm, and actually going to bed," I said suspiciously. "Because being an adult can definitely wait until I've watched at least one show to decompress."

His lips twitched with amusement. "My plan for decompressing involves a lot less clothes. And maybe my mouth on whatever body part you'd like."

I dared Tigger to bounce off the couch as quickly as I did.

Danny chuckled as I hit the Power button on the remote and tossed it on the coffee table. Watson startled briefly at the clatter and looked at us blearily. After verifying that yes, we were still alive and yes, he was still King of Couchville, he gave an indignant snuffle before shifting into yet another contortionist position. For Watson, it wasn't comfortable unless he was exposing his bits.

As soon as I was within reach, Danny locked his hand around my wrist and towed me closer. I was expecting to be groped—demanding it, really—and I was wholly unprepared for him to stick his hand in my pocket. I winced at the crinkling of cellophane.

He pulled out his hand filled with a fistful of colorful miniature wrappers. It was clear he was trying not to smile as he shook his head. "This is disgraceful."

"You married it," I reminded him.

He didn't look upset about that in the least. "Yeah. I did. And now I want *it* in my bed without any clothes."

It was my turn to look mighty pleased. Especially when he turned and headed for the bedroom, giving me a good look at his perfectly shaped rump in those gray sweats. The fabric was thin and worn enough that when he moved, it clung to every curve.

I hoped he didn't think he was ever leaving the house in those things.

Before I could follow, something occurred to me. Something important. "I can't believe you referred to my entire being as an it."

"Rain."

"Coming."

4

Monday morning, the conference room smelled of delicious food, all bought thoughtfully by *moi*. It was the least I could do after issuing the entire team nonrefundable tickets to what was guaranteed to be a shitshow. Bags of body parts and talk of missing—potentially dead—children weren't my favorite way to start a week, either.

I'd bought more food than necessary because we had a Kevin in our department, and he ate like someone was paying him by the calorie. Muffins, bagels, bacon, and eggs were the stars of the show. The fruit arrangement was pretty but consisted of mostly cantaloupe, especially after I'd nicked half the grapes and strawberries while arranging the platter. I finished the spread with coffee and juice and sampled a bit of everything because I take quality control very seriously.

By the time I wheeled my whiteboard in, Tabitha was coming through the glass doors, iPad in one hand and a coffee in the other. She was our resident whiz when it came to technology and kept our department equipment updated, which was great. She was also the reason I now had to struggle to update my expense reports electronically, which was fucked up.

Today, she was comfortable/casual in a gray plaid skirt, a soft-looking black blouse and black flats. Her red hair was pulled up in some complicated bun thing and she had tiny hoops in her ears. Suspects in her custody usually forgot that someone sweet and delicate could still know several takedown holds.

They only forgot it once.

"Those yorkies are darling," she gushed.

I raised an eyebrow as I looked at my murder board. The dogs in question were in a picture with Quinn's best friend, Farrah Bell. She was blond and busty, her makeup overdone in every possible way. I'd written *long shot* under her photo.

"What are their names?" Tabitha asked. "And is that breakfast?"

She didn't wait for confirmation of the obvious before she grabbed a paper plate. Practically mowed me down to get to the spread.

"The yorkies are named Tinker, Toby, and Oreo, respectively," I said dryly. "There's also a couple murder victims up there if you'd like to take a gander."

She waved dismissively. "All in due time, Christiansen. All in due time."

Apparently, *all in due time* was after she'd perused every single bagel option twice and selected an onion one. She followed that up with several strips of bacon and a scoop of eggs before asking, "So who's our vic?"

"Vics, plural. Nate and Quinn Parker and her daughters, Ryan and Regan."

Her brows knitted into a frown. "I think I remember hearing about that like, a decade ago." She added a cup of orange juice and a bowl of fruit to her haul and sat down at the table. "What do the ghosts say?"

They weren't saying a damn thing. Nothing. Zip. Zero. Nada.

That was a good thing. Of course. At one point, I hadn't even been able to take a shower in peace without a ghostly stranger snatching the curtain and demanding I hurry the fuck up because they had important business to tend to, like, yesterday. Nowadays, I saw two or three a week, at most. It should've been a relief. But I knew better than to think I was actually making headway. Something else was going on, and I was determined to find out what.

"Wow, I didn't know there was such an easy way to silence you." I blinked to find Tab still looking at me, one of her tapered brows arched. "And here I was, planning to bring you a candy apple pumped full of caramel and peanut butter. I figured that would buy us at least a half hour of peace."

Before I could respond with persimmon-level tartness, the door swung open, and Nick strolled in. Kevin was right on his heels as they talked over one another. It only took a moment of ear abuse to realize they were arguing about whose team had crushed the other's the night before. As if either of them had done anything more strenuous than sit on the couch and watch, ferrying chips from an oversized bag to their oversized mouths.

No judgment from this quarter, though. I'd medaled in the Potato Chip Olympics several decades running.

"Good grief." Tabitha cut them off mid-argument. "Do you two have any other sound level other than charging buffalo?"

"According to my wife, I do not," Kevin informed her cheerily. "And thank you, Christiansen, for ruining my weekend with a double homicide."

I made a faux sad face. "Well, I missed your anniversary. Gotta make up for it somehow. I thought Self—Self, I ask—what would Kevin like better than a gift card?"

"A summer sausage and cheese gift basket. The kind with the different types of jam." Kevin's eyes widened as he spotted the table laden with food. "Wait, no. This. This is better."

And with that, he fell on my carefully arranged display. I took up refuge on the other side of the table, watching him pile food on his plate like a man who'd been lost at sea for a month and ran out of fellow passengers to eat on day two.

As everyone got settled, I passed out my painstakingly put-together binders to a chorus of groans—clearly appreciation for my hard work. No one bothered to open them until the ding of the elevator sounded. Probably because there was only one person missing from the party and he didn't take kindly to slackers. I hid a grin as Nick hurriedly uncapped a pen.

Sure enough, I spotted Danny a few seconds later through the glass paneling of the conference room. He was walking shoulder to shoulder with Saunders, deep in conversation. Nice to see that he was done playing Match Game, the Body Part edition. They parted at the crossway, and Saunders sent me a dirty look before stalking down the hall.

Hmph. Some people just didn't know how to appreciate a nice gift like bags of body parts.

Danny strode in without a word of greeting. Just grabbed a raisin bagel from the table, poured a cup of coffee, and dropped in the chair next to Tabitha. She offered him a pointed hello and he answered with a grunt. I tried not to smile. It was truly mindboggling how someone could nearly leave me in a puddle of goo with a few simple words and still manage to have the social skills of an orangutan.

Then he doubled down.

"They have no penises," he grumbled.

Welp. That was certainly a way to silence a room. It was so quiet I could hear someone crunching. I glanced at Nick just in time to see him take another juicy bite of an apple slice, his dark eyes nice and wide.

I sighed. If no one was going to send my husband to a *Welcome to Small Talk* seminar, I suppose it *was* my responsibility. I turned to Kevin. "St. James! Nice to see you. How are you doing this fine morning?"

"I'm doing well, thank you," he said with exaggerated politeness. "And you?"

"Just fine." We both turned to Danny, and I sent him a patient smile. "Now you try."

"Both of you can shut it." But his lips twitched with a smile as he struggled to split his bagel. Before I could offer my help, he gave the pre-sliced guidelines an unspoken *screw you* and ripped the bagel in half.

I pushed the cream cheese across the table and Danny caught it before it slid off the end. "Would you like to clarify your earlier ambiguous—"

"And shocking," Nick added. "Don't forget shocking—"

"—statement regarding...er, missing penises?" I finished.

"Saunders was updating me on the duo that you found. Every part is accounted for except their heads and their penises, which appear to have been deliberately removed before someone crammed them in a freezer." He gave me a considering look as he smeared cream cheese on both ragged halves. "Clearly, you have a magnet for psychopaths somewhere on your person."

"I keep things interesting, and you know it, McKenna," I said pertly.

As if realizing he'd forgone a real greeting with no-penis news—never a crowd pleaser—he gave me a sheepish look. He half-stood, leaning over the table, dropping a quick kiss on my mouth that Kevin immediately declared disgustingly sweet. Nick made appropriate gagging noises until Tab smacked him on the back on the head.

I ignored their squabbling. I was too busy giving Danny a onceover as he sat back in his chair. He was wearing a well-worn pair of jeans and a moss green shirt with some indie band logo that I'd never heard of, his dark hair already mussed from his fingers.

I sent him a meaningful look. Sure, the kiss had been a nice consolation prize, especially from someone who hated PDA. But I was expecting a redo later in my office. Something I couldn't also give my grandmother. From the look in his sparkling blue eyes, that trusty married-folks ESP was kicking in.

Those eyes got a whole lot less sparkly as he took in my carefully curated murder book. "I thought you were working on the murder of someone named Franklin."

I shook my head. "His death wasn't so much a murder as it was accidental, and that was just because of Barclay." At his blank look, I added helpfully. "His horse."

Kevin's brow crinkled. "We're investigating the death of a horse? That's not really our department, is it?"

"Are we looking into one of those racetrack insurance scams?" Tabitha asked. "Because I'm all for busting an animal abuse ring."

"And who names their horse *Barclay?*" Nick mumbled around a mouthful of muffin. "If nothing else, we can get justice for the poor horse for living with that name."

"If you will open up your binders to the background section, then we can begin," I said loudly. "As a side bonus, no one else will be able to say something stupid."

"Something stupid," Danny said with a lazy grin as he opened his binder.

I huffed out a laugh.

Well, I suppose I'd left myself wide open for that one.

"Quinn Parker is our primary," I said. "She worked as an Outreach Coordinator for five years at a women's center called the Hope House. She was married to a man named Nate at the time of her disappearance, but her first marriage was to her high school sweetheart, Joshua Keller. They had two kids, Ryan and Regan, who are also missing."

Quinn's picture headed up my whiteboard, all heart-shaped face and big brown eyes. To her left was Nate, clean-cut with a neatly tapered beard and kind dark eyes. And Ryan and Regan, who'd inherited their mother's coloring and her smile.

It was hard to look at them, knowing what I knew.

"Is the ex-husband a viable suspect?" Kevin asked.

I gave him my best schoolmarm look and then gestured at my whiteboard. Joshua Keller—dark-haired, dark-eyed, preppy looking—was right there under the subheading *suspects*. I didn't mind breaking things down, but I didn't plan to do it twice.

"You're so weird about that thing," he groused. "Custody issues, I'll bet."

I hummed because my whiteboard was gospel, and that was just that. "The family disappeared on a Monday. Quinn was sick so she worked remotely, then picked up the girls from school as usual. The family had dinner and watched a movie. She and Nate put the girls to bed and then fell asleep on the couch. Just a normal day like any other."

"Who discovered them missing?" Tab asked absently. She flipped a page before I could answer and made a sound. "Ah, Caleb, the brother. Apparently, he called several times over the next few days and then finally stopped by their house to check. When was the ex-husband's last contact with Quinn?"

"Around—"

She made an *ah-ha* noise as she continued to read. "Oh, there it is. The Sunday before they disappeared. Apparently, he had the girls on the weekends," she said, scribbling something in the margins. "Did he get along with Nate?"

I squinted at her for a moment, waiting. After a few beats, I chanced speaking again. "Well, it seems as though—"

"Wow, they had a dustup the year before and the police had to come and break it up." Her eyes widened. "The plot thickens."

The plot was crunchy peanut butter right about now. "If I could get a word in edgewise...?"

She gave me an innocent look. "Of course. This is your show. Don't let me interrupt."

I harrumphed. "Responding officers who did the welfare check reported that the house wasn't in disarray. The door was locked, security system armed, and Nate's car was missing."

"Looks like their passports and identification documentation were never located, and several pieces of luggage were missing," Tab said with a frown. "No laptops or phones were found in the house, either."

I winced. "The optics weren't great."

"And they haven't improved." Danny rubbed a hand over his stubble absently as he squinted at my whiteboard. "Other than the ex, do you have alternative suspects? And please don't say the lady with the dogs."

"The lady with the dogs," I said, equally ignoring his stifled sigh and Tabitha's *aw*. "Farrah Bell, Quinn's best friend. There was tension in the relationship, and she received a tidy sum from an insurance policy, seven years after the Parkers went missing."

Danny looked a bit happier at that news. By like, a micrometer. "What kind of tension?"

"I don't know, but I think we need to find out."

"And you're sure they didn't just flee?" Tabitha asked. "Seems like they had plenty of reasons to. Money-wise, that is."

"They could have," I said. "But then something happened to make them very dead…Quinn, at least."

"Oh." Tab looked a little deflated. "Well, you could've said something."

"I just did."

"I hate it when he does that," Nick said, unable to fully suppress his shiver. "She's not here, is she? Is she touching me? I thought I felt a little cold on my left side. Just…don't let her touch me."

"For God's sake, Nick. She's not here," Danny answered without looking up. He was already making notes in the margins of his binder. If I had to guess, he was probably figuring out which of us should interview whom. "And you're cold on your left side because you're under the vent."

Realizing the room had gone silent at something he'd said—yet *again*—Danny looked up. "What?"

"I think we're at our quota for fucking ghost whisperers is what," Kevin said, eyes still a little wide.

"Well, rest assured I'm still registering zero on the paranormal scale. When Rain talks to them, he gets this little furrow in his brow. Right here," he said pointing at his own forehead. "Like he finds them horribly annoying but he's trying to be patient."

"You kind of look that way right now," Nick ventured.

"A smart man would draw a conclusion from that," Danny said mildly.

I was still a little stuck on the fact that he'd gotten his masters in Rain-isms and went back for his doctorate. "I can't believe you notice that."

His eyes softened at my dumbfounded look, probably because he loved to prove that he knew me better than anyone else.

"We need to look at this Joshua guy again. For obvious reasons," Kevin grumbled. "Maybe he's the type who wanted a fresh start without all that old baggage."

"Quinn maybe, but what about his kids?" Tab asked skeptically.

"Child support can be a bitch. He could be one of those…those…." He snapped his fingers a few times and then looked my way. "Brain. What's the term?"

"Family annihilator," I said, crossing my arms as I leaned back in my chair. "Shades of John List and Andrea Yates. Or even Ronald Gene Simmons, who killed fourteen family members. And don't get me started on Chris Watts—"

"We won't," Nick said quickly.

"The family annihilator kills multiple close family members in quick succession—children, parents, siblings." I ignored the chorus of groans because yes, I was ramping up for a lecture, and no, it wasn't gonna be quick. "Often there can be no outward signs of the annihilator. They can be very dedicated to their family. Devoted, even."

"Then what makes them finally snap?" Tabitha asked.

"Control. Having it. Keeping it. A sudden loss of it. The male annihilator is usually motivated by a loss of financial control—loss of a job, a divorce, a loss of status." I paused. "And I'm not certain the term 'snap' is always appropriate. Snap indicates a break in reality, or mental illness of some sort."

"If killing all the people that love you the most isn't mental illness, I don't know what is," she protested.

I shrugged. "Yes, but not in the traditional sense. They're narcissistic, certainly. And they might even have a skewed view of the world and their position in it. But when they commit this act, they're making a decision based on a stressor, and that doesn't mean they're mentally ill."

"We'll have to agree to disagree on that," Kevin said dryly. "I'd like to think that if I lost my job, I wouldn't go all Lizzie Borden on the fam."

"It's more than just a loss of a job. Jobs provide income and income provides security." Despite their bitching and moaning, they gave me their rapt attention as I prattled on. "A loss of security in terms of where your children are going to get their next meal or lay their heads at night is the epitome of a stressor."

"With power comes responsibility," Kevin murmured, and I knew he thought of his own large family. "And with responsibility comes pressure."

"Exactly. It's a heavy burden that a lot of people don't even realize they're carrying. If you don't know you're carrying it, you might not know when it's gotten too heavy." I waited for a beat, still thinking. "And as far as Lizzie Borden goes—"

"Jesus Christ, it's like he has a computer chip with a crime dictionary crammed in his brain," Nick said with a groan. "Did Nate have anything suspicious in his history? Anyone who wanted him dead?"

"Not that I could find," I said begrudgingly. I had at least four more family annihilators in the holster I hadn't even got to yet. "No affairs, no criminal history, no crazy exes. Not any that required judicial intervention, at least. On the surface, he seemed like a clean-cut, rule-abiding guy who loved his family."

"Let's make sure that he's exactly what he portrayed," Danny said. "Tab, I want you to work the case as if Nate is the primary. And take Nick with you."

"Hey," Tab protested. "I was hoping to talk to the best friend."

"You just want to meet her dogs," Nick accused.

"Kevin is talking to Farrah," Danny said, turning to Kevin. "And make it absolutely clear that this is just a conversation, not an interrogation. Rain, you should probably follow up with Joshua."

Kevin looked put out. "I wanted to take a run at the ex-husband. Why can't Christiansen talk to Farrah?"

"Surely I haven't developed a stutter and none of you told me about it," Danny said mildly, and Nick smothered a laugh with a cough. "You're talking to Farrah because you're affable and easy-going and bringing up her murdered best friend is bound to be a delicate topic. I'm thinking a touch of sugar might go a long way."

"Hey." It was my turn to grouse. "I've got *plenty* of sugar."

The guffaws really weren't necessary.

"I do," I insisted. "I'm also affable as fuck. Tell 'em, McKenna."

"Okay," Danny said, a smile playing on his lips. "Watson destroyed a pool floaty this morning. Your mom sent me a photo."

I gasped. "Which one?"

I damn well knew which one. He was obsessed with my flamingo floaty, the one with cup holders.

"Your favorite one. Not purposefully," he added when I gasped again. "I think he took a flying leap trying to get on it and got it pretty good with his claws."

"That bastard," I said indignantly. "Suddenly a dog who begs fragility when I ask him to get his furry rump off the couch is pulling a Michael Phelps in our pool?"

"You're the one pumping him full of vitamins and glucosamine," he said easily, like all was right in the world and our child wasn't eagerly auditioning for the Baddest Pup awards. "Still feeling…affable?"

It was hard to shake off visions of Watson gleefully dive-bombing my flamingo, but I managed. Nothing to be done about the tic in my jaw, though. "Absolutely."

He chuckled. "Yeah, you look positively thrilled. So who was the original detective on the case?"

"Um, hang on." I flipped through the file. "Could've sworn I had it."

"Well, if you can't find it, I can just ask—"

"Gimme a sec." I ignored the little smile playing on his lips. He damn well knew I hated leaving a briefing file incomplete. "Got it. Detectives Jonathan Todd and Zachary Owens. And before you ask, I already called. Detective Todd passed away four years ago, but I left a message for Owens."

"Zach?" He looked a little surprised but pleased. "He's in homicide up in Palm Beach. Or at least he was. I haven't talked to him in a long time."

I wasn't too fond of the soft look in his eye when he said that. I raised an eyebrow. "Something you'd like to share with the class?"

It took him a second to understand what I was getting at, and he rolled his eyes. "He's just an old friend. We met in foster care and lost touch. Imagine my surprise when we wound up at the academy together."

My other eyebrow slowly joined the first in surprised solidarity. Mostly because his cheeks had gotten so very dusky. "Oh, that kind of friend."

"Not *that* kind of friend." He made an exasperated noise when he realized I was giving him the Look. I served up the Look with a nice side of suspicious *mmhmm*. "I mean yes, at one point, but not for a very long time."

A slow grin spread across Nick's face. "My, my, my. This meeting has certainly taken an unexpected turn. You think I have time to get that bag of Smart Pop from the kitchen?"

"I already ate it," Kevin said cheerfully. "So no."

"Maybe we can get back on topic," Danny said pointedly. "I believe I was in the middle of handing out assignments."

"No, you were in the middle of a pot of hot water called Zach and Christiansen was adding onions and potatoes," Tab said, clearly ready to settle back and watch the show.

There was a quick rap at the door and Macy waved through the glass. Danny looked a little too grateful for the interruption as he waved her in.

She pushed the door open a crack and stuck her head in. "Detective McKenna? There's someone here for you." She smiled sweetly. "I put him in your office."

"Oh good," he said dryly. "Glad to know someone is unattended in my office along with my personal files and shotgun."

"I wouldn't just put *anyone* in your office," she said with a huff, and we were all nice enough not to remind her that she'd done exactly that before. Several times. To all of us. "He's a fellow detective. He said he knew you."

He raised a brow but pushed back from the table. Innate responsibility made him stop at the door and turn back around. "You guys know what you're doing?"

He received several nods and a disinterested wave for his trouble before striding out the door. Everyone started gathering their things, already focused on their assignments. And me? Well, I was putting one and one together and coming up with Zachary Owens—old "friend" Zachary Owens—in my husband's office.

"I've got to use the bathroom and then we can head out," Tab said, closing her binder. "Nicky, if you have to hit the head, now is the time."

Nick rolled his eyes. "I haven't had anyone monitoring my potty time since I was five, thanks."

"Okaaay. But it's going to be a long day and I'm not driving you around to different fast-food establishments until you find a restroom that doesn't look like a crime scene." When he opened his mouth to speak, she held up a hand. "You also won't be peeing in any cups. And if you make me pull to the side of the road to use a tree like an animal, I'm driving off without you. Do with that information what you will."

His only response was a rude noise as he left. I had a feeling he was headed for the restroom. A smug Tabitha was hot on his heels.

Kevin gave my shoulder a bump. A friendly nudge from linebacker shoulders sent me right into the table. The carafe of orange juice wobbled, and my hand shot out to steady it. "Want to ride with?" he asked. "We can see Farrah first and then head over to Joshua."

I rubbed my hip even as I sent him a glare. *Yeah, like I'm leaving this building with Detective Slept with My Husband on the loose.* I decided to give my poker face another shot. "I think I'll hang out here for a bit."

His grin let me know that my poker face was still the same dismal failure it had always been. "Are you sure? I could use the assist—"

"Get lost, St. James."

He laughed.

5

I stalled for ten minutes or so, trying to think of any excuse to go into Danny's office. It wasn't like I was just hanging around or anything. I contacted Joshua, who agreed to an afternoon meeting around three. I cleaned up the breakfast buffet and even dropkicked the leftovers into the already full breakroom fridge. See? Productive, that's me.

But eventually, I gave up on trying to be well-adjusted and trusting. I knocked on Danny's office door—perfunctorily, because how the hell else do you catch people doing anything—and went right on in.

To be fair, they weren't doing any of the things my imagination had cooked up while I was being so very productive. No one was naked. And no one was putting his lips on my husband, so everyone got to live. For now.

Detective Zachary Owens was handsome. Not the ridiculous kind of handsome I'd married, but close enough. He had rich mahogany hair that fell just so, dark brown eyes, and a dimple creased his left cheek when he smiled. He smiled a lot at my husband. Like, a lot.

I mean, were we discussing murder or not?

I'll admit that I have it better than most when it comes to exes popping up in our lives. Inexplicably, Danny didn't have many—actually none, post-me. So I was lucky that way. But sometimes I was reminded that there was a whole period of time in Daniel Christiansen McKenna's life before me. I wasn't too keen on that reminder landing on our proverbial doorstep. Or being welcomed to stop by any time. And I wasn't loving the warm hug they'd shared or Danny's hearty, *"Zach, it's been too long."*

Not long enough, if you ask me.

And now he was looking mighty comfortable. He was sitting in one of Danny's office chairs, eating a plate I'd put together from the remnants of the breakfast buffet. A few minutes after I busted up their "good to see you" party, Zachary's stomach had growled. He'd sheepishly mentioned that he hadn't eaten this morning. Despite that going very much under the category of personal problem, Danny had given me a hopeful look and asked if maybe I could "rustle up something."

Rustle up something.

Like I was going to grab a loincloth and a spear and head out into the forest.

Before I could tell him to get lost, he used those big blue eyes of his on me that he had all but weaponized. I begrudgingly headed back to the breakroom to "rustle up something." In my world, that consisted of a muffin and a couple strips of bacon. At the last moment, I felt bad at how naked the plate looked and added a handful of melon that we'd all shunned.

Let's just say no one was ever going to hire me to make charcuterie boards.

And now, I was back in his office, posted up on the wall. I had my arms crossed—but loosely, so hopefully I looked approachable and engaged. It was a hard sell because they were both trying my patience.

Danny was doing a lousy job of getting to the point, when cutting to the chase was usually a Danny specialty. And Zach was doing a fantastic job of talking about everything *but* the case. I was already eager to see the last of that pearly-toothed, handsome, dimpled bastard who had a loathsome habit of emphasizing his point with touch.

I gritted my teeth as he leaned forward and squeezed Danny's arm. Case in point.

"So. How is your mom?" He asked.

"She's doing fine. She retired a few years back and now spends her days gardening, cooking, and staying in my business."

Zachary laughed and that dimple flashed again. "Sounds like the Paula I knew and loved." His eyes lingered on the band on Danny's finger and flitted over to the matching one on mine. "And you two are…."

"Yeah." Danny's mouth lifted. "A year next month."

I glared when he gave me that look—*that* fucking look. The one that always reduced me to jelly. That look was dangerous. That look had somehow turned me giving him hell about ruining my favorite copper pot trying to make caramel into me giving him a blow job. I still wasn't sure how that happened. Or how someone who had a hard time making box pudding—just-add-milk pudding—thought he should advance to making caramel from scratch.

Zachary sighed. "Yeah. I figured. You were always that type of guy. Happy?"

"Ecstatic," I said, crisp as a fresh potato chip.

Zachary was a day late and a dollar short. There was no need to feel out Danny's "situation." His situation was solid. Rock solid. You could secure a grapple in his situation and swing from the Empire State Building. And not for nothing, but his Situation felt extremely negative toward homewreckers and carried a Glock.

Perhaps Danny could feel his Situation getting a little stabby because he stopped traveling down the extremely bumpy *Hey Remember When We Fucked* Road and got to the point. "Not that I'm not enjoying catching up, but we should probably talk about Quinn Parker."

"Well, that's easy enough," Zachary said bluntly. "You're wasting your time."

"Care to be more specific?" I asked.

Even though it was clear he was wishing me into the cornfield, he answered gamely enough. "The investigation was solid. Everything pointed toward the Parkers taking off voluntarily." He shrugged. "That's a better outcome than we usually get."

"What makes you so sure?" I pressed.

He looked surprised. "Well, can you ever really be sure about something like this? It's just the most likely scenario. One of the neighbors, Opal Clarke, even saw Quinn getting rid of a lot of her belongings the week before she went missing."

"What kind of stuff?" I asked.

"Purses, clothing, shoes. Opal dug through the Parkers's garbage cans and basically had a thrifting spree."

Danny didn't look convinced. "Spring cleaning."

"Or getting ready to make a move," Zachary countered. "We also put the ex-husband through the wringer. His alibi held up under extreme scrutiny, and he didn't really have a motive to kill his children. No matter how much discord he had with Quinn."

"What's your take on the best friend?" I asked. "She was the beneficiary of an insurance policy for Quinn."

"Minimal," he said with a wave of his hand. "Twenty K at best."

Er...excuse me? "Maybe I need to consider a transfer to West Palm PD. I want to think twenty thousand dollars is chump change, too." I squinted at Danny. "I demand a salary review. Soon."

Zachary barked a laugh, looking a little surprised at himself. He gave Danny a look that was both rueful and knowing. "Okay, I'm starting to get it. He looks like that and he's kind of funny."

It was time to turn my squint on him. I didn't need him "to get" a damn thing about my relationship. Danny cleared his throat, probably because I was throwing off some bristly vibes. Like *wet cat being approached with a towel* bristly.

"I'm just saying that minimal is relative, right?" Zachary shrugged. "For me, that kind of money would be a big deal. Life changing. But Farrah Bell loaned *them* money. She comes from a family with clout and connections."

"They cut her off," I pointed out.

"Because they didn't like her husband," Zachary said heatedly. "He left and she got back in their good graces. She didn't need to kill three people for what amounts to chump change."

"Shall I make a list for you of all the things people have killed for?" I shot back. "I'll organize them in order of *say what* to *you've got to be kidding me.*"

"Okay, let's stay focused," Danny said, rubbing his temples. "What about Quinn's job? Anything there we need to know about?"

"She loved her job."

I grunted. I appreciated his candor, but he was running through my suspect list like a runaway freight train. "Well, let's say Quinn didn't leave on her own—"

"She did," he said firmly.

"But let's say she didn't," I said, undeterred. "Who else would be on your radar?"

"Maybe the brother," he said reluctantly. "Caleb. He's the one who put the majority of the money in the girls' college funds, which Nate and Quinn ran through. Needless to say, Caleb wasn't happy."

"Anyone else?" Danny asked.

"I'll give you my notes." He brightened. "And hey, while your team is re-investigating my flawless work, maybe I can give you a hand on the Sleepy Hollow case."

That was the first time I heard the moniker. Danny, too, judging from the way he briefly closed his eyes. "Seriously?"

"Word gets around. You found two bags of body parts, not one head in sight, on Halloween." Zachary's lips twitched. "Don't expect to get any volunteers down in the PTU for a bit."

Danny gave me a baleful look. Using my trusty married folk ESP, I could only imagine he was thinking that technically *I* found them. I shrugged. I talked to ghosts. Finding bodies was an occupational hazard.

"I appreciate the offer, but I'm sure you have better things to do," Danny said.

"Actually, I'm on a forced two-week vacation. New departmental policy says you use it or lose it. I decided to use it and I'm slowly going nuts." Zachary flashed that toothpaste-ad smile. "So I'm free as a bird."

Danny gave him a considering look. "Well, I guess I could use the assist. I'm heading back down to the crime scene later on today to meet up with a game ranger. I was hoping she could take us a little deeper into the Everglades around the crime scene. Just to make sure no one missed anything."

"An airboat tour through the Everglades? Sounds a lot better than what I've been doing on my vacation so far. I'm over watching TV and my dog is sick of me."

I agreed with his dog. And I'd only known the man for ten damn minutes.

Danny shrugged. "If you think I'm going to turn down an extra set of boots tromping through miles of swampland, you're sadly mistaken."

"Then it's settled." Zachary grinned. Fuck, did he ever give those dimples a rest? He clapped his hands on his thighs before he stood. "I'll just call my boss and make sure it's cool to liaison with your department. Then I'm all yours."

Well, wasn't that just fantastic?

6

Joshua Keller's two-story blue-and-white houseboat was bigger than I expected.

As we sat in the living room on opposing couches, I took a gander around, not hiding my curiosity. I'd expected a gloomy, enclosed space, but a bevy of windows let in a lot of light, making everything seem bright and cheery. And while everything was compact, it was well-appointed—all granite countertops and ash wood and shiny silver bar handles.

It was a very different lifestyle from the one he'd once had. So was his look. Gone was the preppy guy from my whiteboard. This version of Joshua was clad in the South Florida special—shorts, a tank top, and some flipflops. His previously shellacked do was now a full head of wild dark and gray curls. His skin was weathered from the sun, the grooves around his eyes deep. He'd morphed from a guy who was a year late for a meeting with some fiber to laid-back, beach-life dude.

Joshua rubbed his palms down his thighs a tad nervously. "I agreed to meet with you because it was the right thing to do," he said. "But I'm not sure what I can add to your investigation. I didn't kill Quinn."

"I never said you did."

"But it's the husband or the boyfriend, right?" He demanded. "I'm assuming the ex makes that list, too."

Makes it and tops it. I made no apologies for that. Statistics of women killed by a domestic partner was both shocking and self-explanatory.

"You must admit your relationship was rocky," I said. "Not to mention you we're in the middle of a contentious custody battle."

"So that would be a reason to kill *her*. Not my children."

"Not exactly a denial."

"Then you must not be listening," he said, exasperated. "I loved my girls. If nothing else, believe that. And maybe…maybe I still loved Quinn, too. It was just over between us."

"Why did your marriage end in the first place?"

"A lot of reasons," he said, still a little flustered. When I just continued to stare at him, bug-on-a-microscope style, his cheeks colored. "I'm not being evasive, it was just…one of those things. Maybe we argued too much. Maybe we were too young or whatever. The stress of two young kids certainly didn't help. But we parted as friends."

They may have parted that way, but they didn't stay that way. "What prompted you to file for custody?"

"Quinn was talking about moving with the girls to her mom's house in Tennessee, and I wasn't about to let that shit happen." He scowled. "I told her that you and the hubby can go, but Ryan and Regan stay here."

"How did she take that?"

"About as well as you'd expect. But that doesn't mean I killed her," he added quickly.

"You keep saying that," I said, more curiously than anything else. "The general consensus seems to be that she left on her own. Why are you so certain that she's dead?"

"She wouldn't take the girls away," he finally grumbled. "Not forever. Even in her stupid Tennessee plan, she wanted them to spend summers with me. I told her that wasn't enough, and she shot back that I was always working anyway. Which was stupid, because one of my biggest damn expenses was child support—"

"And after they disappeared, you no longer had to worry about that," I said coolly. "Right?"

He eyed me. "Is there something you'd like to say, Detective?"

Nope. I'd say insinuation was doing a damned fine job. "Do you know if Quinn was having trouble with anyone?" I tilted my head. "Other than you, that is."

He gritted his teeth. "Not that I can think of." It was an automatic, throwaway kind of answer, and my pointed look let him know he'd better think harder. He sighed exaggeratedly. "Maybe Farrah."

"Was it the money she loaned Quinn?"

"No, the only thing they ever really argued about was Gil." He shrugged. "Quinn couldn't stand him, and the feeling was mutual. There was a lot of abuse going on in the Bell household. It didn't help matters that Farrah had shit excuses for all her injuries."

"Like what?"

"Like the time she came to the Christmas party with a sprained wrist and had some bullshit excuse about tripping over the cat. Two months later, she showed up to Quinn's birthday party with a black eye and claimed she'd walked into something. We all knew that *something* was Gil's fist." He rolled his shoulders uncomfortably. "She'd stay with us until she was all patched up and then go on home."

"Did Quinn urge her to go to the police?"

"Yes, but she knew that was off the table. Then she suggested the Hope House, but Farrah just wanted her to back off. It got to the point where they just agreed not to talk about him, period."

"Then Gilbert left."

"Then he left," he agreed. "And things got better. Now if that's all...."

"Actually, it's not." I had more topics to cover before he remembered this was a voluntary interview. "Why don't you tell me about the last day you saw the girls?"

"It was the weekend before they disappeared. Just a weekend like any other." His fingers started worrying the rubber bracelet on his wrist. It looked old and worn, and I strained my eyes for a few moments before I could read the faded writing on the side. *Daddy*. "We played soccer at the park and went for ice cream after. Watched a couple movies. We had pizza and chicken nuggets for dinner."

"Sounds like a lot of fun," I said quietly.

He grimaced. "Yet another thing Quinn and I argued about. She was always after me to keep them on their routine, and I'll admit I wasn't good at that. Maybe I spent a little too much time being the 'fun one.' I just...I wanted them to *want* to come to my house, you know?" He sighed. "Anyway. I dropped them off at Quinn's on Sunday afternoon—late, she made sure to say. Then I said some shit and she said some shit...it wasn't our finest interaction. That was the last time I saw any of them."

Maybe it was, maybe it wasn't.

I sat quietly, giving him time to compose himself. I felt like a monster not offering sympathy, but it was a fine line to walk with suspects. You could be sitting in front of someone who'd mercilessly killed his entire family and was now doing his Oscar best to pull the wool over your eyes. Or you could be talking to a grieving father who'd lost his entire world in one day.

I knew my final request would probably get my rump roast booted out the door, but I had to do it anyway. "Would you be willing to take a lie detector test?" I asked. "We can schedule one any time you'd like. Just come down to the station and we'll get it done."

That went over about as well as I expected. His back got so stiff, it would've made a fine ironing board. When he spoke again, it was through gritted teeth. "I'll take whatever test you want if it'll get me off the suspect list. *For good*," he added in staccato beats. "Now I'm afraid I'm going to have to ask you to leave. You'll understand if I don't see you out."

I nodded slowly and stood. I passed his tense form carefully, keeping a watchful eye on his balled-up fists down by his sides. I had stepped out on the porch before he uttered another word. "Detective."

I paused, my hand still on the doorknob. "Yes?"

"Maybe my life is different now. But I changed my life *for* them. Ryan and Regan. Hell, even Quinn," he said fiercely. "I'm living for all of them now because they didn't get the chance. And I can't do that in half-measures."

There really didn't seem to be anything left to say.

I headed down the dock. It was getting darker earlier nowadays—our paltry version of winter—and the sun was low in the sky, glittering over the expanse of oh-so-blue water. A few people were out on their porches, enjoying the scenery and watching the world go by. I exchanged nods and the occasional wave with several of them as I made my way to the parking area.

My phone vibrated with a text, and I checked the screen to find a text from Danny.

> Everything okay with Keller?

I had to smile. I was glad he'd given up on coming up with subterfuge to express his worry and just went full on mother hen with that shit. What had previously driven me crazy was now my most favorite thing. I knew where it was coming from—his oversized heart—and that, as it turns out, made all the difference.

> There's a fleeing suspect and a pursuit down off Biscayne. That's not you, is it?

I scowled. Well, it made *some* of the difference.

> All is well.

> Going to be home a little late, though. Grocery shopping.

I wasn't going to bother to try and foist it off on Danny. It was my turn, after all. And one of us had better do it before the fridge turned itself off in exasperation.

> How late is late

> Maybe a few hours?

> Okay, I won't rush home, then.

> On second thought, I'm going to take Watty to the groomer

As long as he'd dropped off Zachary—that dimpled, pearly-toothed bastard—back at the station, all was right in my world. I decided not to text that, though.

> He needs it

> He said you're just jealous because he's gorgeous

> Tell that mutt he's had his last greenie

I'd made it back to my car before my phone pinged again. I thumbed it open to find a picture of Watson's sorrowful face. I wondered how many takes it took before he stopped smiling his natural doggy smile.

> He said he's very sorry he rubbed his beauty in your face

I chuckled before I put the phone in the cupholder and started the car. I sat there for a few moments in contemplative silence. I knew Joshua was sincere about what he'd said. That he didn't want to live his life in half-measures. The proof was in his actions, and he'd done something that a lot of people talked about but never did—change. He'd overhauled his entire life. His job, his home…hell, even his appearance. It all amounted to a more honest life for himself.

I just had to wonder about the cost.

7

Even after an hour dithering in the store, I was still the first one home. I coasted in the garage and got out with a long stretch, reflecting on how nice it felt to be back. And it *was* nice, right up until the moment I popped my trunk.

I stood there for a few minutes, staring at the sea of bags. I'd over-shopped as usual, lured by the siren song of buy one, get one free. And now that I had to carry all that crap, I realized that BOGO was a creation of Satan.

I sighed. Nothing for it but to get started.

I was halfway finished when my father meandered into the garage. "Hey, kiddo. Thought I heard you come in." He reached over and ruffled my hair like I was six, and I was hard-pressed not to grin as I smoothed it back down. "Where's the big guy?"

"At the groomer's. His nails were getting out of control." I grabbed another four bags. "Watson's, that is. Not Danny's."

I picked up another two bags with the last of my unoccupied fingers. It felt like my ring finger and pinky were going to break off, but oh well. I was willing to sacrifice a few digits if it meant I didn't have to make sixty-five round trips from the kitchen to the garage. I'd put my wedding ring on my thumb if I had to.

My father trailed after me as I shuffled into the house. "You can do that yourself, you know."

"Do what?"

"Watson's nails."

"I have no desire to wrestle that mutt to the ground and hold him immobile while Danny works the Pawdicure over his nails, but you should feel free," I said dryly.

We only worked on them as long as he'd let us, which made for some uneven results. The last time we'd tried, he wound up with nails that were both stubby and sharp enough to cut a bitch. His regular groomer, Robbie, could handle him by herself with just a few murmured words and treats. Better to let the professionals do what the professionals do.

I gave my ring finger a worried glance as it started to turn slightly purple, but I made it to the kitchen island. Gratefully, I dropped the bags on the polished surface. Six down, twenty to go. And five cases of water. Four jugs of cranberry juice. Three cases of soda, two bags of dog food, and a back brace in a pear tree.

By the time I got back to the car for another round of bags, my father was already nibbling on some Oreos. "I hate it when you get the thins," he mumbled around a mouthful of *my* cookies.

"I hear they have double-stuff at the store," I said pointedly. "Pretty sure you have to pay for them, though."

He stuffed another two in his mouth. "The thins will do."

"I thought they might." I wrestled the bag from his paws. Without cookies, I was a lot less interesting, and he meandered back over to his property line. I shook my head with a grin at the Pringles can tucked under his arm. I headed back inside, hitting the garage door button on the way in.

If only that was the end of the journey. I sighed, taking in the sea of bags covering the countertops. Now I actually had to put shit away. And properly, at that!

While I worked, I made a quick call. Two birds with one stone and all that. He answered on the second ring. "Aren't I seeing you on Saturday?"

I grimaced for two reasons. The first was because I did have a session scheduled with Dakota Daydream scheduled for Saturday morning. Early. And the second was because any session with my questionably qualified paranormal advisor involved meditation and yoga.

"Yes, we have a session on Saturday. Regretfully," I said. "Can't wait for you to do your usual routine of tap-dancing on my last freaking nerve. But I need to pick your brain for a moment."

"My brain prefers to be brushed," he quipped.

I sighed. Looks like we were starting the tap-dancing portion of the program a bit earlier than usual. "Why do I call you?"

"Because I'm brilliant and cute and just kooky enough to match *your* kooky without sending you running, screaming into the night."

He was pointedly silent, giving me a chance to deny undeniable facts. Too bad I couldn't. He was quirky and sweet and nerdy all wrapped up into one cute little ginger bundle. And occasionally—I cannot stress that word enough—he gave good advice. If it wasn't for the copious amounts of yoga, I might enjoy his company.

It helped that we had common paranormal ground. For me, it was ghosts. For Dakota, it was a green thumb that really had to be seen to be believed. I didn't know why he could do what he could do. Hell, I was pretty sure I didn't even know *what* he could do—he didn't talk about being a plant whisperer all that much. To be fair, I didn't walk up to strangers and start babbling about seeing ghosts.

Well, not after the FBI put me on psychiatric leave, that is.

"I'm also cheap," he added.

"My PayPal invoices say otherwise," I informed him because he was a snarky little plant whisperer and needed to be knocked off his lily pad sometimes.

"Are you having ghost trouble?" he asked, getting down to business.

"I'm having less-ghosts-than-usual trouble," I said.

"That...doesn't sound like a problem."

"It is when you're trying to solve a quadruple homicide," I said matter-of-factly. "I'm not seeing the volume of ghosts that I usually do...which I'm happy about. Really."

"You sound perturbed about it, actually. Like you miss them or something."

I scowled because how *dare* he imply some shit like that. "I'm only perturbed about what those sneaky ghosts are up to."

He only hummed. All went quiet on his end. I kept putting away groceries because he was thinking, and he'd respond when he was damn well ready. Apples went in the crisper, eggs went in the container, and cookies went in my mouth—er, the pantry. I was pouring the five-pound bag of sugar into the skinny mouth of the sugar jar—and making a right mess of it, too—when he finally spoke.

"You started listening to the ghosts," he said thoughtfully. "Maybe they started listening to you."

"Meaning?"

"Meaning you always told them to go away. And now they have." I could practically hear his shrug. "Maybe they're just giving you time and space."

I grunted as I wiped down the counter. True enough, I had been a little...less than congenial. Maybe I'd been pretty strict lately about the demands they put on my time. I'd certainly exercised the option to send them over the bridge, willing or not. And since I got the protection tattoo, there was no more inhabiting my body. So yeah, maybe word was just getting around.

I couldn't help but feel it was more than that, though. That, as usual, I was missing something important. Every time I thought I had a handle on my paranormal side, the ghosts proved me wrong.

"Yeah, maybe," I finally said. "Do you know anything about them using the stars to communicate? Quinn mentioned it but she was very sketchy when it came to details of how it worked."

"I can look into it," he said. "Meanwhile, I'll meet you at the ley line on Saturday. Bring a better attitude." He paused. "Or snacks."

He didn't wait for my answer as he ended the call. I looked at the cookie jar consideringly before grabbing a Ziploc bag. "Snacks it is," I murmured.

I was curled up on the couch with my laptop and a mug of coffee when I heard Danny's car in the driveway. It wasn't that hard—the vibration of his engine actually moved my mug on the side table. I nudged it back from the edge with a mutter of *good grief.* There was American muscle and then there was disturbing the peace.

He came through the door a few moments later, keys jingling, a stack of mail in one hand and Watson's leash in the other. He leaned down and unclipped the leash, and then it was just a blur of fur streaking around him and bolting toward me.

I greeted Watson with a little grin. It was impossible not to get caught up in his canine joy. He jumped up on me, smelling strongly of powder shampoo and I scratched behind his smooth ears. "Who's a handsome boy?"

"Better be me." Danny leaned over to give me a kiss before flopping down beside me on the couch. He immediately started going through the mail. "I spent a lot of money on this haircut while I was waiting for His Royal Dogness here."

I pretended to look over his perfectly styled hair. Danny was as low-key about his appearance as they came, but he was a freaking prima donna when it came to his hair. It was gorgeous, of course, but I wasn't about to give him the satisfaction.

"Sorry, Irish," I informed him. "In the game of who wears it better, I've got to go with my boy Watty."

"Well, perhaps you'd be interested to know that while I was paying, 'your boy Watty' took a bite out of a woman's purse. Apparently, she had a baggie of ham pieces in there."

"Well, that sounds like a clear case of entrapment," I said indignantly. "Who carries ham around in her purse?"

"It was for her nervous schnauzer, Mindy, who Watson tried to get frisky with."

I waited, but he didn't continue, clearly done tattling for the day. I watched him rip into another piece of mail before I prompted, "Well?"

"Well, what?" he asked distractedly, ripping up a credit card offer. "Was Mindy interested?"

"Wouldn't give him the time of day. She had on a Louis Vuitton collar," he said with a grin. "She was *far* above his station."

I chuckled. "Well, sometimes you gotta shoot your shot anyway." I rubbed Watson's special spot under his chin, and he went stock still to better let me work the stress of rejection away. "Also, as this is a looks competition and not behavioral, Watson still wins."

Danny grumbled as he folded a sheet of coupons from a local eatery and tucked it in the side table. He gave my laptop screen a curious look. "Since when do you use TikTok?"

"Since when do you actually get the name right and not call it TipTop, Oldy McOld?"

"That was once. *Years* ago."

"And I'm never going to let you forget it," I promised. "It was so fucking shocking, I almost signed you up for Life Alert. I need to know if you fall when I'm not home, Daniel."

He looked amused. "Glad to know your sense of humor hasn't changed—despite popular request. Also, you should feel free to stop giving me shit any time."

I smirked. *Not likely, my love. Not hardly likely.* "I'm doing a little research on Quinn's best friend, Farrah."

"Kevin met with her today. Did you get the email with his notes?"

"Yeah. But after meeting with Joshua, we're in follow-up interview territory. I have more questions." I clicked on another video, and a smiling Farrah popped up. For a few minutes, we watched her make a smoothie in what was probably a sponsored mini blender. "I left her a couple messages to call me back so we can set up a time."

"So she makes videos or something?" He squinted at the screen. "When would I ever need a smoothie on the go?"

"Well, Daniel, I'm thinking it might come in handy when you take us twenty-minutes out of our way to hit up *Smoothie King*," I said pointedly, because that little detour had made us extremely late for my niece's Christmas play. Luckily, the wise men bumped into the manger, sending the baby Jesus and several stuffed lambs rolling down the aisle. The bedlam had been perfect cover for us to sneak in the back. "And yeah, she's an influencer."

"Which is?"

"The reason I'm buying these." I showed him a video where Farrah was wearing Copper Fit wristbands. "They're supposed to help with carpal tunnel syndrome."

"Which you do not have."

"Yeah, but I feel like I could any day now," I assured him as I rotated my wrists.

He snorted. "So what, she sells these things?"

"No, she tries out products and gives her opinion on whether they're good or not."

He slow-blinked those beautiful blue eyes at me. "That's...a job?"

"Don't be so close-minded, Irish," I said with a little grin. "I swear, you're not happy unless someone gets up at the crack of dawn, throws on a uniform, and leaves the house with a mug of coffee and a lunchbox."

"Speaking of which, stop pretending to forget the lunches I make for you. We both promised to buckle down on our spending since you got your precious pool."

"*My* pool?"

"That's correct."

"You mean the one I can't keep you out of?" I asked pertly. "And I'm so glad you've finally discovered my master plan. I'm planning to bankrupt us, one ten-dollar value meal at a time."

His mouth twitched as he tried to hold on to his indignation. "Keep it up, Rain. I see spankings in your future." My eyes rounded with hope, and he finally had to laugh. "Oh, for fuck's sake. I have to come up with a real fucking punishment for you. Just tell me about the damn blog."

"Alright, but you owe me a spanking and I'm not about to let that shit slide," I informed him. "It's called Fifty, Fun, and Fabulous with Farrah."

"She's not fifty."

"No one knows that," I said exasperatedly. "You suck at branding, baby."

He squinted at the top of the page. "Yeah, well she certainly doesn't. Are all these people watchers?"

"Good Lord." I stared, long enough for him to raise an imperious eyebrow. "They're called followers, McKenna. And they should give you your AARP card now."

He grinned. Guess getting older was amusing when the devil was still honoring your deal and you were only getting better-looking with age. "I'm going to be getting discounts on shit four years sooner than you and no, I'm not going to share."

Well, damn. I sent him an affronted look. "No need to get vicious."

"And on that note, I'm going to make dinner." He levered himself off the couch with a groan and stretched. "There's this thing I want to try with teriyaki chicken."

I cringed as he headed for the kitchen. "You passed any number of restaurants on the way home."

A few moments later, I heard him puttering about, already pulling out pots and pans. He opened the fridge, ready to do unspeakable things to innocent ingredients. He asked over the ruckus, "Yeah, and?"

"*And* any one of those restaurants would've been better than flirting with food poisoning."

My logic only netted me a dishtowel to the head.

8

I'd admit to having a few preconceived notions about married sex. I knew that we'd move past the "can't keep my hands off you" stage and into something else. And not necessarily in a bad way, either. Just that we'd become more comfortable with one another, and it wouldn't be so much a gas fire as a smoldering flame.

I just hadn't expected that to be so much *better*.

I took my time giving Danny a blow job that made his toes curl, determined to take him there in every way possible. I would not be rushed by threats, promises, or a choked *please* that did wonders for my ego. Instead, I added a new dictionary entry next to the word relentless.

That wasn't to say he didn't return fire. He manhandled me, turning me around before I knew what was what. I thought we were going to pleasure each other at the same time...which made me smug. I never said no to Danny on his knees, lashes like dark fans on his cheeks and brow knitted in concentration as I did my best to wreck his mouth. But much to his embarrassment, his gag reflex was weak while mine was practically nonexistent. In the battle of sixty-nine, I was the undisputed champion. Every time.

I reminded him of that with a smug battle cry of *no mercy.*

Too bad he had other plans.

Two thick, lubed fingers in my ass turned the tables pretty quickly. When he added a third, I forgot what the hell I was supposed to be doing and closed my eyes, resting my forehead against his thigh. I tried not to fuck his fingers, but it was a useless battle. He knew that, and I did, too. Sure enough, a few seconds later my hips started to jerk against my will.

"You play dirty," I accused.

"I'm sorry, weren't you busy driving me out of my mind?" he asked silkily. "No mercy, I believe you said?"

"Doesn't sound like me," I said, trying to get back in the game. I gave him a long lick that made him suck in a breath. And a strong suck at the head that made him buck.

By the time I pushed him flat and took him inside me in one, smooth glide, I wasn't sure who had won or lost. Which was just fine.

"Reverse cowboy?" He sounded slightly scandalized.

I glanced over my shoulder, only to find his face flushed and his gaze riveted on my rear, which I'll admit—one and one time only—had some...jiggly properties. Jiggly properties my husband overly enjoyed. "Don't kink shame me, Daniel."

He gave a pained laugh even as his hand landed on my rear—and not at all gently, either. *Finally.* The man had been promising a spanking and reneging on that promise for far too long, which was just not good etiquette. Nor was tossing me off and pushing me flat on my back so he could pound me into oblivion. I hung on for the ride, my eyes rolling back in my head at how very good it felt.

There was just something wonderful and addictive about being skin to skin with someone who knew you, inside and out. Something that acrobatic sex with a hookup—smoking hot or not—just couldn't even touch. The give and take of it all was fucking next level.

There was no score to settle. No tally to keep track of. If I needed more, he gave me more, and it went both ways. He didn't just know what got me off. He knew what drove me absolutely wild. He had the ability to touch me absolutely everywhere—physically and mentally—because he knew both the good and the bad. Best of all, he didn't seem to see the latter as a flaw, but part of the makeup that made me...*me*. I was finally starting to realize that I'd never get enough.

I was *so* alright with that.

As the pressure crested and built, I tossed my head on the pillows. His corded arm was braced next to my head, and I latched on as I came, fastening my hand around his wrist. Any connection. Every connection. There was no looking away. All I could see was him, his eyes focused on me like I was absolutely everything.

Right back at you.

I came down from my high, glad he'd followed me over the edge. I hadn't had the presence of mind to do anything but enjoy the ride. I'd fully expected to want Danny with the same intensity for the rest of my life. And I now knew that wasn't just an abstract idea but absolute reality.

I winced as I lowered my legs from where he'd hiked them up around his waist. Like I was twenty or some shit. Yet another thing I fully expected—to one day pull a freaking hamstring while we were getting our groove on. I could also do without him collapsing on me after we finished. I mean, he'd earned a rest, but that fucker was heavy. I'd also probably need possession of my ass back at some point, so he was going to have to park that big dick someplace else. Stat.

I informed him of all of this. Loudly.

He chuckled tiredly, still pulsing inside of me. "Gimme...a fucking second. I'm reveling."

"Can't you revel over there?" I grumbled. "Hope they charge you... with my murder. Suffocation in the first degree."

"I'll get off with a slap on the wrist," he predicted, and a damn sight breezily, too. "Especially once I explain that it was a terrible tragedy and I miss you very much. Even your smart mouth. *No one could miss that mouth,* they'll say as they gawp in amazement. *It had to be an accident.*"

"You already thought of your defense?" I demanded, outraged.

He laughed even as he slipped free and rolled on his back. Despite my complaining, I was immediately bereft. Empty in a way I couldn't describe. So it was my turn to insist on contact, stretching myself over him like a human blanket. It still wasn't...*quite* right. And then the possessive hand gripping my ass spread me open a bit, and gave me two fingers deep where I wanted them.

My breath hitched as he gripped my ass possessively with his other hand. Stuffed and a whole lot happier, I gave him a disgruntled look because how dare he know exactly what I needed. He let out a laugh that was mostly a huff of air. "Better?"

I wasn't going to dignify that with a response. Besides, I couldn't quite think of the right word to describe how I was feeling at the moment. Sated? Treasured? Special? I just knew there was no better feeling than falling asleep in a tangle of sweaty limbs with the person who loved me best. I could hear and feel his breathing slow as he fell asleep first.

The night faded away in pieces. I could hear the hum of the air conditioner kicking on. The soft sound of Watson's snoring, who must've crept in the room while we were...er, occupied. Even though he was sleeping, Danny's fingers still filled me possessively. I buried my face in the crook of his neck, so his scent was all I could smell. *When we're close like this, my every thought is you.* I smiled as I fell asleep, the word for the feeling finally coming to me.

Perfect.

The ground was rough and cold, and everything was so very dark.

I looked around in confusion, wondering where I was. I only knew I wasn't in bed anymore, safe and sound. I tried to rub my eyes, but I couldn't seem to move my arms. Or my body. I tried to lift my arms again and realized I was restrained by something rough and abrasive. I struggled for a few seconds before I figured out I was tied with rope. I rocked backward and winced as my head hit something solid and rough. A tree, maybe?

Fuck. I had no idea why I was tied to a fucking tree, but it couldn't be good.

Bright lights suddenly seared my vision. I blinked as I cast a bleary look around. Canned music was coming from somewhere...and voices. I couldn't quite make out what they were saying, but they sounded like they were children's voices. Which was beyond strange. How many of them were there? Did they put me here? And just how the hell was I going to get away from these hellish children of the corn?

My hand moved without my permission, wriggling in my back pocket. My eyes widened as I pulled out a pocketknife. I rarely carried one of those. Danny had often harped on me that I should, but I forgot as much as I remembered. So these probably weren't my pants—shorts, rather. Or my legs, thickly muscled and liberally dusted with dark hair.

My hands sliced through the ropes, and they fell to the ground. I cut the ones binding my feet, too, and then rubbed the chafed skin at my ankles. I realized the "children" talking wasn't live—it was just a recording. I wasn't sure if that was better or worse. Right about now, it just felt creepy as fuck. Their voices were loud and discordant as they sang "Ring Around the Rosie" and I clapped my hands over my ears. I wished the godawful music would end so I could just think.

And then it did.

I only had a few moments to be grateful before I wondered why it had ended so abruptly. There was a long beep, and then the spotlights went off, leaving me in the darkness. My cones and rods struggled to adjust to yet another quick change.

"What's happening?" I mumbled.

The whisper came next, seemingly from all around me. "Run for your life."

My breath froze in my chest. But it wasn't fear, which I should've been feeling. It was rage, an anger the likes of which I'd never felt before. Whoever had this kind of anger certainly needed some therapy. I wished I could poke around in his brain for answers. For now, all I could do was lean into the memory and try to remember everything I could.

"Sharla, you bitch!" I screamed. "Come out and face me!"

There were no answers forthcoming. Just the sound of a gunshot in the distance.

I may've fallen asleep in increments, but I awoke all at once, sucking in air on a gasp.

All was just as it had been when I went to sleep, except Watson had joined us in bed. Danny had fallen asleep on his back. He hated that position, but not enough for me to wake him up. I let his heavy breathing soothe me. It helped. Some.

I directed a squinty-eyed look at a snoring Watson. *You, I can wake.* He slept twenty-three hours a fucking day—surely, he could spare a couple minutes so I could hug the stuffing out of him. The moment my hand landed on his soft and bristly fur, he jolted a bit. Then snuffled and nosed my hand before relaxing again. I rubbed his ears, breathing shallowly as I waited for my heart rate to calm. I was safe. Not tied to a tree. Not running for my life from a woman named Sharla.

Everything had just felt so fucking real.

I eventually gave Watson's ears a good scratch before I let him sleep. I sat up in bed, swinging my legs over the side. As I rubbed at my eyes, the name from my dream teased at the edges of my brain. *Sharla.* I needed to write it down, immediately, so I wouldn't forget. It also wouldn't hurt to do something mundane and normal. Something as far away from that awful memory as I could get.

I got out of bed, careful not to wake Danny. His heavy breathing got lighter for a few moments, before he sighed deeply and turned over, giving me his golden, tattooed back. I closed the bedroom door behind me quietly and padded down the hall to my office.

There was a soft light under the door when I got there. I pushed it open warily, hoping it wasn't the screaming man from my vision. Luckily, it was only Franklin. He was curled up in my wing chair, a book in his hands, and he looked up as I entered the room. His slight smile fell as he took in my appearance.

I yawned sleepily. "You aren't projecting your dreams to me, are you?"

He looked at me over his glasses. "I am not. And you look absolutely wretched."

"So glad you decided to grace me with your presence," I said dryly, making my way over to my desk. "Have I told you that lately?"

"I just meant that you looked like you could use a tad more sleep."

He brightened as I scrounged around in my desk for a marker. "Can I offer you a cup of—"

"I don't want any damn tea," I muttered.

I came across the blue marker first. It wasn't the right one for my color-coordinated system, but it was too late at night—early in the morning, rather—to care. I uncapped the marker and wrote the name Sharla on my whiteboard, then added a question mark on the side.

Realizing Franklin was now looking down at his book in affronted silence—and rightly so—I sighed. "Sorry. I'm a bear until I get my—"

"Tea?" He asked hopefully.

I gave him a tired smile. "Coffee, but yeah, same principle applies."

He looked a lot happier. "So. What has got you out of bed so early in the morning?" He asked. "I would've thought after the…*shenanigans* that you and your gentleman got up to earlier that it would be noon before I saw either one of you."

I narrowed my eyes in his direction. The rice and salt mix we lined the baseboards with was supposed to keep the ghosts from entering any space other than my office…but you could never be a hundred percent sure about this paranormal business.

"And what would you know of it?" I asked suspiciously. "You weren't watching, were you?"

He huffed with indignation. "Certainly not. I do, however, have ears that work just fine." He looked side to side as if he was about to share a doozy of a secret. Then he whispered, "It was quite titillating."

Someone kill me now. "Wonderful," I said sourly.

"So," he said, far too perkily for three in the morning. "Who is this Sharla person? And what has she done to earn a spot of honor on your murder board?"

"I don't know," I murmured. The whisper of *run for your life* was still a little too fresh in my head, and a shiver worked its way down my spine. "But I certainly plan to find out."

9

My Saturday session with Dakota wasn't going well. I'd summoned the wrong ghost using the ley line, proving once again I was right to be leery of using it. In the past, Dakota had given me some long, drawn-out explanation about how the ley line worked. I'd dozed through most of it, but I got the gist. He'd said something about it being an energy line that intersects the planet. With the right stone configuration and a touch of Cascarilla powder, such an intersection could react to excess energy and create a portal. We'd basically created an access point for the return of excess energy. And since ghosts *were* excess energy, it made a perfect doorway. There was more to it, but then he'd whipped out a stack of charts and I'd prayed for death.

I stared at Quinn Harper—*not* Quinn Parker—who'd emerged from the line a scant few minutes ago. She was older, solidly built and not frail in the least, with an iron-gray braid and a thick pair of glasses. Behind those glasses, she had large gray eyes that seemed fed up with my questions. She had no interest in going back to wherever she'd come from, and she didn't need my help. No matter how many times I asked.

Apparently, I'd turned into the ghostly version of an ambulance chaser.

"Are you sure you don't—" I blinked as she started to walk off purposefully, like she was late for some ghostly appointment. "And just where are you going?"

"I must see the new star for myself," she said airily. "No need to trouble yourself, dear."

"What...wait, why do you need to see the stars?"

"Oh, is she talking about the stars like the other ghost?" Dakota whispered and I glared. This wasn't all his fault, of course, but I could blame him in a pinch. At the vehemence of my glare, he startled. "What?"

"It's not the Quinn I'm looking for," I muttered.

"Try again," he encouraged, looking excited. "Maybe we'll get Dr. Quinn, Medicine Woman next time. I used to watch that show with my aunt."

"Okay, A, that's not her real name. And B, Jane Seymour is not dead," I informed him. "You idiot."

He huffed and propped his hands on his hips. "Did I mention that I blew off working on my project for you? I was on the verge of something important. I'm *so* close to developing this really cool watermelon hybrid."

I rolled my eyes because work was the one thing Dakota needed less of. He'd finished grad school and started a nursery named *Root Awakenings*, and it pained me to admit that 'settled' was a good look on him. He was in tan capris, a t-shirt with a science pun, and electric blue sneakers on his feet. He'd stopped using so much product in his do and his ginger hair was doing its own thing on his head.

I thought the messy look worked for him and I'd told him so, earning a blush for my trouble. He'd then informed me snootily that he was over me and no longer had an old man fetish/crush. That little shit. I believed him—mostly. Except when he turned red as a tomato because I gave him a simple compliment.

"You'll be back to your precious watermelon soon enough. But now I need to help...." I cast a look around because that ornery ghost wasn't where I last saw her. "And just where did that blasted woman go—"

"Thanks for your help," Quinn called over her shoulder as she disappeared. "I'll be seeing you, gentlemen."

Well, then.

I turned to Dakota, who still looked a little put out. Probably because Jane Seymour wasn't coming. "You see what I'm talking about?" I demanded. "And this isn't even the first time."

"Actually, I didn't see," he said testily. "As I am not the one who sees ghosts. Remember?"

Oh. Right. That took a substantial amount of wind right out of my indignant sails. "Well, consider yourself lucky."

"I do," he said with insulting fervor. "Every time I drive away from you, I think, *thank fuck that's over.*"

I sent him a narrow-eyed look. "I basically got ghosted by a ghost. She hustled off like she had some ghostly emergency."

"Stop saying the word ghost before it loses all meaning," he said. "Maybe she'll be back."

"They haven't come back."

His eyebrows slowly rose as he looked me over. I didn't fidget under his gaze, but it was a near thing. "Again, I must point out that you sound low-key disappointed about that."

"I'm not," I maintained staunchly. "Just concerned is all. Can't have them out there creating havoc. It is my responsibility, after all."

"Mmhmm." His tone said he saw through my bullshit and wasn't interested in a second helping. "How long has this been happening?"

Too bad. I ladled him out another three scoops. "A few months. And it's not like I don't still see them. They just don't seem interested in sticking around. Which I'm thrilled about," I added quickly.

"You know, I was thinking about this star business." He stared at the ley line thoughtfully. "First, I did some research on stars to see if there was any paranormal connection to opening spiritual doorways. Stars as a being are rooted in the context of astrology and damn near impossible to separate from scientific terminology. And any connection to the spiritual seemed metaphorical rather than actual—"

"Jesus Christ." I sighed, rubbing my temples. I was starting to understand how my team felt when I went on a serial killer tangent.

"My *point* is that I don't think they're referring to an astrological star," he said, used to my impatience. "You're pretty protected right about now. No longer an open vessel for them to use at will. And that's before word got around about all the vanquishing you've done."

"I don't know if it's fair to call it *vanquishing*," I said uncomfortably. "I help them. It's what I'm supposed to do. That's why they call me a bridge, is it not? To help them cross over?"

"Yes, but for those who want to stick around, a bridge who is quick to vanquish isn't exactly ideal. So maybe they applied themselves to finding another light source."

"Another source of…wait." I blinked. "You mean another medium?"

He nodded. "It's possible. That could be what they mean by the new star."

If that was true, I felt sorry for the poor bastard. He had a tough row to hoe figuring this medium shit out. It wasn't easy keeping it from taking over your entire life. And it was downright terrifying trying to keep your loved ones safe. If I made a list of every inconvenience, every bothersome request I'd fulfilled, every time I'd risked my life for those bloody ghosts, the paper would be five miles long. It made me want to find this guy—the so-called "new star" in the ghost community—and bend his ear for a bit. To give him the benefit of what I'd learned the hard way.

At Dakota's raised brow, I realized I hadn't said anything in quite some time. He continued staring a hole into me, probably coming to all kinds of conclusions that were absolutely wrong. "Stop it."

"I'm just letting you finish all your mental acrobatics," he said. "It's very entertaining, watching you come to terms with not being the only catnip in town."

I huffed out a laugh. "Nice."

He hummed. "*And* if I know you like I think I do, you're now worried about the new star going through some of the stuff you went through. So you're planning to find him and help him. Or her." He smirked. "You sure do have people fooled."

It was hard to believe I actually paid for this kind of abuse. "Which means what, exactly?"

"It means that on the outside, you're like Matter-of-fact, Reserved, Analytical Guy. With your whiteboards and your charts and your pressed clothing—"

I narrowed my eyes. "I wasn't aware it was a crime to utilize a dry cleaner now and again."

"And on the inside," he continued with a little grin, "you're an absolute mess with a heart as big and soft as a marshmallow PEEP. They're my favorites, by the way."

I should be able to arrest him for that alone.

"I carry a weapon," I said in measured tones. "You do understand that, right?"

He sent me a placating look, like I was a kid showing him what the Tooth Fairy had left me. If he patted me on the head, I couldn't guarantee his safety. Luckily, he just smiled. "We should start our meditation."

I sighed. "Of course we should."

An hour later, we were still sitting on the grass in the backyard, facing one another. Dakota had put on some weird music that mostly consisted of wind and a pan flute, and it was doing nothing to help me empty my mind. The best I could do was not think about work. Or the mysterious new star, who was probably pulling out his hair by the fistfuls right about now. Or becoming a dad and those stupid bicycles. Or *not* becoming a dad and letting Danny down....

Buzz. I furrowed my brow as the little noise filtered into my consciousness. And the scent of marigolds, much stronger than I'd ever smelled before. Actually, much stronger than the small flowers could produce on their own.

I huffed out a soft laugh. I had a feeling that my mother's

marigolds were now a hell of a lot bigger than marigolds should ever be. She would be thrilled. "I'm focusing."

Dakota hummed. "Not nearly hard enough."

Buzz. And there was that noise again. It took me far too long to realize the buzzing was my phone at my hip. To be fair, my everything had been numb for the last half-hour.

I slowly eased my leg free of its crossed position and dropped my hand casually to my side. I risked a quick glance at Dakota, who was sitting perfectly still, legs folded in pretzel position effortlessly. I worked my hand in my pocket.

Dakota's eyelash flickered and I froze.

He continued to breathe evenly, slowly, demonstrating proper technique—or experimenting with Lamaze, who knows. The buzzing stopped. And then started right back up again. I wriggled my fingers deeper in my pocket.

Dakota sighed. "Will you get that before I strangle you?"

"Now, now," I tsked as I gave up on sneaky and pulled out my phone. "That's not very Zen of you."

"I haven't done you a trace of bodily harm," he said grimly. "Trust me, that is *next-level* Zen of me."

I scowled as he unfolded himself and got off the ground gracefully. Like that position he'd held for half an hour shouldn't require traction and the kind of pain killers that made you see colors. "I'm going to my car to get the rest of the Cascarilla powder," he announced.

"Because summoning the last ghost worked so well?"

"Well, we need one of them to tell us who the new star is. We just have to find someone a little more...cooperative."

Cooperative...*ghosts*? I hadn't seen the phenomenon yet, but I suppose anything was possible. I kept my particular brand of doom and gloom to myself, shaking my head as he practically skipped his ass around the side of the house.

When I checked my phone, I had two missed calls from Danny. Before I could call him back, a text popped up.

> You busy?

>> Depends on why you're asking

> Because I want to know if you're busy

> Your position as the brains of this outfit is in jeopardy

>> You're not at all cute. Two phone calls and a text, someone better be on fire, Irish

I thought about that and added another caveat.

>> Someone I like.

> And just what are you so busy doing

>> Spiritual enlightenment?

> Oh, you're with Dakota? Well, don't let me interrupt

For someone who didn't want to interrupt, he was doing a bang-up job. I pressed his number, and he picked up on the first ring. "One of the torsos has a pacemaker."

His greeting, if you could call it that, was definitely questionable, and I blinked. "Love it when you talk police procedural to me, dollface."

He chuckled. "I figured you'd want to know as soon as possible."

I hummed because he was absolutely correct, and that's why we were a perfect fucking pair. The way to a man's heart—this man, at least—was forensic expediency. But first, I had a bone to pick.

"Your phone manners are woefully lacking and it's time someone told you," I informed him. "It's like you're incapable of saying hello."

Wherever he was, it was quite noisy. I could hear people talking in the background and judging by the volume of one of them in particular, he really liked the sound of his own voice. "Hello just wastes so much time."

"It's one word."

"But then you say hello back, and then we're in *how are you doing* territory," he fussed. "Then there's a *fine, how are* you *doing*, and Jesus Christ, when does it end?"

I couldn't help but grin. "You have the phone manners of an orangutan."

"I don't know any orangutans who would've bothered to put smiley face carrots in your lunch," he said indignantly.

When my sister heard how committed he was to making our lunches, she got him a kit of sandwich tools she used for her kids. When she gifted it to him, his *thanks* had a definite question mark behind it. He looked adorably confused as he stored them in our junk drawer. So imagine my surprise when I started getting veggies and fruits with personality in my lunch.

"You're getting a little out of control with that smiley face press, and you need to know it," I informed him. "I'm tired of having the happiest fucking lunch ever."

"Well, when you start making it, *you* can choose the emotion of your carrots."

He kind of had a point. "Carry on."

"I fully intend to." He sounded amused. "Also, I—hang on a sec."

I listened to the murmur of his voice as he said something to someone in the background. I couldn't pick out everything, but it sounded like a coffee order. And then I realized that it wasn't *people* I was hearing in the background, but one person.

"Is that Zach?" I blurted.

"What?" he asked, sounding much closer as he probably brought the phone back to his ear.

"Zach," I repeated, going for casual. "I thought I heard him in the background."

"Yeah, we're just leaving the ME's office. Now he's making an order for some frou frou coffee on his phone."

"It's not frou frou," I heard Zach insist. "Just because they have a few different types of creamer—"

"Sixteen," Danny said grimly, as if he couldn't imagine a worse fate. "They also have six damn types of sugar, fifteen flavor shots, and cold foam. I don't even know what that is. And I don't want to know," he added quickly.

Zach said something in stringent tones in the background.

"I said I didn't want to fucking know," Danny insisted, but I could hear the humor in his voice.

I was still and quiet as I listened to them go back and forth. Hell, I challenged a German shepherd with his teeth inches from a fleeing suspect's ass to be more focused than me. I wasn't really even sure what they were saying—I was more focused on *how* they spoke to each other. As a detective, nuance was my life, and this nuance spoke of comfort and ease. Fondness.

"Hey, are you still there?" Danny asked.

I cleared my throat, striving for normal. "Yep."

"Oh good, I thought I lost you." At the *ding* on his end, I guessed they were getting on an elevator. "I had to call and share the news about the pacemaker as soon as I heard. Life can be so fucking ironic, you know?"

"Well, Alanis Morissette certainly seems to think so."

He snorted. "Our killer took so much time and effort to obscure their identities, and still left behind things that we can use. Like that tattoo on the first body. Well," he said, considering. "Half a tattoo because of the way the leg was severed. I'll send you a picture."

"Can't wait," I said with a grimace, resolving to eat something before I opened it. I wasn't overly squeamish, but after I saw some shit like that, my stomach would be closed for business for a bit.

"Sent," he said a moment later as my phone buzzed. "Now, here we are with a pacemaker in the torso of body number two, which is even better. Fucking amazing."

"Yes, it truly is like Christmas morning," I said dryly. "Now, gimme a pull at the lever of luck. Did Joshua show up for his lie detector test?"

"Cherry, cherry, lemon," he said, sounding amused. "And the machine is now out of order."

Zach said something that I couldn't quite catch, and I gritted my teeth, making a mental note to *thank* Quinn—maybe with a pie in the face—for bringing this man, however indirectly, into our lives. I looked up as Dakota rounded the corner into the backyard, carrying a small jar and a handful of stones.

"So are you?"

I blinked at the sound of Danny's voice, too lost in my thoughts to even hazard a guess what he'd been talking about. "Am I what?"

He chuckled softly. "That's what I get for interrupting your session. Are you close to finishing? If you're not, I won't rush home."

"No, we're not quite done yet."

"Okay, then Zach and I can squeeze in a visit to a few tattoo shops in the area. I want to see if someone recognizes the ink on the first body."

We chatted for a few more moments before he hung up. I stared at the phone in my hand, wondering why I was letting this Zach thing bother me so. Maybe because there was history there, and history could be a powerful thing.

What're you even thinking right now?

I rubbed my forehead. I was thinking stupid thoughts, that's what I was doing. Sometimes I compared my pre and post Danny lives and wondered how it was even *possible*, finding someone that made me this happy. I guess even the slightest threat to what we had drove me crazy. He'd told me time and time again that I wouldn't be the Rain he loved without all my paranormal quirks. But I couldn't help but wonder if he ever wished for something…easier. Even subconsciously. And maybe a husband who didn't need a defibrillator at the idea of welcoming little people into his life.

"Are you okay?"

My head jerked up at Dakota's softly worded query. His mouth was pursed, his eyebrows knitted together. His whiskey-brown eyes were concerned as he stared at me.

"Of course," I said quickly before that intuitive little plant whisperer figured out I was the nelliest nelly that ever nellied. "We should continue. Sorry about the interruption."

His eyebrows knitted together even more—at this point he was one drop stitch away from them becoming a forehead quilt. "Since when do you apologize for interruptions? You usually *manufacture* interruptions if you can."

"I do not," I said, sending him an affronted look. I mean, it was true, but calling people out on their shit was rather rude.

He gave his jar of crimson powder a little shake, and I barely held back an instinctual flinch. We'd learned the hard way that a little of that powder went a *long* way. Mostly by him blowing up our backyard.

"I've got the Cascarilla," he announced. "You ready to work the ley line?"

"Actually, I think we should meditate a bit more," I said.

He nearly dropped the jar.

Like I said. Rude.

10

F arrah hadn't returned any of my calls. So I popped up on her doorstep on Monday like the worst kind of salesperson—uninvited, determined, and ready to ask uncomfortable questions. I expected the interview to be contentious. I expected a little pushback and a healthy serving of attitude. Maybe even a request that I talk to her through her attorney from now on. The usual.

I did not, however, expect to get punched in the face.

Needless to say, her yard had gotten a tad...*livelier* in the hour since I'd arrived. Like two squad cars and a couple nosy neighbors standing at the edge of their respective driveways lively. I stepped aside to let Officer Casey Hoyt by. He headed toward his squad car, my struggling perp and Farrah's ex-boyfriend—the lovely Lewis—in tow.

I don't know why Lewis bothered. Hoyt's biceps were about big enough to bench press an ox. I was pretty sure if he came out of a supermarket and found his car boxed in, he just picked it up, one-handed, and moved it out of the space. Probably didn't even drop the eggs.

He sent me a wide grin. "Still making friends everywhere you go, Christiansen?"

"I do what I can," I said with a shrug.

He crammed Lewis—now yelling—in the back of his squad car, and slammed the door with a cheery, "Watch your fingers."

Suddenly, peace reigned in Turtle Bay again. Thank fuck. Lewis yelled something that was thankfully muffled, and Hoyt grimaced. "That should be fun all the way to the station. You wanna tell me what went down here again?"

Not especially. It was bad enough that I was going to have to relay the whole thing to Tate. And then write a freaking report. Every time something happened on the job, you all but had to scrapbook that shit by the time it was all said and done.

I gave Hoyt the quick and dirty version. I'd pulled up to Farrah's home in Turtle Bay only to find her on the porch, having words with some guy. Even from the car, their body language seemed a little off. Aggressive.

I'd ambled up the driveway, watching carefully. They were so involved with their arguing that they didn't pay me a bit of attention. My walk turned a lot more purposeful as the man crowded into Farrah's space. I didn't wait, calling for backup. My instincts proved correct a few seconds later, and he slammed her against the door.

She didn't even take a second to breathe—just charged forward and pushed him back. Her small stature meant he didn't go back that far. It did a damned fine job of enraging him, though. She followed up the push with a slap, which didn't exactly help matters.

I broke into a run, reaching the porch just as he sent his fist flying at her face. When I yanked on his arm, it spun him around, which—unfortunately for me—gave him momentum. Lewis swung in a circle and we both had a moment of surprised eye contact...right before that momentum carried a fist Rocky Balboa would've been proud of toward my face. I barely had enough time to turn my face sideways to avoid a full-on hit, and his fist glanced off my jaw. We both stood there in stunned silence. There was no follow-up to what was clearly an accidental punch.

As my jaw bloomed with pain, I cared less and less about the accidental part.

I saw the exact moment he took in the badge at my hip. His eyes flared with recognition. Then fear. Then segued right on into panic. He didn't let moss grow on his feet though, as he darted around me. He sprinted toward the older model pickup in the driveway.

I wasted another two seconds standing there, wide-eyed and bewildered. Wondering how the fuck a simple drop-in had turned into...well, *this* so very quickly. Thankfully, my body started moving without my permission and I dashed after him. There would *not* be a fucking car chase today, despite what the universe was throwing my way.

I slammed into his back just as he yanked his car door open.

Our combined weight slammed it back shut—dented it, too, my bad—and I wrestled him to the ground. It wasn't easy and I was perspiring by the time I eventually maneuvered him to his front and secured his hands behind his back. Then it was just a litany of him begging and cajoling me to let him go until backup arrived.

And *boy* did they arrive. With all the lights and sirens and fanfare they used pulling into the cul-de-sac, you would've thought I'd caught numbers one through five on the FBI's Most Wanted List. I was too glad to turn my perp over to their custody to complain.

I worked my tender jaw gently, moving it back and forth in a way that only made it feel worse. It would probably be quite colorful by morning. I was grateful for the instinctual reflexes that made me turn just in time, though. Lewis's hammer of a fist plus my eye was an equation I was happy not to solve.

The very picture of frustration, Lewis rammed his head on the passenger glass, probably dislodging his last two brain cells that had been holding hands. "That's gonna leave a mark," I said mildly.

"If I'm really lucky, he'll probably spend the first half-hour at the station swearing on a stack that I did that to him." Hoyt gave me a disgruntled look. "And from the looks of his pupils, he's coming down off something. Love it when you give me someone detoxing for transport."

"Stop your whining, Hoyt." I touched my jaw gently and winced. "I'm the one that took a fucking haymaker to the face."

"He barely clipped you," he said with a smirk. "You're probably worse off from that scratch from the wildcat."

Oh, right. My second nasty surprise. Farrah had jumped on my back as I was cuffing her boyfriend. Luckily, she'd only seemed interested in pulling me off him, not causing any real damage. In the process, she'd managed to claw me pretty good down the side of my neck with a coffin-shaped nail. So...yeah, not the best reception I'd ever had.

I dabbed at the scratch. Just a welt, no blood. Broken skin or not, her aggression normally would've earned her a nice little trip downtown. But today, I'd made a judgment call, one Hoyt didn't agree with at all.

"I still think you should press charges and let me take 'er in." He scowled as he looked over my shoulder at the porch, where she was sitting under the watch of another officer. "Obstruction is a thing, you know."

"So is leverage," I informed him. "If she'd truly tried to attack me, this would be a different story. She was mostly pulling at my arm."

That didn't make him look any happier. But I needed her cooperative, not locked up and pissed. Something she should thank her lucky stars for.

It was clear Hoyt wanted to argue some more, but he just shrugged. "It's your call."

Yes, it was. And I already made it, like, ten fucking minutes ago. I held my tongue as we made our way up to the front porch. Farrah's home was small but nicely maintained, with a large yard and several flowering trees. There was a dark green Fiat in the open garage that was crammed full of stuff.

Farrah sat, tense and watchful, tracking our every move. Her belligerence was a thing of the past. That was probably because all the adrenaline had worn off and she still wasn't sure if she was going to jail. I wanted her to worry. Then I wanted to be the solution to that problem. A little goodwill ought to get her over the hump of not cooperating quite nicely.

By the time my boots hit the weathered boards of the porch, she'd worked herself into quite a lather. "Look, if I'm going to jail, just tell me now," she blurted.

"You're not going to jail," Hoyt said, his expression a moue of displeasure. "For that, you can thank Detective Christiansen here."

She closed her eyes briefly and swallowed. "Thank you."

"And an apology might be nice."

I barely resisted walloping Hoyt in the gut. I appreciated the support for a brother in blue, but I had a game plan here. I'd already explained that game plan to him three times, which was two times more than my blood pressure was comfortable with.

"I'm very sorry," she blurted. "I don't know what came over me. I just saw that you put Lewis on the ground. I didn't know you were a cop. I thought I was helping him."

"After he attacked you?" Hoyt stared at her incredulously. "God, lady, you've got a few screws—"

"Thank you, Officer Hoyt," I said loudly enough to make his big shoulders jump. "I'm sorry you can't stick around, though. I'm sure you're extremely busy."

He grunted. He finally left, but not before offering to secure Farrah. "For your protection," he said with mock sympathy.

Too bad I was in full view of a suspect/witness. My fingers itched to give him the double bird. I had to settle for a good death glare. He just smirked and ambled back down the driveway.

"Please, come in." Farrah rose to her feet, still a little shaky. "Let me get you an icepack for your face."

If she was waiting for an obligatory, "that's not necessary," she was going to be waiting awhile. There would be no macho bullshit from this quarter. It was *very* necessary because yes, it hurt. Yes, I was going to pop several painkillers as soon as I got in the car. And no, I did not plan to heed the recommended dosage.

I followed her inside without a murmur of dissent.

Farrah's home was about what I expected—light and airy, with pastel colors everywhere. The floor was large white tile throughout that was polished and practically sparkly clean, which added to the wide-open feeling. We went through a living room with uncomfortable-looking paisley furniture—also spotless—and into the kitchen. That's where the unlived-in vibe ended.

I blinked as I looked around at the mess. Dishes filled the sink and there were ingredients on most of the counters. Two large pots burbled on the stove. Whatever she was cooking smelled heavenly. I wistfully looked at the stack of pink-lidded Tupperware on the opposing counter. Too bad taking anything to-go was out of the question.

She gave me a sheepish look. "Sorry about all of this. I'm a bit of a messy cook. I never quite learned the art of cleaning while I cook."

"I never quite learned the art of cooking period, so we're even."

She cracked a smile before snapping her fingers. "Let me get that ice pack before I forget."

She went over to the refrigerator, which had a glass panel that revealed neatly ordered contents. More pink-lidded Tupperware. Fancy bottled water took up the entire middle shelf. She opened the freezer and pulled out a few small squares in blue fabric.

She zipped the frozen squares in a freezer bag and held it out to me. "Here you are, Detective."

I wasted no time pressing it to my face. "Thank you."

"Of course." She hesitated. "I hate to ask, but could you arrange for someone to get that piece of crap truck out of my driveway?"

The truck of the man she'd defended by jumping on my back like a lemur who'd been told there was a banana shortage at the zoo? Funny thing, that.

"We can red-tag it if you say he's trespassing," I said, suddenly feeling very tired. "Then you can have it towed."

"Good. I want his crap out of here as soon as possible." She nodded decisively, and I wasn't sure which of us she was trying to convince. "I can't believe he turned up again. No, you know what? I can't believe I'm in this situation again. If my father found out, he would never let me live it down."

"Your ex-husband?" I guessed. Gilbert had been a bone of contention between her and Quinn. I'd imagine her father wasn't any more thrilled with the situation.

"And…others. Let's just say I have a track record of trusting the wrong men." She frowned as she went over to her cutting board, which had a bunch of carrots and several rotund onions on the surface. She arranged them so she had enough surface area to work and started dicing the carrots. "None of my family ever cared for Gil and trust me when I say the feeling was mutual. When he left, we were able to start mending fences."

Chop, chop, chop.

"Why did they dislike him so?"

"Take your pick." *Chop.* "He was a little brash and rude with no pedigree. We also had a lot of…disagreements."

"Physical?"

Chop, chop! She stared at me for a few moments, knife poised above the neatly diced carrot, her expression suddenly closed-off and cold in a way that was jarring. "What does my relationship with Gil have to do with anything?"

"Is there some reason you won't answer a simple question?"

"Because you're supposed to be here about Quinn," she said sharply. "Gil is part of the past. He got us in some financial trouble and left. End of story. He was gone long before Quinn went missing."

Yes, I'd read about Gilbert's financial "troubles." He'd embezzled over a hundred thousand dollars from his employer and got caught. Part of his plea deal was to return the money and pay an astronomical fine. The other part of that deal was prison time, and a lot of it. He'd disappeared the Monday before his next scheduled court appearance, sticking his mother with the full amount of his also astronomical bond. You know, an all-around nice guy.

"How did he feel about you lending Quinn money you guys didn't have?" I asked.

"He was furious. I pointed out that he hadn't shared our financial situation with me, so how was I to know? He didn't like that at all." She started in on the onion, her ash-blond hair falling in her eyes. She didn't even pause as she shook it back, so clearly it was a common occurrence. "He wasn't a fan of Quinn, and she didn't like him, either."

"Did he dislike her enough to kill her?"

"Of course not," she said quickly. "He overheard her harping on the fact I deserved better, and that was all he needed to hear. She was too damn idealistic."

I wondered which domestic incident had spurred Quinn's so-called harping. "She wanted to help."

"She wanted to upend my life," she snapped. "She kept trying to get me to leave him and I told her I had no place to go. She told me I could come to the Hope House, and they would help me start anew, but...I just couldn't do that."

"Why not?"

"Gil wasn't the best husband in the world, but I knew what to expect. If I left, I didn't know what my future would look like. It's...it's hard to explain."

Better the devil you know, and all that. It was a powerful kind of logic that kept people mired in bad situations. The strangest part was that while it stemmed from a place of fear, there was also a pinch of common sense in that logic. Probably because we all understood that even rock bottom had a subfloor.

I watched her transfer her perfectly chopped vegetables to one of the stock pots. Steam rose wildly and she waited a few moments for it to dissipate before putting the lid back on. I watched as she wiped her hands on a dishtowel.

"So if not Gilbert, then who?" I asked.

"I don't know," she said with a frown. "Have you talked to Caleb yet? Maybe he'd know."

"Her brother?"

"Yes. He loaned Quinn a lot of money, and he was making a lot of noise about her paying it back. He'd also cosigned her car and when she missed a payment, he was furious and threatened to repossess it. Said he was going to cut his losses and give it back to the dealership."

"Interesting."

Whatever she heard in my tone made her cluck exasperatedly, and she tossed the dishtowel on the counter. "He wouldn't actually hurt Quinn. I just think he'd have a better idea of what was going on in her life."

I nodded. "Anyone else?"

"Not that I can think of." She bit her lip as she glanced around. "I really need to get back to what I was doing. I'm making a ton of food for a benefit at the Hope House and this whole thing with Lewis put me so far behind."

"I thought you didn't use the Hope House's services."

Her gaze flitted away from mine. "I didn't. I'm allowed to support their cause without being part of their program, am I not?"

"Sure."

At her pointed look, I could tell she was waiting for me to *vamoose*. I could've pressed the issue. Told her that we weren't done yet, and I would hate to make this "chat" a formal interview down at the station. But she'd given me more than enough to chew on, so I just nodded and slid off the barstool. My skin was starting to feel the sting of the ice, so I removed the impromptu cold pack from my face.

"Thanks for this," I said, placing it on the counter. "If I have any other questions, I'll give you a call."

"Let me give you a fresh one for the ride home," she said hurriedly.

Before I could demur, she was already in motion, pulling another two fabric ice packs out of the freezer. I closed my mouth and waited patiently. My skin felt too sensitive for another round right away, but it probably wasn't the worst idea.

She popped them in another Ziploc and handed it over with a sheepish look. "I really am sorry," she said. "I was just trying to protect Lewis. Despite everything, he's not really a bad guy."

I made a noncommittal noise. Better than saying what I was really thinking. *While you're so busy trying to protect Lewis, who the hell protects you?*

Her shoulders slumped, probably because I'd let my side of the proverbial *Free Lewis* banner droop. "You know, before my mama died, she used to say I have a bad picker."

My throbbing jaw testified to the fact that mothers do, in fact, know best.

"I'm assuming that went over like a lead balloon," I guessed.

Farrah sent me a rueful smile. "I was about as bristly as a porcupine, but I didn't have a leg to stand on. Not when I was attending her deathbed with a pound of makeup and a pair of huge shades on my face, hiding the handiwork of my boyfriend at the time."

"I'm sorry," I said quietly.

She folded her arms about herself. "We had another two good days before the cancer took her. That last day, she asked my sister Lindsey to give her a damp washcloth. And then she wiped all the makeup from my face."

"No hiding."

"No hiding," she agreed softly. "She told me that she didn't raise her girls to be some man's punching bag. Her words were firm, her voice stronger than I'd heard it in months, but her touch was gentle as could be. She told me that I was worth more. That I was worth everything."

Her voice faltered at the end as she stared off into space. Remembering. I didn't think another sorry would be welcome—or meaningful—so I stayed silent, giving her a chance to compose herself.

"You're worth everything," she repeated, more to herself than anything else.

"Maybe one day you'll believe her," I said quietly.

She raised her gaze, skewering me with an unreadable stare for several moments. Then she gave me a humorless smile. "Anything is possible, I suppose."

11

When I got back to the station, Macy informed me that Danny was in an interview room with Quinn's parents, who'd shown up unexpectedly. I found him in room two, sitting at a table with an elderly couple. Quinn's father, Hal, was a retired postal worker. Her mother Fran had been a second-grade teacher for over twenty years.

Hal was speaking animatedly, hands waving about every so often as Danny listened. I tried to glean how the interview was going from faces alone, but I didn't get very far with that. When God was handing out poker faces, Danny got back in line for a second helping. He apparently did the same thing for looks and personality, then skipped a few people to get the last rockin' ass. Rude, I know.

I flipped the sound switch on the wall.

"Have you spoke to Josh yet?" Hal's gray mustache quivered a bit in indignation. "I never felt like he was fully cooperative with the investigation."

"We have, yes."

"He's with a man now, you know." Hal looked a little scandalized. "Never knew he had sugar in his tank. What kind of man would do something like that?"

I wasn't surprised they'd kept tabs on him. They'd been very vocal against Joshua during the primary investigation. They'd even shown up at his home several times, requiring removal by the police. Joshua hadn't pressed charges, deeming their actions sad and understandable. I could only wonder if all that understanding stemmed from a place of compassion...or guilt.

"I'm not sure what Mr. Parker's current relationship status has to do with anything," Danny said after a moment. "As far as I know, bisexuality is not a crime."

"It's just so *convenient,* don't you think? No more Quinn, no more kids, and Josh gets to be with a *man.*" Fran took up the homophobic torch with vigor. "Not that there's anything wrong with that...that lifestyle. I just think you should consider—"

"We'll check into it." Danny's tone was so chilly it could've turned crème anglaise into ice cream. "What about the two of you? When was the last time you spoke with or saw Quinn?"

Fran's brown eyes widened. "Oh, so now we're suspects? Why would I hurt my own daughter? My grandchildren?"

"It's part of our job to question everyone. Once we eliminate you—"

"Frannie, please." Hal cut Danny off at the pass. "Let's just answer the questions so they can start looking for our girls."

"Don't you tell me what to do, Hal." She took a few calming breaths before she spoke. "I spoke to Quinn the day before she disappeared. She and the girls were supposed to come up and see us that summer. It would've been lovely to see her before...just before. She was so very busy with the girls and her work."

"At the Hope House?"

"Yes. She worked long hours." Fran's mouth turned downward in disapproval. "I told her she was stretching herself too thin, and she told me I shouldn't worry because she probably wasn't going to be there much longer. She didn't know that I knew, but she was looking for property up near us."

Danny's pause was imperceptible unless you knew him as well as

I did. But I could see his surprise. "In Tennessee?" At Fran's nod, he asked, "How did you find out?"

"She used my laptop when she came up to visit. We took the kids up to Blackberry Farm and it was just the greatest day...." She blinked her eyes rapidly, startling when Hal touched her hand. "Well, anyway, she forgot to log out of her email, and I saw a bunch of listings that she'd emailed to herself."

And the optics were getting worse.

It didn't necessarily mean she was going to do anything about those listings immediately. Plenty of people looked at housing in different locations, dreaming and planning of a different future. Hell, I'd done it myself. I'd once clicked on a five-million-dollar house as a lark, just to see the inside. Judging from the emails Zillow zealously sent me on a regular basis, they now had a *seriously* skewed idea of my budget.

But sometimes suspicion wasn't built from one event...but a series of them. The missing passports, luggage, phones, computers. The trouble Nate got them into financially. All the money they owed and couldn't pay back. Quinn telling her ex-husband that she was thinking of moving to be closer to her parents. And now actual listings that she'd emailed to herself?

"Whatever Quinn's plans were, we didn't know about it," Hal said starchily. "Our alibi is rock solid. We were at the lodge the night they went missing, several states away. We didn't even know anything was wrong until Caleb called us the next morning."

"The lodge?" Danny asked as he wrote something down.

"Yes. The Red Rooster Club," Hal said with a sharp nod. "Several people saw us there. We had the roast with potatoes for dinner."

Danny cleared his throat. "That's fine. I don't really need—"

"We had meatloaf and mashed potatoes," Fran corrected.

Hal frowned. "I'm pretty sure it was the roast. They only serve the meatloaf with that spicy ketchup topping on top and you know how spice makes my indigestion act up."

I could practically *hear* Danny's teeth grinding as they went on with one another. Fran snapped her fingers. "You know what? I think we *did* have the roast. Rory was in the kitchen that night and no one makes a more tender—"

"Thank you," Danny said quickly. "I think we have all we need right now."

"Oh good." Fresh tears sprang to Fran's eyes. They looked gigantic behind her bifocals. "The smarter part of you, the logical part, well, you know it's already over. Was probably over before we even knew something was wrong. But hope...it can be such a terrible thing."

"I'm very sorry." Danny's voice was gruff. "I may call you if I have more questions. Wait here. I just need a minute, and I'll escort you out."

I flicked off the sound switch just as Hal started to complain about waiting, and blessed silence reigned in the hallway. He continued to say something that required a lot of hand movement while Danny waited with an intractable expression. I was extremely familiar with that expression. That look said "whatever the hell you're saying won't make a bit of difference, but by all means, feel free to keep saying it."

Whatever he said when Hal finally stopped bitching made Hal's face turn red.

A moment later, Danny came out in the hallway, pulling the door closed behind him with a decisive click. He glanced to the left and did an almost comical double take when he saw me lurking. He gave me a small smile before checking the hallway. Then he leaned down and gave me a kiss. I got caught up in it, as usual, until his fingers grazed my jaw, and I made a painful noise and jerked away.

"What's...." He trailed off as he got a better look at my face. "Oh, shit."

His fingers landed on my jaw again, this time so gentle I could barely feel the pressure. Anger suffused on his face, color rising in his cheeks, and I hurriedly said, "It was an accident," before he spontaneously combusted right there on the spot.

"Farrah?" His voice was tight. "Tell me she's in lockup right now."

"Not Farrah. Her lovely ex-boyfriend, Lewis. And yes, he's in lockup. Probably will be for quite some time." He didn't look any happier after I explained the situation. "It's fine."

"You're a danger magnet."

"You're an innocent victim," I said with a small grin, because surely that's what the hell he'd meant. "There. Fixed it for ya."

He gave me a narrow-eyed look. "Doesn't your mother have a poultice for injuries? I'm sure she'd love to bring it over and make sure you apply it." He waited a beat while that sank in. "I hear it's smelly."

My grin dropped. "Now that's just not nice."

He hummed as he pulled out his phone. "I think I'm going to text her now."

And he actually thumbed out a quick message, that bastard. I huffed when my mother responded immediately in the group text. She informed us all that yes, she had the poultice, and yes, she would absolutely have it ready by the time we got home.

> ROBYN
> I think I'll also prepare some turmeric shots. They promote healing, you know.
>
> LEO
> It is a powerful anti-inflammatory.

I texted back quickly.

> I'll pass. Don't want to trouble you.
>
> ROBYN
> It's no bother. I'll make a special batch that will heal you right up.

I sighed with resignation. Well, I wasn't ingesting any poison voluntarily without an ingredient label.

> What's in it?
>
> ROBYN
> Orange, lemon, and ginger.

"You might as well resign yourself to it now," Danny advised. "Either you take it yourself or wake up choking on it as she spoon-feeds it to you. And those ingredients don't sound all that bad."

"I guess," I said doubtfully. Except the phone pinged again.

> **ROBYN**
> And cayenne.
>
> **ROBYN**
> Rosemary.
>
> **ROBYN**
> Thyme.

I squinted at the screen, hoping against hope that the list was done. This was starting to feel less like an energy shot and more like the colonel's secret recipe to finger lickin' chicken. My phone pinged again.

> **ROBYN**
> Echinacea

Danny bit his lip, clearly struggling not to laugh. "Oh, wow," he managed, trying to sound sympathetic and failing miserably.

And she wasn't quite done.

> **ROBYN**
> Reishi mushrooms

Jesus Christ. My stomach gurgled.

> You know what, I think I'll just be surprised.

In response, my twin sent an emoticon with big watery eyes and told us she was bringing over the healing candle. *The* healing candle —she was very clear about that. Like it was a family heirloom or some shit...which was interesting, because I hadn't even known it existed. Apparently, getting shot hadn't been enough to unearth the mysticism, but a bruise on my jaw had elevated me to healing-candle worthy. I stopped looking for the logic in that thinking pretty quickly. In this group text, logic had moved and left no forwarding address.

The candle probably smelled, too. I pictured the candle and the poultice battling for supremacy around my poor nostrils and my eye twitched. I turned to Danny. "I hate you so much right now," I swore.

Danny put his phone back in his pocket with a satisfied air. Practically dusted off his busybody hands. I wouldn't tolerate any mothering from him, but I had absolutely zero choice with my actual freaking mother.

"Had to be done," he informed me before getting right back on topic. "I assume you saw some of the interview."

"A bit."

"So what do you think of those two?"

I raised an eyebrow. "I think if they'd seen us kissing, they'd have dropped dead of sheer indignation. You know, because of our *lifestyle* and all."

Danny looked amused and mad about being amused. I could tell he was still pissed about the bruise on my face...which was sweet. His caring almost made up for the poultice thing. Almost. "I meant what do you think about their Joshua theories?"

"They're running quite the smear campaign, but it could just be sour grapes," I said with a shrug. "He gets to move on. They don't. He can always replace his partner, but they never get another Quinn."

The eyebrow with the barbell piercing surged upward. "Is that how you really feel? That I would just replace you if something happened to you?"

I didn't speak for a second. Not because I had to think about it, but because just the thought took my breath away. We faced the possibility of dying on the job on the regular. We dealt with people—sometimes on the worst, most unimaginable day of their lives—and people could be unpredictable. Even a simple traffic stop could wind up being so much more. If we didn't pay enough attention or got even the tiniest bit sloppy following procedures put in place for our safety, it could be our last mistake. I *knew* that. I'd come to terms with that.

But what my passing would do to Danny? It was enough to damn near buckle my knees.

"No," I said, my voice a little hoarse. "I don't think you'd just replace me."

"Exactly." He leaned over and kissed me on the forehead. "So maybe let's not talk about what we don't know about."

"You're so annoying."

"And you, dear husband, are getting angry-face carrots from now on."

Figures it would take the threat of losing them to realize how much I enjoyed my happy fucking lunch. It always made me feel *things* to think of my husband working that tiny press with those big hands just to brighten my day. Of course, I loved it when he did other things with those big hands, too. But those carrots certainly made the list.

Danny just waited patiently, a smile tugging at his mouth. I'd disparaged his carrot children one too many times. We both knew that admissions would have to be made. I sighed. "Baby?"

"Yeah?"

"I like the happy ones."

A bit of that gorgeous smile broke free. "Tell me something I don't know."

"I love you."

He got closer, invading my space, and I let him back me up against the wall. And then he gave me that look, that special look that was just for me. "Like I said." His voice was husky and soft. "Tell me something I don't know."

He kissed me then, right under my bruised jaw, a barely-there kind of thing that made my breath short. "What was that for?" I managed.

"Because I love you right back. And you are far too cavalier with the safety of what I very much consider mine."

Before we made the BBPD newsletter by fucking in a hallway, I cleared my throat and tried to pull away. He didn't look like he wanted to let me go—in fact, his grip tightened briefly—but eventually, he did. "My safety was hardly in question. And I actually think things went rather well."

"Depends on your definition of well, I suppose."

"Well." I paused. "I didn't find any dead bodies today."

He looked a bit nonplussed for a few moments before he cleared his throat. "Maybe you have a point."

I nodded sagely. "I usually do, yes."

12

The next day, Danny and I made the hour trip to Glenhill, where Quinn's brother lived. Caleb was a retired banker who'd made a good living for many years and started his second act as a photographer. He was divorced three times over, had no children, and belonged to a bowling league. He lived a quiet, comfortable life. Some would say he didn't fit the profile of a killer, but I disagreed. You name the type of person, and I could find the corresponding murder.

At least his alibi had held up under scrutiny. He'd been working when the Parkers went missing, confirmed by video during most of the day. In the evening, he hadn't been able to account for two hours of time, when he supposedly went home and got ready for a date. Then he was back on the grid, taking a woman named Pamela—who would eventually become the third Mrs. Mercer—out for dinner. Nightfall had he and Pamela having after-dinner coffee at a café, where they talked until the establishment closed at midnight.

So not impossible. But damn near close. He would've had to pull off a quadruple murder in an hour, get rid of any trace evidence, and dispose of the bodies successfully. Unseen, at that. Then he would've had to make it home, shower, dress, and show up for his date with

Pamela. Not only had he made it, according to the ex-Mrs. Mercer, but he'd been on time. With flowers. To say the timeline was a little tight was like saying Watson was a *little* excited that time I'd dropped a platter of bacon.

But that didn't mean Caleb was entirely off the hook. Maybe he just didn't like to get his hands dirty. Murder for hire was a thing, after all.

As Danny pulled up next to the curb of Caleb's home, I couldn't decide whether I found it creepy or sad that he lived in his sister's former home. Maybe both.

"Looks like he's not home yet," Danny said unnecessarily, as if I couldn't see the empty, oil-stained driveway with my own eyeballs.

I reached over and patted his jean-clad thigh. "Those detective skills are still sharp as the day I married you."

"Stating the obvious is highly underrated," he informed me as we got out of the car. "Maybe we should spend our time wisely and talk to the neighbor."

I didn't have to look far for his target. Right next door, a woman was pruning bushes on her fence line. She hadn't cut anything of value since we pulled up to the curb, too busy trying to see just who the hell we were. People like her was the reason crime was practically nonexistent in Glenhill. And the reason it was important to pull your shades firmly shut.

Danny started walking in that direction and I blinked in disbelief. When I tugged on his belt circumspectly, he stopped and gave me a questioning look. "What?"

"For God's sake," I said. "Obviously the only time you've seen the word *finesse* is emblazoned on a bottle of mousse."

He looked at me blankly. "Which means what exactly, Rainstorm?"

"You don't just approach neighborhood busybodies in their natural habitat," I said out of the corner of my mouth. "Much like an animal in the wild, that just makes them suspicious. We have to do something interesting."

He let out a testy sigh. "Like what?"

"Something that will drive her mad with curiosity. Then *she* will come to us, and the information will be that much juicier. Just follow my lead."

I didn't wait for his agreement, trusting that he'd follow as I drifted down the side yard between the two houses. I could feel her gaze between my shoulder blades like an actual touch as we got closer to her side of the fence. I craned my neck, looking into the backyard. It was pretty basic, but I stared at the mango tree in the backyard like it was the tree of life.

"Now what?" Danny asked, clearly torn between amusement and exasperation. "As much as I'm enjoying playing reindeer games with you—"

"Shhh," I said. "Look interesting."

From the look on his face, exasperation was definitely winning. "And how, exactly, does one look interes—"

"Yoo-hoo! Can I help you with something?"

I gave him a pointed look before turning around. My technique for catching busybodies was tried and true. Luckily for them, it was a catch and release program.

The nosy neighbor came right up to the fence, as close as she could get without mowing over her own hibiscus bush. She was taller than I expected, almost the same height as me. She was still wearing her gardening gloves and her hair, thick and white, was pulled up in a ponytail.

"Are you a friend of Caleb's?" she asked, her brown eyes narrowed in suspicion. "Does he know you're back here? You're not selling anything, are you?"

Danny pulled out his shield from his pocket, hustling to identify himself. I followed suit pretty quickly. She looked like the type to mace first and ask questions later.

"Detective McKenna with BBPD," he said smoothly. "And this is Detective Christiansen."

"Opal Clarke." She inspected his shield, looking impressed despite herself. "Is there something I can help you with?"

"We're investigating the Parker case, and we'd like to ask you a few questions," he said. Just that mention made her gaze soften. "How long have you lived in this house?"

"Long enough to remember the Parkers," she said promptly. "That was a terrible time for Glenhill. All of those reporters and police officers and helicopters and looky-loos…it was absolute chaos."

"Did you know them well?"

"Not especially. But we exchanged the occasional hello. And when I made strawberry oat bars, I always made an extra pan. Regan loved those best. I miss having children next door." She smiled wistfully. "It's just too bad about all the trouble they were having."

Danny frowned. "Can you be more specific?"

"Well, everyone knows their finances were a mess. All those debts piling up. They were even in danger of losing the house. I heard the two of them arguing about it many a time," she said importantly. "Sound carries well over that fence."

I'm sure it does. Especially when you've got your window open and your ear to the wall.

"And don't get me started on Caleb."

When she just stood there, blinking at us expectantly, we exchanged a look. I cleared my throat. "I'm gonna need you to get started on Caleb."

"Oh. Well, since you asked," she said coyly. "I'm no gossip, you know. Nothing good comes of sticking your nose in other people's business."

"Words to live by," Danny said dryly. He sent me a quick wink before taking a page from my self-published book, *How to Entice a Busybody*. "Well, if you don't feel comfortable talking about it, we understand. Maybe we can find someone else who has their finger on the pulse of the neighborhood—"

"In this case, I'll make an exception," she said loudly. "I'll just say that they owed her brother a lot of money and he was getting tired of waiting for them to pay it back. Especially when he realized their spending habits hadn't changed."

"What do you mean?" I asked.

"He came over one weekend and found Nate setting up a new

tricked-out grill. Oh, you should've seen Caleb's face! I thought his head was going to pop right off his shoulders."

"What did he say?" Danny asked.

"What didn't he say? I wouldn't be surprised if Caleb decided that he was done waiting for his money," she went on in a stage whisper. "Maybe he decided to settle the score, if you get my drift."

A five-year-old busy watching *Paw Patrol* could still get her drift. "Is that so?"

She nodded eagerly. "He could've been arguing with Quinn and Nate and things got out of control. And then he had to finish the job, if you get my—"

"Yes, yes, I get your drift," I said impatiently. "You've lived next door to him for quite some time now. Do you get a dangerous vibe from him?"

"Well…no," she admitted. "But two days before the Parkers disappeared, Caleb stopped by and saw the box for a sixty-inch TV in their recycling bin. He went apoplectic."

Danny and I exchanged looks. I could see how frustrating that would've been. With them owing him money, even the most mundane of purchases could've looked like they were rubbing it in his face.

"He and Quinn went in the garage, fussing at each other. The door was half-lowered, and I couldn't hear much," she went on, clearly put out that someone would try to have a private conversation. "Well, it turned out to be such a windy day that my sunhat just flew off and sailed over on their driveway."

"Sunhats are aerodynamic that way," I said dryly.

She narrowed her eyes at me because that was her story and she was sticking to it. "When I went over to pick it up, and I heard him yelling at her. He told her that it was high time she grew up and stopped making bad decisions. He was furious that she'd missed a car payment or something, and said she was ruining his credit."

"What else did you hear?" I prompted impatiently when she didn't continue.

"Nothing. They closed the door!"

She gave the Parker house an indignant look for good measure as I exchanged a look with Danny. Right then, I was sure of a few things. One, I was pretty sure she'd thrown the sunhat like a boomerang. Two, if she was my neighbor, I'd close my garage door behind me so quickly I'd probably catch my own foot. Daily. And three, Caleb wasn't coming off our suspect list any time soon.

At the sound of a car, I turned just in time to see a dark blue Jaguar pull in the driveway next door. Caleb, perhaps? A tall, lanky man got out of the car and started unloading bags with the Walmart logo.

"Yoo-hoo!" Opal called, waving like someone just crowned her queen of a float. "Hello, dear."

Caleb gave a perfunctory wave back before continuing up the walk. He didn't seem all that interested in conversation. The presence of two strangers could've been the reason for that. Of course, it could also be because anything you told Opal was bound to wind up in the *Miami Herald*.

Opal waited until he was inside for her smile to drop. "And don't you think it's odd that he bought their house? I mean, who does that?"

Danny cleared his throat. "Yes, I suppose. That is a touch—"

"Now, if it wasn't Caleb, it could've been Nate," she whispered. "I wouldn't be surprised if he killed the whole family and took off for a fresh start. And don't get me started on that ex-husband of hers. He called me an old gossipy woman. Can you *imagine*?"

She propped one gloved hand on her hip and stared at us. Waiting.

Oh. So this wasn't one of those rhetorical things.

"Um, no?" Danny finally answered, rubbing a hand over his stubbled jaw. "Why don't you tell me more about Joshua?"

As Opal chattered on, accusing everyone under the sun, I touched Danny's shoulder and jerked my head toward the Parker house. He bulged his eyes at me, and I pretended not to notice. And when he tried to snag my belt loop when I passed, I dodged his finger. If I stayed any longer, I was going to say something I meant but regretted dearly.

I moseyed across the yard. I knocked five or six times before I finally heard the lock turn on the other side. Caleb pulled open the door with a frown that quickly changed as his gaze dropped to the badge and gun at my hip. He sucked in a breath. His eyes widened. "Quinn."

"Well, I'm Detective—"

"The girls," he blurted, uninterested in letting me finish identifying myself. "You haven't...you didn't find...."

"I would've said that straight away if we had," I said gently. "There have been some developments in the case, and I'd like to ask you a couple questions. If you have the time."

"I guess...I just thought it was done, you know? So much time passes, and everyone forgets." His eyes widened as he realized how that sounded. "Not to say you're not working on it. It's just...I'm glad she's still important to someone other than those that share her DNA."

"Of course," I said simply. "Can we go inside?"

He swallowed. Frankly, he looked like he'd rather try to kiss a honey badger. But in the end, he gave me a short nod. "Follow me."

Caleb's home was odd.

It wasn't because of the décor—the colonial was roomy with high ceilings and whitewashed wood beams. Everything seemed to be done in a mélange of shades of brown, making it feel warm and cozy. It wasn't showroom neat, either. There was a coffee cup and a stack of mail on the coffee table and a crumpled-up blanket on the couch, right next to a pile of laundry. A pair of worn-in slippers was next to the table and a laptop was on a fuzzy recliner that had seen better days.

The only thing keeping it from looking like a nice, well-loved home was that only half of it appeared to be in use. I took in the living room silently, not bothering to hide my confusion. Even the furniture had been arranged so that half the room was literally just empty space.

I turned to Caleb with raised brows.

"Feng shui," he said defensively.

Looked more like feng-*something was going on over in that side of the house.*

"Sure," I agreed.

He waved at the couch as he hurried over to scoop up his laundry. "Have a seat. I'll be right back."

He was back in a jiff with a drink I didn't ask for and refreshments I wouldn't touch. I looked at the plate of scones longingly. I could see the flecks of cranberry and orange peel—one of my favorite flavors.

"So." Caleb rubbed anxious hands together. "You said there were recent developments on the case?"

"I can't really discuss them with you," I said apologetically.

"Well, have you found Quinn and my nieces? Nate?"

I shook my head. "Not yet, no."

He stared at me for a few seconds before looking skyward with a long-suffering sigh. "Ah. Got it."

"Excuse me?"

"No, it's just that I knew this shit was a possibility."

"What is?"

"I'm a suspect, right?" He demanded. He didn't give me a chance to answer before he charged on. "I already went through this a decade ago. Then two years after that. And any other time a reporter digs through Glenhill's history looking for a story to fill some airtime. Don't get me started on these fuckin' true crime podcasts always looking for a quote—"

"Trust me, I won't," I said dryly. "This is all part of our investigation. You wanted Quinn to be important to someone other than family. Well. She is."

"I don't know what you expect me to say. I've already told the detectives everything I knew way back then."

"I like to ask my own questions," I informed him. "So. How was your relationship with your sister?"

He blinked, clearly not expecting such a softball. He didn't need to worry—it only got harder from here. "Well, we had our good days and bad days, just like everyone else. But we were always close. Our parents were good people, but they worked long hours and rarely took time off. Since I was so much older, I was more like a father to Quinn than her brother. Fourteen years. That dynamic followed us into adulthood."

"Long-standing habits are the hardest to break."

"Tell me about it." He gave me a wry look. "I babied her a little too much, and I acknowledge that. But she was my sister and I loved her."

"She *did* owe you a lot of money, though. And she wasn't taking paying you back seriously."

"Family is there for family," he said sharply. "No matter what the cost."

"Even when it came to the car loan?" I asked. "She had you over a barrel, Caleb. You either had to catch up the payments or watch your credit be destroyed."

"She was only a few months behind," he shot back. "I'm the one that decided to take that risk in the first place. Yes, I was a little upset, and maybe I said a few things I shouldn't have. But I was just trying my hand at tough love. I wasn't that great at it."

I hummed. I loved it when people said shit I could disprove. "I don't know, you seemed to have the hang of it to me. At least, that's the way a witness tells it. You were laying into Quinn in that garage."

"That fucking busybody Opal," he said, his face suffusing with color. "I swear on everything that is holy, my next move is going to be to get that fence raised as high as the association will allow."

I gave him a faux-understanding look. "I can understand you were frustrated."

"No, it's not—"

"Tired of being taken advantage of."

"I was not—"

"And maybe things got a little out of hand. Then you had one hell of a cleanup job to do—"

"Hey," he snapped. "That's enough. You're twisting everything and making it seem like something it wasn't."

Perhaps. Or maybe I was just a little too close to home. I couldn't shake the feeling that he was hiding something. I didn't know if that something was the abominable act of killing an entire family. But he wasn't telling me everything—that much, I knew. I felt it in my bones, deep down where instinct resided.

Caleb's phone vibrated on the table, and he gave it a quick glance. When he reached for it, I shook my head. "We'll only be a few more minutes."

"It's work."

I figured if I kept talking, he'd realize I didn't give a damn. "I'm going to level with you, Caleb. I'm running a little short on suspects here. So if you didn't have anything to do with the disappearance of the Parkers, who did?"

"How would I know?"

His mouth was saying one thing, but his flustered face was saying something else entirely. I waited quietly, long enough that he started to fidget. And only when his eyes got a little watery did I speak.

"This doesn't have to go beyond this room," I said quietly. "Unless there's a reason that it needs to."

"I don't want you to think badly of her," he blurted. "You're the guy looking for her and I don't want to make the same mistake this time around."

I tried my very best not to look lost, but I wasn't sure I pulled it off. "I'm not here to judge your sister. I want to know what happened to her, and I can't do that without your help."

It was another few moments of silence before he spoke. "She was cheating on Nate," he finally burst out.

Hell, at this rate, I was going to need a ratchet to get my eyebrows back to their proper level. "Why do you say that?"

"She had this friend that she was a little too close with, if you know what I mean."

"Spell it out for me," I said impatiently. "Who was this guy?"

"Woman," he corrected. "And her name was Raven Lee. Quinn said they met at the gym, but I think they actually met at the Hope House."

I chewed over that for a few moments before I finally asked, "What did they do that was suspicious?"

"I came over one night and Regan let me in, telling me that her mom and her mom's *friend* were on the back porch. I didn't think much of it, but as I approached, I smelled smoke. Quinn was very sensitive to smells, and she didn't allow any smoking around her." He gave me a meaningful look. "Except apparently, Raven."

Sometimes people had different rules for different people in their lives. If we didn't, a few days ago I wouldn't have been forced to wear a smelly poultice and sit next to an equally smelly healing candle. "That doesn't mean—"

"They were talking," he said quickly. "Almost arguing. I heard my sister tell her that they were in too deep. That Raven couldn't leave her now."

Well, damn. When I asked for something suspicious, I really didn't expect him to actually produce the goods. I pulled out my phone and pecked in a few notes. I knew it wasn't productive, but I found myself demanding, "Why didn't you say something before? This could be important."

"I told the detective," he shot back. "He said he'd look into it."

I furrowed my brow. "Detective Owens?"

"I guess. Yeah, that sounds about right."

I kept my poker face as I kept making notes. I knew Danny was fond of the guy and all, but he'd left more than a few stones unturned. Maybe this Raven lead was nothing. Maybe it was everything. Either way, I'd seen no mention of any of it in the case file, and there should've been.

Caleb's phone vibrated on the table again and he let out a long sigh before grabbing it. He gave me an apologetic look. "I've got to get this. It's my assistant."

I waved him off. "Go ahead."

He stood, swiping his finger across the screen. "Yeah? The Peterson wedding again?" He sighed. "No, only basic edits are available for the package the bride chose. No, I won't. Because I can't. Vivian Peterson is a pain in the ass, that's why...."

He made his way down the hallway, his voice fading to a murmur as he closed a door behind him. I certainly didn't mind the break—it gave me time to organize my thoughts and finish making notes. I glanced up at the sound of a soft shuffle of feet, but Caleb hadn't returned.

I waited for a few seconds, listening, but all I could hear was ambient noises from the house—the hum of the air conditioner and the whirring of the fan. And the murmur of Caleb's voice as he continued disparaging Vivian Peterson. To be fair, she really did sound like a pain in the ass.

I shrugged off the strange noise and finished making my notes. Then I stood, indulging in a long stretch before I moseyed on over to the bay window. The yard was pretty much immaculate, and I smiled at the sunflowers blooming in the flower beds. They were Quinn's favorite, and it was nice to see her remembered in that manner. I had the feeling she'd approve.

I spotted Danny still talking to Opal next door. A white Volvo SUV was now in the driveway and a gray-haired man in golfer plaid had joined them. The husband, maybe? I could only assume from his "stab me now" expression that he found Opal's gossip as trying as I did.

And then I heard that shuffle again.

I turned slowly, frowning as I surveyed the room. Thanks to Caleb's strange decorating choices, I had a clear view of the entire space. No places to hide. Except...my gaze landed on the short door built into the wall of the stairs. I went over to the door cautiously, pressed my ear to the wood, and...there! There it was again. The softest shuffle of feet. Living person? Or other? At this point, I wasn't sure which one I preferred.

I drew my weapon even as I took a few steps back. "Whoever is in there, it's time to come out. Now," I said firmly. "You're not in trouble, but we need to talk."

I could've sworn that I heard a little *eep*.

Quinn, maybe? I had a feeling she hadn't been completely honest with me from the beginning, and every interview I had with her friends and family only increased that feeling. She wasn't interested in solving her murder. She just wanted her girls and once she had them, I had the feeling I wouldn't be seeing her again. That made me wonder who, or what, she was so afraid of.

"Show yourself," I commanded firmly. "I'm not going to ask you again."

The door cracked open, and a little face appeared...right before it slammed shut again.

My heart sank to my toes even as I holstered my weapon. In my line of work, you had to get used to seeing dead people. Yes, it still knocked me for a loop to see someone, once alive and vibrant, as just a husk on the coroner's table. But I'd be lying if I said I hadn't developed a bit of a shell. Cold, maybe, but the distance between me and the victim was critical. It helped keep me sane enough to get them the justice they deserved. It was the reason I could still laugh and joke and make lunch plans right next to someone whose entire existence had just ended.

The kids, though...it never got any easier. And to be perfectly honest, I'd be worried about my humanity if it did.

I knocked on the door gently and tried the knob. It didn't open. Didn't even turn. Which let me know that if she didn't want me in there, I wasn't going in there.

"I'm sorry," I said softly. "I thought you were a bad guy. But it turns out that you're not, and I'd really like to talk. Would you like to talk to me?"

I didn't receive a response.

"I'm a police officer." I felt like an absolute idiot cajoling a door, but I kept the same steady tone. "Do you know what we do?"

Silence.

"We find bad guys who hurt people and we put them away so they can't ever do it again." I paused, waiting. "You know what? You don't have to come out. Maybe it would be better if I came in. Could we do that?"

The door opened a bit. Just an inch. "Are you really a police officer?"

My heart squeezed again as I held my badge up to the crack. "You see this? You can only have one of these if you're one of the good guys."

Small fingers grazed mine as she traced my badge with her fingers. Then her hand disappeared back into the shadows. A moment later, the door opened a little wider. "Can I sit with you?" I asked, clipping it back to my belt.

"I guess," came a small, reluctant voice.

I grimaced as I really looked at the small door and realized just how I was going to have to contort my body. But if she was too scared to come out, then that's just what the hell I'd do. I stooped and tried to enter, hitting my head neatly on the door frame. I held in a curse even as I rubbed my head. I had a feeling yelling out *fuck* was a good way to get that door slammed in my face permanently.

Eventually, I decided crawling was the way to go. There was a soft rug under my knees as I inched along, which was strange for a storage space. I got no other sensory input other than *dark*. Oh, and there was a stack of something soft in the corner. I reached out my hand to make sure the lump wasn't living, then gave it a squeeze. Pillows, maybe?

The little girl was tense and still beside me, clearly unsure of how she felt about having me in her space. I wanted to get some information before that feeling leaned too far into negative territory.

"What's your name?" I asked.

"You're a stranger," she whispered. "I'm not supposed to talk to strangers."

"Well, that's true. But maybe if I tell you my name and you tell me yours, then we won't be strangers anymore." I waited, listening to her hushed breathing. "What do you think?"

She didn't seem convinced, and I was strangely proud of her. "You first."

"My name is Rain."

She scoffed. "I'm Ryan. And rain is a thing, not a name."

A smile tugged at my lips. "Well, you're going to have to take that up with my mother, Ryan." I paused, thinking. "And while you're at it, tell her that Moonbeam is not a good middle name. Maybe she'll listen to you, because she sure as fu—heck isn't listening to me."

"Moonbeam," she squealed and giggled. Then she slapped her hand over her mouth, as if she'd forgotten not to make noise.

It was a struggle not to react to that realization. "How long have you been here, Ryan?"

"I dunno."

"Can you tell me who put you here? Was it your mom?"

"No, I put myself here," she said indignantly. "This is Ryan's corner, only for Ryan."

I rubbed my chest again. Good Lord, she was going to kill me, one miserable tidbit at a time. "Please tell me it's not for when you're bad."

She giggled again. I was going to have to make her tell my friends and family that I was, in fact, hilarious. At least to the under eight set. "No, it's my reading corner, dummy."

Well, that certainly made the pillows and rug make sense. Now that my eyes were adjusting a bit, I could see shadow-shapes and what looked to be some letters on the wall. I was sure if I could see them, they'd spell out her name. I reached out and traced one of the letters, my fingers finally telling me it was a curlicued Y.

I hated to change the mood, but I had to get information from her before she disappeared. "Tell me something, Ryan. Were you reading in here…that day?" I asked quietly.

She sucked in a breath. I heard movement and it seemed like her shape changed a bit, like she turned away from me.

"I'm sorry to ask. I just…it's really important, okay?"

She remained stubbornly silent.

"You can tell me, and you won't get in trouble," I cajoled, making sure to keep my voice soft and easy. "Did you sneak down here to read after your mom put you to bed?"

She did something with her head that I couldn't really discern. A shake? A nod? "I need the words, sweetheart," I said softly.

"I came down to tell Mommy that my throat was scratchy. I think I was getting her cold. But she was crying and holding Regan. And Regan wasn't moving." Her words came so quickly that they started to jumble. "Nate was saying that it must've been the cake."

My mind raced as I realized that Quinn had lied to me from the very beginning. "What cake were they talking about?"

"It was on the counter," she said miserably. "Just an itty-bitty piece. We asked for some, but Mommy said we'd had enough sweets for the day and maybe she'd share it tomorrow. She promised."

"But Regan snuck some anyway?" There was more movement from her corner, and I reminded her, "Words, Ryan. Use your words for me, okay?"

"*No.*"

"But—"

"I'm tired," she announced. "Your questions are stupid and so are you."

"Ryan—"

"I want to read," she said loudly. "By myself."

I held in a sigh. Danny actually wanted one of these little tyrants? "In a minute. Can you tell me what this cake looked like? The one your mom made?"

"I'm done talking," she said sullenly.

"Okay," I said slowly. And then another idea hit me. It wasn't my favorite thing to do, but now that I had the protection tattoo, I felt safe enough to try it. "Maybe...maybe you could show me."

"Show you?" she asked hesitantly. "How?"

I held out my hand and she shied away. I put it out there again, slower this time, and waited. Quiet and still, there in the dark. "At your pace."

She never touched my hand. I felt a light touch on my thigh instead.

I wasn't sure how I knew things had changed on the outside of that door. It was still pitch black, and there was still a sliver of light coming from under the door. But things just felt...different. Maybe it was Ryan beside me, breathing shallowly, her fear an almost palpable thing. What we lacked in vision, we made up for in sound.

I could hear doors open and shut. A *thump, thump, thump*. And then something moving across the floor slowly. Something heavy. Someone was breathing hard and exerting himself, and I couldn't help but wonder if someone was dragging a body across the floor. No...those were wheels. Like luggage?

I opened my mouth to speak, and Ryan shushed me urgently. "But I—"

"Shhh," she said anxiously. "They're not in a good mood. They said lots of bad words."

"What kind of—"

"Shhh!"

I huffed.

The footsteps went back and forth past our little hideout—sometimes fast, sometimes slow. It was practically *killing* me not to know what the hell was going on out there. There wasn't a damn thing I could do about it. This was Ryan's memory, her vision, and I wasn't able to do anything she hadn't done.

A ghost had once forced me to play about in a memory and to do that, I'd had to lose my corporeal form for a bit. It wasn't something I liked to even remember. And even if I'd known how she made that possible, it wasn't something I wanted to do ever again. So I listened, feeling all kinds of helpless, straining to hear any identifying factors.

Eventually, I heard a door slam. Then a car started up in the garage. Moments later, Ryan got up slowly and crept toward the door. I was relieved when the suffocating darkness gave way to light and suddenly, we were in the living room. Everything looked different than it did now—brighter, lighter, messier, homier. Toys littered the carpet, and a cup of cooling dark liquid was overturned on the table.

I drifted closer, feeling the strain of the connection between Ryan and me. It was like an invisible bungee cord tethering us together.

There was only so far I could go, only so much I could do in her vision. The dark liquid on the table was now soaking and staining a folder and I tried to read the name on top. It looked like…Moira. Moira McDaniels. There was a Stacy Pittman, too. I strained to see more until my eyeballs actually ached. I only caught the words Project Halo before I had to give up.

Ryan was already pulling me away. I noted the luggage by the wall —two duffle bags and five suitcases. Two of them were child-sized, and one of them was open. I caught a glimpse of some neatly folded clothing and toys. *Favorite toys?* I wondered grimly as I strained to see. Favorite things to keep a child placated while driving through the night to get out of town?

We made our way through the kitchen, which was clean and tidy. And there was a four-inch cake, tiny and heart-shaped, and frosted with white, pillowy-looking frosting. The perimeter of the heart was neatly defined with thinly sliced strawberries and there was a plump strawberry cut in the shape of a rose sitting in the middle. A small corner of the cake was missing. Regan's doing?

I stared at the still dripping dishes and a pink-lidded Tupperware container, draining on the dishrack. A pair of bear-paw potholders hung neatly by the stove. It was hard to imagine what had happened here this night. There had to be more disarray from killing four people than an overturned cup of coffee. How had they incapacitated Nate and Quinn so easily?

The door that led to the garage flew open and I blinked in surprise to see Quinn rush through the door. "Ryan, honey, there you are. I was looking everywhere for you." Her eyes were glassy and red-rimmed as she lunged forward and grabbed Ryan's hand. "We have to go now."

Ryan pulled away and demanded, "Where's Regan?"

"She's…she's already in the car," Quinn said. "Remember I said there might be a time when we needed to leave immediately?"

Ryan frowned mulishly. "I don't want to go. I have soccer tomorrow."

"That doesn't matter!" Quinn took a deep breath and started

again, calmer this time. "We always have fun at grandma and grandpa's, don't we? Now, come on, it's time. Be a good girl and—"

"What is taking so long?" Nate appeared in the doorway, looking frazzled. "We should've been on the road by now."

"She's a little girl," Quinn snapped. "She doesn't understand—"

"We'll explain on the way," he grated out before disappearing back in the garage.

But none of the promised explaining happened.

There was fast driving though, and tense silence. It was dark and rainy, the road was deserted. The windshield wipers kept a steady beat, fending off sheets of rain as best they could. At one point, Quinn reached over and switched on the radio. She was trying to be positive, but there was no hiding the tears tracking down her cheeks that she dashed every so often. When I caught a glimpse of Nate's face in the rearview mirror, it was tight and tense. Regan was beside me in her car seat, a blanket tucked snugly around her. Her serene face looked like she was sleeping, but her stiff body told a different tale.

She was clearly long past help.

I swallowed as I looked away. We whipped past a green sign, and I craned my neck to read it, almost instinctively. *Marlon Junction, 3 miles.* There was nothing but water on either side of the highway. The wheels skidded a little on the slick pavement and a yellow sign warning about a sharp curve flashed by so fast I barely saw it. I didn't know which waterway we were passing, but I had a sinking feeling I was about to find out.

"Slow down," I whispered.

"Slow down," Quinn said almost simultaneously.

"We need to get as much distance between us and this place as we can," Nate said grimly. "They're coming for us. You know that as well as I do."

"We can't do that if we run into a goddamned tree," she snapped.

"Bad word," Ryan whispered, and I gripped her hand.

We hit the sharp curve and I thought, just for a second, we might actually make it. Then the car hydroplaned, and we flew off the road like the car weighed nothing at all. There was a scream and a yell and then we hit the water with unbelievable force, nose first. Water flew up around the car like a tsunami.

And then there was chaos.

Ryan's eyes tightly squeezed shut and my world went dark. I strained to see, but Ryan wouldn't look. She couldn't look. I didn't need to stick around for the rest. And damned if I'd let her relive it, either.

"Come back with me now," I said in a normal tone, because we sure as hell weren't lingering in this memory a moment longer. She gasped, shaking her head. "*Now*, Ryan."

When her eyes opened, we were back in the closet under the stairs.

I felt along the wall for a switch of some sort and touched all the letters of her name. When my fingers found the flat of the wall beyond the big R, I felt a bump under my fingers. I pressed the switch and suddenly the space was flooded with light.

I blinked for a moment, adjusting to the sudden change. When I looked down at Ryan, her cheeks were wet with tears, her arms tucked securely around her knees as she rocked. "I couldn't look."

"Honey, I'm so, so, very sorry." When I reached for her, she scuttled back away from my outstretched hand. I silently cursed. "Sorry, I forgot."

I knew she was comfortable here—this was her corner and she'd probably retreated here many times. This spot was safety. But I didn't want to leave her alone, there in the dark, reliving the worst moment of her life.

Not one day longer.

I bit my lip, thinking how best to phrase my next request. Finally, I just came out with it. "I want to take you someplace. Someplace special."

I winced as I reviewed my words. She looked scared and not a bit interested in my special place. All I was missing was a windowless van and a promise of candy.

"Your mom has been missing you very much," I tried again.

"You know where she is?" Her eyes widened as she shrank back. "Wait. Did you kill her?"

"Of course not," I said quickly. "I mean, yes to the first, and of course not to the second."

She stared at me suspiciously. "I think I'd like you to go now," she finally said.

"But—"

"I want to be alone in Ryan's Corner," she said loudly. "Mommy said I could be in here whenever my mind got too busy, and even Regan wasn't allowed in here."

"I'm not trying to take Ryan's Corner away from you," I said soothingly. "I just—"

"Get out," she said, her little breaths coming short and fast. "Get out, get out, get out, get out—"

"Okay, okay." I got to my knees before she went all exorcist on me. "I'll come back when you're—"

"Detective?"

Caleb.

Oops. Guess I *had* just kind of disappeared in his house. I glanced back at Ryan and her eyes were just dark circles in her pale face. She disappeared, quick as a blink.

I wasn't sure how I would explain my curiosity with the closet under the stairs to Caleb, but figured I'd come up with something. I crab walked my way over to the door, wincing the whole way. I needed to figure out how to generate more cartilage because I wasn't going to make it to eighty with this particular set of knees.

As it turns out, an explanation was unnecessary.

He was standing there as I emerged from the little closet. His face was about as white as a sheet as I straightened to my full height. "Sorry about wandering through your house. I, uhm...thought I heard a noise." As he continued to stare at me wordlessly, I scratched my neck. "Turns out it was nothing, really. Probably just a rodent or something."

"I had the house tented last year," he said, his voice a little hoarse. "I don't have any pests. Not any that I can see, anyway."

"What do you mean?"

I knew exactly what he meant.

"That door doesn't open. Ever. Even the pest control company tried prying it open. We took the hinges off, and the door still wouldn't budge. Not...not until today, that is." He swallowed. "Guess she was waiting for the right person."

"I don't know—"

"Don't bullshit me," he said, his face blazing with color. "Is it...is it Quinn?"

"No," I said honestly.

It took him a second to realize that while I hadn't confirmed it was his dead sister, I hadn't denied that "it" was someone else.

"Oh God," he squeaked. "I knew it. All this time, I just knew it. It's been a misery living here, Detective."

"Then why didn't you leave?"

"I bought this house because I thought I should. Quinn loved this place, and I didn't want it to go to strangers. And then, when I knew there was...something there," he said in a rush, glancing at the door, "I figured it had to be her. This was her home. Her safety."

"And you didn't want to leave her alone," I said quietly.

He fisted his hand to his mouth, stifling back a sob. "She deserved that much."

There was no hiding the sound of the door creaking open. No point, either, as Caleb's eyes got big as fifty-cent pieces. Ryan peered up at him curiously. "Why is Uncle CJ cryin'?"

He looked into the gaping maw of the door and sucked in a little breath. Then he hit the floor like a sack of potatoes.

I winced at the thud. At least he landed on the carpet. It was pretty thin carpet, but still. I knelt and felt for a pulse. It took a few seconds to find, but there it was under my fingertips, steady and strong.

I sat back on my haunches. "Well. That could've gone better."

Ryan nodded vigorously.

13

Luckily, Caleb wasn't out long—a few minutes at most. I insisted on helping him off the floor, which led to the discovery that his lanky, thin frame was deceptive. My back and middling biceps could testify that he was a lot heavier than he looked. I ignored the ominous creak of my back as I straightened. While I was busy 3D printing a new set of knees, I should probably look for the blueprints for a spine.

He assured me that he was okay before I even posed the question, then shuffled off to the bathroom because he "needed a minute." From the way he muttered to himself the entire way, I thought that minute might be accompanied by something pharmaceutical.

"Is Uncle CJ okay?" Ryan asked anxiously. "I didn't mean to scare him. I tried to play with him a few times, but he just got all weird. So now I only come out and play when he's at work."

I waited until the click of the bathroom door to answer. "He'll live. He's just going to have one hell of a headache."

"Bad word," she whispered.

Christ almighty. If I didn't have sarcasm and bad words, I might as well turn in my tongue. I sighed, running my hands through my hair. "I should probably call someone for him before I leave."

But I didn't want to leave alone. I eyed her, wondering if I should even bother her again about coming with me. She spoke before I could. "So…I was thinkin'."

"Yeah?" I prodded when she didn't continue.

"I want to see my mommy," she said quietly.

I swallowed a sigh of relief. "Kid, that's about the best fuc—flipping news I've heard all day."

"But I'm not leaving without my bear," she said assertively. "Mr. Buttons."

"Okay," I said slowly. "Tell me where we can find it, and we'll grab Mr. Buttons and giddyup."

Clearly, using *giddyup* was a bad move. She did a galloping horse impression all the way upstairs, whinnying included. When I chose to walk—like a human with common sense—she sent me a petulant look over her shoulder. Then she stuck out her lip farther than I thought was possible. I rolled my eyes and gave a half-assed whinny. "Better?"

"Much," Her Highness assured me.

Some days, this ghost whisperer shit wasn't all it was cracked up to be.

I startled as she tucked her hand in mine. I stared down at her for a few seconds. *Well, if that's the cost of admission….* I did a whinny that would make Seabiscuit proud, and Ryan grinned.

She tried to drag me through a room door, and I barely pulled her to a stop before my nose hit the wood. When I opened the door, I found what was clearly a kid's room, done in pink and pale yellow. Unicorns were painted on two of the walls. I stared, my brow scrunched in confusion, wondering why the room was so perfectly preserved after all these years. The sheets on the bed were rumpled, a crumpled bathrobe on the floor.

Ryan let go of my hand as she skipped to the bed. "Mr. Buttons!"

My head spun at the sudden transformation of the room. Without her hand tucked securely in mine, it was a bland guest room—beige walls and fluffy pale-blue carpet. I knew that ghosts kept the form they liked best. Apparently, that could extend to their surroundings.

"Holy shit," I whispered.

"Bad word," she said, skipping back with bear in hand.

"Sorry," I said absently.

"S'ok. Uncle CJ says bad words all the time." She presented her bear for me to admire. "Ta-da!"

"So. This is who all the fuss is about?" He was an ugly thing with a torn ear and only one eye, and clearly a victim of being loved damn near to death. His one eye begged me to be humane and end his suffering. Instead, I greeted him politely. "Nice to meet you, Buttons."

"*Mister* Buttons," Ryan said threateningly.

Jeez. Didn't I get any credit for talking to an inanimate object? *Kids.*

"Can we go now?" My tone was undeniably testy. "Please?"

I held out my hand again, but she didn't take it, instead holding out her arms. And while I didn't know much about kids, I knew the universal gesture for *up, up, up.* That she trusted me was all well and good, but I only had one bloody back and I wasn't about to fuck it up for a ghost kid. They might be specters, but they were real to me in a way that surprised me every time. That included things like weight.

I gave her a gimlet eye. "You have legs."

She stubbornly maintained her position, arms upraised like she'd caught the holy spirit. "Up," she said pointedly, in case I was dumb as a box of rocks.

Christ. I reached down and picked her up. She went from light as a feather to solid and real in the span of an eyeblink. As we made contact, the room transformed again. I barely held back another *holy shit.* I knew it was just smoke and mirrors, but it was enough to make me dizzy.

She hung in my grip, looking at me in confusion. *Oh. Right.* That was probably because I was holding her like the giant bags of dog food from Costco that Danny insisted that we buy. I readjusted her in my hold, resting her on my hip. She linked her thin arms around my neck, resting her head against my chest trustingly.

I glanced down at her face, what I could see of it, anyway, her cheek flushed with pink to the soft bow of her mouth. I was reminded anew that what I did wasn't easy, but it was important. It didn't matter where I'd come from or why it had taken me so very long. But I could see her. Talk to her. And that meant she no longer had to live in the dark.

It was probably time to say something reassuring. Something sweet.

I may have gone in a *slightly* different direction.

"Let's find your mom before I need a freaking back brace."

Her mouth curved. "Bad word."

"Yeah, yeah, yeah."

I was glad to see Caleb on the couch when we came back down. He still looked a little out of it, and I furrowed my brow in concern. "Do you need me to call someone for you? Or maybe I could take you to the hospital to get checked out—"

"I don't have insurance. Unless there's a bone sticking out of someplace it shouldn't be, then I'm going to have to self-triage."

I grimaced, feeling a tad guilty. We got paid peanuts, the hours were long, and the job was dangerous at worst and tedious at best. But the one thing we had was great health insurance. "Caleb—"

"I'm fine." He didn't look so fine as he put his head in his hands. He looked haggard and worn and at least ten years older than he actually was. "I just…I don't know if I can take this shit anymore. The slamming doors, things not being left where I put them, turning the TV off and watching it come right back on…."

He looked close to tears, and I felt his pain. It was a special sort of hell being haunted by a ghost you *could* see. I couldn't imagine knowing something was there and not being able to do a damn thing about it. "It's going to be alright now."

"You don't know that," he said tiredly.

"I promise you that I do."

"How can you possibly—"

"Caleb," I said in measured tones. "You said that door doesn't ever open, right? No matter what you do?"

"Yeah."

"Well, it opened for me."

He furrowed his brow as he put together some very obvious clues that his mind told him couldn't be true. I hoped he got my gist, because I wasn't about to confirm some shit like that out loud to a virtual stranger. And a suspect to boot.

Luckily, his eyes got nice and round. "So you...*oh*."

"Trust me when I say it's going to be alright." *Especially now that you don't have a scared little ghost in your house.* I kept that little tidbit to myself. "Lie down and get some rest."

"Here? I need to be upstairs behind a locked and bolted door," he said anxiously. Even as he talked about his nightly ritual of barricading himself in like the zombie apocalypse was upon us, he followed my instructions and laid down on the couch. "I just can't...."

"You can," I said firmly. "And no one's going to bother you for a little while."

One-handed, I grabbed the throw that was folded neatly on the back of the couch. It would be easier without my ghostly burden, but when I eyed her, she just gave me a sanguine smile. For someone who'd been averse to even holding my hand, that was quite the pivot. She was probably already planning to beg a top surgeon to do conjoined twin surgery on us but in reverse.

Caleb was already half-asleep as I shook out the throw over him and let it settle on his shivering form. I missed his feet, but it was the best I could do with one hand. "I'm never safe," he murmured around a yawn. "And I'm always so cold."

"Things are going to get better," I said. "I promise."

When we came back outside Danny was still talking to Opal, and looking like he was regretting being born. But he had his phone out and was taking notes, so clearly everything couldn't be a complete waste. If he was curious about why I went straight for the car, he didn't comment. Instead, I heard the *beep beep* of the car as he must've pressed the remote. I gave him a little wave of thanks before I maneuvered myself in the passenger seat with my bundle.

I closed the door with a sigh and looked down, only to find myself the focus of two big brown eyes. Our faces were so close, my eyes tempted to cross. "Um, hello."

She smiled. "Hello."

Clearly, I was the only one disturbed about being so close I could count her eyelashes. "This is awkward, no?"

"Are you taking me to my mommy now?" As I hesitated, a tiny wrinkle puckered her brow. It only took a few seconds for her to get belligerent. "You promised. You *said*."

Tiny freaking tyrant.

"I know what I said," I shot back. "And yes, I am. Just...not right now."

First, I've got to figure out where the hell she is.

Ryan looked satisfied with my reassurance, lame as it was. I wriggled in my seat, trying to get more comfortable. She wriggled a bit, too, and I caught her foot a second before it connected with some very important bits. Then her head clipped my still-sore jaw.

"Sweet Jes—you know, this is a pretty big car," I finally ventured. "I can put you in the backseat if you'd like."

She shook her head. I wondered how soon was too soon to ask her again. For someone who wasn't touchy-feely on the best of days, this was a lot of closeness. There was only one person on the planet that I let maul me to his heart's content, and he was a wee bit taller than this small fry insisting we remain touching at all times.

I needed my ley line, stat, so I could summon Quinn. Although if she didn't show up— because ghosts were fucking contrary that way —I guess I'd have to keep Ryan around until she did. I wasn't sure how we would get around the ghostly safeguards I'd put in the house, but we'd figure something out. If nothing else, she'd be safe in my office.

I rubbed my forehead. I was pretty sure Franklin wouldn't be thrilled with the new development. He didn't strike me as a kid person. Or a people person. The only thing he continuously asked me for was peace and quiet. When I pondered how fucking noisy a graveyard had to be for a ghost to crave peace and quiet, he said cryptically that the soil was always talking. Then he shushed me.

Fine by me. If he didn't want me to disperse of the rave that was clearly going on next to his tombstone, then whatever.

The driver's side door opened suddenly, and Ryan let out a little gasp. I patted her back awkwardly. "Good Lord," Danny said as he slid in and slammed the door. "Next time, you take the chatterbox and *I'll* take the grieving brother."

"You had your chance, McKenna, and you made your deal."

"Actually, you slunk off at the first opportunity, leaving me as a sacrifice."

"Which you did not do," I said, hiding a smile. "You have to be a part of your own rescue."

He snorted. "Something I will keep in mind in the future."

"Did she at least give you something usable?"

I listened as he relayed everything he'd learned—some of it useful, some of it downright gossipy. The most important takeaway seemed to be the mystery man Opal had seen across the street. She'd seen his dark-colored Camry on three occasions, and two of those occasions had been when Quinn's friend had been visiting. She didn't have a name for the friend, but she agreed to meet with a sketch artist. I was betting that friend was probably Raven Lee.

So who was the mystery guy? Raven's husband? A lover? Someone very invested in finding out exactly who Raven was spending all her time with? Someone who knew how to bake a poisonous cake and leave his wife's lover a slice?

"I don't suppose she caught the tag of this mystery man?" I asked.

Danny snorted. "Of course she did. This is a woman who actually got kicked off neighborhood watch for watching too damn much and—" He gave me the once-over, his brow crinkled. "Why are you holding your arms like that?"

"Hmm?" I looked down only to remember he couldn't see Ryan on my lap. It probably looked like I was giving myself a weird-ass hug, one in which my arms couldn't touch my body. "I have...er, a passenger."

"One who's clinging to you like a lemur?" He raised an eyebrow. "Should I be worried?"

"Only if you want to report me to the BAU-3 for child crime," I said sweetly.

His amused look faded. "Oh, so that's...oh."

"It's a good thing," I said quietly. "What happened already happened. She was just alone in a dark room, reliving the worst. This way, I can reunite her with Quinn and things will be better."

He was quiet as he started the car and pulled away from the curb.

I tried to distract him by relating everything I'd learned. I spoke carefully, mindful of Ryan on my lap. She didn't seem to be paying us much attention, but you just never knew. Danny did more listening than anything else, processing in that quiet way of his. When I finished, he went exactly where I thought he'd go.

"So we're potentially dealing with a poisoning that was both intentional and accidental," Danny surmised. "Nate and Quinn realized that once the perpetrator realized she was still alive, he'd try to finish the job."

"They decided to leave immediately," I said, picking up the story. "Only Nate was nervous, and it was dark and rainy. The road was slippery, and he took a curve too fast and...well, you know the rest."

"So where did Quinn get the cake?" Danny asked.

It was a logical question—one I had no answer to.

Yet.

I listened with half an ear as Danny called in the potential location of the Infiniti and requested a dive team. He looked irritable when he finally hung up and didn't hesitate to tell me why. "It's a fucking shame they didn't know about Raven Lee when this case was fresh," he said. "Who knows where she is now or if she's even alive. It drives me crazy when people hold back shit that could be important."

"Caleb says he did." I hesitated before I spoke because I had a feeling the next part wouldn't go over well. "And he's pretty sure he spoke to Detective Owens."

He frowned. "I sincerely doubt that."

"Because?"

"Because Zach is conscientious. Always has been," he said patiently. "And I'm not going to take the word of a suspect over the word of someone I consider a friend."

Loyalty. He had it in spades. He wasn't about to let me besmirch a friend's good name without proof and I had to respect that. That didn't mean I had my doubts. If Caleb was telling the truth—and I felt like he just might be—then Zach had dropped the ball in a big way. The smallest little detail could make the difference between a case being solved or languishing in the evidence room.

I didn't plan on making the same mistake.

I updated our team by text as he drove, staying busy to keep awake. But Ryan's heavy weight on me was soothing and warm and it was damned hard to keep my eyes open. I pretended not to see all the looks Danny kept shooting my way. It wasn't like he could even see her, so I wasn't sure what all the staring was about.

Not only could he not see her, but he couldn't smell her scent—something lavender and vanilla. Or see her face pressed against my shirt. He couldn't see the crown of her dark silky head, tucked under my chin. Or the way she was holding on to her teddy bear like he was her very best friend in the world. I looked back at the road because I certainly didn't find those things adorable.

Not in the least.

The traffic was light, and it was smooth sailing on the highway. Eventually, I gave up the battle of trying to stay awake. The last thing I felt was Danny's hand, resting lightly on the back of my seat. I didn't bother not to try leaning into it.

Guess Ryan had her security blanket, and I had mine.

14

Star-shaped cucumbers. They were the perfect accompaniment to the smiley peanut butter and jelly sandwich I'd unearthed a few moments earlier. The press had made the sandwich small, so Danny had packed two. I already knew he'd stuffed his face with the pieces that hadn't made it.

I grinned as I unpacked the rest of my happy-faced lunch at my desk. If he thought I didn't realize he was adding shapes to the kit my sister bought, he was wrong.

I certainly could use the pick-me-up.

It had taken the dive team three days to find the submerged Infiniti, three scant miles past the Marlon Junction sign. Danny was currently down at Nova Willow, supervising the dive site as they pulled up the car. I decided to stay at the office, mostly because I already knew what they'd find inside—four skeletons and a carful of secrets.

According to the text he'd sent me an hour ago, my suspicions had been correct. He'd also let me know that the dive master had just radioed, "We've got a bravo," which was code they used when they found something important. Danny also let me know that Tate had officially removed me from her Christmas card list.

It was just as well. Seeing her hugging people voluntarily and smiling always freaked me out anyway.

I had my hands plenty full trying to track down the origins of a random piece of cake. I'd asked Ryan for more detail, but she wasn't much help. I sent a glare her way, but she didn't notice, too busy playing with my iPad on the floor. Her version of "help" consisted of telling me the cake had been strawberry with chocolate and she hated both strawberry and chocolate.

Two days in the company of a child who never seemed to *stop talking* had taught me to pick my battles. But I wasn't about to let that nonsense slide. "You told me your favorite candy is M&Ms."

"That's *different* chocolate," she'd said aggressively, looking feral enough to fight for the honor of M&Ms, and I immediately changed my mind about challenging that shit.

At least Danny and Zach were making progress with the body parts. Our first victim had been identified by his pacemaker. Bennett Hayes had been a fifty-six-year-old retired architect from the town of Crestwood, married to a therapist named Rhonda. He'd probably thought his cardiac issues would eventually take his life. Guess life had other plans.

According to Rhonda, she'd been blindsided by his abandonment. She knew he'd been seeing someone, and hoped she could convince him to go to therapy. But life had other plans. Bennett drained their bank account and left town while she was at work. He even took the damn dog. She could only guess that he was finally fulfilling his lifelong dream of traveling the world with that woman—his assistant named Brandy.

"Trollop," Danny had clarified after telling me about his interview with Rhonda. "She actually used the word trollop."

We'd stopped for coffee on the way to work, and we were posted up at a table, waiting for our order. Okay, fine, we had the coffee already and we were waiting for my cinnamon roll. Sheesh.

"It's a good word," I said with a smile.

"Yeah, but when would you really get the chance to use it?"

Soon, I realized when the barista who brought over my pastry decided to flirt with him. Never had delivering coffee required so much cleavage and touching. After she sashayed away, I shook my head.

"Trollop," I'd muttered around a mouthful of cinnamon goodness.

Danny had nearly choked on his coffee, laughing.

He also had a lead on the tattoo for the second victim. One of the tattoo artists recognized the work as belonging to an old buddy of his. Now they just had to track him down. It was hard to reconcile the fact that identification of our victim could possibly hinge on the memory of someone who went by the name Thrall.

I sighed. *And so it goes.*

For every answer we'd found, we'd also unearthed another question. And I sure would love to find Raven Lee. I also needed to know more about Moira McDaniels, Stacey Pittman, and Project Halo, which meant a trip to the Hope House. The original detectives on the case had already met with Quinn's coworkers. Guess it was our turn.

No time like the present.

I gave Ryan one last glance and headed out the door.

As I walked around the compound with my guide Maya, I realized *house* was a bit of a misnomer for the compound. It was large and imposing from the outside and surrounded by metal bars, almost like a prison. But once I was allowed through the iron gates, the correctional facility décor was left behind.

The compound reminded me almost of a mini campus—three connected buildings and a larger building near the tree line. The latter of the four looked residential—someone had attempted to domesticate it with flowers and yard ornaments. Various items of clothing hung on a rack on the side of the building and there was a small playset in the back.

"What is this place?"

I startled as I glanced down, realizing Ryan had followed me. I tried to move my hand before she could grab it, but I might as well have saved my time. A second later, her hand was tucked snugly in mine as she looked around curiously. It had only been two damn days, and I'd already held hands with her more than anyone in my whole fucking life.

When I didn't answer her question, she gave my hand a vicious tug. I rolled my eyes, but dutifully asked Maya. "What is that building over there?"

"The living quarters," Maya informed me as we passed. She was a chatty little thing, only about five feet on a good day, and thought the sun shone out of their CEO and founder's ass. I'm sure it helped that Evie was her mother.

"My mother wanted it to look and feel like home," she continued. "We can house about nine women at a time, depending on if they are alone or bring children."

"Is there a playground?" Ryan wanted to know.

"What's your position in the organization?" I asked instead, and Ryan gave me a quick kick in the shin. "*Ow,* fuc—fudge," I managed, giving a concerned Maya a smile. "And is there a playground here?"

"Of course," she said with a chipper smile. "Just right over that hill there. Swings, slides, and a jungle gym."

Ryan let out a little cheer that I ignored. Tiny tyrant. If she thought I was going to take her over there after trying to take me out at the knees, she was…well, probably right. I glared. But it would be on *my* fucking timeline. I mean, unless she got all pouty and shit.

"And your position here?" I reminded Maya as we meandered along the picturesque path.

"Residential coordinator," she said. "I help the ladies get settled and even try to recover parts of their old life if possible. Pictures, clothing, and the like. It would probably be easier to buy new things, but it's important to reclaim any parts of themselves that they can."

I'd only known her for ten minutes, but I could already tell Maya's job was a perfect fit. I imagined her assaulting everyone walking through those gates with friendly chatter. It would probably be a relief to some, especially those shell shocked by a mountain of upheaval. You didn't have to talk or think—you could just be. That also meant she'd probably met everyone at some point, which was good news for me.

"Do you remember Quinn Parker?" I asked.

"Sadly, no," she said, waving at a passel of kids charging by. "Walk!"

They slowed to a skip, which was about as good as it was probably going to get. Ryan nearly tugged my arm out of its socket. "Can I?" she whispered.

I nodded. She squealed and took after the rowdy group. It wasn't like she needed my permission. But maybe I represented a safety net. An adult had entered the chat, and it was probably comforting and easy to defer to my judgment.

"I've only been here for five years," Maya continued, "so Quinn's employment period would've been a bit before my time. Sad story, that."

I felt a little deflated because that meant she wouldn't have met Raven Lee. And since the files of Moira McDaniels and Stacey Pittman had been on Quinn's coffee table all those years ago, she probably wouldn't know them, either. I asked her about all the women, just to cover my bases, and she shook her head in the negative.

"Sorry. But maybe my mother will know."

At the sixty-watt smile Maya sent me, I was tempted to check her back for a battery compartment. I wasn't about to make any sudden moves, though. I was the only man I'd seen thus far on the compound and the few women we'd passed had given me a thousand-yard, *tase first, questions later* stare.

We continued along the path, passing a fountain with a statue of a girl in the middle. She was caught mid-twirl as if dancing in the water, her outstretched arms forming a graceful arc.

"Lissette Pemburton," Maya said before I could ask. "Daughter of our primary benefactor, Arianna Pemburton."

"What happened to her?"

"She was killed by a sexual predator," she said quietly. "She was snatched in a mall parking lot at knifepoint."

There wasn't much else to say about that. Not anything productive, anyway.

We passed a dark-haired woman sitting on a bench, reading a thick paperback. With her head downturned, her hair swept away from her neck. I could see the bruising on her pale skin. My jaw tightened. The marks looked fresh.

The woman glanced up as we approached and her ready smile dimmed, even as Maya called out a friendly, "Hello, Helena."

She bobbed her head in response. I caught a glimpse of bright green eyes before she looked back down at her book quickly, as if so engrossed that even a word past a cursory greeting was too much. I had the feeling she wasn't even seeing the page anymore. Her entire posture had changed from relaxed to still and ready. Like a rabbit that had spotted a pair of glowing feline eyes in the tree line. It was almost like she was used to fleeing but trying to make herself stay put. To remind herself that she was safe.

"It must be very hard, working here," I said quietly.

"Sometimes," Maya admitted. "But it's also extremely rewarding."

A few seconds before we reached her bench, Helena lost her inner battle. She closed her book and got up, hustling in the other direction. The grounds might be beautiful and picturesque, but it was impossible to forget why the entire compound was surrounded by bars. Some of these women were hunted. In fear for their lives.

And people running scared tended to have monsters at their heels.

Maya informed me that Evie was in the community garden and left me at the entrance with a smile and a wave. I spotted her straightaway, kneeling in the flowerbeds as she dug a hole with a small gardening trowel. Underneath a wide-brimmed, well-worn sunhat, her red-gold hair gleamed in the sun, a riot of waves and curls down her slender back.

I cast a shadow over her as I approached, but she didn't look up. "Detective," was all she said as she kept working. She had a large bucket next to her that was half-full of dirt—pungent dirt, I noticed with a wrinkled nose. Fertilizer, maybe? She also had a few trays of seedlings on a cart nearby. As I watched avidly, she reached in and spread a handful of fertilizer into the hole she'd dug.

"Thank you for meeting with me," I said. "I just wanted to clear up a few things."

"Of course," she said simply. "Anything to help. But I don't know what I could possibly add to the original investigation. We were very cooperative."

I knew that to be true. They'd met with Zach several times and answered a host of questions. But they hadn't mentioned a few things that I found very interesting. "Why didn't you mention Quinn's impending resignation?"

She glanced up at me, clearly surprised. The feeling was definitely mutual as I saw her face for the first time. She was classically pretty with a heart-shaped face, cornflower blue eyes, and a smattering of freckles across her face—well, half of it, anyway. On the left side, the skin was mottled and scarred from some sort of burn. And from the looks of her arms, the damage wasn't contained to her face.

She was clearly waiting for my reaction. I wasn't going to insult her by pretending I didn't have one. "Accident?"

She shook her head, her half-twisted mouth lifting. "Very much an on-purpose, Detective. This was a gift from my uncle when he set my aunt's room on fire."

I grimaced. "I'm sorry."

"I was a child." She waved a gloved hand. "And it was a very long time ago."

"I'm still sorry," I said, because one had nothing to do with the other.

She inclined her head before she got back to planting her seedlings. "If Quinn intended to resign, it's certainly news to me. I thought she was very happy here. She was certainly well-liked and did wonderful work. She loved being a part of something bigger than herself."

"Did she have discord with any of her coworkers?"

"Not at all," she said. "Our mission statement is women helping women, Detective. That isn't just lip service, and that attitude extends to our staff."

"What kind of services do you provide?"

"Support services. Counseling, education, legal advice...even healthcare in our clinic. Most of all, we provide a sense of community, which can be critical." Her voice grew impassioned as she warmed to her topic. I had the feeling she'd given this speech many times. "Breaking free of an abuser physically is sometimes the easy part. It's the mental grip that's made of unbreakable alloy."

I nodded. "One of an abuser's most valuable tools is making their victim feel alone."

She glanced up at me again with a tiny smile. I had a feeling that if she had a gold star nearby, she would've stuck it to my forehead. "Clearly, this isn't your first rodeo. I can only assume you've seen your share of domestic violence in your line of work."

Too much, quite frankly. Every time I thought I'd reached the bottom floor of human depravity, the Down button on the elevator dinged.

"I have," I said simply.

"Well, our first step is to let them know that they're *not* alone. That people have walked through the same fire and came out on the other side. Maybe not unscathed, but you can draw power even from your scars. And I would certainly know." She finished planting a row of seedlings and checked the bucket. She tsked, realizing she'd gone through most of the fertilizer. She rose, using the edge of the cart for leverage, and then dusted off her knees. "Walk and talk? I need to grab a fresh bag."

I nodded and fell in beside her as she led the way. I followed her down the manicured brick paths that led deeper into the maze. The gardens were extensive, a profusion of color that felt vibrant and alive. The air was thick with the fragrance of the crops, a mix of beauty and function. Every crop was meticulously labeled with a ladybug shaped sign. It was a place to come think and relax. Maybe on one of the stone benches, weathered by time and nestled against the trees.

"Quinn had an abusive boyfriend in college, so our mission statement was very close to heart," she said, picking up right where we'd left off. "She loved what we do here, and she was glad to be part of it."

"Did she ever have the need to partake of your services herself?"

Evie's brow furrowed. "As far as I know, she and her husband were doing just fine."

We stopped by a row of ten silver drums along the garden wall. There were stacks of burlap sacks with a picture of a dragonfly and the word *Bloom Blast* printed on the front. Several plump bags of fertilizer had already been filled and were stacked on a cart.

I squinted at the tiny writing on the bottom of the sack. It was a mission statement about sustainability and using the earth's natural resources from a company named BioHarvest. "Do you sell this?" I asked.

She nodded proudly. "I may be a little biased, of course, but it's the best fertilizer around. We compost it ourselves and sell it to local nurseries. It's quite an unexpected source of revenue."

"Every little bit helps."

"That it does." She pointed at one of the bags. "Would you mind?"

I stifled a sigh. Not because I minded helping, but because that fertilizer smelled like it wanted to be alone. It also looked pretty heavy, which meant I couldn't carry it away from myself using the tips of my fingers.

I bent and hefted one of the bags in my arms. When I turned, she was struggling with one of the bags herself and I inclined my head at my arms. I barely held in an *oof* as she piled it on top of the first. Well, I'd asked for it.

We made our way back to the seedlings. "What can you tell me about Raven Lee?"

If she hadn't been walking in front of me, I would've missed the slight stiffening of her slender back. "I'm sorry?"

"Raven Lee," I repeated, readjusting the bags in my arms. "Were you trying to help her disappear?"

"I don't recall that name and I have a great memory. And we don't make people disappear, Detective," she said starchily. "We help them find new purpose."

"In a different city under a new name with a new look," I said dryly. "Yeah, we have a lot of people in WITSEC finding new purpose."

Her eyes narrowed. There was a beat when I wondered if she'd end the interview and ask me to leave her garden oasis. In the end, she just gave me a tight smile—maybe because I was in the middle of providing her with free manual labor. "And just what would you have us do? If we did something like that—and I'm not saying we do—we would be helping women who don't have any other remedy."

"I expect you to help people within the constraints of the law," I said mildly. "It's the same reason I can only arrest a child abuser instead of pushing them into traffic."

The moment we reached her half-finished flower bed, I wasted no time offloading my smelly burden in the dirt. I straightened and tried dusting off my shirt where the bag had rested but gave up pretty quickly. It was destined for the trash pile. Luckily, it wasn't one of my favorites.

"The law only protects us so far," she finally said. "What do you suggest a woman do when she has an angry, abusive ex-husband at the door?"

"That's what restraining orders are for."

"A fat lot of good it will do her then." She snapped her fingers. "I know! Maybe if she shows it to him and asks nicely, he'll just go away. You know, right after he bashes her face in."

Her color was high, splotchy pink paint splashes on her high cheekbones—courtesy of being a redhead. As a blond, I could relate. I watched her quietly as she tried to gather herself. The woman who looked ready to chew nails was a stark departure from the cool, collected, confident CEO she'd been. I couldn't help but wonder at how easily she flipped that switch.

"Speaking from experience?" I asked, my voice soft.

"You know that I am," she said stiffly. "I didn't grow up in the nicest household. And I followed that up with some...mistakes of my own."

"Like Raven Lee did?" I asked casually.

She stared at me for a few moments. Assessing. We both knew she'd heard of the name. If I wasn't sure before, I was damn sure now. "I don't remember her."

"What about Moira McDaniels?"

"Again, I—"

"Stacey Pittman?"

"I don't know any of those names." From the look she gave me, I had a feeling our "limited interview" was about to come to a sudden end. Sure enough, she said, "So if that's all, I need to get back to—"

"What can you tell me about Project Halo?"

"I can tell you that it's a painful topic," she said stiffly. "Do you enjoy reopening wounds?"

I would reopen the rip in the ocean floor that Megalodon came through if it meant solving my case. "Is it named for Lissette Pemburton?" At her look of surprise, I clarified. "I saw her statue earlier in the courtyard."

"Project Halo has nothing to do with the Parkers. Or Lissette. It's how we classify our most severe cases of abuse, so we can make sure they have the right resources. I named it in honor of my aunt, Angel Ruiz." From her expression, I could tell this was a topic she didn't broach often, if ever. "And all the other women who didn't make it out on the other side."

"I'm sorry for your loss," I said awkwardly.

"As I said before, it was a long time ago," she said in crisp tones. "And now I must insist we say goodbye, Detective."

It didn't take a rocket scientist to understand that everything she'd been through was represented in the walls of this place. Every room, every program, every fiber of the Hope House reflected Evie Sinclair's struggle. And her scars, both metaphorical and physical. If she was hiding something—and I wasn't sure she was just yet—she would protect this place with every breath.

I kept my tone and my face neutral. "Thanks for meeting with me. I'll let you know if I have any other questions."

She hesitated, clearly debating how to respond to that. After a moment, she lifted her chin. "Maybe you should let my attorney know instead."

So much for cooperation.

15

Chevy called first thing in the morning. I was starting to think she didn't know it was possible—and advisable—to call people at a reasonable hour. "Raven Lee doesn't exist."

I tried to speak and failed twice before I got my voice to actually work. "What?" I croaked.

"She doesn't exist," she reiterated, slower, as if I was crazy, not sleepy. "She does, however, have a defunct Facebook page. Apparently, she's married with two kids and works in retail."

I peered blearily at the time, wondering if this was a horrible dream and some harridan hadn't woken me up on a Saturday morning with news about work, of all things. Maybe if I closed my eyes, I'd realize I actually still had more time to sleep before Danny inevitably woke me for breakfast.

It wasn't so much that he would wake me, per se, but he would dump breakfast sausage in the air fryer and let it do its thing. The smell of sizzling sausage was tantamount to smacking me in the face with a pillow. I'd zombie-shuffle to the kitchen and after a caffeine pick-me-up, scramble some eggs. Danny would fix the toast and ten minutes later, *voila*—a breakfast even we couldn't ruin. So surely this was a dream, and I was about to be woken at Jimmy Dean o'clock, as God intended.

Although if this was a dream, Watson's butt probably wouldn't be in my face.

I gave his furry rump a push. He pushed back, smacking me in the face with his tail. Now that I was a little more awake, I could hear the shower running. That probably meant Danny had gone for his morning run already before I'd even cracked open an eye. That also meant he'd seen Watson's butt in my face and left it there. I fought the urge to rearrange Watson's rump against his pillows.

To dog butt or not to dog butt, that *is the question.*

Oblivious to my dilemma of revenge, Chevy nattered on. "I also looked into the Hope House. Evie Sinclair seems to run an aboveboard operation. They do really good work for women and the community in general."

"So I heard," I murmured. "At length."

"As for the half-plate you gave me, I did come up with some possible matches for a black Camry." She hesitated. "A lot of matches."

I figured. It was too much trouble to hold up my phone, so I put it next to my head. It immediately slid under my face, and I couldn't be bothered to move it away. "How much is a lot?"

"Seventy-five," she said cheerily, as if she hadn't mixed six boxes of Legos, dumped them all over my desk, and ripped up the instructions. "If I expand the parameters to include dark blue, add an additional fifty-six."

"But—"

"Dark green and we're talking another twenty-nine."

Christ.

I yawned so wide that my eyes teared up. "It's Saturday," I told my pillow. "My plans involved convincing Danny that the lawn doesn't need mowing until next week, taking Watson for a nice, long walk, and maybe ending the day with a dip in the pool. Nowhere on that list was chasing down a possibly black/blue/dark green Camry in

South Florida owned by a possible stalker who possibly thought his wife/girlfriend was possibly cheating with Quinn."

"That was flagrant usage of the word possibly."

I snuggled deeper into my pillow. "Possibly."

"You told me you needed the results soon, did you not?" she demanded.

"Yes. Soon like…like, *I need to organize my spice drawer* soon. Or *I need to make room in my closet by getting rid of the clothes with rips and tears* soon. Good grief." I fought back another yawn. "When people tell you they need to drop a few pounds soon, do you overnight them a BowFlex and storm their snack stash with a garbage bag?"

I could almost feel her shrug. "Yes."

"Figures."

"Now that we've gotten all of your bitching out of the way, would you like me to forward you my list? Because I pulled strings for you, Christiansen." Her tone was light on sugar, heavy on spice, and not at all nice. "I would hate to think that you'd wasted my time. More importantly, I would hate to think of a punishment for someone who wasted my time."

I shivered. "One of these days, you're going to have to make good on those threats, you know."

"You act like that's going to be a problem for me. I already have plans in place and an alibi on tap. Someone else who owes me a favor," she said pointedly.

I huffed. "Send me the list."

"Already done."

She hung up before I remembered my manners. I said *thank you* to dead air.

A few moments later, my phone dinged with the promised list from Chevy. And then a text with a link for a Facebook page. Before I could click on it, the bathroom door opened. I glanced up just in time to see Danny coming through the room, a towel tied at his waist, rubbing another over his hair. I'd been so engrossed in my sleuthing that I hadn't even heard the shower turn off.

He glanced my way and did a double take. "Oh, hey, you're up."

And a good thing I was, too. Who else would ogle him getting dressed? I admired the lines of his golden, muscled back as he rifled through his dresser drawer. "Yep," I confirmed. "Every part of me is up."

He chuckled. "Pervert."

"Hey, I'm allowed to ogle you," I said as I pulled up Chevy's second text. "I locked all that hotness down. Made it legal and everything."

"And you're lucky I didn't know what I was signing up for." Stonewashed jeans and a white t-shirt seemed to be on deck as he pulled them from his drawer and tossed them on the bed. "Did you just send me a text?"

"Yep. Chevy sent me...."

Oh, and there went the towel.

He sent me a grin. "Chevy sent you what?"

I sent him a dirty look because he wasn't that cute, and he needed to know it. And so what if seeing the man naked still had the ability to make my mouth dry? I tore my gaze away with effort.

"She sent me a list of possible matches for that partial plate," I said, scrolling down the list, which was extensive. "Maybe we'll find whoever was stalking Mrs. Raven Lee...who doesn't exist, by the way."

He said something muffled in response. I was far too sleepy to figure out what the hell he'd been trying to say while pulling a shirt over his head. "What?"

His head popped through and he raked a hand through his hair. Well-behaved and well-trained from the school of Mousse and Sculpting Clay, it fell back into place. "I said that our mystery guy probably doesn't have the car anymore. That's if the car was his to begin with."

I squinted at Mr. Positivity. "Well, aren't you just a ray of sunshine this morning?"

"My particular brand of sunshine is realism. It's an acquired taste."

"I haven't yet acquired it," I informed him. "And just where are you headed so early this morning?"

"A fancy old folks home in Miami Beach named Golden Haven Shores. I hear it's practically a resort," he said. "I have an appointment to speak with Arianna Pemburton."

I frowned as I thought about where I'd heard that name before. "The Hope House benefactor?"

He nodded as he came around my side of the bed. He sat on the edge and started putting on his boots. "She wasn't happy with us poking around her pet project. Tate told me to have a face-to-face meeting and smooth things over."

I grimaced. "Sorry. I didn't mean to ruffle any feathers."

"You're just doing your job," he assured me. "Besides, Zach is going to help me schmooze. He gets a lot of freaking mileage out of those dimples."

"So he does," I murmured. I bit back words better left unsaid. I wasn't thrilled about the two of them fannying off together to Miami Beach on a sunny Saturday morning.

I watched as he laced up one boot and started in on the other. "How did you guys meet, anyway?"

"Foster care."

I waited to make sure that was it and...yeah, he was done. Good Lord. It was like he thought he was getting charged by the word. "Care to expand on that, Daniel?"

"Not really," he said mildly. "They call it the past for a reason."

"Sorry." I gave him a sunny smile. "What I meant to say was, *Expand on that, Daniel.*"

He huffed out a laugh. "There's nothing to know. We shared a room with five other kids, but we were the closest in age. The oldest of the bunch. Of course we gravitated to one another." He paused. "It was nice, I guess. Having someone around who understood exactly what I was going through."

"Because he was going through it, too," I murmured.

"Exactly. I thought we'd be lifers, to be honest. We weren't cute little kids or the babies that everyone wants. And I was known as a problem because I kept getting into trouble." He shrugged. "Really, that was the only thing we really ever argued about. He was desperate to find his forever family and I wanted to stay."

My temper flared because I knew the reason for that. I managed to keep my anger on a low simmer but God, that fucking Rachel McKenna had a lot to answer for. His mother would pop up every now and again, finally clean enough to take advantage of her supervised visitation. She'd take him out with the social worker, buy him a bunch of junk he didn't need, and use their time together to fill his head with all kinds of nonsense.

As soon as I get up the money, sweetheart, I'll be back to get you. It'll be just like old times. Just you and me.

We had fun, didn't we? No one will ever love you like I do, will they, Danny love?

Of course I'll be back for your birthday, and I'll bring you something special. Remember when I used to make your favorite cake? No one makes it like I do, do they, honey?

She would always flake on his birthday and there was never any goddamned cake. She'd been manipulative and calculating, framing their relationship to meet only her needs and purposefully filling his head with lies so she could keep his love. He'd even acted out with the two families who'd been interested in adopting him, just so they wouldn't take him away. All she'd cared about was hanging on to the most important title in his life without any of the responsibility.

Danny sent me an unreadable look over his shoulder, as if he knew what I wanted to say. I gently bit down on the inside of my cheek to keep from saying it. I'd disparaged her before, and it had gone just about as well as one would expect. Besides, he was one of the most observant people I knew.

I wouldn't be telling him anything he didn't already know about Rachel McKenna.

"Which of you got adopted first?" I asked when I could finally speak normally again.

"Zach, of course. Like they had a chance against those dimples." He gave me a half-smile. "It was always a good day when someone found their forever home."

And a bad one, too, I'd bet. I didn't say that, either. One, because it was obvious. And two, that wasn't how Danny rolled. Emoting all over him any time he gave you a nugget of his past was a good way to get him to clam up.

He'd have to deal with me squeezing his hand, though.

From the way he squeezed back, he didn't seem to mind all that much. "Stop giving me the look."

I widened my eyes, trying to stop looking however I was apparently looking. "I'm not giving you any look."

"You're *so* giving me the look. And tilting your head to boot." A half-smile curved his mouth. "Stop treating me like I'm the last cat at the shelter and I just pawed your pantleg."

I chuckled when I realized that yes, my head had definitely taken on an acute angle. "Sorry. Habit."

He gave my hand one last squeeze and stood. "Are you going in?"

"Nah, I'm working from home today."

It took him a minute to get what I would absolutely not say, and then he hid a smile. "Interesting."

I scowled. "I don't see what's so bloody interesting about it."

"Admit it. You want to work and be able to keep an eye on your ghost kid."

"Now, now." I narrowed my eyes at him. "Those are bold words for someone who *knows* I can make it look like an accident."

He chuckled. "I think it's sweet. And creepy." He paused. "Which means it's so very...well, *you*."

"Thank you," I said dryly. "Clearly our vows were the last sweet thing I'm going to get outta you."

He leaned over and planted a kiss on my scowling mouth. Then another two in quick succession. "You're the love I never expected to find and the one I'm not sure I deserve," he said, reminding me of part of his vows. "And I told *everyone*."

"True," I allowed, trying not to turn into the biggest sap that ever sapped.

"I also cried, Rainstorm. That can't be undone."

I grinned at his aggrieved tone. God forbid anyone should

remember that his eyes got red and a little watery. A *couple of* tears had escaped for a few seconds before he dashed them away. Apparently in his world, he'd fallen to his knees and wailed his love to the heavens.

"It was very sweet." It was my turn to lean over for a kiss. I tangled my fingers in his silky dark hair when he would've pulled away, because one kiss was never going to be enough. By the time I let him go, I was very sorry we'd decided to be productive human beings today. "I think my sister was recording it, too."

"And if she wants me to keep looking the other way about her pot habit, it'll never see the light of day. There's a fine line between personal usage and distribution, Rainstorm, and your family does the electric slide on it every damn day."

I chuckled. "But you love 'em."

"Yeah, I do."

And you love me.

I didn't bother to make him say the words. Some things were just too damn obvious. As he bustled around, finishing getting ready, I figured another hour of sleep wouldn't hurt. I quickly did some mental math about the absolute *latest* I could get up and still get stuff done for the day. Then I set my alarm for ten minutes after that.

I fell asleep shortly after I set my phone on the charger. The last thing I felt was a soft kiss at the nape of my neck and the words *love you* at my temple. I reached up and sleepily patted his stubbled jaw.

Love you right back.

Three hours later, forced out of the cocoon of our bed by my alarm, I finally got moving. A shower helped. So did coffee. By the time I threw on some jeans and a shirt and headed to my office in my socked feet, I was feeling close to human. Watson, trailing behind me, stopped cold a few feet short of my office door.

I chuckled at his slightly anxious little face. His German shepherd roots wanted to herd me to safety. But the part of him that made him my Watty—slightly lazy, a bit cowardly, and oh-so-lovable—wasn't going near my office and all its paranormal visitors. I leaned down and rubbed his ears fondly. He scooted off, leaving me to face the "dangers" within.

"Nice guard dog you are," I called after his swishing tail as he disappeared in the living room. A moment later, I heard the squeak of his Kong toy. Clearly, he'd gotten over his sadness at my potential demise. "I'm not even dead yet!"

Squeeeak.

Well. I huffed.

The moment I opened my office door, a kid-shaped blur flew at me. I barely held on to my coffee cup as Ryan wrapped her thin arms around my waist. Startled, I lifted wide eyes from her dark head to Franklin, sitting in his favorite chair with yet another book.

"You haven't found her mother yet?" he asked, looking displeased. "The girl *does* natter on so. I've been reading this same chapter for an hour."

I narrowed my eyes at him as I walked to my desk. With Ryan clinging to my legs, it was more of a stagger. "You're always free to find someplace else to read."

He huffed and flipped a page so hard that I heard a little rip.

"I'm bored," Ryan announced. Done strangling me to death, she flopped on my rug. "Can we go to the park?"

"I have to work," I said as I booted up my computer. "Maybe Franklin will take you."

"Franklin will do no such thing," came from his corner as he continued to read.

Ingrate. I shot him a look and he stuck out his tongue. I turned to Ryan, who was now drumming her heels on the floor. I winced at the noise. It didn't help when she started humming some tune to herself in rhythm with the beat.

"Maybe I can…." The noise increased. "Maybe we'll just…Ryan!"

She paused, looking at me questioningly. I rubbed my temples because I'd only been awake for an hour, and I already needed two Tylenol and a codeine chaser. "Maybe I can take you later."

"But I wanna go *nooooow*."

"We'll go later," I said firmly. "Right now, you can...um...." I looked around for inspiration and my eyes lit up as they landed on my iPad. I grabbed it and powered it on, relieved to see the battery bar was full. "For now, you can watch this."

"Mommy said I can only have an hour of screen time a day," she said even as she took the iPad with greedy hands.

"Well, with any luck Mommy will come and tell me that herself," I muttered.

I gave the ley line in the backyard a grim look. I'd tried to reach Quinn for hours—and released another two Quinns into the atmosphere—but I was thinking it was never too soon to try again. And again. Whatever it took.

I set Ryan up with a cartoon that was so brightly colored and loud that my eyeballs shrank in their sockets. Franklin gave me the dirtiest look he could manage. But what was I supposed to do? She'd been in a dark room long enough. We'd just have to deal.

I got to work. Used to silence when I was working, it took me awhile to stop reading the same sentence over and over, but I adjusted pretty quickly. I combed through Chevy's list, comparing the owners of the Camrys to any names in our investigation. Strangely, I came back with two hits—distant hits, but more than I'd expected. I made notations to that effect next to the names Allen Porter and Javi Santos.

Allen Porter worked at a café near Quinn's gym. He had no criminal history, but he'd seen her nearly every day when she stopped by for an after-workout latte. A deep dive into his social media showed that he posted a lot. Like three to four times a day a lot. It made it easier to get a general picture of Allen and what was important to him as a person. As far as I could tell, his girlfriend Gigi made the list. So did his dog, a lab named Bruno. He loved coffee art, got into arguments about politics with strangers, and his mom liked every comment he ever made.

The other hit looked even better. Javi Santos got my interest due to no other reason than being a PI. He had no social media presence, which wasn't all that suspicious given his profession. It was his job to observe without being observed. He had no connection to Quinn and no criminal history.

But what were the odds that the car of a PI would be in front of her house?

His address was familiar, too, and I realized that Nick only lived about five minutes from his house. So instead of schlepping my ass all the way down to Marina Mile, I decided to shoot Nick a text, asking him to check this Javi character out.

Helpful as usual, he texted back.

> **GONZALEZ**
> I'm busy.

> Doing what.

> **GONZALEZ**
> Doing me.

> I don't need to know about your masturbation habits, I need a favor.

> **GONZALEZ**
> It's early, Christiansen.

> It's five minutes away from your door! You can probably see him from your window.

He didn't respond and I mentally dusted off my hands. Perfect.

It suddenly hit me that I hadn't checked the other link Chevy had sent me. So I clicked on it, waiting as it took me to the Facebook page of Raven Lee. I enlarged the picture of the smiling woman. She looked to be in her mid-twenties to thirties—I was shit at determining ages, so I never tried. She was on the thinner side, pretty, with dark eyes and a profusion of dark curly hair that threatened to overwhelm her face. It kind of looked like...a wig?

A guy was standing behind her, arms linked around her middle, and I didn't need the matching red plaid shirts to know they were a couple. His rolled-up sleeves showed a shark tattoo on his right inner forearm, but she had no visible identifying marks.

My gaze lingered on the man's face. He was big and blond and fairly handsome, but what drew my attention was that he wasn't smiling a bit. And despite the placement of his hands indicating his familiarity with her body, they didn't look all that comfortable with one another. Maybe they were just bad picture takers. Or maybe I'd just found the reason Raven Lee had been at the Hope House.

I quickly sent the picture to Nick.

> See if Javi Santos knows either of these people.

He sent me back a thumbs-up, and I went back to Raven's page. There were only ten pictures on her profile, and I clicked through them all. She had a boy and a girl—young—and they both were blond and tall like their father. There was one of them on the beach, at a family picnic, and one at a park.

On a hunch, I pulled up Instagram and tried my luck with her name. When I actually got a hit, I nearly clapped for joy. When I got fifty hits, I was a lot less happy. I resigned myself to sorting through them all, which I did after getting a fresh cup of coffee. I compared profile after profile, until I came up with a relatively good match for Raven S. Lee.

More photos, twenty in all. More typical Americana. But according to the FBI database, this slice of Americana didn't exist. So who was Raven Lee really? Why was she using a fake name? And what, if anything, did that have to do with the Parkers?

I was still pondering that question when my phone buzzed. I picked up when I saw it was a call from Nick. "Yeah?"

"Javi Santos is a dick," he growled. "He also has a very annoying habit of answering questions with questions."

"Hazards of talking to someone whose entire career is ferreting out the things people don't want him to know," I murmured.

"Yeah, well, that doesn't mean he wasn't fucking annoying. And condescending. When I suggested that his cooperation wasn't optional, he threw a whole bunch of legalese at me and shut the door on my nose."

"So...what I'm hearing is you didn't find out anything."

"I'm not really feeling the love here, Christiansen."

"In case you've forgotten, I got punched in the face on my last suspect drop-in." I shrugged. "Almost losing the tip of your nose to a quickly slamming door is a vast improvement."

"I'm sure you wouldn't feel that way if it was *your* nose," he said with a growl. "Anyway, he couldn't have said no more if I asked him to. He doesn't know either of the people in the photo. He's never heard of the name Raven Lee. He doesn't know Quinn or Nate, and he wasn't hired by either of them to spy on the other."

Well, shit.

"Any more terrible news you'd like to impart before I hang up?" I asked dryly. "You seem to be on a roll."

"I don't know," he said with a sigh. "I'm getting a vibe from this guy. Like he's not on the up and up. I think I'm going to stake out his place for a bit. Maybe even follow him."

He sounded a little too amped about that, so I felt it was my duty to remind him to be careful. And follow Santos without making contact or a mess.

My kindness was rewarded with the sassy rejoinder, "So you're the only one who can chase a suspect into a canal?"

The *nerve*. I mean, yes, I did that. But the nerve of it all.

"I terminated that pursuit several minutes before he took a dip in the Woxahatchee Canal," I said hotly. "I also fished his ass out of the water, sans assistance."

"Well, I suppose you should be commended for not letting him drown."

"That's all I'm sayin'," I said with feeling. Now yes, the canal wasn't deep. But fuck, there were gators in it, and that made my rescue efforts a big hairy-ass deal. "You gotta give credit where credit is due."

He snorted. "You know what? I think I'm good on surveillance tips from you."

I shrugged as I pulled up a photo of Raven and her two kids in front of an ice cream truck. "Suit yourself."

Maybe they were close to home. Touching the screen with two fingers, I enlarged the picture. They were clearly in *a* neighborhood—and a newer one, at that. The replicated architecture and uniform colors and carefully manicured lawns made that pretty obvious. Now I just had to find something that would differentiate this cookie-cutter area from the hundreds of others popping up all over the damn place.

"So." Nick's voice made me jump because I forgot I even had him on speakerphone. "What're we doing for Thanksgiving?"

I glanced at my phone's display to make sure it was still connected to the right person. *Gonzalez* still read across the screen. Still. It didn't hurt to make sure that he hadn't been taken.

"Hi, this is Detective Christiansen," I said cautiously. "I'm going to help negotiate Nick's safe return, okay?"

"You're a riot," he said. "I'm serious. My family is going out of the country to see my grandmother."

"Aaaand you hate them and her?" I asked slowly.

"My girl can't get time off from work," he said impatiently. "I mean, I was looking forward to seeing my grandma, but it kind of works out so someone can watch Cupcake and Sugar."

I resisted checking the display again. "Who are?"

"My mom's beagles." He let out a long-suffering sigh. "The boarding service fell through, and she is fanatical about those spoiled mutts. You should see the fucking binder full of instructions on how to watch them. It's like an inch thick!"

I tuned him out, going back to the ice cream truck photo as he continued complaining about Cupcake and Sugar who, quite honestly, sounded like lovely little dogs. There was a reflection of a statue in the polished surface of Raven's sunglasses that caught and held my attention. It looked like a statue of some sort. Maybe of a jumping fish?

"Anyway, I'm not really digging a Hungry Man dinner on a holiday," Nick finished, wrapping up his *incredibly* long—and boring, don't forget boring—diatribe.

"That really seems like a personal problem," I said absently. I made the screen so big that it was blurry, so I went down a pinch until the reflection came into focus.

"Shouldn't you guys be throwing holidays at your place anyway?" he complained. "I mean, that's what you do when you're married and old and shit."

"You just want someplace to park your considerably sized fanny and eat free food."

"Nothing you or the boss man have prepared, but yeah," he said in his best no-duh tone. "And if you could throw in some free beer and a big screen to watch football, that would be ideal."

I brightened the picture and increased the contrast. The dolphin likeness, caught in bronze right in the middle of a playful arc, came into focus. I recognized it as the Dolphin Serenity Statue, an iconic landmark located in the heart of Oceanfront Park. It was hard to tamp down a surge of excitement. Yes, I only had a general area, but it was a hell of a lot more than I'd had a few minutes ago.

I printed out that picture and the one where Raven was standing in front of their house. The two carved pumpkins and the "It's fall, y'all" sign were probably long gone. Hopefully, the rest of the porch décor still remained.

"Well?"

I looked at my phone and barely held in a groan. "Good Lord. How are you still here?"

"I swear to God, my two-year-old niece could beat you in a concentration competition," Nick said with another sigh. "Are we a go for Thanksgiving or not?"

"Not. Very much not," I said decisively. "Honestly, I'm still trying to wrap my mind around you having the hutzpah to invite yourself over to *my* house on one of my precious and extremely necessary days off from seeing your face."

"I want to bring the yams," he announced, as if he was hearing impaired. "Technically, I guess it's more of a sweet potato casserole.

But they have the same flavor profile and I'm not bringing two dishes to this thing."

"What thing?" I asked as I shut down my computer before grabbing my printouts. "There is no thing."

There was a suspicious pause on his end. "Do you just not want me to bring the yams?"

"Goodbye, Gonzalez."

I hung up on his plaintive, "But I even put marshmallows on top!"

I was halfway out of my office before I remembered that I had unusual responsibilities this week. Little responsibilities. I eyed Ryan, still happily watching her cartoon, her chin on her hand. I guess it wasn't like I *needed* to stay. She certainly didn't need me in any way. Hell, she looked happy as a clam, lying on her stomach on my office rug. I just felt like she'd been alone enough.

A soft laugh came from the corner near the window. I found Franklin giving me an indulgent look. "I'll watch her. It's not like I'm going anywhere at the moment." He paused. "As long as I don't actually have to *do* anything with her."

"You're a prince, Frankie."

"I don't like that," he informed me with a sniff. "And I don't enjoy children."

"I told her I'd take her to the park," I said.

He stuck his nose back in his book.

Boy, it was tough to find good help these days. Especially ghostly fucking help.

With a sigh, I headed out.

16

It took two hours of driving slowly through Oceanfront Park before I found the house. I crept to a stop at the curb, eyeing the small split-level home. There was a guy in the driveway wearing cutoff shorts and not much else, washing a blue Dodge Ram. Earbuds in his ears, he was blissfully unaware as he bopped along to a beat only he could hear.

I pulled the picture of Raven Lee and her beau up on my phone, right before I smiled with satisfaction. If that wasn't the same guy, I'd eat my nonexistent hat. He had the same floppy dirty-blond hair, build, and height. And when he squeezed out a sponge over a bucket, I was able to see the same shark tattoo on his arm.

Yahtzee. I got out of the car and made my way up the walk. He glanced up as I rounded the hood of his truck, and then gave me a double take when he saw the badge. He pulled out his earbud so quickly that he almost bobbled it.

"Can I help you?" he asked with a frown.

"Maybe you can. Detective Christiansen with BBPD." I showed him my badge as he slowly pulled out his other earbud and pocketed them both. "I just have a few questions for you Mr. ...?"

"Matthews. Jason Matthews."

"Do you mind if I see your ID?"

We both knew I was phrasing it as a question when it was really a request. And not an optional one. He reached in his pocket and pulled out a frayed wallet. He handed over his ID reluctantly. "What did you say your name was again?"

"Detective Christiansen," I said, taking a quick picture of his ID before I handed it back. "Do you know a woman named Raven Lee?"

He quickly schooled his expression, but it was much too late for that. It was very clear from his face that he'd definitely heard that name before.

Because it wasn't a normal day if someone wasn't lying to me, Jason shook his head slowly as he pocketed his wallet. "Can't say that I do."

I nodded. "Interesting."

"Now, if that's all, I'd better get back to—"

"If you don't know her by that name, maybe you know her by face," I said casually as I unfolded my printout. I handed it to him with a smile. "I mean, I don't go around linking my arms around the waists of people I don't know. But you do you."

His throat worked as he stared at the picture. He seemed to be having a hard time with words. Being confronted with a lie will do that to you. "It's a long story."

"Luckily for you, I've got time."

He handed me back the printout with a sigh. "Her name is Caitlin Closs, and we never were a couple. She's my cousin."

I kept my eyebrows under control, but it was a near thing. I was pretty sure that kind of relationship was illegal in quite a few states. "What's with the family photos?"

"She asked me to do her a favor." He blew out a breath and then looked down at the water now flowing down his driveway. "Do you mind if I go turn off the hose?"

"Go right ahead," I said with a nod.

He hustled off around the side of the house as I watched him carefully. Luckily for me, he didn't seem interested in running. He trudged through the soggy grass and was back in less than a minute.

"So about that favor," I prodded.

"I didn't ask for the details. I figured she was just trying to make her life seem better than it really was. You know, on social media or whatever." He shrugged. "Maybe to make an old friend or ex jealous."

"Was that something she'd done before?"

"No. Maybe. I don't know." He shook his head. "I was just so happy that she was doing well, holding down a job, and showing interest in something other than drugs. She also gave me...um, a hundred bucks." He seemed to be embarrassed that his cooperation wasn't entirely altruistic. "I needed the money, so...I did it."

"And I think I know, but just for the sake of clarification, what is *it*, exactly?"

"She wanted a day of my time for a photo shoot. I had to bring the kids and a couple different outfits, and we'd go to a few places, take pictures, and act like a family unit. That's it." He shrugged uncomfortably. "There was another woman there who took the pictures—"

"Quinn?" I asked sharply.

"I didn't get a name." He gave me a sheepish look. "I was just doing my cousin a favor. It seemed harmless enough."

I pulled out my phone and scrolled through a few pictures before finding one of Quinn. I turned it around. "Is this the woman?"

"Yes," he said, surprise wreathing his features. "What did she do? Was it some sort of scam? I asked Caitlin about it, but she refused to talk about it. The whole damn thing was weird, and that was *before* they brought Nina into it."

I barely kept from rubbing my temples, but it was a near miss. A new name popping up this late in the investigation was a bit of a nightmare. "Nina?"

"My kids' mom. She's a makeup artist." He looked at me earnestly. "She's amazing. Works at a local theater, you know?"

"I'm sure. But about Quinn...."

"Oh. Right. Well, when she found out about that, she asked if Nina would do Caity's makeup." He scowled at my expression, which

I was pretty sure was a dead ringer for, *Yeah, and?* "Not regular makeup. Bruises."

Well. No chance of keeping a poker face when he dropped that little bomb on me.

It took me a second to get with the program. "She wanted you to cover up bruises?" I finally asked.

"No, she wanted Nina to create some. Makeup magic and all that. Like I said. Weird." He rubbed the back of his neck, looking a little uncomfortable. "Per her request, Nina gave her a black eye and some fingermarks around her throat. And then that Quinn woman took pictures."

"Why did...why?" I couldn't hide my confusion. "Did she explain why she'd do such a thing? Did you even ask?"

"Of course I asked," he said indignantly. "She said she couldn't give me all the details for my safety, but she said she was working on something big. Trying to do a little good and make us proud." Regret crossed his face. "We didn't tell her that enough, you know?"

My mind tumbled over the possibilities. I was trying to cram this new puzzle piece in with the existing ones, and it wasn't fitting well.

"I need to speak with Caitlin," I finally said. "When's the last time you saw your cousin? Do you have any contact information?"

He looked a little disgruntled. Probably because I hadn't answered any of his questions but kept posing more of my own. "We don't talk much nowadays. She has a phone, but she's not all that great with paying the bill. I swear it's off more than it's on," he said with a tinge of frustration. "I can give you her last address, but I doubt she's still there."

Wonderful. I held in a sigh. "Does she ever come see you?"

"She shows up every couple of months, usually asking for money." He shrugged. "It's not like I can spare all that much, but the kids love seeing her, so it's whatever."

"Would she come if you called?"

"I could try."

He stood there, just looking at me, and I was hard-pressed not to grind my teeth. "Could you try now?"

He scratched the back of his neck, looking like he was wondering if he could get away with refusing. "Well...."

"Just a conversation," I said quickly. "She isn't in any trouble."

Looking about as reluctant as a person could manage, he pulled out his phone and made the call. When I instructed him to put it on speaker, his look segued from reluctance to full-blown irritation. But he did as I asked. His call went to voicemail, and he left her a vague message about calling him back because it was important.

We didn't talk much longer. I asked a few more questions, but his answers got shorter and terser, and it was clear that he was quite finished with me. I decided to take my leave, but not before giving him my business card. I instructed him to contact me if Caitlin called and got a grunt for my effort. Before I was halfway down the driveway, I could hear water on metal as he went back to washing his car.

No matter. I had a lead. And a hot lead on a cold case gave this detective very warm feelings. Just what kind of game had Quinn been playing? Why did she need those photos of the picture-perfect family? And the fake bruises? I...didn't know what to make of that.

My phone started buzzing the moment I started up my car. I checked the screen expecting Danny and found *Unknown* instead... which was cute. I didn't answer calls from people I knew, but way to keep hope alive. I checked the message after my phone stopped buzzing. I froze at the written text. *This is Harper from the adoption agency...*

My grip tightened on the phone so hard, I feared for the safety of the screen. I loosened my fingers with effort and forced myself to tap the message. Her cheerful voice started immediately. "This is Harper from the adoption agency. Can you give me a call at your earliest convenience? Okay. Hope to speak to you soon. Thanks! Bye."

Listening to the entire thing did little to relax my shoulders. And what was with people leaving long fucking messages that told you absolutely nothing? I only knew what I had known *before* I checked the damn thing. Was it more paperwork? Something we forgot to sign? A follow-up interview? Or....

I forced myself to call her back. I was an adult, and avoidance was not cute. Even though she'd called me a scant five minutes ago—excuse me for penciling in time to hyperventilate—the call went to voicemail. I glanced at the clock and realized it was after five. I must've been her last call of the day. Monday, then.

I'd be lying if I said I wasn't relieved.

I blew out a breath and checked my other messages. I had one from my mother asking me to "try and stop by the store when I had a chance." Because I'd been her child since the moment I'd taken my first breath of oxygen, it was a simple matter to decode that message. "Try and stop by the store" meant stop by the store. And "when I had a chance" meant right the fuck now.

The third was from Nick.

> GONZALEZ
> Javi is following some guy named Michael Lawrence.

I texted back immediately. It didn't escape me that I defaulted to work first. I wasn't sure if it was from habit, or because it was so damned comfortable. Yes. Murder and mayhem went under the category of comfort for me. Like a blanket and a cup of hot cocoa.

> Why?

> GONZALEZ
> If I knew why, I would've said why. I think we need to reevaluate your status as the brains of this operation.

I glared at the phone. So at least we knew who our next dead body would be. Nick Gonzalez. Age 34. Cause of death: got on my last fucking nerve for the last fucking time.

> I think we can cross off Nate as the primary.

> GONZALEZ
> Yeah? Why's that?

I tried to think of a quick way to summarize all I'd learned in the past twenty minutes.

> Because it looks like Quinn stirred up something the likes of which she wasn't prepared for.

In that, we certainly had something in common.

17

My mother's health and wellness store did brisk business. Her inventory always seemed to be a blend of things people needed and things they didn't need but were willing to try. Crystals, candles, and aromatherapy led the sales pack, with incense, skin care, and relaxation aids trotting not too far behind.

The wind chime on the door sounded as I entered, and my mother looked up from the front desk with a smile. That smile got bigger when she saw who it was. She was a rainbow of colors today, with her lilac shirt and flowered skirt. Her blond hair was free from its usual braid, held back from her face by a headband made of feathers.

"I didn't expect you so soon." She leaned over the counter to give me a hug and buss my cheek. The scent of lemongrass enveloped me. "Thank you for the compost, dear."

I'd visited the Hope House's website to research more about Evie Sinclair's organization and came across the BioHarvest link for her *Bloom Blast*. I ordered some, figuring it was win-win. I got to support the cause and make my mother happy.

"You're welcome," I said absently, looking at the mess of papers on her counter. There were some colorful charts, and some had different zodiac signs on them. "What is all this?"

"Child astrology charting," she said with a smile. "Using the exact positions of the celestial bodies at the exact moment and location of the child's birth, astrologers can provide insights into his or her future life path."

I blinked and asked the question again, hoping I'd garner an answer this time that actually made sense. "What's all this?"

She laughed softly. "It's more useful than you think. It can predict personality, tendencies, strengths, weaknesses…the moon sign can even predict how the child will process and express feelings." She shuffled through some of the charts until she pulled out one with a bull on the top. "I used your and Danny's signs to figure out the most compatible one. You need a Virgo in your life."

"Mother."

"I would settle for a fellow water sign. And they'll certainly mesh with Danny's earth sign because he's so grounded."

I rubbed my temples. "Robyn."

"A Scorpio, then. You can give me a Scorpio," she insisted. "You need to know these things now before you make a move."

"And just who said we were making a move?"

"Paula seemed to think so, and she's usually right about these things."

That was because she prided herself on being all up in Danny's business. We were lucky she didn't check him for polyps while he was sleeping, and that was probably because she couldn't get her mitts on a good endoscope.

"Also, that Harper woman at the agency called us to check your references. We gave you boys a glowing one," she said with a smile. "Danny's was easy. Yours was a bit more challenging, of course, but don't worry. I didn't at all mention any of your…ways."

"My what?" I demanded.

"The ghost stuff," she said at the same volume a cook would use to say *order up*!

I shushed her as a couple of her patrons looked our way. "Maybe it would be easier to spread the news if you just buy ad space during the next Super Bowl."

"Sorry. Just trying to help." She snapped her fingers. "That reminds me. I made up some more vitamin shots for you. I'll be right back."

I did my best to contain a shiver. "Can't wait."

She bustled off to the back of the store. I picked up the astrology chart on top that she'd so carefully put together. Under Danny's name in flowy script was a picture of a bull. Apparently, they were known for a stable and reliable nature. Patience. Persistence. They were hardworking and diligent and possessive.

Well, hell, she might as well have left off the bull made of constellations and put a picture of Danny at the bottom.

And then there was my side. Pisces were known for their empathy and compassion. They could be emotionally responsive, attuned to subtle energies around them, and drawn to mystical or spiritual pursuits. They could also struggle with setting clear boundaries and absorb emotions and energies of those around them.

And when you put the two signs together? Well, apparently the Taurus's practicality provided a stabilizing force for the Pisces.

I shook my head with a wry smile. My mother may have some offbeat ways, but sometimes she was right on the money. Still, I wasn't about to turn a child away because he wasn't the perfect astrology sign. So if we wound up with a Leo or something, she'd just have to deal.

Look at you, talking about adoption without hyperventilating.

That was progress, right?

I heard the slap of my mother's sandals as she came back through the curtain and put the chart back down just in time. It wouldn't do to seem *too* interested. I just got her to stop emailing me a daily horoscope.

She had a large shopping bag with her that rattled when she set it on the counter. When I peered inside, I saw an assortment of glass bottles filled with brightly colored liquid. "No more than one of those a day," she cautioned.

"There's absolutely zero chance of that," I assured her. I had enough trouble choking down the one. Then I usually spent the next half-hour making sure it *stayed* down. "I'd better get going."

"Of course." She gave me another hug. "Did I mention how nice it is to be able to do this whenever I want?"

I chuckled when I finally freed myself from the folds of her peasant blouse. "Once or twice. A day."

"Well, it's true. Those FBI years were hard on us. All of us."

I blinked, caught a little off guard. That's what happened when things were light and breezy, and someone unexpectedly got deep as shit. I wasn't about to sweep it under the rug. "You never said anything."

"What was I supposed to say? You were doing something that you wanted to do. I was proud of you, even if it took you all over the country at any given time. And even though you were working in close proximity to murderers. Although I suppose you still do that." She peered up at me. "I have mentioned how much I hate that, haven't I?"

"Not today," I said dryly. "But thank you for rectifying that."

She patted my cheek. "Welcome. Anyway, I like to think of this as my reward for being patient while you lived out your dream. Then your dream changed, and I'm so happy that I get to be part of this chapter of your life." She paused, thinking. "I'd be happier still if it contained a whole lot less murder."

"Robyn," I said with a sigh.

"I'm putting it out there in the universe," she said with a wave. "You have to manifest these things, Rainstorm."

I looked at her fondly. In my younger years, I'd always taken my parents' presence in my life for granted. I'd seen a lot since then, though. I knew that love could be conditional, even from those that gave you life. But my parents? The well of their love never seemed to run dry. They gave it freely, unconditionally, and as much of it as you could handle. I winced, thinking about the sexual wellness gift basket my mother had given us for our anniversary.

Like I said. As much love as you could handle.

And then a teeny bit more.

"How did you know you wanted to be a parent?" I blurted.

She lifted a shoulder as she began gathering the astrology charts in a nice little pile. "I didn't."

"Well, how did you know you were ready?"

"Again. I didn't." She gave me a considering look. "Still don't."

I glared. "Thank you. *Mother.*"

"Yes, yes, I know you're my child, but I'm assuming you want the truth."

"I guess." I mentally reviewed my insurance policy and confirmed that therapy was indeed covered. "Alright. Go ahead and scar me."

She pretended to cut my arm with a knife. "Parenting can be hell. When you two were young, we never got any sleep. Taking care of myself was an afterthought. Going to the bathroom alone was a freaking luxury." She shook her head, clearly caught up in the trauma of raising us to be functional human beings, and I scowled. "People would always tell me that when you two got older, things would get better, which was true. They failed to mention that it also gets worse."

I was going to put her in a home and make sure that playing shuffleboard was a daily requirement. "How so?"

"Because then I had absolutely zero control. Not over the petty things like what you eat or what you wear. But over who hurts you. It's hard to step back and let your kid navigate the world. To hope you've taught them all the things they need to know." She smiled faintly. "And you *still* get no sleep. Now it's not a little person waking you up at an ungodly hour, ready for breakfast and cartoons. It's thoughts of where they are and hoping that they're safe that has you sitting up in the middle of the night."

Alright. Maybe I'd get her a room with a view. "You're not exactly selling it, you know," I said quietly. "This parenting business."

"I don't intend to. I love you and your sister. You're quite literally the best thing I've ever done. But can I pinpoint a time when I looked at Leo and said, *yes, now, we're ready?* Absolutely not."

That...was actually rather helpful. Because I didn't ever see that happening. I wasn't ever going to have that lightning bolt moment when I was a hundred percent sure we were ready. When I looked up, she was gazing at me fondly.

"I know," was all she said.

"You know what?"

"I *know*. I know what you're thinking and it's hard to make that leap."

I didn't bother to deny it. "It truly is."

"It's okay to be scared. I may've held back on the ghost stuff with that lady at the agency, but I was a hundred percent truthful with the rest. You're going to be an amazing dad."

Talk about presenting facts not in evidence. "But—"

"Don't argue with me, Rainstorm. I'm still your mother." At my testy huff, she gave me a warning look. "You *will* be an amazing dad. As long as it's something you really want to do. It's a thankless job sometimes and one that has no bloody end, by the way."

"You are aware that you're affecting the value of your Mother's Day gift?"

"Facts are facts," she said, because doubling down is a thing. "As long as I walk this earth, you'll be my responsibility and I take that job very seriously. What you need from me will vary, and I'll always do my best to provide it. Sometimes you'll need a listening ear or a shoulder to lean on."

"You're good at that."

"I know, right?" She looked smug. "Sometimes you'll need a hug—"

Did I mention what a treasure she was? "Always."

"Some home cooking, maybe—"

"Dear God, no," I blurted.

She pinched me and I yelped. "And right now, you needed some good, sound advice, which hopefully I've provided."

"You have," I said begrudgingly. Even if I could've done without the abuse. "But what if I'm not enough?"

"Love will carry you through. It's everything you need."

I made an irritable noise. "Yeah, along with money. Space. Time. Patience. Did I mention money?"

She pinched me again and I wasn't fast enough to dodge those evil little fingers. "Love," she said again, firmer this time. "Is the most important thing."

Did I say she was a treasure? I meant she was a menace.

When I squinted at her, she made pinscher claws again and I capitulated fairly quickly. "Love," I agreed with a heavy sigh. I eyed her because she hadn't covered one very important topic. "Tell me the truth. You love me better than Sky, right?"

Pinch. "I love my children exactly the same."

"Ow." I rubbed my poor, abused arm. "That was the same fuck— flipping spot, Mother!" I aborted the curse a bit late, but I was hoping we could let it slide. I had no desire to have my mouth washed out with ethically sourced, cruelty-free, vegan soap.

"And there's more where that came from," she threatened.

I glared. Okay, now no view. I was going to make sure they put her room next to the bingo hall and she would fall asleep and be jerked awake to the sound of someone calling, "O-52!"

"I love you both for different reasons," she said firmly. "I love your logical nature. The way you have to make sense of everything. And your determination. The way you will hunt to the ends of the earth for every little answer. I love your sister for her whimsy and the way she sees beauty in the little things."

"I see beauty in the little things," I muttered.

"I also love the way she's a great listener and doesn't interrupt people when they're talking."

I couldn't help but laugh. "Point taken."

"I love her trusting nature and the way she embraces the universe's plan for her. The way she trusts that everything will work out. Maybe not the way she wanted it to, but the way it was supposed to. Even if it hurts." She eyed me critically. "It wouldn't have taken her so long to acknowledge the ghosts, Rainstorm."

I huffed. Probably not. "At the moment, the scales are leaning a bit heavy toward Sky."

She rolled her eyes even as she reached up and brushed my hair out of my eyes. "I also love your grounded nature and the way people know within seconds of meeting you that they can count on you. It's what makes you such a good detective. It's also what will make you a good parent." She gave me a secret little smile. "If that's the path that you choose."

I needed to invest in a bulletproof vest for fucking feelings because damned if she hadn't hit me dead center in the chest.

"Thank you, Ma," I said gruffly. Nothing made you understand your parents more than contemplating taking on the job yourself. "Love you."

Her eyes widened a fraction. It wasn't something I said all that often. Maybe that was something else I should work on. It wasn't something I wanted to use as fucking punctuation in a conversation, but I also didn't want someone's eyes to fall out of their head when I did.

She cleared her throat. "Get back to work, love. I know you're doing something important, and I know it can't wait."

I half-smiled as I leaned down and kissed the top of her head. Lemongrass. I'd never be able to associate the scent with anyone or anything else. "I'll always make time for you."

"You absolutely will." She patted me on the cheek. "Everything that came out of my uterus will respond to my summons."

I stifled a sigh. "Yes, Mother. Less of the uterus talk, if you don't mind."

"We'll see." She tucked the astrology charts in my bag before giving it a push closer to my side of the counter. Then she looked at me expectantly. "So?"

I gave her a blank look. She'd given me a lot to chew on. Surely, she didn't expect me to declare myself ready for little person patrol—for life—right this bloody minute. "So what?"

"What are we doing for Thanksgiving?"

I groaned.

As I approached my car, I could see it was already occupied.

Quinn sat in the passenger seat, trying to rifle through my attaché case—emphasis on *trying*. It was damn near impossible for them to harness my energy now, and I'd gotten an earful about it from several irritated ghosts. Too bad, so sad.

I hit the key fob, and the piercing *beep beep* startled my would-be snoop. She grabbed her chest as I slid in the driver's seat. I was already mentally shuffling through greetings. I figured I could either go with the benign, *hey*. Or the more accurate, *Where the hell have you been?*

She spoke before I could decide. "I'm starting to think I made a mistake contacting you."

"And just what is that supposed to mean?"

"It means you're doing a lot of poking your nose around where it doesn't belong, and not a lot of finding my child."

"If you hadn't disappeared for so long, I would've been able to tell you that I found Ryan," I said with more patience than she deserved. "*Days* ago."

"You...you what?" Her eyes flew wide. "I can't believe...you found her?"

I raised my eyebrows. "Still think I'm poking my nose where it doesn't belong?"

She swallowed hard. "Take me to her. Please."

"That's the plan," I said as I pressed the Start/Stop button, and the car came to life with a smooth rumble. "And while I do that, you can tell me everything you know about Caitlin Closs."

If I hadn't been listening so carefully, I would've missed her soft hitch of breath. "I don't know who that is," she finally said. "Things get awfully confusing on the other side."

"So you've said," I said noncommittally. "But just know that I'm going to find her. And I'm going to ask her some hard questions that I think you know the answers to. So why don't you just save us all some time?"

She didn't seem inclined to do that as she sat looking out the window, watching the passing scenery like there would be a test on it later. So be it. I sighed, wondering what was so appealing about always choosing the hard fucking way. I was almost home before she spoke again.

"She stays at the Blue Palm Motel in Hallandale," she finally said. "But I don't want any part of that. Now that you've found Ryan, I just need Regan and we can—"

"Fuck off to parts unknown, leaving me with several unsolved mysteries and dead bodies on my hands?" I asked mildly.

It was another five miles before she spoke. "I'm sorry. I know it seems like I'm stonewalling you, and that's a poor way to pay you back for finding my daughter."

"Let me guess. It's not like that at all."

"That's right," she said sharply. "I'm helping you."

It was difficult to keep the frustration out of my voice. "How so?"

"Because I thought I knew what I was getting into, but I had no clue." Her tone was a mixture of sadness, regret, and underneath it all, there was anger there, too. "So take my advice. Stop while you're ahead."

We both knew I couldn't—*wouldn't*—do a thing like that.

The rest of the drive home was silent.

18

I decided to milk my only lead on Caitlin's whereabouts for all it was worth. I invited Danny to stake out the Blue Palm with me, telling him that, "It's like they always say, the couple that stalks together, stays together."

He was having no part of it. He just stared at me before saying, "They don't say that. Not even a little bit."

So off I went to do my dirty work myself.

I couldn't complain too much. He'd had to meet with Arianna Pemburton again, smoothing feathers faster than I could ruffle them. He told me about their visit as I skulked about in the motel parking lot. She'd asked him to take her to Pemburton Acres, her family estate, so they could have their chat. On the way, she instructed him to pick up lunch from her favorite café, and a bemused Danny found himself having an impromptu picnic with her on a picnic table that her grandfather had built.

I was starting to think she just liked his company.

Because of her mobility issues, Arianna Pemburton had been forced to leave her treasured family estate. The massive house was a tad rundown but still beautiful, surrounded by ten acres of woods. She'd willed the entire property to the Hope House, and Evie Sinclair had floated the idea of moving her entire operation there. With that kind of space and privacy, she could finally create the oasis she was looking for.

It was yet another sign that the Hope House was exactly what it purported to be. That was great for the women they helped. Not so great for my investigation.

Sitting in front of the dreary, almost abandoned Blue Palm Motel didn't seem to be working out that well either. After several days, Caitlin's room remained undisturbed despite the manager's assurances that she was paid up for the month. I left her several messages on her cellphone, and a scant day later, the phone was no longer active. It was then that I had to acknowledge the obvious.

Caitlin Closs had no intention of speaking to law enforcement.

I mulled over my next steps for a while. I shifted around a bit, getting lower in the seat. I was pretty sure I could think better if I was more comfortable. And maybe if I closed my eyes.

Just for a minute was my last thought before I drifted off.

The ground was hard and cold, and my bindings were rough against my skin. I struggled to get free as the voices began, those children singing that nursery song, loud and cheerful as ever.

Ring around the rosie, a pocket full of posies....

The lights came on, bright. So very bright. My eyes watered as I wriggled my hand in my pocket for my knife. I had the ropes off before the song ended, and I scrambled up. My feet prickled as the feeling surged back into them. That was a very good thing. If I remembered anything about this dream, I knew there was a hell of a lot of running involved.

"Ashes to ashes, they all fall down!"

Buzzzzz.

There was that long, ominous beep as the spotlights went off. Darkness enveloped me once again. "Run for your life."

"Sharla, you bitch!" I screamed. "Come out and face me!"

A gunshot sounded and I jumped.

Buzzzzz.

My eyes popped open at the nonstop buzzing. I looked around blearily for the source and saw my phone in the cupholder.

Christ. The buzzing stopped and I rubbed my eyes blearily. Fat lot of good I was on a stakeout. While I was busy examining my eyelids, Caitlin could've sauntered in and out of her hotel room accompanied by a ten-piece band playing the Pink Panther theme song.

The buzzing started again before I could even check the screen. I picked up the phone, my brain still so sleep-addled that I fumbled it twice. The content of my dream certainly hadn't helped. I felt rested and tired all at once.

I cleared my throat a few times before I answered. Damned if I'd let anyone know I'd doddered off like Grandpa Simpson. "Yes?"

"If Nick is bringing the yams, then I should be able to bring the potatoes," an insane person said.

"Wha?" I rubbed a hand down my face tiredly at the sound of Kevin's voice. "The hell are you talking about, St. James?"

"Carole is a little miffed that she's not hosting, but she's agreed to help. With her expertise, we can make them any way you'd like. Mashed, au gratin, scalloped...." He paused and I could've sworn I heard his stomach growl. "I mean, is there any bad way to have potatoes?"

As someone who'd sat next to him during countless meals—countless, I say—I knew the answer was *probably not*. "Not to sound repetitive," I said with a yawn. "But what the hell are you talking about? And why are you bringing a variety of potatoes to my house?"

"Thanksgiving, of course. Nick was bragging about being on deck for yam casserole, and yams are usually my specialty," he said with a huff. "If I'd known you were assigning dishes already for this thing—"

"There is no thing," I said loudly. "Please tell me there's another reason you interrupted my slee—er, stakeout."

"I met with Moira McDaniels today."

That certainly perked me right up. I scrubbed my gritty eyes again. "Yeah, and? What did she say about the Hope House and Project Halo?"

"She couldn't say enough about Evie Sinclair. She had been in an abusive relationship for many years and after a particularly nasty fight, she landed in the hospital. She made up her mind then not to go back, but she wasn't sure how she was going to make it work," he said. "The Hope House took her in straight from the hospital."

"What happened with the husband?"

"Well, in a stroke of luck, Marcus wound up leaving her for his ex and moving back to Vegas. So she was able to go back home and keep the kids. Best case scenario."

I hummed. "I don't suppose you talked with Stacey Pittman?"

"You would suppose right. Tab is handling that one."

I didn't waste any time, grabbing my phone and texting her quickly. "What did Moira say about Project Halo?"

"Not a damn thing. She's never heard of it."

"That makes no sense," I said with a frown. "Her name was in the folder. I saw it on Quinn's table."

"It makes perfect sense," he said patiently. "She's *lying*. I'm sure you've heard of the concept. You know, like when you told us there were no Snickers bars and we figured out that you'd squirreled them away in a decoy box of granola bars?"

I sighed heavily. "I don't suppose they lived to tell the tale."

"Eaten like a motherfucker," he said cheerily. "Now about the potatoes for Thanksgiving...."

My phone beeped with another call. "Gotta go," I said happily. "Tab is ringing in."

"But—"

I switched over. "Hey."

"Is that idiot really bringing the yams?" Tabitha wanted to know. "If he gets to pick, then so do I. You have to taste my slammin' mac and cheese. I make it every year for my family."

Sweet Jesus. I scowled. "Maybe they'd like to taste it again this year."

"I'm not about to travel cross country for both Thanksgiving *and*

Christmas. Especially not since my sister had tubal ligation and my mother is now on my ass about grandchildren. Theresa did her part, now it's your turn," she said in a voice injected with low-country drawl. "It's enough to put you off your dinner."

I didn't respond, mostly because I'd noped out at the words *tubal ligation*. I was fairly certain I wasn't qualified enough—or mature enough—to have *any* of this conversation. Besides, I was having my own "providing grandchildren" crisis, fuck you very much.

"I'll have a little more information about Stacey Pittman, if you don't mind," I said crisply. "And a fuckton less about procreation."

She sighed exasperatedly. "Fine. You try to open up—"

"Let's close it up tight. Lock it. And throw it in a river," I suggested.

She mumbled something about me being emotionally devoid, which I ignored. "Seems as though Stacey was in an abusive relationship with her ex-boyfriend, Tate Robards. They were together for two years, each one worse than the last. She saw an ad for the Hope House and decided to give change a chance."

"Lemme guess, she sang the praises of Evie Sinclair?"

"It was a struggle to get her to hang up," she said with a long-suffering sigh. "She's now in a loving relationship with a woman named Julia and they have two kids. Her life has completely turned around and she claims that she owes it all to Evie."

"And Tate Robards?"

"What about him? According to his renewed registration this past May, he's slithered his way down to Miami. I'm on my way to see him now."

Judging from her tone, she was looking forward to it. I resisted cheering her on and channeled my inner responsible Danny instead. "Walk lightly," I warned.

"That's going to be hard to do in my steel toe boots. I wore them special, just for this meeting. But I'll certainly try," she said solemnly. "I'll treat him with the same courtesy he treated Stacey with. And Courtney Kidd. And Sabrina Marshall."

"Who are...."

"Domestics on his rap sheet for the past twenty years."

I mentally sent thoughts and prayers to Tate's balls if he even stepped one micrometer over the line. Her family probably knew her as the sweet, soft-spoken Tab who never forgot anyone's birthday and was a whiz at baking. But that Tab had to be merged with the one who recently kneed a handsy suspect in the groin and growled, "like I said, keep your hands where I can see 'em."

"I'm sure you won't do anything you wouldn't mind writing in a report," I said pointedly. "One that Danny and Tate will read."

"McKenna's good judgment is rubbing off on you," she informed me. "It's gross and you need to know that."

"Hey, maybe I won't nearly get anyone killed this time."

"Let's not get ahead of ourselves," she predicted. "Now about the mac and cheese...."

"I gotta go," I announced and hung up.

I ignored her follow-up text.

> TAB
> Four different types of cheeses, Christiansen.

19

I got home late.
I didn't bother to check the house for Danny—I spotted his striped towel on a deck chair through the kitchen window. I headed to the bedroom and grabbed a pair of shorts and a wrinkled t-shirt from my "going to put the laundry away any day now" chair and changed. Then I headed for my office to see Ryan. I remembered halfway there that she wasn't here anymore and stopped cold.

Huh.

It had been harder than I thought it would be to let her go.

I should've been happy to get on with life without a little ghost constantly at my heels. She'd been understandably clingy, and that had been hard to get used to. But somewhere along the line, I had. And now...well, things were a little weird. There was no chatter—fucking nonstop chatter—every time I entered my office. No one tugging on my shirt when she wanted my attention. And no one randomly plopping herself on my lap for reasons only she knew.

I wasn't going to make it out like it was all sunshine and roses. I certainly wouldn't miss all the freaking questions. Or realizing how much I didn't understand about the world by being forced to answer all those questions. No, I don't know why they chose red, yellow, and green for the stoplight colors, and no, I don't know why butterflies are so pretty and no, I don't know why unicorns don't exist. And I certainly wouldn't miss explaining to one more person why I'd put my iPad on a blanket in the corner of my office and let it play kid movies until the battery was ding-dong dead.

"Just doing a battery test," I'd told a questioning Kevin lamely. "It seems to be dying quicker these days."

He'd squinted at me. "And playing *The Little Mermaid* on repeat helps that how, again?"

"It just does."

"What about the candy wrappers and...." He peered closer. "Is that *actual* candy on your floor? Since when are you such a slob?"

Since a little ghost can't get it through her head that she can't eat candy. "Mind your business, St. James."

He'd left with a raised eyebrow...but not before eating two fun-sized Snickers that had been on the floor. "Five second rule," he said, actually blowing them off like that accomplished anything regarding sanitation.

"It's been down there longer than that," I informed him, and he pretended not to hear.

So yeah, maybe I'd gotten used to having her around a little bit. So sue me. But she was back where she belonged, and that was something to feel good about. I only had to remember her flying into Quinn's arms so fast that she fell backward on her butt. Quinn hadn't bothered to try and catch herself, too busy clutching at her daughter.

"I'm sorry I took so long," she said as Ryan buried her face in her shirt. "I had to make sure things were safe."

"Why wouldn't they be safe?" I wanted to know and was summarily ignored.

"I was so scared," Ryan cried.

"I know, darling. But I've got you now."

I managed to ask Quinn a few questions that she half-heartedly answered before she snapped at me that now was not the time. At my silence, she'd sent me an apologetic look...and just in time, too, as

Ryan frowned. "Don't yell at Rain, Mama. He's my friend. He saved me."

"I know, darling, I just...I'm sorry."

And then they disappeared, leaving me alone. Well, almost alone.

Franklin was still in my office. I peered in the door and gave him a baleful look. He didn't notice, too busy puttering around the room. He looked completely at home, and clearly wasn't in any hurry to go anyplace else. I was pretty sure if he ever figured out how to get some ghost tea, he was moving in for good. Luckily, he loved peace and quiet almost as much as he loved rearranging the books on my shelves.

My stomach growled, which reminded me that it was my turn to fix dinner. I headed for the kitchen and did a leisurely perusal of our fridge contents. Our leftovers might be questionable, but they hadn't crossed into the "this might kill you" zone. Probably. I picked up one of the bags of prepped veggies that Danny made on a weekly basis and fished out a carrot stick. Then I perused some more.

I was contemplating pouring some chili we got from somewhere over what was left of a baked potato we got from somewhere else when my phone buzzed. I fished it out of my pocket, only to find a text from my mother. And because the universe sometimes likes to make you go huh, she was texting about food.

> ROBYN
> We're coming over for dinner.

I stuck the rest of the carrot stick in my mouth like a cigar so I could text her back.

> I believe there's a question mark missing from that statement, Mother.

> ROBYN
> I gave birth to you.

> ROBYN
> Our relationship is centered around exclamation marks and periods.

> **So telling me what you're going to do and telling me what you're going to do with emphasis?**

ROBYN
> Exactly.

ROBYN
> So...we're coming over for dinner.

ROBYN
> !

Damn woman thought she'd gotten the drop on me, but I had an ace in the hole.

> **We don't have food.**

I looked at her three dots smugly. *Your move.*

ROBYN
> Leo and I will stop at the Vegan Barn. What would you like?

Well, that was easy.

> **I'd like you not to stop at the Vegan Barn.**

By the time I polished off another carrot stick, my phone pinged with another text. I opened it only to find a link to the Vegan Barn menu. I sighed, scrolling down their offerings. I got as far as avocado lime tartare before I closed the link.

> **Surprise us. We like to live dangerously.**

ROBYN
> Yeah, I got that the second time you got shot.

I scowled before I texted her back.

> I only got shot once. I was shot at a few times, but that doesn't count.

ROBYN
> Thank you for making my point so succinctly. Couldn't have done a better job myself.

> Goodbye, Mother.

I ignored her cat smiley face with heart eyes.

Well, at least dinner was done. The leftovers would live to see another day. An entree from the Vegan Barn was a far cry from the chili I'd been contemplating—which could only be described as meat on top of meat with a sprinkling of beans. But still.

I headed out the sliding glass door to the deck and made my way down the stairs before trudging across the grass to the tiled pool area. I kicked off my flip-flops, lowered myself to the edge, and dipped my feet in the cool water. It felt so good that I scooted forward a bit more to submerge my legs.

Danny swam with practiced ease, back and arm muscles visibly flexing, his dark hair sleek as a seal. He had a rhythmic, powerful stroke that moved him effortlessly through the water. He had me at endurance, no question. But his heavier musculature meant I had *him* at speed. Should the occasion arise, I wasn't a hundred percent sure I'd get away from a shark first. But I liked my chances.

A glance at the sky made me realize we had about a half hour left of sunlight, if that, and I closed my eyes briefly, relishing the last fading rays. This late in the year, it should've been nice and cool, but it was a little nippy at best. Not even worthy of the lightest of sweaters. I felt lazy and content, like a cat in a sunny window with a belly full of catnip.

Danny came up at the end of the pool, water sluicing over his head and shoulders as he broke the surface. I smiled as he swept his hands through his waterlogged hair, looking like something out of a magazine ad for cologne or some such nonsense.

"You know, for someone who lobbied pretty damn hard not to get a pool, you use it very often," I said, and his head jerked in my direction.

His cheeks creased in a smile as he started moving through the water toward me, keeping his head above water. "I never said I hated the idea."

"You just thought it was costly, took up a lot of real estate, and proclaimed we'd never use it."

He chuckled as he reached the side, putting one hand on either side of me. I was only midway along the pool, so when he stood, the water only came up slightly above his waist. "Is there a reason you're disturbing my swim?" he asked, a smile playing on his lips. "Because there needs to be a reason you're disturbing my swim."

"Well, I'm disturbing you for two reasons."

"Which are?"

"Well, first, I was watching you through the kitchen window and it looked like you could use a kiss."

"It did, huh?"

"Indeed."

I leaned down and met his lips with mine. They were cool from the water, but they didn't stay that way for long, warming as the kiss went on...and on. I finally pulled back, but only because he'd forgotten where we were. Those big hands were secure on my hips, and I wasn't about to be dragged into the pool. Again.

"And secondly," I said a little breathlessly, "my parents are bringing us dinner, so if you want any input, now is the time."

"I already ate." He paused. "Although I guess I could eat again since the meal was so fucking small and pretentious."

"Tell me you didn't pick the place without telling me you didn't pick the place," I said, biting back a grin. "All of your favorite restaurants pass out shovels instead of spoons and forks."

I yelped when he splashed me. "Zach picked the place," he admitted begrudgingly. "And I find your maligning of my appetite interesting. Especially since the last time you requested a to-go box, the server looked at your plate and couldn't figure out why."

I didn't respond to that nonsense because if I wanted to save a scoop of mashed potatoes and a half a chicken strip, then I could do so. Besides, I was still a little stuck on the idea of him going out for a sit-down meal with Detective Slept With my Husband. But trust was earned, not given, and Danny had more than earned it.

So I'd just have to deal.

I suddenly realized I'd been silent on the whole Zach topic a little too long. I blinked when I looked at Danny only to find his searching gaze on my face. He was silent for a few more seconds, as if he was making sure he was coming to all the right conclusions. Then he made an exasperated noise.

"You're being absolutely ridiculous," was all he said.

I squinted. It was sad that I didn't know what part of my behavior he was referencing. "Regrettably, you're going to have to be a little more specific."

"If you could see inside my head and how desperately I wanted this...how long I've wanted what we have right now...." He shook his head and smiled ruefully. "You'd laugh yourself silly to even think I'd look at someone else."

That damned man. He wouldn't even let me build up half a wall before he smashed it to bits. Also, our improving communication skills were really getting in the way of having a good snit now and then.

"Sorry," I said hoarsely. "I'm being stupid."

"Yep." He sent me a cheeky little smile. "And it's not even the first time today."

For that, I got splashed again, and this time I splashed back. Didn't have quite the same punch on someone completely wet, but still. At least Flipper Jr. had to knuckle water out of his eyes.

"You can talk to me, you know," he said quietly. "If something makes you unsure or nervous. Because I can put up with you doubting a lot of things, like whether our water meter is right—"

"The bill seemed excessive to me," I said suspiciously. "Every month it's around the same thing and then *bam*, thirty dollars extra."

"Or whether Watson destroyed your new pool floaty, even though another suspect was seen and identified in the vicinity—"

"Yes, yes, I know," I said with a huff. My father had claimed it was the work of a raccoon, but that was a little too convenient for my taste. "Don't you think it was odd that he disposed of the evidence before I could see the scratches for myself?"

"He probably did that because he didn't want you to arrest our dog," Danny said mildly. "Everyone was a little concerned when you tried to Mirandize him by telling him he had the right to remain frisky."

I glared. "I'm sorry, was there a point to all this?"

He huffed out a laugh. "My *point* is that you may doubt many things, Rainstorm, but *us* better not ever make the list. You got me?"

A smile tugged at my lips. I liked it when he got all bossy and growly, which clearly proved there was something wrong with me. "Loud and clear." At his snort, I widened my eyes. "I'm listening."

"Sure." He hummed. "You don't listen to me about a goddamned thing, but I love it when you pretend."

I could only laugh. Still a little embarrassed to be caught doubting him, even for a second, I made a move to get up. Unfortunately, Danny didn't seem remotely interested in letting me move a muscle. His hands held me in place, thumbs absently playing with the skin under my shirt, right above my waistband.

"So." I cleared my throat. "How're things dead body wise?"

His mouth curved, but he didn't call me out on my strange small talk. Or my instinct to flee. "The tattoo artist was right on the money. Our dead guy is named Gary Black. He was married to a woman named Sabrina—well, separated," he amended.

"Is she a suspect?"

He hummed. "Of course. And not just because that's usually the way of it, either. He disappeared two days before a hearing on a custody case. Everyone seemed to think he just ran off, except his mother."

"She didn't think he'd leave his kid?"

"No, she admitted he wasn't much to write home about as a father."

"Damn. It's a cold world out there." I shook my head. "Tell her we don't need any help with the eulogy, please and thank you."

He snorted. "Well, to be fair, Gary sounded like a really shitty person. She said she could definitely see him leaving his kid, but he would never let Sabrina win."

"Yikes."

"Exactly. Needless to say, Gary's particular brand of charm makes the suspect pool rather…vast. I also met with his sister, who reluctantly told me some guy was asking questions about Gary before he left. Guess what his name was?" Before I could answer, he waved a hand. "You'll never guess. Javi Santos."

I furrowed my brow. "Why…would a PI following Quinn also be asking questions about your victim?"

"I don't know but I'm pretty sure we need to find out." He sighed. "So. Where's the ghost kid?"

"How do you know she's not right there?"

"Because you're different when she's here. More careful. And you certainly wouldn't have kissed me like I just got back from war. I touched your hip to move you aside in the kitchen, and you practically accused me of bending you over the kitchen island." He looked put out at the memory alone. "I mean, really, how do parents get laid?"

"Quickly. And quietly," I said with a little grin. "You're also correct. Ryan is with Quinn now."

"And just where the hell has she been?" He demanded. "Did you tell her how many times we had to fucking watch *The Little Mermaid*?"

"You liked it."

"Yes, the first ten times," he groused. "Then I thought that crab was fucking annoying, and I was extremely tired of everyone bursting into song for no damn reason."

My mouth twitched. "They're not that bad."

"No?" He arched a brow. "Could you imagine if you asked me where the ketchup was, and I proceeded to answer with a three-minute choreographed song and dance about how much I love ketchup? And never really fucking answered the question?"

I chuckled. "I think it could be entertaining, yes."

He huffed, still clearly mentally detailing everything annoying about the world of animation. "But on to more important things," he said after a moment. "Can I see your phone for a second?"

I sent him a blank look as I fished it out of my pocket and handed it over. "Of course."

I frowned as he placed it on the tiled deck. "Where's your watch?"

"On my dresser. Why do you a—*ack!*"

I went in with a splash as he playfully toppled me in the water, and the world turned blue. I came up sputtering, rubbing water out of my eyes as I tried to look mad. "You. Are. Such. A. Bastard."

He sent me a wicked grin as he swam closer, caging me against the textured wall. Instinctively, my hands came up to his shoulders. *Oh.* "So it's like that?"

"It is," he said as he pressed a kiss to my jaw. "I'm still irritated about the Zach thing. Clearly, I've been remiss in proving to you that you're mine."

"I think we both can agree that I was being stupid and—*oh wow, that's nice,*" I mumbled as he continued to mouth his way down the side of my throat, his five-o'clock shadow scraping nicely against mine and making me shiver. "You could've at least let me take off my clothes first."

"That's my job."

It was hard to argue with that, especially with his lips pressing open-mouthed kisses to the side of my throat. Those big hands found their way inside my shorts and immediately gripped my ass. I liked a good frotting session as much as the next guy—sometimes. This wasn't one of those times. I squirmed in his hold, wishing we were skin to skin. I either needed more or less, because right now I was just frustrated.

Before I could even ask, he was unzipping my shorts. *Fucking finally.* I let out a low moan when he took us both in hand. I tried to reach down and help, but he batted me away. *Bossy, thy name is Danny*, and I wasn't mad at it.

I let him do the heavy lifting, too busy making a feast of his mouth. I nipped and bit and licked until he opened for me, and then tongue-fucked his mouth to my heart's content. His dick jerked against mine, and I knew he wasn't far from the finish.

I was absolutely correct as he came a few seconds later, breaking away from my kiss with a curse. He pressed his face against my neck as he rode it out. I rubbed his back, holding him tight. I loved it when we were in sync enough to come together. But watching him go first had its own merits. Nothing made me want to growl *mine* more than seeing my reserved, careful husband come apart in my hands.

He didn't move for several minutes after, just breathing into my neck. But it was definitely the calm before the storm. Before I knew what he was about, I was out of the pool and on the side. Sans shorts.

I glanced over my shoulder worriedly and he read my mind. As usual. "Your parents are still out."

"Well, last time I checked, they're coming back," I said dryly. Despite my words, I made absolutely zero effort to locate my pants or put them back on. "That's kind of how it works."

"Then I should hurry," he said sagely.

And then he sucked me into his mouth and all thoughts of everything important—like getting caught getting a blow job by the pool—sailed right on out of my head. The only thing that mattered right then was Danny's perfect mouth. And getting him to let me fuck it. This licking and sucking business was nice but a little leisurely for how desperate I felt.

I held on to every reserve I had, trying to remain still. My hips jerked a little and he stopped sucking completely. I shivered as the cool air hit my damp cock. "Please," was about all I could manage.

"Not yet," he said before swallowing me down again. He swallowed a few times, throat working around me. I didn't so much as close my eyes as squeeze them shut in desperation.

"How about now?" I asked a few seconds later. "I'd really like to move right about now."

"Nah. Love the way you taste, you know?" He slowed down even further, sucking just the tip in his mouth before releasing me with a *pop*. Then gave me another long, leisurely lick like he wasn't driving me clear out of my mind. "Love the way you beg."

"I don't beg," I said archly.

"No?" He pulled off completely and lifted each of my legs out of the water so my feet were braced on the side, leaving me all but spread-eagled. He leaned in and started licking and laving my balls, which gave me a full-body shiver. My poor, lonely dick jerked against my stomach. I knew if I so much as touched it, I'd only extend my own torture. "How about now? Do you beg now?"

"I do not," I said crisply.

I did some wordless begging though, as that clever tongue dipped down below in my taint. It was close enough to my crease that I scooched down, hoping he'd take the hint.

Danny's mouth curved. He was great at hints. Not so much with mercy. "And now?" he asked pointedly.

"Please," I finally uttered. "I just need...."

I didn't even finish the thought before his tongue speared my hole, rewarding me for losing our little game. I anchored a hand in his damp hair, holding him in place unnecessarily as he ate me out. His technique was something to be studied and preserved for posterity—his tongue swirling and dipping inside me and then darting away to lick up and down my crease. I barely knew what I was saying, but I was saying it pretty much on repeat. Some slurred, nonsensical combination of *please, love you, fuck you,* and *fuck me* maybe. He finally wrapped a hand around my dick and started stroking while tongue-fucking my ass. I only had a few seconds to enjoy it before I came with a hoarse shout.

My breath sawed through my lungs, ragged and uneven as I loosened my death grip on his hair. I lay there, sprawled like a wanton thing while he licked my release from his fingers. I smiled fondly. I loved how nothing was off the table with him sexually. I never would've expected it from the cautious, reserved way he approached life.

But that was probably why he only slept with people he genuinely cared about. People he could see a future with. I wasn't sure if it was possible for him to give less than all of himself in bed, and he wasn't about to be that vulnerable with a stranger. When you got Danny, you had *all* of him.

I planned to keep every bit and guard them with my life.

"The fuck brought that on?" I asked when I could finally manage words again. It had to be more than the Zach thing. Although if that *was* it, I was pretty sure I could whip up some more jealousy. Every day, if necessary.

"There's not one moment that I'm looking at you, or touching you, that I don't want to take you apart." He gave me a rueful smile, those blue eyes soft and warm. "I'm just usually damn good at controlling myself."

"Maybe you shouldn't be."

"I'll keep that in mind." He gave my thigh a squeeze. "Alright, Rainstorm. Time to get up."

Yeah, that wasn't looking likely. "You're the one who reduced my knees to jelly," I said lazily. "Maybe you should think about that next time when picking the location of an impromptu sex-fest."

He hummed. "I'll do that. And while I'm thinking of better sex-fest locations, you should know that I heard your parents' van pull in a few minutes ago. They're also awfully spry for their age, so you don't have long." He looked me over critically as I continued to stare, dumbfounded. Mostly because he'd sucked my brains right out through my cock. "You should probably start with finding your shorts."

That certainly got me moving in a hurry. I yelped and cast a frantic glance around for anything resembling my cargos. I came up empty. "I told you not to take them off. Gimme yours."

Desperate, I tugged at the waistband of his dark blue board shorts, and he danced away "Then I'll be the one bare-assing it," he said indignantly. "Get lost, skinny dipper."

"Me?" I squawked. "I'm only skinny dipping because *you*—"

At the sound of the sliding glass door opening, I made a quick battlefield decision. I slipped into the pool and the world turned blue again. I came up with a sputter, wiping water out of my eyes. I braced my arms on the edge just in time to see my mother step out onto the deck. Watson barreled out behind her and came to a skidding stop at the edge of the pool. I gave his head a scratch as he huffed a greeting near my ear.

I saw the moment he spotted my new floaty, innocently drifting on the fringes of the pool. I gave him the gimlet eye. "No."

He whined. When I didn't relent, he sat back on his haunches. He let out a very human-like sigh before consoling himself with a good, long scratch.

My mother waved in greeting, and we waved back. She was in cotton candy colors—a light pink off-the-shoulder blouse and a flowing skirt in pink ombre that blew slightly in the wind. "Oh, good, *there* you two are. Dinner is ready." She smiled at me. "I got you a plant burger, Rain."

"Mmm-mmm good," I said wistfully, wondering if it would be rude to top my plant burger with bacon.

"And Danny, I got you the Big Green."

He looked at me questioningly and I shook my head. Who the fuck knew? My plant burger got *extremely* desirable in comparison to something only identified by size and color. Judging by his stifled sigh, Danny agreed. "Thank you, Robyn, we'll be right in," he said. "We're just...looking for something."

"Okay." She beamed. "I should also tell you that Watson gets a good report today. He ate well and had two bowel movements. And at the park, he only chased two ducks."

I squinted at him, trying to impart my disappointment. That sounded like a so-so report to me. "Only two, huh?"

He panted, giving me a doggy smile. Like he was the goodest boy and screw what I thought because ducks *deserved* to be chased.

My mother turned to go back inside, which was great because everything south of my border was starting to shrink. "And Rain?"

"Yes?" I asked, trying to quell my exasperation. It wasn't her fault we'd gotten freaktastic in the pool like a couple of frisky sea monkeys.

"Your shorts appear to be caught on the drain."

"Thank you," I said with as much dignity as I could muster as Danny guffawed.

"You're welcome, dear." She winked before disappearing into the house with a swish of her cotton-candy skirts.

I let my head drop on my folded arms. "I hate you," I said with a sigh.

"Yeah, but where do we stand on more pool sex?" I could hear the smile in Danny's voice.

Like I'd ever be able to resist him. If he wanted to have sex in a supermarket, I'd probably just resign myself to having my picture put under the counter with the rest of the sexual deviants. "Fine," I mumbled. "But next time, *you* get to lose your shorts."

Danny huffed out a laugh against my nape before he pressed a kiss there. "Deal."

20

I woke on the ground, trussed up tight.
 No confusion, this time. I immediately knew where I was, and everything was horribly familiar. The cold, hard ground. The complete darkness. The rough feeling of rope tied around my body.

I didn't bother to struggle free this time because I knew how this ended. The voices began, children singing that nursery song, the sound grating in my ears. I waited, my breathing harsh and fast as my host came to terms with his situation.

Ring around the rosie, a pocket full of posies....

I squeezed my eyes shut, trying for a little autonomy in someone else's memory. I managed for just a second, right until the bright lights came on. Then, my eyes popped back open without my consent. My hand worked in my pocket as I grasped for the pocketknife. Then the ropes were off.

I clapped my hands over my ears, but it didn't help. It never did. So I staggered to my feet. Waiting.

"Ashes to ashes, they all fall down!"

There was that long, ominous beep as the spotlights went off. Darkness enveloped me once again. *"Run for your life."*

"Sharla, you bitch!" I screamed. "Come out and face me!"

A gunshot sounded and I jumped. It was far away, but not nearly far enough. I started to run, crashing through the trees. It was strange, keeping someone else's pace in his body. I might hate exercising, but I forced myself to stay in reasonable shape. If I couldn't keep up with my partner on foot, then I would leave that person to head solo into a potentially dangerous situation. Thinking about that person being Danny was all the motivation I needed. So normally, I was pretty fast and agile.

But now? I was clumsy and uncoordinated, struggling for each and every breath. My back and hips ached, and I cried out as I stumbled on a root and landed on my knees. Pain arched through my body.

I scrambled to my feet as another shot sounded, closer this time. I was giving it my all, but the writing was on the wall. Had been before I even started. Whoever was running me—him—down would succeed, and it would be lights out.

I didn't deserve this. Yeah, Sharla and I had gotten into it a few times, but not enough for her to fucking have me killed. And she was responsible for this, I thought, feeling rage suffuse my body all over again. She had to be. Her and her fucking brother Marlon.

I stumbled again as the terrain changed and found myself ankle deep in water. I slogged forward another few feet, mud sticking and squelching at my shoes. When I lost one sneaker in the muck, I staggered to a stop. I rested my hands on my hips and looked up at the night sky. The stars sparkled like diamonds on a backdrop so inky and black, it looked like paint.

"Giving up so soon?" A woman laughed somewhere in the distance. The mysterious Sharla, maybe? "But we just started to have fun, Vin."

"When I find you, I'm going to fucking obliterate you. Make sure that your pretty little face ain't so pretty anymore," I raged. "No one is going to want you, I promise you that. No one is going to love you like I do. You hear me, bitch?"

"Oh, I hear every word," she said silkily.

"You're going to beg me to take you back and when you do, I'm gonna—"

I woke at the crack of a gunshot, and I knew it wasn't just the end of the memory.

It was the end of *him*.

I lay there, silent, looking up at the ceiling. The fan rotated slowly above me. Now that I knew Vin a little better, it didn't seem like much of a loss. I knew that the angry ghost was probably somewhere close, sending me the vision over and over again. I was also pretty sure why he wasn't giving me any messages in person. From what I'd seen and heard in just those two memories, he had been far from a model citizen. And like Dakota said, word of my vanquishing was starting to get around.

Little did he know that it was my job to investigate *all* crime. It wasn't my job to pick my victims. Or my perpetrators.

My eyes widened as I realized that the memory this time had been a little different. She'd said his name. *Vin.* I hadn't had much luck with just the name Sharla—hell, I'd gotten so many hits that I hadn't bothered to print them. I needed more parameters. But Sharla and Vin?

I sat up straight. And Marlon. He'd said something about her brother, Marlon. That should be enough to make some connections.

I couldn't have gotten out of bed faster if it was on fire. I headed to my office, already making plans.

Watson broke the cardinal rule an hour later and interrupted my research. He'd done it no less than four times, giving me the potty signal. With him, it was a fifty-fifty chance that he was playing you. Sometimes he had to go, sometimes he just wanted to stretch his legs —and the treat he got after he came in. Like he'd actually done something worthy of a Milk-Bone.

Either way, it was a game of Russian roulette I had no desire to play—especially since the prize was poop on my floor. When he put his head on my knee and looked up at me with eyes so liquid and dark and full of hope, I caved.

"Fine, you mutt," I groused as I closed my computer. "But if you don't really have to go, you're not getting a fucking treat."

He knew I was full of bullshit, evidenced by the way he spun in joyful circles all the way to the front door. So that's the story of how I found myself standing on the top step of the porch at four in the morning, watching my dog deliberate over every blade of grass in the fucking yard. Clearly, the process of determining which patch of lawn was worthy of his poop was extensive.

As if to punish me for even a slight delay of bringing him outside, he faked me out a couple times with a half squat before circling some more. "Will you just go already?" I complained.

He cast a look over his shoulder, looking at me with those inky eyes. If I had to interpret his expression, it was shades of, "*My dude, the vibe is just off.*"

I sighed and sat on the top step. To be honest, I had time. I wasn't all that interested in getting back in bed and going back to that memory. It wasn't all for naught—I now knew the ghost's name. Vincent Mitchell. I knew that he wasn't missing but murdered. And considering what happened to his wife, Sharla Mitchell, they were bound to have an interesting conversation when they finally found one another.

The door creaked open behind me, and I glanced over my shoulder to find Danny standing there in his pajamas—sleep shorts and a gray t-shirt—knuckling his eyes. He had something dark in his left hand and only when he stepped out onto the porch could I tell it was a hoodie. He joined me on the top step, examining the wood carefully before he graced it with his posterior. I hid a grin. Like father, like dog, I suppose.

"What're you doing out here?" The volume of his voice was normal, but in the stillness of the night, it seemed loud. He seemed to think so, too, because the next time he spoke, it was in a much quieter tone. "It's late. Or early, I guess."

"Watty apparently likes to do his business in the middle of the night now." I shook my head when he held out the hoodie. "We won't be out here much longer."

He arched a brow even as he kept holding it out. I huffed out a laugh even as I took it and shrugged it on. It took me a minute to realize it wasn't mine because of the fit, and I was suddenly very glad I'd taken it. "Why don't you tell me about it?"

I looked at him blankly. "Tell you about what?"

"About whatever has you up first thing in the morning."

"Watty—"

"Is an opportunist, as you know." Danny gave him a fond look. Our errant dog was currently investigating a tree at the edge of the yard...where he knew he damn well wasn't supposed to go. "He's smart enough to know we worship the ground his spoiled rotten butt walks on, and he'll give the potty signal whenever he damn well pleases."

"Slander," I said loyally.

"Not if it's true." Danny snapped his fingers and Watson bounded back from the perimeter. "So. What's up?"

I didn't make him ask again. I proceeded to tell him all about the memory—word-vomited over him, really. He didn't interrupt, listening with his brow furrowed. By the time I got to the end, my heart rate was up again. I could hear that shot, reverberating in my ears, and that spooky disconnect from the ghost giving me the memory...because that was the last thought he'd ever had.

Danny's face was rather grim by the time I got to the gunshot. If I had to guess, that was probably less because Vincent had kicked the bucket and more because someone was playing a game called *run for your life*. And we both knew Vincent wasn't the only victim.

"I'm sorry you had to experience that," he finally said.

"He wasn't a very nice guy."

"What does that have to do with my sorry?" He bumped my leg gently. "It has to suck reliving his death over and over again."

"I know that, I just...." I picked at a piece of thread on my sleep pants, even knowing I was going to create a hole. "It feels wrong to care about someone like Vincent Mitchell meeting his end. The man has a rap sheet a mile long, mostly for hurting other people."

"You're human, Rain. That doesn't mean you're going to love watching him die. Hell, I'd be worried if you weren't affected."

"I guess."

"Where is this Sharla person?"

"Car accident. Happened four years after Vincent allegedly went missing." I didn't bother using the very obvious air quotes. "A trucker fell asleep and smashed into the back of her Honda. The bump—as he called it—jarred him awake but he didn't realize he'd hit her. He dragged her for another ten miles before someone flagged him over. Let's just say there wasn't much for the road crew to haul away."

He winced. "Shit."

That certainly seemed to encompass the thoughts of the first officer responding to the scene. I'd watched the video from his body cam, and he'd said that quite a bit as he rushed to the obliterated car. It was only a few seconds before he gave the code for dead, no rescue, on his radio. The video had been released to the public, so most of it was blurred as he'd examined the wreck. But the bits of hair and brain matter and a mangled hand among the twisted and smoking metal told a pretty clear story.

"It's small consolation, but at least she got a few years of peace from Vincent before she died." I paused as I thought that over. Morally grey didn't even cover it. "Although I certainly don't condone her methods."

Danny hummed. I cast a glance his way. That hum had sounded more thoughtful than commiserative. "What?" I asked.

"I was just thinking about Gary."

"While I was emoting all over you?" I swatted his arm. "Nice multitasking."

He huffed out a laugh. "I was just thinking about his mysterious disappearance."

"Yeah, what about it? He took off for greener pastures."

"So they say. And what about Gil?"

"Farrah's husband?" I blinked. "He fled the country so he wouldn't have to answer for impending embezzlement charges."

He raised an eyebrow. "So they say."

Well, fuck. "And what do you say?" I asked slowly.

"I say that's a hell of a coincidence."

My gaze met his in perfect understanding. "So it is."

21

I spent much of the morning organizing the conclusions Danny and I had come to the night before in whiteboard format. I added pictures of our potential victims and connected them with different colored lines to demonstrate degree of similarities. Seeing it laid out before me, I had to admit it seemed...farfetched. But plausible. We didn't have a smoking gun yet. I only knew that those coincidences had to add up to something.

But did they add up to murder?

Right now, all my conclusions added up to was a lot of flak from my fellow team members.

My phone buzzed in my pocket, and I checked the screen just as it went to Voicemail. *Harper.* I grimaced, realizing the ball was in my court once again. But now just wasn't a good time. *Tomorrow,* I promised silently. I'd call her back tomorrow for sure.

"A murder ring," Nick said slowly, looking at my whiteboard like it could potentially bite. "A murder ring orchestrated by a women's support group."

"Well...yeah," I said as I pocketed my phone. "If you just follow the connections I drew, you'll see an undeniable pattern."

"Follow the connections.... Good Lord, Christiansen, there are lines everywhere," he fussed. "It looks like you fell asleep with a fistful of uncapped markers in both hands."

I huffed, ignoring Kevin's snicker. "The lines in *blue*, Gonzalez. Red is for suspects and green lines are for people we've cleared. The purple is for employees at the Hope House that could potentially be involved, and black...." I squinted. "Well, I'm not sure what the black is for, but you get the point."

He grumbled as he got up to get a closer look. I paid him no mind as he exaggeratedly followed my blue lines with a finger.

I glanced up at the clock again because we were still missing two people. Tabitha had sent a text through the group chat, saying she was running down a lead and she'd be a bit late. And Danny had gone upstairs to present our theory to Tate an hour ago. Before he'd left, he guesstimated he would be no more than a half hour.

I could only presume he was delayed bandaging his ass from the chunk our supervisor had bitten out of it. That left me explaining our theory solo to the two skeptical audience members of the infomercial who didn't believe you could really "set it and forget it."

Kevin rubbed his temples. "All I know is that there are four more people on this board than there were last week, and that's four too many. And where are the snacks?"

"You just had lunch," I said. He'd strolled in the room ten minutes prior, crunching ice from a Wendy's cup. There was also a suspiciously empty Krispy Kreme box I'd found on the table when I first came in. I didn't know for sure that Kevin had anything to do with it, but I knew how to place a smart bet.

"I'm still a little peckish," he said, patting his stomach.

"Well, I'm not dipping into my 401K to finance your eating habits," I said tartly.

"Hey, you bring me dead people, you bring me food," he said, stabbing a finger at my whiteboard. "I can only assume that those fancy little Ds you've written underneath their pictures mean they're dead."

"It's a sophisticated system," I said with a modest nod. "And while I did not bring snacks, I did make coffee."

"*I* made the coffee, actually." I turned to see Danny coming in, a little smile on his face as he handily took back the credit I stole. He touched the small of my back as he passed, before taking a seat at the table. "You're welcome."

Zach was hot on his heels, the tall, dark, and handsome to Danny's tall, dark, and handsomer. *Annoying.* I did my best to keep my face from doing anything strange, but judging from the little smile Kevin hid behind his Wendy's cup, I didn't entirely succeed. I glared and he sent me a jaunty little salute as he crunched some ice. I was over my jealousy—mostly—but I was damned tired of him hanging around. I was *more* than ready for his vacation to be over and for him to vamoose back up to West Palm Beach.

"We're married, McKenna," I informed him, much to his amusement. "I think they said something about us being one or whatever at the ceremony."

"I don't think that's how it works," he protested, his blue eyes crinkled at the corners. "And I'm so very glad you were sort of paying attention during one of the most important moments of our lives."

I sent him an exaggerated wink. "I was too busy waiting for my cue to seal the deal."

Danny laughed, causing my mouth to quirk in return. I wouldn't ever get tired of looking at that smile or listening to that laugh. It had been a rather long kiss with a background of our friends and family hooting and hollering. And yes, I was fully aware I shouldn't be getting sentimental in the middle of a murder investigation. But was there ever a better reminder to appreciate someone you loved?

I happened to glance over at Zach and nearly dropped my marker. He didn't just look annoyed, he looked...angry. Really angry. There was a brief moment where that anger warred with jealousy before he wiped them both away.

"I'm assuming you didn't call this meeting so I could watch the two of you fawn over one another." Zach's words and his sharp tone made him the immediate focus of pretty much everyone at the table. He flushed. "I'm just saying."

"You're just saying a lot," Kevin said, a small frown on his usually affable face. "Relax, Owens."

He continued to look flustered, raking a hand through his hair. "Sorry. I just...we do things a bit differently at PBPD."

"Well, you're not at PBPD," Danny said, giving him a raised eyebrow. "But you can feel free to make the switch if you're uncomfortable with our conduct."

Which only confirmed what I already knew—the only hedging Danny knew how to do was with a pair of garden clippers in his hands. I searched my mind for something to say that would ease the sudden tension in the room.

Luckily, Nick had turned back to my whiteboard and was ready to get back to the special of the day—murder and mayhem. And was that a marker in his hand? "Marcus McDaniels. Isn't that Moira's ex-husband?"

"I talked to her," Kevin said slowly. "She said that he left her for a waitress and moved to Vegas. No foul play was suspected."

"Don't you think it's strange that he hasn't had any work history in twelve years?" I asked. "No apartment, no mortgage, no utilities...not even so much as a phone in his name."

Nick tried to write something on my board, and I smacked his treacherous hand just in time. "*Ow,* fuck! The hell is wrong with you?"

"You know the rules," I said, plucking the marker from his fingers. "Tell me what you want me to write, and I'll write it."

"Write Vegas underneath. And then write *you're a fucking maniac* under your picture." He rubbed his hand dramatically as he went back to the table and sprawled in his chair. He turned to Danny and demanded, "He makes love to that thing when we're not around, doesn't he?"

Danny bit his lip, clearly holding back a laugh. "What Rain does with his whiteboard in his spare time is his business."

I ignored them both as I printed *Vegas* in small letters underneath Marcus McDaniels's picture. He was a big bruiser of a guy with a neck that seemed as thick as it was long. His eyes were cruel and cold.

It was hard to believe he'd willingly found a woman to go to Vegas with him. I wouldn't accompany him to McDonald's, no less across the country.

Kevin leaned back in his chair, tipping it back on two legs as he mulled that over. "And Bennett Hayes?" he finally asked. "Isn't he the torso with the defibrillator?"

"Yeah, the architect." Danny fielded that one. "The wife, Rhonda, said he drained their bank account and left to be with his assistant."

"The trollop," I supplied, and he huffed out a laugh. "Then we have Sharla and Vincent Mitchell—"

"I don't remember hearing those names during the course of the investigation." I turned to see Zach's brows knitted together as he stared at my board. He'd been unusually silent since Danny told him he could pack his shit and take off. Apparently, he was done projecting hurt vibes and was ready to put my feet to the fire. "Where did you find those names?"

"I was searching the database for other cases that fit the pattern. Four years ago, Sharla Mitchell filed a restraining order against her husband, and he disappeared not long after." I shrugged. "Then I looked for a connection between her and the Hope House and found her on the donors list last year. A nominal amount, but still."

"Vincent Mitchell disappeared on a fishing trip," Zach said, his gaze unwavering. "They found his abandoned boat in the middle of Jackson Creek, along with all his gear."

I cleared my throat as his intense gaze shifted to my poker face, which was admittedly not the best. "Is that a question?"

"It can be."

"It doesn't matter how he came up," Danny said firmly. "The pattern fits, so he added Vincent Mitchell to the data."

Zach could stare at me until the end of time. I knew he'd heard the rumors just like everyone else. Stick around BBPD for more than an hour, and someone was bound to tell you some gossip about the resident ghost whisperer. I swear, the station was held together by duct tape and rumors. That didn't mean I was about to admit jack shit.

"Gary Black," Kevin murmured. "He disappeared right before a custody case with his wife Sabrina. Strange timing for a guy who said he'd rather die than let her win."

I gave him a meaningful look. "And to that, I say, be careful what you wish for."

I led them through the other cases, detailing the strange circumstances of their disappearances. By the time I finished, we had a list of six people who'd miraculously vanished off the face of the earth. And two who had accidents, the timing of which could only be described as fortuitous.

I leaned against the wall, arms crossed, marker tucked firmly in my grip. "I bet if I could get my hands on the Project Halo files, I'd find even more."

"There's no way Evie Sinclair would allow us access to those files," Zach predicted. "And we're going to need a bit more than circumstance and conjecture before we can force the issue legally."

"We might already have more," Kevin said, snapping his fingers. "Farrah Bell's husband, Gilbert."

My eyes widened because fuck yes, that made sense. "The catalyst," I said, uncapping my marker. I drew a line from Farrah Bell to the subheading of the Hope House. "Quinn was clearly suspicious of Project Halo, but she couldn't prove anything. It isn't impossible for someone to have an accident on an early morning fishing trip."

"Or run away with a waitress," Kevin agreed.

"Exactly. But Gil?"

"She knew him personally," Danny said, following my train of thought effortlessly. "She knew he'd never leave Farrah. Actually, he'd never give up *controlling* Farrah. Not of his own accord. Maybe she even found something in their house to prove it."

I hummed. "Then Farrah tells Evie that Quinn is on their trail—"

"And Evie tells her to take care of it," Kevin finished. "Javi Santos is on retainer to do their investigating and dirty work. He probably figures out the best way to make each person disappear without raising too much suspicion."

"And then Farrah makes her bestie that *let's make up and be friends* cake I saw in the kitchen," I said. I always got a feeling when things were falling into place, and I had that feeling right about now. "But instead of strawberry on the inside, it's laced with poison. Regan sneaks a couple bites and dies, and Quinn knows Evie is going to send someone else to finish the job."

Zach's eyes widened slightly, and I reviewed my words. *Oops.* Guess I *was* confirming jack shit. Maybe not in so many words, but there were only so many ways I could know that Regan had died long before Nate sent the car flying into the lake.

Sure enough, I was once again the target of that intense, dark stare. "How would you—"

"I'm guessing," I said casually.

"It's one hell of a guess," Zach said cautiously. "We're going to have to be very careful before we accuse a well-known, well-*loved* member of the community like Evie Sinclair of being a—"

"Godamned serial killer?" Nick threw a pen at me, and I barely had enough time to duck. I stooped to pick up his death missile and popped back up, blowing hair out my eyes with an indignant huff. "Fuck, Christiansen. Not again."

"You're forgiven," I said firmly.

"I didn't apologize for anything."

"Well, it just sounded like you were blaming *me* for this clusterfuck to end all clusterfucks, and I know that can't be the case. So." I gave him a sweet smile, right before I winged his pen back. My aim was righteous and true, and he squawked as it hit him in the shoulder. He was lucky I hadn't aimed for his big empty noggin. "You're forgiven."

Nick's eyes were lively and amused as they met mine. But before he could throw it back, Danny reached over and confiscated the pen, muttering an exasperated, "*Children*," that I pretended not to hear.

Strangely, Zach didn't seem to mind our antics. In fact, a little smile played on his lips as he watched. Guess he only had a problem with our methods when it interrupted him making moon eyes at my freaking husband.

Hey, I did say I was *mostly* over my jealousy.

"I just want to know where your serial killer divining rod is," Nick declared.

"Statistically, there are always a number of serial killers operating under the radar," I argued.

"Yeah, well. I could do without you proving it all the damn time." He looked me over critically. "You know, I'm surprised they don't try to kill you ahead of time before you ferret them out. That's what I would do."

"That's enough of putting those kinds of thoughts out into the atmosphere," I said dryly. "Please and thank you."

"The beauty of it all is that it sounds so nutty that no one would ever believe it." Kevin had his fingers laced behind his head as he stared off into space. He sounded almost as if he was talking to himself. "The fact that they were douchebags certainly helps conceal the crime. We all say that we work as hard for every victim, but you know that shit ain't true."

I'd like to think I avoided that pitfall. It was our job to be impartial and follow the evidence. But I'd be lying if I said I wouldn't put in double and triple overtime for a missing kid. Happily. Not so much for a guy whose favorite hobby was using his wife's head as a speedbag.

I listened with half an ear as the team debated our latest theory. I found myself looking at my board again, but not at the victims. At our suspects. The wives, girlfriends, and partners. And in Timothy Todd's case, his stepdaughter. Her mother had died in a car accident when Wendy was eleven, and she'd had no other family to take her in. Timothy Todd, her stepfather, had been lauded for letting her remain in his house. For still caring for his deceased wife's daughter. The community didn't know all the things that went on behind those walls while they were busy patting him on the back.

I'd put up their best pictures, but we'd all seen the photos of their injuries in the case file. Some of them were horrific. It was hard to imagine doing some shit like that to a stranger, no less someone you loved.

Suddenly, Danny sat up straight in his chair. "Javi Santos."

I frowned. "Yeah, what about him?"

"*Javi Santos*," he stressed, as if that explained everything. He turned to Nick, and I hoped he was going to buy a couple vowels and a shit ton of consonants. "Weren't you following him last week?"

"Yeah," Nick said with a shrug. "He was tailing some guy named Michael Lawrence. It was kind of anticlimactic, really. I followed him to the grocery store, then the gym, and back home. It was almost like he was just trying to see—"

"His routine." I pushed off the wall, letting my arms drop as I met Nick's widened eyes. *Christ*. "He doesn't happen to be married, does he?"

"Live-in girlfriend, I think," he said with a wince. "A yoga instructor named Leah. They've been together for six years."

I had a feeling Leah wasn't looking to make seven.

"We've got to put some protection on him and bring Javi in," Danny said.

"Do we have to?" Nick grumbled. "He broke her arm in two places, you know."

Danny's face did something complicated, like he didn't quite know where to go with that. If I had to guess, he was probably imagining giving Michael a matching set of breaks on *his* arm. But eventually, he landed on the side of all that was legal and right. "We don't get to pick our victims," he ground out.

Nick didn't look pleased as he opened his mouth to speak. Before he could, the door swung open and Tabitha came striding in, plastic Starbucks cup in hand. Her iced coffee was mostly gone, but the remnants of the cold foam still lingered at the top. She dropped into a chair that squeaked in protest and set her coffee cup on the table without looking. Zach moved his phone just in time and sent her a dirty look.

"What a day," she groused. She didn't seem to notice—or care—about the complete silence in the room. "This is the third day in a row I've tried to hunt down Tate Robards and came up empty. And you know what's strange—*ooh*, donuts."

Her face fell as she opened the box and revealed six grease spots ringed by hardened glaze. She immediately belted Kevin in the stomach, and he yelped. "Fuck! You know, I'm not exactly loving the energy you've brought to this meeting."

"Well, buckle up, because there's more where that came from," she threatened. "Donuts are meant for sharing. Not inhaling."

"Preach," Nick murmured, raising up his hands in peace as he became the target of Kevin's glare.

Tabitha raised her iPad in front of her face, waiting for a beat. Then she made a noise of frustration before pasting on a sweet smile, and the iPad opened.

"Good Lord, it doesn't even recognize her human face," Kevin muttered. He gasped and covered his stomach as she raised a hand to belt him again.

"*Anyway*, it's like this Tate guy doesn't even exist," she complained, fingers busily moving across the screen. "After he left Stacey Pittman, he disappeared like a ghost. Not that anyone is missing his abusive ass."

And the body count went up again, just like that.

Tabitha blinked as the room suddenly became a cacophony of sound—chairs scraping as everyone got up from the table in a hurry. Michael Lawrence might deserve his fate, but that wasn't up to us. We were in the business of protecting life, not playing judge, jury, and executioner. That meant we had a job to do. And a potential murder to stop.

"Hey," Tabitha called after us as we headed for the door. "What'd I say?"

If ever there was an operation that needed to happen simultaneously, it was this one. So we split up. Danny, Zach, and I headed down to Javi Santos's townhouse, while the rest of the team went to pick up Michael Lawrence from his job.

"Tell him we need to take him into protective custody," Danny instructed. "But don't tell him anything other than that."

"I'm sure that's going to go over *really* well," Tabitha said with a sigh.

Yeah, well. We were saving his ungrateful life, so he'd better get on board. They completed their task before we reached Javi's, and my eyes widened at the text Kevin sent.

> **ST. JAMES**
> He tried to deck Tab.

I texted back quickly. If I knew Tab—and I *did know Tab*—that hadn't gone *quite* like Michael had expected.

> Is he okay?

There was a long pause as the dots disappeared and reappeared. And then finally, a text came through.

> **KEVIN**
> Um, all I can say is that she used appropriate force.
>
> **GONZALEZ**
> Agreed

I snorted. I'll just bet she did. It sounded like a mess to untangle, but as long as Lawrence had been the aggressor, Tate would stand behind her. She might be a harridan, but she knew how to support her team. And kick us in the ass, but mostly it was the support thing.

Things didn't go *quite* as smoothly on our end at Javi's place.

From the moment we reached his townhouse, we could all tell something was off. There were tread marks on the corner of the lawn edging his driveway and the mailbox was slightly askew, like he'd pulled out in a hurry. As we headed up the front walk, the garage was wide open, and I saw bags sprawled by the back door...almost like he was interrupted by something.

Had someone given him the heads-up that we were on the way? How? And more importantly, who?

We searched his townhouse and found exactly what I knew we'd find.

Nothing.

I wandered through the living room, looking at the whirlwind Javi had left behind. A desk in the corner had been ransacked, the drawers still open, a few stray papers on the floor. Cords dangled where a computer had been taken. I touched one of the cords, only half-listening as Danny and Zach argued over whether we had enough evidence to pick up Evie Sinclair.

I already knew the answer to that. Nope. Not even close. We had a lot of conjecture and one hell of a theory. But nothing solid enough to haul her in for more than a voluntary interview that she could leave at any moment.

As for searching the Hope House, well, that was a catch-22, wasn't it? Maybe we'd find something more concrete if we could search the premises. But in order to get that search authorized, we needed something concrete to take to the D.A. It was the kind of circular logic that stalled an investigation rather nicely.

I sighed as I stooped to pick up one of the papers underneath Javi's desk—an old cable bill. I already knew what the rest of our night looked like. We'd tear the place apart, piece by piece. Open every drawer and closet door, go through every scrap of paper. We'd interrogate his neighbors and question his family and friends. But in the end? It wouldn't matter.

Javi was in the wind, and he'd taken everything of value with him.

22

The house was quiet as I headed back down the hall to my office. It was a bit of a lazy day, as I was in sweats and socks, but there was always time for a coffee break. Watson plodded along behind me, his Kong toy gripped in his jaws. He tossed me an irritable look, as if telling me to get settled so he could settle, too, and get chewing.

We had the house to ourselves because Danny had taken off early to do errands. Usually, I would've tagged along, but he mentioned going to Home Depot—his mothership—and I quickly begged off.

"*Work,*" I'd said desperately. "*I just have so much to do.*" Then I started shuffling through papers like my life depended on it.

He eyed me suspiciously. "I thought we were going to the dealership. You told me your car needed an oil change last week."

"I'm at 5%," I said breezily.

"You were at 5% last week. How can you still be at 5%?"

I didn't answer what was very much a rhetorical question.

"I'm just buried, you know?" I reached the end of the pile of papers with a surprised *eep*. I shuffled through them again—slower this time—and his mouth twitched. I don't care if he saw right through me. I would do whatever I had to do not to spend three hours in a hardware superstore again.

"I guess I'll take care of it while I'm out," he said, proving he was indeed better at this hubby stuff. I thanked him as I busily scribbled something on one of the papers. Danny grabbed my car fob, clearly trying not to laugh. Then he kissed me on the cheek and left.

For the first time in a long while, Watson nosed open my office door and followed me in as I sat down at my desk. My office was quiet, too. Franklin had taken off days ago, and I rather missed his comforting presence. Not that I'd ever admit that kind of shit aloud.

Before he'd left in a huff, he told me that things had gotten rather noisy around these parts. I'd listened, brow furrowed, trying to see what he was talking about, but I remained befuddled.

"Your soil," he said, aggrieved. "It talks. The soil is always *talking*." And off he went.

And here I thought I'd have all this luxuriously thick hair well into my sixties before I started getting my father's balding patch. Turns out I was going to yank it out long before then.

"Oh, good," I'd called after him. "More fucking riddles."

I spun around in my chair a few times, spinning with my chair like a gameshow wheel until I landed on my whiteboard. I blinked up at it, waiting for the dizziness to settle. The case was stalled. There was no other way to put it.

We'd planned to shuffle Michael Lawrence off someplace safe, where he could lie low until everything was resolved. But thanks to his near assault of a police officer, he was cooling his heels in lockup. We'd alerted the guards to stay alert, just in case Evie's reach was even longer than I'd imagined.

Despite putting out feelers with corresponding agencies, Javi hadn't been spotted. I wasn't really all that surprised. He was an old pro, and Project Halo had been going on, unnoticed, for quite some time. Their little game worked smooth as silk, and it was going to take some real digging to find a cog in the machine. But we would. Of that, I had no doubt.

My phone buzzed with a text from an unfamiliar number. It only took me seconds to realize it was from the manager of the Blue Palm.

I frowned at the unfamiliar number before opening the text.

> **UNKNOWN**
> Looks like a light is on in Caitlin's room.

I thumbed a quick reply of thanks, bemused that he'd put down the pot long enough to actually come through.

> **UNKNOWN**
> Should I make a citizen's arrest?
>
> **UNKNOWN**
> I'm ready.
>
> **UNKNOWN**
> Pretty sure I can take her.
>
> **UNKNOWN**
> I think.
>
> **UNKNOWN**
> You're on the way, though, right.

I bit my lip to hold in a laugh as I responded.

> Don't approach or do anything. I'm on the way.

I hustled out into the garage and froze, blinking at the empty space. *Oh. Right.* I growled and rushed back in the house to grab Danny's key fob. Honestly, I couldn't believe Caitlin had managed to evade Javi this long. I was glad that she was still alive. And not just because I might've just unearthed a *living* witness. You know, someone who could sit in front of a jury and not just send me fucked-up dreams.

I probably needed to hurry so she'd stay that way.

A few moments later, I was in Danny's Charger, headed for Hallandale.

I made the twenty-minute drive in ten and wasted no time driving straight to Caitlin's room. I slowed as I found a car backed in at her door. The trunk was up. I squinted, but I couldn't tell what she was doing. Was she loading luggage before she got out of town? As if to buttress that thought, the car rocked a bit as something heavy hit the trunk.

I sent up a prayer of thanks that the manager had taken my offhand request to call me seriously. I pulled up to the car, nose to nose, to block her in. I was halfway out of the door when the trunk slammed. And I found myself face-to-face with someone familiar.

Javi Santos.

I furrowed my brow as I tried to process what I was seeing. As I looked past him into the motel room, I could see it was in utter disarray. The lamp was broken on the floor along with the TV, and the desk and chairs were turned over. I stared at the smear of blood on the doorjamb. It looked like one hell of a fight had gone on. I stared at the smear, which upon closer inspection looked like a handprint.

A fight had gone on and someone had lost.

I had another split second to process that before Javi leaped into action. He jumped in the driver's seat and threw the car into gear. He revved the engine a few times. I pulled out my weapon as I shouted for him to stop. I almost rolled my eyes at myself. A suspect actually complying with my demands? *Yeah. Like that'll happen any time soon.*

He stopped revving his engine and put the car in gear. I barely had time to jump out of the way before he slammed into Danny's car.

Holy fuck.

"Get out of the car," I yelled for shits and giggles. "Javi Santos. You need to—"

Crunch.

I winced as he rammed the car again. Ohh, Danny was going to kill me. That's if Javi didn't, of course. He backed up to the motel room door with a terrible screech, hitting the wall and caving in his own bumper. I knew what the fuck was coming next. I dived out of the way just in time to see him positively *floor* it.

The crunch was loud enough to make my ears ring as fender met fender. This time, he'd nosed Danny's car out of the way enough that he could get around it. But not without a terrible screech of metal against metal as he scraped the entire driver's side.

I ran to get in the car as he sped out of the parking lot, but the door was too dented to open. And from the looks of things, that was now the best-looking part of the car.

I sprinted after Javi's rapidly disappearing car even though I knew it was futile. Maybe I could get a shot off and take out one of the tires. I knelt down and squinted as I took aim. *Pop, pop, pop!* I hit one of them and the back window besides, which splintered but didn't shatter. He fishtailed onto the road and disappeared with a squeal of tires.

I barely had time to process that before a car whipped into the lot so quickly that I gasped. I rolled to the side and the car came to a stop mere inches from my body with a squeal of rubber. I opened my eyes slowly, unaware of when I'd even squeezed them shut, only to find myself face-to-face with a tire.

A door slammed and I heard heels on the pavement as someone sprinted to my side. "Oh my stars!" Someone exclaimed.

My heart thundered in my chest. Stars didn't quite cover it. I was damn near tempted to check my underwear.

I looked up to find a woman staring down at me, one hand over her mouth. She was pretty, tall and thin, her long legs seemingly endless in tight black jeans. Her rose-scented raven hair swept in my face as she leaned over me, babbling how she hadn't seen me. I looked beyond the silky hair curtain to see the car that nearly took my head off. I raised my eyebrows at the red mustang.

Yeah. That'll work.

"Are you sure you're okay?" she asked worriedly. "You aren't...you know, *saying* all that much. Maybe you're concussed."

"I'm not concussed," I reassured her. Probably. "I do, however, need your car."

She reared back. "Excuse me? I save your life and you're fucking carjacking me?"

"What? I'm not carjack—I'm a cop," I snapped. "And I need to requisition your vehicle in the interest of public safety."

"Well, I don't know what all that gobbledygook means, but this is my birthday present to myself," she said, aggrieved. "You're not taking my car."

"Except I am," I told her as I got up off the ground. I hobbled over to the driver's side as she followed, arguing loudly. I hopped in and closed the door.

She glared at me, clearly regretting missing her opportunity to imprint Goodyear on my face. "I'm going to call the fucking cops. The *real* cops."

"You do that," I said as I revved the engine. Too bad it was stick shift. I was rusty but it roared under my hands. "Tell 'em we need backup at the Blue Palm Motel."

She was still yelling as I peeled off.

I wasn't worried about finding Javi's car. Thanks to his roller derby behavior —and the plastic of his newer car against Danny's reinforced grille—it was wrecked to hell in the front. I was more worried that he'd jumped out and rabbited somewhere.

I called in backup as I headed for the interstate. Hopefully he was trying to get as far away as possible. Kevin might be a big goof, but he was all about that business when the situation called for it. "I'm on the way," he said briskly. "What else do you need?"

"Um, send a unit for Danny."

I could hear his car door in the background and his car fire to life. "Oh, you've got his car?"

I grimaced, remembering his precious Charger, now a scratched, banged-up heap at the Blue Palm. I mean, it wasn't my fault, but that wasn't going to go over well. Like, at all. The man used the hose on the lowest setting to wash his car with a lint-free mitt. I've seen people treat babies rougher when washing them in a sink with No Tears shampoo.

"In a manner of speaking," I finally said. "And maybe you could text me the number to a marriage counselor. I think I'm going to need one."

23

I hadn't seen Danny speechless very often.

He hadn't said a word since he'd arrived at the Blue Palm Motel parking lot. He'd walked a circuit around his car, though, and more than once. On his fourth go around, he still hadn't uttered a bloody word. I exchanged a wide-eyed look with Kevin, standing next to me with his hands planted on his hips. Tabitha meandered over with a low whistle as she surveyed the damage.

Somehow it looked worse than the last time I'd seen it, which... just didn't seem possible. In my mind, the damage had been mostly cosmetic. But what I was looking at wasn't even drivable.

Finally, I couldn't stand the tension anymore. "Okay," I blurted. "Say something."

He slow-blinked at me. "This...this is almost grounds for divorce."

I was pretty sure he was being dramatic. But just in case....

"I'll get you something better," I swore.

"All they have is older Crown Vics."

"I'll work my connections," I insisted. "I know a guy in asset forfeiture."

Tabitha clucked as she picked up the driver's side mirror,

dangling by two wires. She let it drop and I winced as it banged against the metal. Not that it could get any worse without the use of a compactor, but still.

She squinted at Danny. "Between your speeding and his penchant for car chases, how are you guys even insurable?"

"Now *really* isn't the time," Kevin said out of the corner of his mouth, sending another worried glance at his best friend. I wasn't sure if it was his sage advice or Danny's growl that got her moving, but either way, she skedaddled with a waggle of her eyebrows.

Danny blew out a breath, deliberately turning his back on his car. "The important thing is that you're okay. The rest is just replaceable stuff, and you are not." He paused. "You are okay, aren't you?"

"Peachy," I assured him.

"Then that's all that matters. To me, that is," he added, glancing over at Lieutenant Tate, who was talking to the motel manager. From the look on his face, I was pretty sure she was terrorizing the man, but better him than me. "Her? Not so much. For your sake, tell me we have a suspect out of this."

"We do have Caitlin Closs, who was tied up in the trunk," I said. "She's refusing to speak to us at the moment, but still."

I'd popped the trunk shortly after the chase ended, and she came out swinging. I caught her arm on the downswing out of sheer instinct. Even after I identified myself, she continued to try to attack. She'd clearly been too scared to comprehend that I wasn't the same guy who'd put her in the trunk. And if I had to guess, she'd spent most of her confinement preparing herself to die.

She'd stared at me, wide-eyed, breathing shallowly like she'd run a marathon, even as I identified myself once more. No recognition. I knew that if I even let go of her arm a micrometer, she'd swing at me again. So I tightened my grip on her wrist until her fingers spasmed and the knife fell to the ground, landing with a clatter.

"I'm a cop," I told her. "He can't hurt you anymore."

If anything, the news that I was law enforcement made her even *more* squirrely. The only thing she bothered to say after that was that...well, she had nothing else to say. "*Especially* to cops," she emphasized.

Well. Isn't that a kick in the rump?

Danny didn't look impressed with our bounty, either. "Anything else?" he asked delicately. "Other than a reluctant witness who—judging from her ten years of silence—is really, *really* good at keeping her mouth shut and hates cops?"

"Um," I said.

"Well," Kevin agreed.

"What about Santos?" Danny asked, a little exasperated. "He seems like the type to make a deal to save his own skin."

"About Javi," I hedged.

"Javi," Kevin agreed.

Danny sighed. "Holy fuck, you two."

I cleared my throat as I proceeded to explain the events that ended the car chase. By the time I'd spotted the damaged blue Corolla, I had backup in the form of two squad cars, with Kevin and Tab pulling up the rear. I pulled back to let the squad cars take the lead and fell in behind them. Unfortunately, a slow-moving car didn't hear the sirens in time, and the first unit t-boned him in the intersection. The second squad car pulled over to assist, which left me in the lead again.

Danny opened his mouth, but I already knew what he was going to ask. "Everyone is okay," I assured him. "They transported the driver of the Kia to the hospital with minor injuries and she's already released. And both officers are bruised but okay."

I'd radioed it in and was told to continue the chase. They also informed me that Stop Sticks were being deployed five miles ahead of our current location. So I kept on. It was a delicate balance. I had to keep enough space between us, so I didn't get caught up in the wreckage if he topped out. But I had to keep close enough to keep the pressure on him.

He was able to evade the Stop Sticks, unfortunately, almost hitting the officer who'd thrown them standing on the side of the road. And let's just say that escalated things a bit. I got the greenlight to end the chase "however I needed to." So I waited until there was no traffic and PIT maneuvered him.

"Into a tree," Kevin finished, scratching the back of his neck. "Certainly wouldn't have been my first choice, but it worked."

Interesting. I glared. Because the way I remembered it, he'd cried out, *"Ohhh, got that motherfucker,"* only to be followed up with Tab's extra sensitive, *"That's how you fucking do it."*

"He was also okay," I hurried to say when Danny opened his mouth again. It would *really* be better just to hear the whole thing on this one. "Until…he shot himself to avoid capture."

He stared. "So…what do we have again?"

Other than another dead body? I tugged at my ear. "Well."

"Well," Kevin agreed.

"Christ," Danny muttered, scrubbing his hands down his face.

Kevin's phone buzzed and he checked the screen. "It's Carole. Gimme two seconds, I gotta take this."

Could she be calling me? I glanced down at my silent phone as he walked off a short distance. *'Cause I really feel like she could be calling me, too.* Especially since Tate was on her way over.

It was clear that our lieutenant had been on her way to something fancy, judging by her fitted black dress and heels. Her hair was a riot of tiny braids that she'd pulled up in a bun, and a simple but beautiful gold lavalier necklace sparkled at her throat.

Tate smiled at us, like a shark who knew her prey wasn't a seal but was gonna take a bite anyway. Just to be sure. "Tell me why I'm missing my anniversary dinner, Christiansen."

Oh, boy. I straightened my shoulders. "I assume Detective McKenna here caught you up on our work on the Parker murders."

"Yes," she drawled. "Right up to the point where an upstanding citizen is probably a serial killer, who has been operating under our noses for the past ten years. At least."

Her mild tone didn't fool me. Or that carefully arched brow. She was furious. Not at me, of course. But with Tate, the hurricane path of destruction could be wide.

"And who the hell is the dead guy they're scraping out of that fucking Corolla on 153rd Street?"

Barbarians. I worked with barbarians.

"That would be Javi Santos. He was a PI that we think was working with the Hope House." I gave her a sheepish look. "We were hoping to ask him about that, but…well, you know."

"Sure," she said dryly. She swept a stray braid out of her face, and I was startled to see our No-Frills Lieutenant had French tips. She caught me staring and her brow creased. "What?"

Not even on a dare. "Nothing," I said quickly.

She eyed me some more but moved on to her most pressing concern—and mine as well, to be honest. "If Ms. Sinclair is our killer—and that's a very big if—it looks like she's in cleanup mode. How'd she even get wind of this?"

Danny rolled his shoulders, looking all kinds of uncomfortable. He seemed to be having a hard time picking his way through this unexpected minefield, and I wasn't about to join him without a bomb-sniffing dog at my side. I did my best impression of a statue—if I needed to plop a crown on my head and hold a torch aloft, I would.

"We might have a leak," he finally admitted.

She gave us a killing glare. "A leak? In my department?"

"That's the only thing that makes sense," I said cautiously. "We don't know how far her influence reaches. That's why I'd like to bring in Sinclair for more questioning."

Her answer was immediate. "No. Absolutely not. All you have is conjecture at this point."

"How are we supposed to move *past* conjecture without questioning her about it?" I asked, because sometimes it's fun to play with fire. At least until you lose your eyebrows.

"I want you to question this Caitlin Closs until she cracks, you hear?"

I cleared my throat. "Lieutenant, she just went through something very traumatic. Pressuring her right now might be extremely counterproductive."

"Christiansen, that wasn't a question." She tilted her head and her gold teardrop earrings swayed. "It was a directive."

Well, then.

"Yes, ma'am," I said with a sigh.

She stomped off, presumably to terrorize someone else. "Warn the villagers," I murmured.

Danny let out a laugh that was mostly air.

24

Three days in lockup for unrelated outstanding warrants had done its job.

Caitlin Closs had changed her stance on speaking to cops...at least, that's what she'd said. Sitting across the table from her, I saw no evidence of that. In fact, she mostly seemed obsessed with the large square mirror behind me. At one point, she'd gotten up from the table and examined it, end to end, before flopping back down in her chair.

She looked better than the last time I'd seen her. Her eyes weren't wide with fear, but clear and alert. Her wild and tangled dark hair lay neat and shiny right above her shoulders. Her thin frame was dwarfed by the orange jumpsuit, and the standard issue orange sandals looked like clown shoes on her tiny feet.

She glanced at the mirror again.

I raised an eyebrow because enough was enough. I had to get her talking before she pulled out a screwdriver and dismantled the thing, piece by piece. "I assume you called me down here for a reason."

"I'm ready to talk," she said. "But not in here."

"Unfortunately, this is the only option."

She bit her lip, looking at the mirror again. I was almost tempted to look, too, just so I could see what the hell was so interesting over there.

"Who...." She licked her lips. "Who's behind that window?"

"No one," I assured her.

She didn't look convinced.

I bit back any terse words. I'd had a long day of chasing down leads. It didn't help matters that Tate was still riding my ass like I was a bucking bronc, and this was her last chance at winning a rodeo belt. I was also nursing an injured shoulder. I was pretty sure I'd jammed it when I'd done that PIT maneuver—which was textbook, no matter what my micromanaging husband implied after he watched Kevin's dashcam video.

But none of that was her fault.

Whatever I'd been through, at least I hadn't spent time duct-taped in a trunk, certain I was going to die. And I hadn't spent much of the last decade dodging the long reach of Evie Sinclair.

"You've done well carrying whatever burden Quinn put on your shoulders," I said quietly. "But maybe now it's time to set it down."

She didn't look all that sure as she frowned down at the table. "Yeah. Maybe."

"Your parents called me on your behalf. And so did your cousin, Jason." I let that sink in for a few moments. "They're worried about you."

"They probably think I've relapsed," she said darkly.

"They don't, in fact. They're just glad you're okay. But if you want to keep being okay, I think you need to level with us." I paused, trying to think of a delicate way to phrase my next words. "I'm pretty sure Javi Santos wasn't working alone. And whoever sent him to make sure you didn't talk isn't going away."

She continued to look at me, a little lost. "I don't know where to start."

I shrugged. "Why don't we start with Quinn?"

"She...she was a nice lady. I worked at a food truck near her job.

She came by at least twice a week for our cinnamon rolls. I used to tease her about her sugar addiction, and she was amazed that I could work around those rolls all day and not have it go straight to my waistline. And I told *her* that if you're around it all day, you get pretty sick of it fast. Like the three years I worked at Pizza Hut. I never wanted to see another piece of pepperoni as long as I...." She faltered, probably because my eyes had begun to glaze well enough to cover a Krispy Kreme donut. "You probably don't care about that."

"I want to hear it all," I said honestly. *I might need someone to splash me in the face with water, but I definitely want to hear it all.* "Go on. You're doing fine."

"Okay, so...one day, she came by, and she was really upset. When I asked her what was wrong, she wanted to know what I'd do if I discovered something bad. Something really bad but done for the right reasons by good people." She shook her head. "I was so fucking confused, but I told her she had a responsibility to do the right thing."

"Did she say what the bad thing was?"

"Not at first. She just asked, 'What if I'm wrong?' And I told her to make sure that she wasn't. She just nodded and left." She started nibbling the ragged cuticle of her left thumb. "I didn't really expect to hear about it again, but she was back the next week."

"What did she say?"

"That she needed my help. She'd followed my advice and tried to be sure, but she needed more evidence."

"The Hope House," I said quietly.

She glanced at the mirror again. "Yes. And some secret project."

"Project Halo?"

She nodded slowly even as she let her thumb go and moved on to her index finger. "She said that she needed a way to get more information, and that would only happen if she had someone on the inside. Someone the women of Project Halo trusted. I didn't want to get involved at first."

I bit back my irritation at Quinn. I couldn't believe she'd involve an innocent bystander in something so dangerous. "Was she upset?"

"No, she gave me a hug and thanked me for being a sounding board. I hoped we'd be cool the next time I saw her."

"And were you?"

"I never got the chance. I got fired the next day. Drug testing." She swallowed. "I've always struggled...."

"I know," I said softly. I reached over and gave her hand a little push away from her mouth. She was picking at her nail beds so feverishly that one of them started to bleed. "We're not here about that."

She stuck her hand under her leg.

"My boyfriend called me worthless when he found out that I wouldn't be able to contribute to the rent and kicked me out. I asked my parents if I could store all my stuff in their garage and they agreed, but not without chewing me out pretty good." She paused. "I thought that maybe everyone was right. I hadn't done anything good in a long time. and this was my chance."

"How did you get in contact with Quinn?"

She blinked. "I went right up to the Hope House and asked. I figured it would be a great start to our ruse. And that was the jump-off. We took all the pictures to establish my 'relationship.'"

"With your cousin."

"Yep. I made a couple fake accounts and updated them religiously. Then I had Jason show up to the Hope House a few times when I was there and act like an absolute ass."

"Why the bruises?"

"They were trusting me, but things weren't moving fast enough. Project Halo seemed to have four stages and I was stuck in stage two. We realized that things weren't bad enough for them to offer me the ultimate solution. And when Quinn disappeared?" A shadow crossed her face. "I knew...I fucking *knew* she hadn't just run off. No how, no way."

I sat there for a moment, processing everything she'd told me. "So you decided to disappear."

"Not until a man showed up at my new job looking for me. And before you ask, I *did* go to the police." She looked down at the table. "I was encouraged to rethink the things I thought I knew."

I looked at her in stunned silence. It was a moment before I could speak. Because if she was saying what I thought she was saying.... I had to work to relax my shoulders so my body language would look approachable again. "By whom?"

She glanced at the mirror again. "And you're sure—"

"It's just you and me here."

"Detective Owens." After the name burst from her lips, she sucked in a breath as if she couldn't believe she'd actually said it. Like she'd been holding on to that for a long time. "He didn't believe me, and neither did his partner. They both seemed convinced that Quinn and Nate had left town. He told me that the Hope House was a solid organization, and I was making unfounded accusations."

I unclenched my jaw with effort. "What else did he say?"

"That I'd be destroying a community service that a lot of women really needed and counted on." Her voice was a whisper at this point. "His partner told me I should shoot up some more and leave the detective work to the real cops."

I gritted my teeth. *Idiots.* Tunnel vision and sloppy police work had destroyed many a case. "I'm sorry that happened to you," I said slowly. "But *we* are not those detectives. And I want to hear everything you have to say."

"Everything?"

"Everything," I confirmed grimly.

Her gaze darted here and there. She looked happy that she'd finally word-vomited her entire saga but also like she wanted to throw up because she had. "And no one heard us?"

"This isn't the two-way room," I said, feeling a bit guilty. But it would only make her more afraid to know the truth. "That's just a mirror."

"Okay. That's...okay." She slumped in her chair, the very picture of relief. "I don't suppose I could have something to drink?"

"Sure," I said easily. "Water? Tea? Coffee?"

"Coke, if you have it. I need the sugar."

"Give me a sec. I'll see if I can rustle you up a snack, too."

She gave me a tentative smile. "Thanks. Confession may be good for the soul, but it's not so great for your stomach."

I chuckled. "I'll see what I can do. Hold tight for me, okay?"

My smile died the minute I exited the room and saw Danny and Zach standing there. Judging from the tense silence between them, *things* had been said. Zach gave me a wary look, probably because he knew I had some shit to say about what I'd just heard, too.

He was absofuckinglutely right.

"Every single murder," I said, my tone positively frigid.

"What?" he snapped.

"Every single fucking murder since she told you and your partner, Detective Dipshit, about her suspicions. They're all at your feet."

"She didn't seem credible," he said wearily. "Just one hint of impropriety and the Hope House would've been shut down. And you know how valuable they are to the community."

I peered at him. "Refresh my drink, are we referring to murder as a hint of impropriety in this scenario?"

"I didn't know it was murder," he shot back. "For fuck's sake, Caitlin didn't look like she does now."

I widened my eyes. "That's your excuse?"

"You're telling me some junkie comes up to you talking shit about a respected member of the community, and you'd take her word for it? Without a drop of proof?" He sent me a scathing look. "Get real. She had more track marks on her arms than skin. My partner agreed with me that she was probably full of shit."

"Then he should be standing here, too," I said without a trace of understanding. "No wonder your department was so eager to lend you out."

His cheeks flushed as he turned to Danny, clearly done trying to bring me over to his way of thinking. "She was a junkie, and junkies lie. You *know* how they are. Like my father." He paused for emphasis. "And your mother. You remember all those times she swore she was coming to get you? You'd get all excited and bounce down to the living room when she finally fucking followed through. What was that, two times out of ten?"

"Zach," Danny said quietly.

"And when you got back, you'd be full of stories of how soon you were going home with her. And how long it had been since she'd used." He made a sound of disgust. "You remember that birthday that she told you she'd take you to SeaWorld? She showed up all fucked up on something."

"Yes, I fucking remember," Danny said, his tone hard. "I don't need a refresher, thanks."

But Zach wasn't quite done proving his point. "They wouldn't let her see you and she was screaming your name downstairs," he charged on. "Then her drug-addled ass had to be dragged out of there in cuffs. Then that kid did impressions of her for weeks to piss you off—"

Danny was in motion before I even realized what he was going to do, his hand gripping Zach's collar. Zach grunted as his back hit the wall. My eyes were probably the size of quarters. If he wanted to continue that shitty little story he was so fucking determined to tell, he was *probably* going to need some air in his windpipe.

"Hey," I said urgently, latching on to Danny's tense arm. "Hey. That's enough."

I was pretty sure our vows wouldn't survive me tasing him and leaving him twitching on the station floor. But I wasn't about to let him ruin his life, either. Luckily, it only took another couple *heys* before he finally eased up his iron grip.

Zach sucked in air, patting his throat. He seemed to really want a repeat, because he kept right on. "Lies," he spat, his voice a little scratchy. "That's all they do. You and I both know it."

Christ. I readied myself to intervene again.

Danny's hands flexed and he took a step back. As if he didn't completely trust himself not to go after Zach again. "I'm telling you this as a friend," he said evenly. "Shut your mouth about my mother."

We had a tense few moments—so tense, in fact, that a passing officer paused and asked if everything was alright. I assured him that it was, and he kept walking. None of us spoke until he got on the elevator and the doors slid closed.

"Look," Zach said, straightening his collar, which was wrinkled beyond repair. "Clearly, I was in the wrong. I'll go apologize to her."

I let out a laugh of disbelief. "You're not getting near her. You're off the case." It wasn't my call, but damned if Danny could do it right now. He still looked extremely capable of doing his old friend bodily harm. "And I will be filing a complaint with your supervisor."

Zach didn't seem to think my word was the final word on the subject. Not judging by the way he stared at Danny for confirmation. When Danny didn't counter my edict, his nostrils flared. "D?"

Danny's jaw flexed. "I'm assuming that you're not also hearing impaired along with being a complete asshole."

Zach stared at him for another moment, his throat working. After a tense moment, he hit the wall, hard enough to make me flinch. Then he stalked off, headed toward the elevator. Danny watched, expression hard, until the doors slid closed behind him. And even then, he didn't turn.

"Hey." My touch on his shoulder wasn't enough to get his attention. I had to squeeze before he looked my way. "He was just trying to get under your skin."

He sent me a wry smile as he blew out a breath. "Well, he certainly did that."

Fucking Zach. He'd been in the small circle of trusted people who knew Danny's past. The parts of him that had been small and vulnerable and susceptible to the word of the woman he'd loved the most. Before he'd become capable of defending himself. Part of being a member of that trusted circle was knowing where the soft spots were, exactly where to press to make it hurt. But never doing so. For that alone, I wanted Zach's head on a pike.

"I'm sorry," I said.

Danny arched a brow. "I wasn't aware you were in control of that douche's actions."

"Not for that," I said. "His actions were his own. But I'm pretty sure you hadn't wanted me to hear that story, or you would've told me by now."

"I'm an open book to you," he said simply. "Zach only knows

those things because he was there. You get to know because I *want* you to know. My past, my present, my future—it's all yours. Remember?"

I remembered every word of our vows. Every single word. He was lucky I didn't tattoo the whole thing on my arm so I could look at it whenever I wanted. "Yes, but you make me drag it out of you."

"Yes, I do," he admitted with a crooked little smile. "Sorry."

I looked around quickly to make sure the coast was clear before I leaned in and kissed him. Just because.

"We don't have enough to pick up Evie yet, do we?" I asked.

He shook his head. "I'm going to talk to Andi and see if we have enough for a search warrant at least. But...yeah, probably not."

"We'll keep working it," I finally said.

He gave me a half-smile. "Like we always do."

I enjoyed his proximity for another moment before I stepped away regretfully. "Sorry about your car," I said. "You can drive mine until I find you something else."

He grunted, which made me give him an affronted look. That was BMW slander, and he needed to know it. "Maybe you can stop acting like I offered you the keys to my clown car and not a fine, world-class automobile."

"Foreign cars aren't my thing. You know that." He bumped my shoulder. "Besides, I meant what I said. As long as you're here in one piece, I don't care about the rest."

That was a nice sentiment...even if it was a lie. "Don't you, though? When you saw your car, you looked like you were going to cry."

"I did not," he said with a glare.

"Your eyes got all watery."

"That was dust!"

"Like the dust you got in your eyes when Watson mastered the command *shake paw*?" I inspected my nails, giving them a quick buff on my shirt. "Or the dust you get in your eyes every time we see that ASPCA commercial with the dogs shivering in the snow?"

Even with everything that had happened, I could see the reluctant amusement in his eyes. I would always treasure the fact that I could make him laugh. Always. "Why do I put up with you again?"

"Because I'm your fucking soulmate, McKenna."

His lips twitched as he tried not to smile. "That's as good a reason as any, I suppose."

.

25

Considering the shitshow Friday had been, Saturday was damn near perfect.

Danny suggested we go out for breakfast, which sounded great. Getting frisky in a shared shower—you know, to save water and whatnot—turned that breakfast into brunch, which was even better. Then we went to a little place near the beach that served pancakes the size of a dinner plate, and then took a little stroll down the boardwalk...*because* we'd stuffed ourselves silly with pancakes the size of dinner plates.

I wasn't sure what the calorie tradeoff was, but hey, it was an effort. All I knew was that when I finally got back in the car, my jeans were cutting me off in a way they hadn't been when we arrived.

"That was a nice walk, don't you think?" I patted my stomach. "Pretty sure I worked off that pancake."

"Yes, you definitely worked off a pancake," Danny said with a grin. "Which would be great if you'd only eaten the one."

I waved a hand before putting on my seat belt. Semantics. His pancake math was way off. "I'd expect as much from someone who pours his syrup in a little cup on the side of his plate."

He chuckled and started the car. Then glanced over at me as he buckled up. "Hey, do you mind if we make one more stop before we head home?"

"'Course not," I said, relaxing in the seat. "I've got no place to be."

He smiled and reached over to give my thigh a squeeze before pulling away from the curb. I didn't even need to know what the stop was. Full of one of my favorite breakfast foods and spending the day with my favorite guy, I was as mellow as I was going to get.

Halfway to our destination, buildings and scenery started looking familiar and I cared a bit more. When we passed the Walmart, my suspicions were confirmed, and I realized we were headed to his mother's house.

I swallowed a sigh. I rewound our perfect day to the moment Danny asked if I minded making another stop. I tsked as past-me—that poor, unknowing idiot—smiled and declared he had no place to be. Insert rude buzzer noise. *The answer we're looking for is, "You go ahead, I'll take an Uber, thanks."*

My relationship with Paula had undergone many changes over the years. The first time Danny and I had given things a go, she'd been skeptical and fond of me all at the same time. But I left, and that fondness morphed into a hatred with the power of a thousand suns. When I came *back*, she'd added a few more suns to that total.

Danny had made it clear that I wasn't going anywhere, and she could either get on board or...well, he never finished that ultimatum. That's mostly because he's a big ol' momma's boy, and we all knew any version of that *or* would've been complete bullshit.

Still, Paula had gotten the point. It helped that by accepting me in her life again, she had yet another son to pester. When she wanted company, her ability to drive/see/stand suddenly diminished, and one of us needed to come in a hurry because she was feeble. Well, she was feeble until she wanted to play pickleball with the girls, that is. Then we were told—not so subtly—to bugger off.

In any case, we'd grown fond of each other. None of that fondness was apparent as she confronted us before we even got one foot inside her ornate French doors. I got my usual kiss on the cheek, though, so I couldn't be in too much trouble. Maybe.

"I just had a very interesting call from your mother, Rainstorm," she said crisply. "I have an issue with the two of you."

The "you look lovely today, Paula," died on my tongue. Especially since we clearly weren't getting in the house. How she managed to block such a large doorway with her small frame was beyond me. She *did* look nice though, clad in a fuzzy peach sweater, a pair of fitted black jeans, and a black pair of fuzzy slippers. While her outfit was approachable, her stance was not—arms folded, eyes narrowed, one foot tapping.

I gave Danny a glance and he returned it with a shrug, which was not at all helpful. I mentally detailed all the things it could be. As far as I knew, we were here for a "surprise." There had been nothing in the invitation that indicated the surprise was a beatdown. I wasn't sure why Danny was in trouble too, but I was glad. Strength in numbers and all that.

I cleared my throat. "Care to be more specific?"

"Thanksgiving," she said with a huff. "You're under no obligation to include me, of course, but I would've thought you'd at least ask my advice for hosting."

Oh, that. Danny looked at me and it was my turn to shrug. "Ok, so maybe I told my folks they could come over. Then they told my sister, who texted something about bringing some Tofurky nonsense, and I didn't have the heart to tell her no." I scratched my neck as I tried to remember all the holiday-related promises I'd offhandedly made. "Then Nick was all, 'how come you're not inviting us to the thing?' And I was like, 'Shut up, there is no thing.' But I realized we were having six people over for dinner at that point, so yeah, it's kind of turning *into* a thing—"

"Rain—"

"Then Dakota sent out this email…I mean, he says he didn't, but who else would've brought that level of organization into a holiday?" I narrowed my eyes as I thought about his shady denials. That ginger was guilty, and I wouldn't rest until I proved it. "Then Nick renewed his request to bring the yams, and I agreed."

Actually, my exact words were, *Jesus, fine, whatever.*

Danny seemed to be having trouble finding words, so I motored on. Couldn't seem to stop, really.

"Tab wanted to bring mac and cheese and that seemed like a better plan than us attempting to make it again." I nudged his shoulder. "You remember, the noodles were all hard and we couldn't quite get the powdered cheese to dissolve—"

"*Powdered* cheese?" Paula gasped, looking like she might take a header right down the porch stairs.

Danny pressed fingers to his temples, looking like he might toss me off right after her.

"So anyway, Kevin, Nick, and Tab are probably coming," I finished hurriedly. "Oh, and whoever they want to bring."

Danny sighed. "Lord."

I had the feeling if Paula wasn't there, that *Lord* would've been surrounded with expletives. Probably because I'd just blithely invited a crap ton of people to our home—our sanctuary—and he wasn't the most social on his best day. Frankly, I was having doubts myself. Especially now that I realized exactly how many folks would be showing up to our place with empty bellies and holiday cheer. *Shudder.* I was the very picture of regret as I stood there biting my lip.

But then I straightened. I'd always been quick on my feet, and the way to salvage this was standing right in front of us with rigid shoulders and a hurt air.

"Paula, I have an idea," I said with an *ah-ha* snap of my fingers that was hopefully convincing. "Why don't you host the meal instead? Let's face it, you're the obvious choice. Your dining room is also so lovely, and you have that huge table."

Her arms slowly dropped to her sides as she peered at me hopefully. "Really? You wouldn't mind, dear?"

"Well, I—*oof.*" I rubbed my side as I glared at Danny, he of the sharp fucking elbows. There went any plans of milking it a bit more. "Not at all."

"My dining room table has leaves, too, so there'll be plenty of room for everyone. And if need be, we can set up a few card tables for the kids and whatnot." She frowned as she thought. "It's only a few days away, but I'm sure I can even rent some chairs if necessary."

"We'll help you set things up. And Danny and I can bring something, so you don't have to do so much cooking," I offered—generously, in my opinion.

She gasped. "That's...quite alright."

I scowled. Not at her gasp, which was pretty much the universal response to us bringing anything edible. But slapping a hand over her heart was over the line. "If you're sure."

She looked a lot happier. "Positive. And now that everything is settled...." She reached into her pocket and handed me something so tiny that I nearly bobbled it. "This is for you. Well, both of you, really."

I looked down at the micro flash drive, blinking down at the neatly printed label on the end. I could only wonder how the hell she fit *Christiansen McKenna* on something so bloody small. "What's this? Other than the obvious, I mean."

"I gathered all the footage from everyone's phones at your wedding and put together a little video."

"Really?" I wasn't much of a picture guy, which is why the only wedding photos I had were a few crappy selfies of the two of us. I was surprised and touched. "Thank you, Paula, that's really thoughtful."

I handed it over to Danny so he could see it, and the bastard pocketed it. I gave him a squinty-eyed look. If he thought he was making off with my wedding memories, he had another think coming.

"It really is," Danny said, leaning over to give her a kiss on the cheek. "Thanks."

"And that's not all." She looked really jazzed as she threaded her arm through his and mine and finally let us in the house. "Follow me, loves."

Follow me apparently meant bumble down the hallway as a three-headed hydra. I turned sideways so we wouldn't get stuck, wincing as I nearly knocked a picture off the wall with my shoulder. Eventually, we made it to the den in one piece. She led us over to a piece of furniture occupying the middle of the room and gave us a little *ta-da*.

Ta-da?

I blinked because I suddenly found myself face-to-face with a crib, and I was *really* hoping that mahogany monstrosity wasn't the surprise. Paula patted my arm and finally let go.

Too bad. My buckling legs could've really used the support.

She clasped her hands together. "Isn't it just lovely?"

That...really wasn't the word I was thinking. I glanced at Danny, hoping he had more in the arsenal than *fuck*. He only gave me a nonplussed look in return. So I returned the elbow in the side he'd given me earlier. With interest.

"Er," he said with a cough.

Always the wordsmith, I agreed. "Er."

Luckily, Paula hadn't lost the absolute ability to use the English language. "You remember the Reeds who live down the block? Their son, William, builds custom furniture and the woman who consigned this had a miscarriage. Poor dear." She shook her head. "She's pregnant again, but she wants an entirely new piece for the new baby. So he gave it to me for a song."

I tugged on my ear, which was so very itchy all of a sudden. "That's...nice of him?"

"It is, isn't it? I figured it should be used, not sitting in a dusty warehouse someplace." She ran a hand over the mahogany front. The wood was inlaid with curlicue designs and flower patterns, and I had to admit it was beautiful. Someone had clearly taken a lot of time and put a lot of love into the construction of the piece. "I immediately thought of the two of you."

Danny cleared his throat. "Mom, this is great, but like I told you with the bikes, we don't know how old the child will be. Or *when* it will be. Or *if* it will even be." As her mouth turned downward, he hustled to say, "But thank you."

"Oh, *she* bought the bikes," I blurted.

He raised an eyebrow. "Of course she did. Who'd you think...oh."

And then I was in the crosshairs of an intense blue stare. Yowza, I hated to be the focus of that patented *I'm gonna grill you until it hurts* expression.

For her part, Paula was still lost in the world of decorating a nursery for a child we didn't even have. "Well, it's not like it *couldn't* be a baby," she ventured.

"Yeah, I guess that's true," Danny said, clearly striving for patience. "It's just that—"

"There's no harm in hanging on to it," she said quickly. "If you can use it, fine. If you don't, that's fine, too."

"I guess I can put it in the shed with the bikes," he said with a sigh. "But I'd really rather you give it to someone who can use it right now. Not just maybe at some point in the future."

"Well, if I find someone who needs it, then I know where to find it," she shot back.

"We should probably leave it here," he said, a thread of annoyance seeping into his voice as they tried to out-nice one another. I stared at them, wide-eyed, wondering if they'd just start shouting compliments next. "It makes no sense to haul this thing here and there. Especially since it's such a solid piece."

Solid, backbreaking, hernia inducing…so very many adjectives we could use for that crib she apparently wanted us to cart around in our trunk like groceries.

She sighed. "If you're sure…."

"We are," I said quickly. Too quickly, probably, as Danny sent me an unreadable look.

I tugged on my ear again.

"Well, I guess that's that, then." Paula sighed as if we'd crushed all her dreams and blew them back in her face in powder form. "Maybe I could call one of my friends from book club. Last week she was going on and on about her daughter's pregnancy."

She gave us a pointed look that I ignored. If she wanted a grandchild to trot around so badly, she could watch Watson for the day. I cleared my throat. "Please tell William that's not a slight against his beautiful work."

"William." Danny's brow furrowed. "Isn't he the one who lives in Virginia? I think I remember him visiting his parents last Christmas."

"Yes, well." She patted her hair, suddenly flushed for no reason at all. "He's decided to move down to Florida and he's staying with them for a bit. Just until he gets on his feet and establishes a customer base down here."

Oh boy. He was doing a little more than that if those were his boxers I'd found in the hamper last week. It's not as creepy as it sounds and no, I wasn't digging through her hamper like a weirdo. It all started with me knocking over a crystal container in the guest bathroom, sending bright blue hand soap racing toward a stack of cream-colored hand towels. In my haste to grab something to mop it up with, I'd blindly reached for a towel in the hamper and come out with a scrap of fabric that amounted to a red and blue plaid mind-bomb.

I hoped she was ready to discuss it with Danny. Very little got past him when it came to his mother. And I was sure he was going to be very interested in her being in a relationship with someone closer to our age than hers. It would probably help her fly under the radar if she didn't blush every time the name William was mentioned.

"While you two are here, you might as well stay for dinner," she said happily. At her suggestion, my stomach growled in agreement. "You can build my new bookcase together while I cook."

Jesus Christ in an IKEA store.

I sighed as the good son, Danny, readily agreed.

We trudged to the living room, where several ginormous boxes were leaning against the couch. As we started unboxing them, Paula headed to the kitchen, promising to return soon with something to drink because we were "bound to work up a thirst."

I hope that was code for alcohol in a big glass.

The last time Danny and I had built something together—an entertainment center—it hadn't gone well. I'd handed him an A piece when I was supposed to give him a B piece, and we only realized it eighteen steps later.

We argued for hours—which was, coincidentally, about how long it took us to disassemble and reassemble the whole shebang. I'd been tempted to send a strongly worded email to the company about how a simple labeled sticker could save a marriage.

It took us a good fifteen minutes just to unbox what was surely going to be the last thing we did before we died. We had enough building materials and hardware to replicate Noah's Ark. "How big is this thing gonna be?" I asked.

"I think it's a five-part thing," Danny said absently, looking at the manual. "She wants the bookcases to cover the entire back wall."

I just nodded. I wasn't sure but I thought it was probably better than my knee-jerk instinct to scream, *Dear God, why?*

"Maybe we should organize all this first," he suggested. "You know, put all the As with the As and Bs with the Bs."

I grinned. Clearly, I wasn't the only one who had PTSD about the entertainment center. "Maybe we'll make it to our next anniversary after all."

He chuckled, his eyes sparkling. "Let's not get ahead of ourselves."

26

Despite my dire predictions, the bookcases came together fairly quickly. We established a system, working together seamlessly. And wonder of wonders, since there were five separate units to build, I got to manage two of my own...which, now that I think about it, was probably why we were working together so seamlessly.

We shot the shit as we worked, talking about nothing and everything. I'd just finished complaining about Dakota's latest session idea—birdwatching, of all things—when Danny said something completely out of left field. "Harper left me a message yesterday." He waited a few beats to let that sink in. "Her third attempt, she said."

Crap. I hadn't remembered until just that second that we'd played a damn good game of phone tag, but never connected. I didn't have a good excuse. When I wanted to track something down, nothing got in the way.

It took me a minute to gather my thoughts...and even then, I only came up with the lame response of, "Harper?"

At his arch look, I rubbed a hand over my face. "Yeah, okay. What did she want?"

"Who says I called her back?"

"You're you," I said with an eye roll. Avoidance wasn't really in his arsenal. The man returned calls to startled telemarketers. "Of course you called her back."

He kept screwing in pieces that connected the L-shaped frame to the other L-shaped frame. *Square, here we come.* My L-shape didn't look quite like his, but I was ignoring that as long as I possibly could.

After a few minutes, I made an irritable noise. "So now you're not going to tell me?"

"So now you care what she said?" He raised an eyebrow. "You know, instead of leaving her message unanswered for a week?"

I winced. "Sorry. Time really did get away from me."

"What if I told you that it was about a baby?"

My eyes got so wide, I was pretty sure they looked like hazel dinner plates. "I don't...oh, wow, I don't think...that's, *wow*—"

"Sweetheart, just take a deep breath," he instructed, looking vaguely alarmed. Like he was ready to bust out some of those certified CPR skills.

Yeah, I guess I was spiraling a bit. I took that recommended deep breath...and said the first fucking thing that came to mind. "I don't want a baby," I blurted.

Okay, so I kind of shouted it. Danny's eyes widened a bit. It might've been a tad more subtle to hire a skywriter.

I rubbed the back of my neck uncomfortably. Maybe I hadn't meant to say it in that manner, but I wasn't taking it back. Not when I checked the veracity of those words, and there was no lie detected.

Something else struck me then. Danny only looked surprised at *how* I'd said it. Not *that* I'd said it. He always claimed that he knew me better than I knew myself.

Guess he wasn't lying.

I blew out a breath. "I think we should leave the whole infant thing for someone who really wants that experience, start to finish," I said quietly. "If we have to do this, I think I'd rather someone a bit older."

"We don't *have* to do anything," he said, his brow furrowed. "It's not a deal breaker and I'm sorry if I made you feel like it was."

I put down my screwdriver and laid the piece I'd been working on flat on the floor. This wasn't a "two birds with one stone" kind of conversation. Danny seemed to agree, as he stopped kneeling and sat flat on the floor. He draped his hands over his upraised knees and waited, watching me patiently. Giving me time and space to marshal my thoughts.

"Did she really call about a baby?" I asked hesitantly. When he shook his head, I squinted at him. "Scare tactics, Daniel? Really?"

"How else am I supposed to know what you're thinking? Baby...." He spread his hands a little helplessly. "I need you to talk to me. What're you so afraid of?"

"I'm not afraid of anything," I said automatically. "I mean, other than spiders, bugs, snakes, heights, geese—"

"Geese?"

"They're mean, and don't bother to try and tell me that they aren't." I gave him an arch look. "One of them chased me in a parking lot."

He looked all too interested in the visual of me getting run to ground by waterfowl. Then he confirmed it. "I would've given good money to see that."

"Well, I'll ask the good people at Burger Barn to see if they'll hand over their security video." I plucked a few loose strands on my ripped jeans. "It's...it's a person, Danny. An entire person depending on us for everything. I understand the gravity of that."

"And I don't?"

"I never said that."

"Maybe not, but you *did* say that you were on board. I would've never started the process if I knew you were having doubts."

"*Doubts* is a strong word for what I'm feeling, I think," I murmured.

"So is, *Honey, we made a mistake, and I don't want the two-point-five kids we adopted*," he said dryly.

I squinted at him, wondering what happened to the nice boy that I'd married. Apparently, if you live with a sarcastic bastard long enough, that shit rubs off. "Technically, those were strong *words*. Plural."

He treated me to a long-suffering sigh. "When it comes to you, one really has to be careful when using the phrase *tell me what you're thinking*."

"Sorry. But what do you want me to say? If I say no and put a stop to all this, will you hate me? Resent me?" Just the thought sent a spear of pain through my heart. His gaze dropped to my chest, and I realized I was rubbing it. Like the pain was very much physical instead of metaphorical. I dropped my hand back in my lap. "I don't think I could live with that."

"I could never hate you. And believe me, I've tried." My gaze flew to his, but he wouldn't meet my eyes. His hands moved as if he needed something to do with them and sure enough, he picked up his cordless drill. "Hand me that hinge, will you?"

Sure thing. And then maybe we can talk about this trying to hate me shit some more. I checked the manual he'd spread out on the carpet. After a moment, I plucked one of the hinges from the pile on the left and handed it over. He gave me a half-smile and a murmured *thanks*.

"So." I drew out the word for about five syllables. "About your membership to the I Hate Rain Club. How much are the dues and are you current?"

He gave me an apologetic look. "Maybe *hate* isn't the right word, exactly."

"Then what is?"

"Frustration? Anger? Jealousy, maybe? Whatever the word, I wasn't exactly feeling warm toward you during our five-year hiatus," he said wryly. "Not when you were trying to fuck me out of your system with other guys."

I'm sure it hadn't helped that he'd been courted by several monasteries to do lectures on chastity. I knew it was too much to ask that my cheeks weren't doing their world class tomato impression.

"It wasn't that many guys," I said, because it was never a bad time to deploy a weak-ass argument. "And if I had known—"

"That wasn't a criticism, Rainstorm. I only brought it up because I wasn't able to hate you then, and I can't do it now. Even if I wanted to." He finished screwing in the hinges on one side and I wordlessly handed him the one for the other side. He looked at my face and sighed. "I'm not doing this right."

Alarmed, my gaze flew to the manual. Dear God, I refused to have another assembly-based blowout again. "No, this definitely goes to part C. I triple-checked."

He gave a short laugh. "Not *that*. I was talking about...you know what? This is one of the most important conversations we're going to ever have, and I'm not about to have it building a freaking bookcase."

He stood and dusted off his jean-clad rear before stretching out his hand. "Come with me."

I gave him a skeptical look. "Where are we going?"

He arched a brow. "Does it matter?"

"Not really." I smiled crookedly. Wherever he was going, I was going, too. And that was just that.

I slipped my hand in his and he pulled me to my feet. As I followed him down the hall deeper into the house, I could hear Paula humming in the kitchen. The smell of something delicious wafted through the air and my stomach growled.

We'd come a long way from the woman who'd nearly had an aneurysm when Danny referred to me as family. But I still felt weird as he led me into her office. Done in cream and the palest of lavender, it was pristine and organized. Danny dropped into her cream-colored desk chair and started up her desktop.

I lingered in the doorway, glancing over my shoulder in the direction of the kitchen. "Should we be in here?"

He chuckled as he keyed in her password, and her computer came to life with a cheery noise. "It's fine. She's not like you about her office."

He beckoned me over. With one last doubtful glance over my shoulder, I went. I was fully prepared to post up behind the chair, but he pulled me down on his lap instead. Startled, I nearly slid right off. I looped my arm around his neck just in time.

Once I was sure I wasn't going to make a crash landing on the cream carpet, I patted his chest with my free hand. "Hey, Santa."

He grinned. "I'm not asking because I *know* which list you're on. Pretty sure you have a lifetime membership."

He yelped when I gave him the pinch he so richly deserved. I followed that up with a sound of faux dismay—certain parts of him were a lot more awake than they should be. Especially in his mother's fucking office in his mother's fucking chair.

"What do you expect?" He gave me an unrepentant look. "You're on my lap and you're wearing those jeans."

"You *put* me on your lap and what's so special about these jeans?"

He arched a brow. "Fishing? Really?"

My lips twitched. I'd have to be dumb, deaf, and blind not to understand how fond he was of my ass. And I didn't mind choosing jeans that did wonderful things to it, just to torture him in public.

That didn't mean I was going to admit a damn thing.

"I'm absolutely certain I don't know what you mean," I said with my nose in the air. I was going to wear these jeans every chance I got until I finally expired from loss of circulation to my restricted legs. "And not that I'm complaining, but aren't we supposed to be working?"

"We'll get it done," he said confidently as he plugged in the micro flash drive. "Or, at least, I will. Yours looked a little wobbly."

I smothered a laugh as he clicked on the video file. "Shut up. Once I add the shelves, it'll look better." Or buckle and collapse. Whatever. "You'll see."

I expected the video to start with a snippet from our wedding. Instead, it started with a black screen with just our names in fancy script and the date we'd been "established." Like we were fine wine or some shit. I eyed the beginning date because no way in hell was I that fucking old.

"You've been in my life too long," I informed Danny. Needling him was a far superior option to acknowledging the burning sensation in my tear ducts.

"Seems longer every year," he agreed readily.

I tried to pinch him again, but he grabbed my wrist and kissed my palm instead.

The pictures from the courthouse were about as hilarious as I'd imagined. Everyone was wearing something different—hell, it didn't even look like we knew each other, much less that we were going to the same event. I chuckled under my breath at the next picture of Paula standing to the side of Danny and me. She was looking at our outfits yet again—*not* riot gear, despite what she kept saying—and the look on her face was priceless.

There was a series of stills featuring members of our team. Kevin and Nick laughing. Tab straightening Nick's collar…I peered closer. No, she was strangling him a bit. That tracked. That segued into a photo of Danny and I sitting shoulder to shoulder on the floor. My head was resting against the wall and my eyes were closed, the very picture of excitement.

Then there were some of my family. My mother, her flowing skirt elegant and her sandals dainty as she dabbed at her eyes. My father in a Bermuda-shirt and old man sandals—with tall white socks no less. And my nieces facing off, their expressions thunderous, clearly mid-argument. If I recalled, they were fighting over who was going to be the flower girl, a position that entailed them tossing all of ten seconds worth of flowers my sister had brought.

I was surprised that the next picture was not wedding-related, but of Danny and I sailing on his uncle's boat. We'd fished all day in the Keys and then ordered pizza because the fish were all too cute to eat. The next photo was of the two of us at a baseball game, wearing jerseys. I wasn't into sports, but our lieutenant had given us the tickets, which meant we *had* to use them. Danny had his arm slung over my shoulders and I was wearing a backwards cap that he'd plopped on my head. I kept telling him that I didn't have a hat head, but he'd insisted that I looked cute.

"Where'd she get these?" I asked, my voice a little hushed.

"She asked me for some of my favorites. I didn't know what she wanted them for." He shrugged. "I thought she was doing some *Mixtiles* shit or something."

I chuckled as a photo came up of Watson. That fucking ham. He was wearing sunglasses and grinning, backlit by the sinking sun on the beach. I'd propped the shades on his snout as a lark, then had to chase him to get them back. Cue me shouting, "Those are Tom Ford, you mutt," as I sprinted down the beach. Luckily, they fell off Watson's face before he dived in the surf in a desperate attempt to avoid capture.

My laughter faded as a more serious segment of pictures from our wedding came up. No tuxes or flowers or fancy church for us, but the gravitas of the situation was palpable. And the look on Danny's face when he put the ring on my finger, well…I hadn't held it together then and I was hard pressed to hold it together now.

Not to be corny or anything, but sometimes I just looked at him like…I found you. *How? How the fuck did I manage that? In the wilds of dating and love, I found you.* Sometimes it had felt like digging through a discount bin of scraps, looking for a potential mate—*not you, not you, oh dear God, definitely not you*. And somehow, I'd come up with not just a potential winner, but The One. Because every time I looked at him, I knew that's exactly what he was.

That's not to say things are absolutely perfect. He can be anal about certain things. Heaven help me if I tracked mud in on his precious hardwood floors. The phrase, *Jesus, I said I'd clean it up later* may have been used. And I couldn't leave the bed for over fifteen minutes. I'd come back to bed, eager to slide right back into my comfy nest, only find it already made with my pillows fucking fluffed. He also wouldn't leave any dishes in the sink overnight—not even soaking. But as it turns out, I can live with a lot, as long as I get to live with Daniel Christiansen McKenna.

Fuck, I even loved that we had the same last name. We didn't make a fuss at work about it, and most people still called us by our individual last names. I also refused to go through the trouble to change anything other than my license…not until I absolutely had to. I was sure that would bite me in the ass at some point. But for now, *we* knew what it officially was, and that was enough. It made me grin like an idiot any time I had to sign something. It also made me have to write really small to make it all fit because goddamn, a signature line is only so long.

The more I looked at the montage of our life, the calmer I felt.

We'd already been through so much—good and bad—and there would be even more still to come. This would be just one more step on our journey. One more thing to link us together. And those links weren't breakable—they were titanium strong. It was hard to believe that as good as it was, we could have more. And I'd never been good at moderation.

I wanted it all.

I looked at the words Paula had written across the photo of our entwined hands. I smiled a little because he must've told her about the inscription in our rings. "All roads lead to you," I said softly.

"I've been completely lost on you since the first time I laid eyes on your face," he said with a wry chuckle. "So I think this goes without saying, but I'm going to say it anyway. I don't need anything else. You're enough—what we have is enough. Always has been. Always will be."

"Ditto," I said, my voice a little scratchy.

"So tell me what you want, because I want to do this with you. But only if that's what you want, too."

I didn't even have to think about it. I'd thought about it enough. Now all I had to do was give him the answer in my heart. "Yeah, it is. We're good, Irish."

He searched my face to see the truth of it. And whatever he saw made a slow smile spread over his mouth. "Yeah?"

"Yeah."

I thought it would be best to seal that deal with a kiss. A very long kiss that involved mapping his mouth thoroughly. And then going back in to make sure my take on the topography of his tongue was correct.

"I wasn't aware there was so very much kissing involved in building furniture," a starchy voice said from the doorway.

I broke away from Danny with a startled noise. Not a squeak. Okay, maybe a squeak. He slowly spun us around in the chair to give his mother an apologetic look. "We're working on it."

"You're certainly working on something, that's for sure," she said.

"Ma—"

"Don't *Ma* me. You're the one making out in my chair."

He sighed in exasperation. "Can we not?"

"If you wish, dear. I'm nothing if not accommodating." She looked particularly pleased with herself. "Daniel, I need your help to pick up something."

That netted her a groan and a heartfelt, *oh God*. He rubbed a hand down his face, lingering on his scruff. If I had to guess, he was probably debating if he needed to shave.

Yes. The answer was always yes.

"No more baby furniture," he finally said.

She huffed. "No more baby furniture, I swear. Unless I see something *really* good that you can't live without." Before we could object, she powered on. "It probably would've been more accurate for me to say we're picking up *someone*. Not something."

"Who?"

"William. The neighbor's son."

Ooh, she was playing with fire. Three William mentions in a very short time was two too many. Sure enough, Danny frowned. "Since when are you on such good terms with their son?"

Her cheeks turned fetchingly pink. "Just doing a favor for a neighbor. You know how it is."

I could feel Danny's gaze on my face as he tried to puzzle things out. If it wasn't his mother, I was pretty sure he would've put it together by now. I busied myself by disconnecting the flash drive properly. This formerly "not a picture guy" now had grand ideas for the boring wall in our den. *Mixtiles* here I come.

"Rain, would you mind keeping an eye on my stew?" she asked. "In a half-hour, just fish out the bay leaves, turn off the stove, add a bag of frozen peas and put on the lid." She snapped her fingers. "Oh, and give it a taste and add salt and pepper if you need to. And if the liquid is too low, I have beef stock in the fridge. But not too much, it should be perfectly seasoned at that point."

Stock? Bay leaves? I was pretty sure everything she was talking about was beyond Level Scrambled Eggs—which I fucking aced, thank you very much—but I nodded gamely. *No big.*

"Maybe we should just turn the stove off, and you can finish the stew when we get back," Danny said hesitantly.

Judas. I pinched the inside of his arm and he yelped.

"It's not a problem," I said breezily.

It was a problem. It was a very big problem.

No matter how much I stirred, the bay leaves remained elusive. And all my fussing about with a wooden spoon started mushing the peas. I gave up on it pretty quickly. We'd just treat each person's bowl like a box of Cracker Jacks, with a bay leaf as a prize. As if that wasn't bad enough, I over-salted and over-peppered, then tried to make up for it by adding too much stock. That made the stew too bland, so I salted some more.

Aaaand we were back at salty.

More…stock, then? Container of beef stock in hand, I stared at the still burbling stew. Then at my reflection in the mirrored cooktop. I realized with wonder that I would probably keep going until it was actually inedible.

I decided to leave well enough alone and put the lid on confidently. My prior plan had been to partake in the stew. Maybe even have a few of the buttery rolls Paula hadn't baked off yet. My new plan consisted of my being long gone before anyone dipped a spoon in it and figured out what I'd done.

I decided to leave kitchen things to those who knew better and scampered off to finish up the bookcases. And that was going great until one of the drawers wouldn't go in properly. I took it out and reseated it, but it still wouldn't fit. I blew out a breath that sent my hair flying.

This just wasn't my day for assembling.

I tried to be smart and patient. I watched two YouTube videos of people putting it together perfectly, then tried again—with their useless fucking tips—to no avail. Then I got my degree from the University of Brute Force, jamming the drawer in two more times before common sense prevailed. If I broke it, I'd have to buy a new one. *And* build that fucker again.

I laid on the carpet—sprawled, really. The errant drawer rested on my stomach. I stared at the rotating ceiling fan for a few minutes before I closed my eyes. If it was my bookcase, I would've given up eons ago. But this was Paula.

Paula.

She needed smelling salts when I forgot to use a coaster.

"You installed one of the drawer hinges upside down."

I opened one eye to find Quinn kneeling by the bookcase and examining the slot where the drawer went. "Oh, thank God," I muttered. "I'm starting to think I have a problem."

"It's a tad...wobbly, isn't it?"

I glared. "Did you just show up to bust my balls about my building skills?"

"Or lack thereof," she muttered. "No, I came here to...well, to apologize."

"For what?"

"You know exactly what." She lowered herself to the floor and pulled up her knees, then wrapped her arms around them. "I should've helped you more with the Hope House situation."

"No argument here," I murmured as I examined the drawer slot myself. It didn't look like I'd have to take anything else apart to fix it. Thank the Lord. "I guess the question is why would you protect people whose actions led to the demise of your entire family?"

"Because what was done was done. How would sending Evie Sinclair to prison help anyone?"

"I'm thinking all the people she killed while you were debating that question are probably raising their hands right about now," I said dryly. "I don't understand. You were so desperate to flush out their crime that you hired Caitlin Closs to infiltrate Project Halo."

"I know, I know." She winced. "It's hard to explain. I was just...so conflicted. I'm a rule follower at heart, and an advocate for using the systems we have in place as a society. But sometimes those systems don't work. I shouldn't have to tell you that."

Finished putting the hinge on the right way, I sat back on my haunches. The drawer slid in seamlessly, and I resisted the urge to spike my screwdriver with triumph. "If everyone dubs themselves judge and executioner, then the entire system collapses. I shouldn't have to tell you *that*."

She bit her lip as she debated on what, if anything, to admit to me. "If you're sure," she finally whispered.

"What?"

"I don't suppose you've heard of Bonnie Light."

I shook my head as I mentally rifled through my case files. "Was she a member of Project Halo?"

"No," she said softly. "She was one of my biggest regrets."

I eased to a sitting position. I copied her pose without realizing it, my arms locked around my knees. "Tell me about her. Because right now I don't understand, and I really need to."

"She was...well, she was lovely. She married young, mostly to get out from under her conservative family's thumb. They were extremists that wouldn't even let her wear pants or cut her hair. You know the type." At my slight nod, she continued. "Unfortunately, she wound up with a guy who made her upbringing seem like a picnic. His favorite move was to beat her with a belt, and he always left marks with that enormous buckle."

"Did she refuse to report the abuse?"

She nodded. "He had her convinced that if she left him, she'd have nothing. She'd *be* nothing. And she'd never see her boys again. I tried to convince her to stay at the Hope House, but I couldn't break through the wall of fear he'd built."

"So what happened?" I asked quietly.

"She showed up at my house one night with more bruises across her back and buttocks. This time, he'd even broken skin, which he was usually careful not to do. When I examined her in the bathroom, she left blood marks on the counter."

Color had suffused her sweetly rounded face, sending her perpetually pink cheeks into the red zone. I could certainly relate. I actually had to work to relax my jaw. "Surely, that was enough to keep her from going back."

She shook her head slowly. "I thought I had her. She finally agreed to move into the Hope House and spent the night on my couch. But her husband showed up the next morning. I blocked the door and threatened to call the police. I didn't even know how he found my address until Bonnie calmly ducked underneath my arm and stood next to him." Her lips tightened. "She'd told him where she was. I could see the decision written all over her face."

"Sometimes the first time leaving doesn't take," I said. "That wall of fear you spoke of can be pretty high—"

"I know that!" She blew out a breath and gave me an apologetic look. "I *know* that. We saw that a lot. You just provide support and a nonjudgmental safe space until they can do it in their own time."

"But you just had a feeling."

"If you're sure." Her eyes looked a bit glassy. "Those were the last words I ever said to her. She was dead by the next morning."

The sorrow came off her in waves, and I felt horribly inadequate to offer her comfort. "I'm sorry," I finally said. "I know that had to be heartbreaking."

"For lack of stronger words." She sniffed a couple times, rubbing her nose. "So yes, Detective, my first reaction to Project Halo was horror. But then I started to think maybe they were right."

I certainly wasn't going to lie—I would've loved to see Bonnie Light have more time on this earth while her husband rotted in the ground. But justified murder was a slippery slope that we weren't equipped to handle. Where did the line begin and where did it end? And more importantly, who got to make that call? I never wanted to become the thing I despised.

No matter what the cost.

I took in the pugnacious tilt of her chin. Clearly, she was expecting me to argue with her into the next century. I didn't oblige. I didn't need her aggressive body language to know I wasn't about to change her mind, no matter what I said.

I decided to focus on more prevalent matters. "How did you know something was amiss with Farrah's story about Gil?"

"I was so happy when he took off. He left a mess behind, yes, but he was *gone* and that was the most important thing. Everything else would come out in the wash. But then....." She bit her lip. "I was helping her clean out the house and all the crap he'd left behind, and I felt like something was off."

"Why?"

"The vibe was just wrong. She wasn't nervous at all. They're always nervous, even when there's no possibility that he's coming back. Years of living under someone's thumb can do that to you."

"People are allowed to react in different ways."

"True," she allowed. "But I also saw her at the Hope House. She was helping in the garden, and let me tell you, manual labor isn't really a Farrah thing." She frowned. "I asked her about it a few days later, and she flat out denied even being there. That made me even *more* sure that something was wrong."

"What was the tipping point?" I asked.

"I found the box when I tripped over a piece of upraised carpet in her bedroom," she said. "While I was trying to smooth it down, I found a latch. I opened it and found a little hidden box no bigger than a drawer."

"Did you open it?"

"Of course I did. I found his wallet and passport, which was disturbing enough." She swallowed hard. "Then I found the medal."

I looked at her blankly. "What kind of medal?"

"Gil's grandfather was in the Olympics. He was so proud of that thing, you'd think he earned it himself." She shook her head. "Maybe he'd leave his wallet behind if he was starting anew. Or even his passport if he knew where to get a fake one. But there was no possible way he'd leave that medal behind."

"So you knew he was dead," I surmised.

She nodded. "And I wasn't sorry," she said, a touch defiantly. "I just wasn't sure how it happened. Farrah isn't that kind of person...at least, I thought she wasn't. I knew whatever terrible thing had happened was an accident. Or maybe he'd even killed himself. I figured if I gave her time and space, she'd confide in me."

"But she didn't."

"No, and my suspicions grew."

"Moira McDaniels and Stacey Pittman," I guessed.

She gave me a sad little smile. "Gold star, Detective. Evie kept touting these cases as positive results, but like I said, I've been doing this a long time. It's not usually the abuser that disappears."

I let out a sigh. "So you recruited Caitlin to help you infiltrate Project Halo and confirm your suspicions."

She nodded. "She's alright, isn't she?"

"In a manner of speaking," I said, rubbing the back of my tense neck. *Probably wishing she'd never laid eyes on you, though.* "I don't suppose you know what she does with the heads."

She shook her head. "We only got to stage three of Project Halo."

I already knew exactly what stage four was, no infiltration required. Somehow, Evie or maybe even Javi got the abuser in their custody, drugged and trussed up like a turkey. They took them out to some remote location and gave them the means to cut their ropes when they woke up. And then?

Run for your life.

"I should've told you," she said, her voice small. "I can make this right."

"You're making it right by telling me now."

"I just...I want to do more." She brightened. "You're looking to adopt."

I furrowed my brow at her as I tried to follow her sudden change of topic—and her worrisome interest in my private life. "Whatever you're thinking, the answer is no."

"I can help! Regan has this friend. I think she'd be the perfect match for you."

"You found Regan?" I smiled a little at her nod. "I'm glad. I was a little surprised she wasn't with Ryan."

"I should've known where I'd find her. She's always been my

social butterfly, whereas Ryan preferred books to people's company." She looked at me eagerly. "So about her friend—"

"Thank you, but no," I said firmly.

Her chin jutted out stubbornly. "She needs you. Both of you."

That went without saying—maybe not me, but someone. I'd seen the website link Harper sent to us. Pages upon pages of children up for adoption, listed online like puppies or some shit. *Brad is sweet and well-mannered and loves riding his bike.* Waiting for someone to choose them. Waiting for a good home. For someone to swoop in and show them that they were worth more—that they were worth everything.

"They all do," I said, more to myself than anyone else. "But no. We'll handle our personal lives ourselves."

She sighed, looking let down. "Okay. But maybe I can give you something else." Before I could open my mouth to deny her again, she shook her head. "Not the adoption thing. Although I'm not ruling that out entirely—"

"Quinn—"

"The bodies," she said quickly. "I can tell you how she repurposed them."

Good Lord, would folks ever stop coming up with new and inventive ways to destroy my faith in humanity? "Repurposed?" I asked warily.

"Detective," she said, biting her lip. "What do you know about compost?"

27

In the end, we didn't spend Thanksgiving in Paula's beautifully decorated dining room, parked in front of a table laden with food. Instead, we found ourselves at BBPD in a briefing room packed with law enforcement. A serial killer was on the loose, and we needed all hands on deck.

Because the room was overcrowded, the air was hot and stagnant. We were short on chairs, space, pens, and—when the coffee ran out—patience. I hadn't been afraid to use elbows and managed to snag one of the four squeaky rolling chairs. I sat next to an agent named Marks, who seemed to think my former FBI credentials made us good enough friends to bump elbows. He'd already discarded the jacket from a wrinkled suit that had once been crisp. I knew from experience that the tie would follow soon enough.

As for me, years in the PTU had finally done the trick on my attire. I was at my casual Friday best in dark gray trousers and a navy button-down shirt, the sleeves rolled to the elbows. And a slim gray tie. A silver, understated watch. Shiny hard shoes....

Okay, fine. I still had a way to go on the whole "casual" bit.

Technically, the PTU was still in charge of the case. But Tate's superiors had thought it a good idea to "liaison with other departments." A lot of them. Tate was at the front, standing next to my whiteboard as she led the briefing. Danny was half-sitting on a table to her left, arms folded across his chest. He'd been out in the field, so he was all in black, his off-duty badge hanging from a silver chain around his neck.

Tate started making arrows in red marker...on *my* carefully curated whiteboard. I grabbed my chest as I shot out of my chair. Danny gave me a wide-eyed look and a slight head shake. My trusty married folks ESP said he was begging me not to do something we'd both regret dearly.

I sank back down in my chair with a huff of indignation.

All in the name of justice, I suppose.

"I'm just going to be blunt," Tate said, her face etched with tired lines. It had been a long seventy-two hours for all of us. "We've got a serial killer out there, and we need to act quickly and efficiently. The media is already sniffing around since we executed a search warrant on the Hope House. By the time they get the whole story, I want Ms. Sinclair in cuffs."

Easier said than done.

It had been three days since anyone had seen Evie Sinclair. Or her daughter Maya. And three days since we'd shown up, fast-tracked warrant in hand, to search the Hope House. I hadn't been the least bit surprised to find her gone. We'd already proven she had friends in mysterious places. Guess one of those mysterious friends had given her the heads-up.

Considering what we found when we executed that search warrant, she'd better *stay* gone.

"Christiansen?" I sat up in my chair and it gave an ear-piercing squeak. "Yes?"

"Why don't you give the room a rundown on what we found at the Hope House?"

I grimaced as I gave them a summary on human composting.

It wasn't a crowd pleaser.

There had been half-decomposed remains in a barrel of compost, which meant—and let me see if I can phrase this in fancy legalese—

Evie Sinclair was in deep shit. We'd also rounded up several of her cohorts, who claimed they'd seen others. That meant the deep shit had a nice sublayer of quicksand.

Ghoul that he was, Saunders had been thrilled to encounter something in practice that he'd only heard about in theory. His human composting lecture had been *long*. And gross. All I'd known about composting was that it recycled organic waste into fertilizer. What I *didn't* know was that the human body could be considered as organic waste.

"*When they put the body in a container with carbon-rich materials, they created an environment in which decomposing organisms could grow,*" Saunders had said excitedly. "*Like bacteria. Fungi.*"

My stomach wobbled. "Sounds...lovely."

He gave me a happy smile that was incongruous with his grumpy face. "Those decomposing organisms feed on the carbon, while nitrogen allows them to reproduce and grow."

"How long does the process normally take?"

"Eight to twelve weeks." *He still seemed a little too excited about the possibility of becoming mulch.* "And of course, you can speed things along by adding protozoa and bacteria. It's all perfectly legal in some states."

"Not this one," I said grimly.

"Understood. But there is something to be said for the green burial movement."

Yes, there was plenty to say. We could start with the word creepy and go from there.

He peered at my face as I sucked in a quick breath. "Are you alright, Detective?"

If I had to guess, I was probably a little gray. Mostly because I'd just remembered that I'd bought a few bags. And gifted fertilizer to my parents where the first ingredient was humans.

So. Yeah. That happened.

I couldn't help but remember Franklin's irritated face after my parents spread the fertilizer. *The soil is always talking.*

And now I knew why.

By the time I finished, one of the detectives in the front had his hand over his stomach. He looked like he was holding down his lunch with sheer will. I hurriedly took my seat.

Tate cleared her throat, looking a little green herself. "As you can see, I've brought in extra help. I've reassigned cases to free up that extra help, and I am approving overtime. I've done whatever I can do to dissolve all the obstacles hindering you, so give me results. *Fast.*"

I half-listened as Tate continued to list all the things she'd done to help us do our job.

When I'd broken the fertilizer news to my parents, they'd only cared about the bad energy that it must've carried. My mother was also seriously considering green burial for herself, which was rather on brand.

"I want to be a daffodil," she said, peering at me earnestly. As if that wasn't the weirdest shit she'd ever said to me. *"I don't expect you to compost me yourself, though."*

Aaaaand we have a tie.

"That's probably for the best," I'd said dryly. "Especially considering it's highly illegal in the state of Florida."

"Traditional burials have such negative effects on the environment," she fussed. *"And did you know that embalming uses eight hundred gallons of toxic chemicals annually?"*

"Cremation, then," I said a little desperately. "The process of cremation—"

"Releases carbon dioxide and mercury into the air." She tsked even as she advanced on me with motherly menace. *"You wouldn't want that, would you? You'd think someone with such a spiritual name as Rainstorm Moonbeam would care about the earth."*

"My name isn't—ow!" I rubbed the ear she'd tweaked. "Fuc—frick, I do care about the earth, woman."

Composting her in the backyard was starting to look like a fine option, legalities be damned. Although I supposed that would get in the way of my ultimate plan, which was her never dying. Ever.

"Christiansen, are you coming?"

I looked up to find Nick giving me a strange look. I heard chairs scraping the floor and a lot of movement around the room, and realized that sometime during my mental meanderings, the meeting had been dismissed.

I sighed. "Of course."

It was late when I finally left the station. There was still so much to do with the murder ring that I almost felt guilty going home. But Danny firmly told me to get some shut eye. He was currently harassing Andrea, the D.A., to let him write up an arrest warrant for Arianna Pemburton. She hadn't been pleased when he and Kevin showed up on her doorstep—on a holiday, no less. That displeasure grew by leaps and bounds as they explained the situation to her in her grandmother's cozy sitting room.

Apparently, we didn't meet the standards for evidence.

I was a little tired of hearing that.

I knew I just needed to be patient. The Hope House's network hadn't been built in a day. Dismantling it wouldn't take a day, either. As long as we chopped off the heads of the snakes, we could round up the rest of the wriggling pieces later. Or something less disgusting.

I groaned as I coasted to a stop in my driveway and spotted the Crown Vic parked slightly to the side. After the day I'd had, I wasn't in the mood for company. I *really* wasn't in the mood for that company to be Zach.

He looked about as happy to see me as I was to see him. I waited on the porch as he got out of his car and ambled up the drive, the fading sun glinting on his chestnut hair. He was a lot less handsome now that I knew him better. He wasn't a dirty cop, but he had ridden that line so closely that it was a near miss. And I had no use for that in my life—professionally or personally.

From the way he just stood there at the bottom step, eyeing me, I was wearing that conclusion all over my face. "I'd hoped to speak to Danny," he finally said.

Well, you can use this thing called a cellphone.

"He's still at the station," I said. I was too tired for snark. Too tired.

For snark? I was tempted to check my pulse. "If you hurry, you can probably catch him."

"Thanks," he said stiffly.

"No problem."

We didn't bother with any other pleasantries. He just turned and headed back down the drive. I watched him walk back to his car, almost feeling a little sorry for him. There was no getting back into Danny's good graces at this point. He'd destroyed their trust and trust was everything to Danny.

Zach had known him a long time, so he really should've known that.

My phone rang in my pocket. I answered as I closed the door behind me. "Yeah, Chev, what's up?"

"Hello to you, too," she said. "I'm not sure how you got me officially assigned to this shitshow, but thanks a lot."

I snorted as I kicked off my loafers. "Hey, all I did was suggest we bring in the FBI. The rest was just the magic of bureaucracy."

I lined up my loafers by the door and dropped my keys in the bowl. Nice, normal things that let me know I was well and truly home. As I shuffled to the kitchen on bare feet, I acknowledged how very tired I was.

I was already jonesing to put this day behind me. In the morning, I'd be refreshed and ready to chase down an elusive serial killer again. Right now, I was good for only two things—inhaling some food and getting some sleep.

"Did you find out something I should know?" I asked,

"Yes, but it's not as fun if I'm *supposed* to be doing it," she whined.

I chuckled. "Spill it, Sullivan."

She huffed. "Well, I was doing a little digging about the whole Project Halo thing and Angel Ruiz."

"Danny already told me about Angel Ruiz."

"Did he tell you everything?" Chevy asked, sounding a little put out.

"Well, how would I know if I know everything if I don't know what I don't know?"

She paused. "What?"

I rubbed my weary eyes. "Please don't ask me to untangle that," I begged. "It's...been a long fucking day."

She laughed. "Well, luckily for you, all you have to do now is listen."

I flicked on the kitchen light and made a beeline for the fridge. I was rather comforted by the fact that she wasn't asking for permission. Whatever she had to say, I was going to hear it. Might as well skip the kicking and screaming part.

"Well, as you know, Angel Ruiz was Evie's aunt. Angel had been encouraged by her family to leave her husband Patrick for years. And let me tell you, after seeing his rap sheet, I'd say that was pretty solid advice."

"All domestic?"

"Well, abuse was certainly his favorite flavor," she confirmed. "But he dabbled in grand theft, fraud, extortion and the like."

This Patrick Ruiz guy sounded like a real treat.

I grimaced as I opened the fridge. Then, I moved a smoothie out of the way to take a gander at the contents. As I mentally cataloged them by degree of edibleness, Chevy detailed the worst of Patrick Ruiz's crimes.

After taking a bite of cheese and a spoonful of chili, I eyed the smoothie again. It was hard to ignore the smiley face Post-it with my name on the bottom. Clearly, my mother had been busy making healthy shots again. Every time I managed to choke down my supply, the woman had already whipped up a fresh batch.

I sighed as I took it off the shelf. I had a routine physical scheduled next month and my labs better be fucking *fantastic*. I took a sip of the green sludge and shuddered. Chevy was still prattling on in my ear about Patrick Ruiz and his laundry list of crimes.

"I mean, really, who steals from a children's charity?" she demanded. "The man had no morals to speak of—"

"What does any of this have to do with Angel Ruiz?" I asked, well aware I was risking my very life by interrupting.

"I'm getting there," she growled.

"Hop in and let me give you a lift," I said, thoroughly exasperated. I was dead on my feet, and I was ready for a hot shower and a long nap on the couch that started with me pretending to watch TV.

She huffed. "Angel left her husband a few times, but he threatened to kill himself if she didn't come back. Finally, she had enough and left to stay with her sister, Marta."

"Evie's mother," I said.

"Exactly."

I took another long sip of my drink. It wasn't half bad, which either meant my mother was getting better at this smoothie business or my taste buds had finally given up and died. Maybe I was just hungry as hell, and anything would taste like the nectar of the gods.

"So after about three months of living with her sister, Angel filed for divorce. That happened to be the catalyst that sent Patrick over the edge," Chevy went on. "He broke into her sister's house during the night, dousing Angel's bed with gasoline and lighting a match. Everyone in the room was burned including Evie—"

"And Angel and her child, Tomas, died," I said, wincing. "Unfortunately, I'm aware."

"Well, I did a little digging and talked to one of the firefighters on the scene. Jim Flannery. He's retired now, about 80 years plus and chatty as all get out. I only talked to the man for an hour, and I can tell he's equal parts forgetful and sharp as a tack."

I chuckled. "I'm guessing anyone who told him a secret in the past will be a suspect in his future murder."

"Pretty much," she agreed. "And as it turns out, the baby did *not* die. But they weren't about to turn him over to his father's side of the family. Not only was he a murderer, but Patrick had ties to a street gang based in Miami called *Los Lobos Salvajes*."

The wild wolves. "So what happened to the baby?" I asked.

"They gave him a new identity and entered him into foster care."

I polished off the rest of the smoothie and took the container over to the sink. It wasn't my mother's usual recyclable bottle. This one was fancy-looking and made of glass. I decided to wash it immediately because if I had to guess, she was probably going to want this one back.

"Let me guess, the child disappeared into the system?" I asked over the sound of water as I gave the bottle a good wash.

"I *am* the system," she said smartly. "When will people learn there's no getting away from Chevrolet Sullivan?"

"God bless your poor fiancé," I said fervently. "Tell him that I can at least help him to the border. After that, he's on his own."

She huffed. "Do you want the name or not?"

"Lay it on me."

"Zachary Owens."

I couldn't say a word, processing those two words. Just two itty bitty words.

I proceeded to add a third.

Zachary fucking Owens. The same Zachary Owens that had been working the original case and "missed" a ton of clues that even the greenest detective would've seen? The same one who Caleb had informed about Caitlin Closs, whose name miraculously never made it into the case file?

Realization after realization tumbled over one another in my mind like falling dominoes. Honestly, it felt like she'd hit me over the head with a 2x4.

The same Zachary Owens who'd shown up unexpectedly at BBPD and inserted himself into our investigation? The same one who talked to Caitlin Closs and let her know, in no uncertain terms, what would happen if she kept running off at the mouth about the Hope House?

The same Zachary Owens that I'd sent to find my husband?

The bottle fell from my fingers and clattered in the sink. Chevy was still prattling on as I made my way to the living room quickly. "Apparently, he's currently on suspension from PBPD."

I wheezed. "Not on vacation?"

"No," she confirmed. "He gave an abused woman a gun and several lessons on how to use it, just in case her father violated her protective order. She shot him a couple weeks later."

"Sounds like legitimate self-defense if the father violated a PO," I said slowly.

"She went to his house and hunted him down, supposedly at the advice of Detective Owens. Which he denied, of course," she said dryly. "Allegedly, he told her that waiting is the difference between becoming the deer or the hunter."

Run for your life.

I closed my eyes briefly as I stuck my feet in my loafers and grabbed my keys. "I gotta go, Chev," I said hurriedly as I practically flew out the door, slamming it shut behind me. "I need to call—"

"No one," a voice said firmly. "You're calling absolutely no one."

Well. I guess there was a bright side to all of this. I swallowed hard as I looked from Zach's cold, resolved face, and back to the gun. At least he wasn't off killing my husband.

Yep, my inner bitch confirmed, who didn't seem to care whether I lived or die. *He's not off killing Danny because he's penciled you in first.*

"Rain?" The fact that Chevy was using my first name summed things up. Shit had just got very real. "I thought I heard...was that Owens?"

"Yes. You can absolutely come for Thanksgiving," I said calmly as Zach gestured for my phone. "I'm going to have to call you back."

I hung up on her intake of breath. Okay, so she'd gotten my message and the cavalry was coming. I just had to last until then.

Easier said than done.

I handed over my phone wordlessly, watching as Zach gave it a major league pitch into the thick foliage next to the house. We stared at each other, the moments stretching into something dark and ominous. I shivered slightly. It wasn't all that chilly outside so I could only assume my body was reacting to the situation.

This wasn't some junkie with shaking hands. Or someone who got their gun training from watching TV. He was as trained as I was. The same *way* I was. Which meant I was in some serious trouble. I was just glad my parents weren't home. And whatever was going to happen needed to happen before that changed.

"So." I was proud that my voice was steady even though I felt the cold down to my bones. "What's the plan?"

"I'm sorry." He looked genuinely regretful. "This is going to hurt him and that's the last thing I want to do. But you threatened the mission and now she wants you gone. It's the only way I can make things right."

"That's...that's crazy," I said, licking my lips. My tongue felt thick and strange in my mouth, and I swallowed a few times. "There's an arrest warrant already prepared for Evie Sinclair. If you really want to make things right, you'll get her to turn herself in—"

"That's not going to happen, and we both know that," he said calmly. Like it would be nothing to put a bullet between my eyes.

A trickle of sweat eased down my back, making me flinch in surprise. I felt like a human popsicle, so I wouldn't have thought sweat was on the docket. I wanted to dab at my perspiring temples, but I wasn't about to make a move. That casual finger on the trigger wasn't fooling anyone.

He held out a pair of cuffs. I gave him a, *you gotta be kidding me* look. "I'm going to have to check the 'not a chance in hell' box for cuffing myself and being led to my death like a docile little lamb."

"And sometimes the lamb, docile or no, has already lost the fight with the opponent he can't see."

I shivered again even as sweat trickled in my eye. My eyes stung immediately. I forgot my own edict not to make any quick movements as my hands darted up automatically, dabbing at the sweat. My vision was a little blurry and I rubbed at them again.

My heart rate kicked into high gear when I realized it wasn't the sweat compromising my vision. And my legs...they felt so *wobbly*. I looked around blearily, confused, almost expecting someone to be behind me. *Someone* had to have kicked my legs out from under me.

I sank to my knees.

"Don't feel very good," I mumbled. It didn't escape my notice, even in my condition, that I was complaining to the last person who would care.

"You're about to feel much worse," he said, tilting his head to the side as he observed me. I was now shivering like I was on day three of a detox program. "Tell me something, Detective. How did you enjoy your smoothie?"

I couldn't answer him, too busy trying to catch myself as I listed to the side. It didn't work, and I hit the deck hard. Stunned, I just lay there for a moment. Gazing at the thicket of woods beyond the house. It was undeveloped and there was always something so serene and peaceful and *right* about the land being untouched. On the rare occasions that I had time, I could sit on the porch for hours with a cup of coffee and a good book. Of course, I was usually curled up in one of our Adirondacks, Watson at my feet. Not lying on the floor.

I blinked blearily. And just why was I on the fucking floor again?

The boards of the deck were smooth against my shirt. Someone had carefully sanded those boards with his own hands. I searched foggily for the name. Danny. Yes, that was it. Halfway through the job, I'd bought him an electric sander and informed him exasperatedly that we weren't Amish. He told me that we could certainly do worse when it came to craftsmanship which, well, wasn't wrong. Craftsmanship and butter, that is.

It took me a few seconds to remember why I was dazed and confused, daydreaming like an idiot when I was very probably about to die. The edges of my vision were starting to fade to black, like a burned photograph. It was a slowly closing circle that I couldn't get to expand no matter how hard I tried.

The blurry image of a man approached the porch, not a drop of hurry in his step. He was wearing boots—brown and well-maintained with thick black soles. I got an even better look at one of them as it headed right for my cheek.

And then the dark circle of my vision closed completely.

28

I woke up confused.

    Disorientated.

Everything was dark and quiet and still. And *cold*. I knew I was outside, that much was for certain. And was that the rough bark of a tree at my back? My head throbbed like a separate entity from my body, and there was something thick and solid encircling my throat. I tried to reach up and check, but something was restricting my movement. Something else was binding the rest of me.

I looked down at my body only to find ropes crisscrossing my midsection. They were tight, but not so tight that I couldn't find any give. Maybe too much give. I couldn't help but think that was purposeful, which left me with even more questions. Who would've tied me to a tree, but not securely enough so that I couldn't get myself free?

Had I been in an accident? The last thing I remembered was driving home after a really long day. No, that wasn't it. I frowned as my sluggish brain tried to spin a little faster. I'd been talking to Chevy and then....

And then....

Oh God.

It was then that I realized I wasn't alone. I blinked at the man across from me, also tied to a tree. Judging from the blood trickling down the side of his face, he'd been hit in the head. More than once.

Zach.

It took a few seconds for me to even recognize him. To be fair, I wasn't exactly crisp at the moment. I was even more confused than before. The last thing I remembered was his boot coming at my face.

My temples ached anew as I made a quick battlefield decision. There would be plenty of time to figure out what was what and how I got here. And what the hell was restricting my throat. Right now, I needed to get myself free and find a phone.

I worked my shoulders side to side, flexing my arms to make them bigger and then smaller. Bigger and then smaller. After a good two minutes of wriggling, I was finally able to work my fingers under the ropes. I used my hands to pull the coil wider and wider, until I had enough room to wriggle free. I staggered to my feet, using the tree for leverage, then worked the ropes down until they pooled like a coiled snake on the ground at my feet.

Immediately, my hands flew to the circle of plastic around my throat. It was sturdy and didn't budge. Not even when I tugged on it so hard that I was sure I'd bruised my skin. Frustrated that I was stuck being collared like an animal for the time being, I made my way over to Zach. I briefly itched with the desire to repay him for that boot in the face—*that,* I remembered in technicolor. But I needed him. He was the only one of us who probably knew where we were and how we could get free.

Didn't mean I was going to wake his ass like a Disney princess, though.

I shook his shoulder, hard enough to send his head lolling. One whiff of the metallic scent of blood, and I knew he wasn't faking his injuries at least. I knelt down beside him. "Zach, you bastard." He moaned faintly and I shook him a bit harder. "You need to wake the fuck up, right the fuck now."

His eyelids fluttered as he coughed weakly. "Stop shaking me, for fuck's sake. I'm awake."

"Well, that's good because my next step was to slap you silly."

He coughed again. "That's not exactly the best way to rouse someone from unconsciousness, you know."

"Maybe not, but it would certainly make me feel better," I said, yanking at his ropes. "Now you're going to help me get the hell out of here."

He didn't seem remotely interested in helping as I struggled to get him free. In fact, he seemed mildly...amused? My hands had been tied behind me so long that I was clumsy where I was normally dexterous, and the sensation of pins and needles made my job that much harder. But there was no time to waste. We needed to get out of here—wherever *here* was. The sooner the better.

I wriggled enough room in his ropes for him to get free...and waited. As he just continued looking at me, I made an impatient sound. "Well, I hope you don't expect me to carry your ass. Get up, princess. Let's go."

He coughed, sending a small spray of blood across his shirt. "She's not going to let me go. I failed to protect the mission." He gave me a drowsy smile, teeth stained with blood. "I thought by bringing you as a gift, I'd earn her forgiveness."

"I'm guessing by the state of you, forgiveness was denied."

He winced as he prodded his side with careful fingers. When he pulled his hand away, it was dark with blood. "Evie does enjoy her knives. She's such a fucking bitch sometimes."

I winced. Not in empathy with that sick fuck, but because I was now under the control of someone who reportedly *enjoyed her knives*. Christ.

"Why me?" I demanded.

"Because you fucked with her mission. And the mission must be—"

"Yeah, yeah, yeah," I muttered, stabbing my fingers through my matted and muddied hair. "You people and your fucking mission."

"You still don't get it, do you?"

Oh, I was certainly starting to. I furrowed my brow, staring at him. "You warned her ahead of time, didn't you? And Javi."

"Do you really want to spend your last moments asking questions you already know the answers to?" He coughed again. Clearly, he had some internal injuries, which wasn't the best news in terms of him living long enough to help me escape. "If you use that big brain of yours, I'll bet you can even hazard a guess at where we are."

"Arianna's estate." I felt cold down to my very bones. Because if I remembered what Danny told me about this place, the grounds were massive. "Is she involved?"

"I don't know how high up the food chain goes."

Well, wasn't that just peachy. "So what, you just woke up one day and decided to join a murder ring? What is *wrong* with you?"

"It wasn't like that," he said wearily. "I wanted to know where I came from, and I started doing some research. Looking for biological family. Most of my father's family is either locked up or deep in a gang—"

"You didn't really luck out on your mother's side, either," I said dryly. "You should've chosen the gang."

"Shut your mouth," he said without heat. "I wanted to get to know my mother, and Evie helped me with that. Then I asked her what happened the day she died. She refused at first, but I kept asking."

"And did she tell you?"

"Eventually. He burned her. *Killed* her. Would've killed me, too," he said, his eyes blazing. "My mother asked for help several times from the authorities, and no one helped her with shit."

"I'm sorry," I said stiffly. "But there's no excuse for—"

"Evie still didn't tell me about the program. It was another two years before I found out, and only by accident."

"How?"

"I stopped by her house on the weekend to surprise her with a desk I found at the flea market. She's always looking for shit like that for the Hope House. When I went around the house to put it in the garage, I smelled decomp. You know that smell."

I nodded. Every cop knew that smell. It was unmistakable.

He leaned his head against the tree trunk and looked up at the sky. "I almost turned her in," he said, somewhat conversationally.

"Are you sorry you didn't?"

It was a moment before he answered me. Mostly because he was coughing up his own blood. His breathing was a lot more labored than it had been before. But his answer was strong and sure. "Not at all." At my expression, he smiled/grimaced. "Maybe one day you'll understand."

My answer was just as sure. "I hope I never do."

Suddenly a bright light came on, piercing enough to make my eyes water. A small green beam appeared in the trees about the size of a penlight, and I squinted into the glare. I looked down at Zach. I could finally see the full extent of his injuries and I sucked in a breath. Getting him to his feet was going to be a challenge, to say the least.

And was that…a ring of skulls? Some of them had holes in them. I looked at the circle that surrounded us, our macabre skeletal audience.

"Well," I murmured. "At least I finally know what she does with the heads."

Zach's face was white as could be, probably from blood loss. He gave a bitter laugh. "I guess everything is ready for the game."

I didn't need to ask what game. I knew. Oh, fuck did I know. The memory of Vincent running through the woods and screaming at Sharla had never been so vivid and fresh in my mind. I touched the collar at my neck. "Is this—"

"A tracker," he said with a bitter laugh. "Do you finally understand what's going to happen here tonight?"

A speaker crackled and I jerked, looking wildly into the trees. I couldn't see a damn thing in the spotlight. I whirled, but there was nothing but darkness beyond our circle. She could be two steps away, and I wouldn't even know.

"Let's play a game!" Canned carnival music followed the child's eager voice. And then he asked eagerly, "Is everybody ready?"

Hell to the no, I wasn't fucking ready.

"We've got to go," I said urgently. "And we've got to go now."

Zach laughed. "I'm not going anywhere, Christiansen. And you're not going anywhere, either. I'm not going to spend the last moments of my life trying to avoid the inevitable."

"Let's play a game," the child said again. "Is everybody ready?"

Fuck your game, lady.

I knelt down hurriedly and finished pulling Zach free of the ropes. When he just sat there, leaning heavily against the tree, I was once again tempted to introduce my boot to his forehead. I yanked on his arm instead. "Do you want to fucking die?"

"Hell of a time to ask that question," he said.

"You *are* showing me the way out of here," I snapped. "And you can either come with me voluntarily or you can be dragged."

He snatched his arm from my grasp. "Don't you get it?" He shouted in my face as I reared back instinctively. "Everyone who plays this game loses. That's the fucking poin—"

His head exploded, spraying blood all over my face.

I just stood there for a few seconds, stunned, looking at the gore painting my hands. I'd seen a lot of people die a lot of different ways. That was just part of the business. But I'd never seen someone's head explode a few scant feet away from my face. I'd never been so covered in their blood that I could almost taste it. I knew I wouldn't forget this moment as long as I lived.

To be fair, that probably wouldn't be long.

"Let's play a game," the child's automated voice said excitedly.

I stumbled backward, looking around the clearing. And then there was the whisper—that voice I'd heard in my dreams—that signaled the start of her horrid little game. "Run for your life."

That was probably good advice.

29

I tore through the trees, running at top speed. Adrenaline surged through my veins as I made my way through the dense woods. The canopy above was so thick that I could barely see anything other than shadowy shapes, and I prayed I wouldn't run headlong into a tree.

Occasionally, a patch of moonlight would break through, and I could see for several glorious minutes before it was dark again. Branches clawed at me as I stumbled over tree roots. I cried out as one snagged on my shirt and ripped the fabric, leaving a long scratch on the skin beneath.

The noises didn't help. Every now and again, there was sinister laughter. Then wind, whistling through the trees much faster than it really was. And the sound of a low growl, somewhere to my left. I poured on speed in the other direction, wondering how much of the atmosphere was real, and how much was simulated. Everything was designed to be a mindfuck, to remind me that I was in Evie's playpen where she made all the rules.

Was she watching me on a security camera? Hell, she didn't even need that. She just needed to use the handy little tracker in my collar. I tried to work my fingers under there again, but there was hardly enough room to fit my pointer finger, much less actually move it around. I crooked my finger and tugged, but all I did was chafe my neck. I wasn't going to break it with my bare hands, and I couldn't seem to find a release mechanism. So...yeah, everything was going smoothly.

As long as I had the collar on, I was probably a moving dot on a map somewhere. Distracted by that realization, I stumbled over a branch and fell, face first, into some water. Darkness enveloped me. Stunned, I sank into the black, freezing water. And then my brain kicked in and I swam hard for the top.

I burst free of the surface, gasping for air. Breathing felt like ambrosia. The sound of a bullet whizzing by my ear wasn't *quite* as welcome.

Okay, so back under I go.

I took a few quick breaths, then one long one before I sank down below. At least a dip in the river would get rid of Zach's blood and... other bits...all over me. Christ. I had to remind myself that there would be time to wrestle with that later.

If I had a later, that is.

I moved through the water smoothly, only coming up for air when I absolutely had to. Something sharp singed my arm and I gasped, surging for the surface once more. I raised my arm slightly above the water, staring at the torn fabric of my sleeve and the red wound on my arm. It was only a graze, but it hurt like hell.

"There's more where that came from, Detective," a disembodied voice informed me smoothly.

I looked around for the speaker, but I had no idea where it could be. It could be designed as a rock or hidden as a plant. Or maybe just mounted in one of the trees. This was Evie's playground, and she wasn't about to let me forget it. She was playing with me. And I wasn't supposed to win.

I spotted an outcropping of rocks and sank below the water again. I swam for it, expecting a bullet to the back with every stroke. I was almost surprised when I felt the rough rock against my palm. I came up behind it, breathing shallowly. I wasn't sure if I was directly in her sight or hidden completely. I just hoped my head wasn't about to explode.

A hand grabbed my arm and I gasped. "It's just me," a familiar voice said.

"Franklin?" I knuckled water out of my eyes and coughed as a small wave of water caught me in the face. "What're you doing here?"

"I live here." As I continued to stare at him blankly, he made an impatient noise. "Barclay and I used to gallop through these woods long ago. It's one of my favorite places to be. Or at least it was."

"Why didn't you...why didn't you tell me about this place?" I sputtered.

He scratched his head. "Well, I kind of did."

"No, you gave me body parts and a mystery. That is *not* telling me about it."

"I beg to differ. Besides, I was a bit conflicted." He scratched his head. "On one hand, murder is just terrible. But on the other hand, they were *really* bad men, you know?"

I stared. "Maybe when I get out of here, I'll create a seminar called, *Killing Is Wrong*. I invite you to attend."

"I said I was sorry."

"You actually did not, in fact."

"Sorry," he burst out. "But I was talking to Quinn, and she told me about this woman named Bonnie Light—"

"Seriously?" I croaked.

"Well, anyway," he said, flapping his hands. "There's no time for that. She can't see you right now, but she has a drone that she sends out for her craftier prey."

Jesus Christ. If she sent that thing out, I was pretty much done for.

"You just have to hang on a little while longer," he said urgently. "And I'm going to help you."

"How?"

"I've been disabling cameras," he said proudly. "Otherwise, she would've had you long before now."

I beat back another wave, coughing. I thought back to the aerial view of Arianna's estate and remembered it was surrounded by a large iron fence. "I need to get to the fence."

"That collar will shock you."

"Okay," I said slowly. "Add getting the collar off to the list."

But one thing at a damn time. Right now, my main concern was keeping my head attached to my shoulders.

I wriggled a finger under the blasted thing again. It didn't feel indestructible, but I was going to need more than the strength of my index finger. "I need tools," I murmured.

Franklin brightened as he snapped his fingers. "I have just the thing. Follow me."

And then he fucking disappeared.

"Franklin," I hissed.

Bloody ghosts. If I could fucking do *that*, I'd just poof myself back home.

After a moment, he reappeared, a sheepish look on his face. "Sorry." He held out his hand, wispy and pale in the moonlight. When I hesitated, he gave me a chiding look. "I'm about the only friend you've got right about now."

I took his hand even as I murmured, "You're not exactly lifting my spirits."

He dragged me under in lieu of response, and I wished I'd taken one more breath. One-armed, I swam along so as not to lose my grip on my ghostly guide. Every now and again, I'd tug him to the surface. He'd wait impatiently because I had the temerity to need air, before pulling me under again. And then we were across.

I crouched in the shallows, my gaze on the bank. I'd be fully exposed if I made a break for it. But I couldn't stay here forever. "How're we looking?" I whispered.

"Go," he said urgently.

I charged through the shallows until I hit the shore. I stumbled up on the bank, reeds and muck grabbing at my boots. Franklin floated ahead, nose lifted like he was scenting the air. Then he shouted, "Down!"

I didn't hesitate, flattening myself to the ground.

A bullet whizzed over my head so close that I heard the whine. Smelled the smoke. I kept my eyes on Franklin, hoping I looked just like one more log on the bank. When he nodded, I scrambled to my feet and darted for the trees. I ran on stiff and rapidly tiring legs, trying to keep him in sight.

"The shed," he said excitedly. "There's the shed."

The building in the distance was small, about the size of a one-car garage, and made of sheet metal. I never thought I'd be so glad to see a rustic shed that looked like a tetanus shot. I hurried up to the building and tugged at the door. The door didn't budge. I spotted the keypad entry just as I was about to give the door handle another yank.

Fuck.

"0842," Franklin said urgently. "Hurry."

I keyed in the code and gave a silent prayer of relief when the keypad turned green. I hustled in the building and slammed the door behind me. I stood there in the darkness for a few moments, my chest moving with my heaving breaths. I wasn't foolish enough to think I was safe, but I really, *really* liked the idea of being behind walls and a closed door.

"There's a hanging bulb over here," Franklin said from somewhere to my left.

I almost said I didn't think that was a good idea, and then I remembered the fucking collar. Right. She knew exactly where I was.

I reached up in the air, feeling around until my hand knocked into something solid. I grasped the bulb and felt my way up the fixture until I found the switch. When I turned it, the room lit up with low, lazy light. I turned and took a good look at my surroundings.

My mouth fell open.

The room was mostly wood, with shelves against the wall and a long table in the center. Sharp-edged tools hung from the ceiling—half of which seemed to be saws of some kind. My shocked gaze flitted between one with a circular wicked-looking blade and one that looked like a fucking cutlass. There were dark stains on the walls and floor, and it took me a minute to realize it was dried blood.

I stared at a few coagulated bits before I turned that shocked gaze on Franklin. "You brought me to her kill room?"

"No," he said defensively. "This is where she cuts up her victims. But everyone who comes through those doors is dead. Or mostly dead."

As I continued to gape, he huffed impatiently. "Fernando survived the hunt even though he'd taken a bullet to the head. Remarkable, really."

I closed my eyes briefly, just to reflect on the iffy business of asking a ghost for help. On the positive side, I had tools now, and one of them was going to get this fucking collar off my neck. Then all I had to do was take another jaunt through Evie's Forest of Horrors and head for the fence line.

I perused my options before I settled on a long bone saw with a thin blade. Without revisiting my fears that the collar had a failsafe that I wouldn't like, I slipped the tool between my neck and the collar, the steel of the blade cold against my skin. And I went to work.

Franklin watched quietly, his arms wrapped around his middle as if he was cold. "He's going crazy looking for you."

That went without saying. "I know."

"I tried showing him where you are, but that didn't go so well." He bit his lip. "He's not very...approachable."

I scowled. "What did you do? Did you fucking—"

"I didn't touch a hair on your precious Danny's head," he said with a huff. "I've just heard you two talking before, and it doesn't seem like he's very amenable to the ghost situation."

"Yes, but he's extremely amenable to keeping me alive," I said dryly. "So what did you do?"

"I blew a flyer about the Pemburton Foundation off his desk," he said proudly. His smile dimmed just a bit. "He just picked it up and put it back. The second time I blew it off, he paused and got really still. Then he crumpled it up and threw it in the trash."

I continued to hack away at my collar. I pulled it away from my neck slightly only to see it was actually fucking working. And as long as there wasn't a bomb in the clasp, I was getting this thing off.

There you go, I thought, giving myself a mental pat on the back. *Thinking positively, as usual.*

"So what did you do then?" I asked, realizing Franklin had left his story very much unfinished.

"Well...nothing. It looked like he was waiting for something. So I waited, too. We stared at that paper for a bit." He frowned. "And let me tell you, it was very boring."

I resisted smacking myself in the head. "He can't see you like I can," I said slowly. "He was waiting for you to do something else. So he could see if it was just a coincidence or supernatural."

"Oh." He looked a bit nonplussed. "Well, I just gave up and decided to try and help you myself."

Yet another update for the "Dear God, what did I do to deserve this" files. No help was coming.

Franklin disappeared, but I didn't have the spoons to wonder where he'd gone. Instead, I kept working on the collar and trying not to panic. The collar finally broke apart under the persistent saw of the blade, and I breathed a sigh of relief that I didn't explode like human confetti. I doubted Evie had ever let anyone get far enough to worry about collar removal. I threw it on the ground.

I jumped as Franklin reappeared, wringing his hands. "The drone is ready."

Well. At least I had the tracker off. So while an incoming drone wasn't exactly the best news I'd ever gotten, I didn't panic. I pocketed a few small weapons I might be able to use in a pinch, just in case. A switchblade and a couple screwdrivers made the list. If the drone found me, they'd be about as good as a paperweight. But at this point, I was just about out of ideas.

"Do you know the way to the fence?" I asked urgently.

Franklin nodded. "Let's go."

I followed Franklin's wispy form through the woods for what felt like hours. Really, it had probably only been ten minutes. But the effect of being in Evie's playground was starting to play tricks on my mind. At one point, we passed a man in torn and dirty clothing on his knees, moaning. He caught my gaze and I stumbled to a stop. Blood dripped down his forehead and into his gaping mouth. "Help me," he whispered.

I briefly started in his direction before I realized he wasn't real. A ghost of Evie's victims?

"Help me," he screamed as I charged past.

I chanced a glance backward and his head fell off.

Christ.

There was a faint buzzing noise, too, one that had been itching my ears for a bit. It seemed to grow louder the farther I ran. I was far too tired to track down the origin of the sound or wonder why it was...*following me.* I gasped as I remembered the fucking drone.

I looked about, searching for cover. Any cover. There was a dense thicket of bushes dead ahead, but the buzzing was getting louder and louder. And then I saw it hovering overhead, a dull gray specter of death. It flew in front of my face like it was checking me over.

Time's up.

I stumbled to a stop and looked up. The canopy had thinned in this part of the woods, and I could see the wide expanse of dark sky, sparkling with stars. I felt tired. Dirty. Scratched up and bruised. And thoroughly defeated. I imagined the fates of all those before me, realizing that this was it. This was the end of the road, and the consolation prize was a bullet to the head. The drone whizzed away, and I froze at the sound of laughter.

"You should be proud of yourself, Detective."

I didn't bother to look for the speaker. "Yeah? Why's that?" I asked tiredly.

"You made it farther than any of the other bucks."

The term just added more insult to injury. But that's how she saw her prey at this stage. No longer human. Just a target to hunt down and kill.

"That's fucking fantastic," I said tiredly. "And we're not fucking bucks, we're—" I had another surprise when I saw Evie emerge from the trees, rifle in hand. "People," I finished faintly.

I'd gotten so used to hearing her everywhere that it was a bit surreal to see her in person. She was dressed in dark camouflage, looking for all intents and purposes like she was a hunter who had just chased her prey to ground.

"You did well," she said firmly, ignoring my words. "But at the end of the day, it ends as it always does. With a whimper."

She didn't look as smug as I'd thought she would. Or angry. She looked...determined, almost. Like she was going to do what needed to be done, and that was that. Unfortunately, I knew what came next.

On your knees.

I'd seen this play out before, only I'd just been a spectator then. But this show? Yeah, this one was just for me.

"On your knees," she said firmly.

I shook my head slowly. "You know I can't do that."

"This isn't personal, Detective," she said quietly. "You weren't an abuser like the rest. But you tried to hurt the program, and Project Halo must be protected at all costs."

"Project Halo," I said with a tired laugh. "You can give it all the fancy names you like, but it's just fucking murder."

"For people who deserve it," she shouted. "They're fucking abusers who hide and cower behind the law. The court system is flawed, created by men to *protect* men. Do you know how many times we encouraged these women to file reports, only to have the fucking police tell them that there's nothing they can do?"

"And this is how you fix the system?" I sent her a look of disgust. "You're no better than the rest."

"I give them back their lives," she snapped. "They didn't have to go on the run and look over their shoulder for the rest of their lives. I gave them back their friends, their children, their finances. I let them go *home*. And just what the fuck do you do to help them, Detective?"

"Everything that's within my power. Every legal thing," I shot back, even as I mentally acknowledged that antagonizing someone holding a rifle trained on you wasn't the best idea.

"Like what?" She laughed an ugly laugh. "Give them a restraining order and pat them on the head? Maybe that piece of paper turns into a gun when their abuser finally shows up. That'll be a neat trick."

"And your way is better?" I demanded. "You make them willing accomplices to murder."

"*My way....*" She took a calming breath. "My way is the only way. The only way that actually saves anyone."

"We'll have to agree to disagree."

The drone was back and flying low. We both watched it as it lazily drifted between us. She gave me a cold smile, and I knew my original assessment was incorrect. She *was* smug and she was going to enjoy finishing her shitty little ritual.

"I'm done talking," she said imperiously. "Get on your fucking knees."

Not in this lifetime. "You're gonna shoot me? Fucking do it." When she continued to look at me, I growled. "Do it!"

"Maya, darling?" She turned and spoke to the drone. "Let's give him what he asked for."

A small hole opened at the bottom of the drone and my breath caught in my chest as gunfire exploded out of the machine. But...I didn't fall.

I opened one eye, unaware I'd even closed them. I felt my chest and my head, fully expecting to find a wound. And then I heard a choked cry. I turned just in time to see Evie drop to her knees, still clutching her rifle. Blood seeped from several wounds on her chest, and her shocked gaze met mine. Then her eyes rolled up in her head and she slumped over.

I stood there in the silence, staring at her body. I finally got it together enough to go over and kick the rifle away, but there was no point. She'd sustained devastating injuries. She was well and truly dead.

The speaker crackled. "Rain?"

I blinked, my eyes watering at the sound of that voice. That fucking voice that I thought I'd never hear again. I couldn't speak, not even to reassure him that I was okay.

"Rain, we're—how do you fucking work this thing?"

"You're pressing the wrong button." Kevin's voice was next, and I sank to my knees, right there in the dirt and leaves, almost weak with relief. "Isn't it enough that you already shot somebody? I thought you were going to command her to surrender."

"Well, that was certainly the plan, but this thing isn't very user-friendly," Danny said, clearly irritated. "It's been heavily modified. And I'm pretty sure that this one is output and *that* one is input."

Good Lord. I was just glad the drone hadn't been facing me while they tried to figure out which buttons to push. I held in a hysterical laugh. I'd earned one, a good one so long and deep that it hurt my belly. But if I started, I was probably never going to stop.

"You guys are both morons." Tabitha's voice was almost distorted with how close she was to the speaker. "You're broadcasting, but he can't answer back."

"Well, he can signal us or something if he's okay, can't he?" Nick this time. "Gimme that, I can do it. I've piloted planes before, you know."

"You fly toys with your nephew on the weekends," Tab said dryly. "That is, in no way, cause to wear aviators and a *Top Gun* replica jacket out to a bar, and hope women assume you're in the Navy."

As they argued, the drone buzzed closer, moving up and down my entire body. I gave it a wave and a thumbs-up. As it scanned me yet again, I glared. I was this close to giving it a grand slam hit into the stratosphere.

Whether they could hear me or not, I snapped. "Will you get that thing away from me? I just saw it execute someone. And apparently, that wasn't even the fucking plan."

"Well, I don't know what he said, but he looks pissed." Kevin sounded amused. "So, yeah. Guess he's alright."

"Which way?" I asked tiredly, hoping they could read my lips.

"Oh," Tab said. "How sad. The poor thing doesn't even know what day it is. You've been gone for two days," she said loudly.

"Not which day," I said exaggeratedly at the drone's camera. "Which. *Way?*"

"I think he wants to know which direction," Kevin said after a moment. "You're pretty far from the main building. About three miles out."

The sky finally made good on its promise of rain and droplets starting hitting my nose. It felt...good. Cleansing, almost. A lot of bad things had happened on this property. It could use all the purification it could get.

The soil is always talking.

"Three miles?" I asked the drone.

"Three miles," Kevin repeated. "Do you think you can follow the drone?"

"I can try." Despite my words, I made no effort to move, just standing in the rain, grateful to be alive.

"I think he said bitch, bye," Kevin said, sounding a little put out.

"You know what?" Danny said after a moment, sounding like he'd made a decision. "Just stay where you are. We're going to come get you with the ATVs."

"Sounds good," I said, as I lay flat on the ground. The rain came down stronger, soaking me. I took a cleansing breath, enjoying the fanciful notion of it washing away the evil and making things right. "Sounds really good to me."

30

It was a nice day for a Thanksgiving redo.

The scenery passed at alarming speed because my husband didn't know how to drive any other way. I reached for the *oh shit* bar as a Lincoln in front of us dared to use his brakes. Predictably, Danny cruised right around him and slotted right back into the lane a few cars ahead.

When we applied for replacement licenses in our new last names, I suggested he nix the name Daniel Christiansen McKenna and go by his real moniker, Sonic H. Edgehog. He did not find that amusing. At all. Just a month ago, we'd been forced to make a traffic stop and he had the temerity to demand, *"Do you know how fast you were going?"* I mean, the hubris of it all. As the indignant motorist fumbled for an answer, I covered up my guffaw with a cough.

I had to own some of it...a lot of it, really. I'd been determined to make things right after the...er, *incident*. Not that he'd guilt-tripped me or anything. But seeing his feigned nonchalance every time we passed one on the street was pitiful. So...I worked the hell out of my connections. Cashed in hard-earned favors. As a last resort, I begged Ronnie in asset forfeiture, and she'd been all too happy to assist. A few years ago, I'd helped her say goodbye to her grandfather, who'd she'd argued with the night before he passed.

In the meantime, Danny had gone through a variety of rides he'd been all too glad to return to the depot. On his most hated list went a Scion that he'd looked hilarious driving, and a Jeep that had been painted two different colors—one of which was rust. Oh, and a sleek black Benz that belonged to a disgraced real estate mogul who went by the name Big Tone. After a month of tooling around in Big Tone's Benz, Ronnie had finally come through.

She might've come through a little too much.

Riding with Danny was a harrowing experience *before* I'd presented him with the fob to a drug dealer's seized Hellcat. Now? Well, just update your will and buckle up. And pray—praying is good.

On the plus side, I'd gotten to see Danny speechless again. But for a good reason this time. He still insisted that the day we got married was the best day of his life, not "just got a Hellcat day." Let's just say I have my doubts.

"This traffic is ridiculous. Makes me glad I don't have to make the rounds all damn day to see everyone." Danny drummed his fingers on the steering wheel. "Can you believe they all agreed to get together in one place?"

"As someone who tried to coordinate the Secret Santa exchange last year?" I raised an eyebrow. "No, I cannot."

He chuckled. "I think you uttered the phrase *never again* about sixteen times."

"And I meant it," I reminded him in case he had any bright ideas about "delegating" that shit to me again.

We shouldn't have been shocked at how easily it all came together. Paula had wrangled the group with military precision, turning an amorphous idea into a plan with a date and a time and *rules*. Oh, the rules. There had been emails. Phone calls. Group texts. Assigned dishes. And while it was annoying, we'd needed her at the helm. We were a group of people who could spend all of lunch debating on where to get lunch.

For my part, I'd participated in the holiday hubbub as minimally as possible. I got away with it, too, mostly because everyone was still so glad I was...you know, alive and whatnot. I'd actually walked right past my mother's yoga group, mid-stretch on her deck, and no one tried to get me to join in.

When they called out greetings and inquired about my health, I smiled and said, "I'm doing well, thank you." As Mrs. Krantz perked up and patted the empty mat next to her, I added, "Not that well."

Then I added a limp to my step as I walked away. Just in case.

Paula had brought me so many baked goods that I'd started bringing them in to work. And yes, I generally believe that sharing baked goods is a sign of psychosis. But there are only so many mini muffins one can consume without letting out his pants. Not that I would know. Anyway.

I was getting perks at work, too, and I wasn't hating that shit at all. I had a feeling it was less because they cared that I'd made it out alive and more because I was integral in bringing down a murder ring. I didn't really need the details. All that mattered was my mail was being delivered on time and my forensic results were getting priority.

When I'd hacked Chevy's credentials yet again, she let me use the FBI database for twenty-six whole minutes. That was as good as a declaration of love from her. And Tate had only said she regretted ever laying eyes on me twice this week.

Had to be some sort of record.

I wasn't sure how long I could milk the "got kidnapped by a serial killer" angle, but I was going to ride that gravy train until the tracks ran out...and even then, I might try to push that bitch a few more miles in the dirt.

We were still dismantling the Hope House's murder ring and finding out how deep their roots stretched. The women we'd brought in with connections to Project Halo were a mixed bag. Some had been stalwart in their denial of any wrongdoing. Others had been trembling on the ledge and just needed a push. And one savvy woman, Farrah Bell, had immediately expressed interest in a deal. That was probably for the best, seeing how we'd recovered Gil's most treasured belonging—his grandfather's medal—from that hidden compartment in their former bedroom. It had been nestled in a box along with his wallet and passport, just like Quinn had said.

When I'd asked Farrah why she hadn't disposed of the items in all this time, she just looked a little sad. "It didn't seem right to get rid of him entirely."

But it felt right to turn him into fertilizer? I'd nearly bitten my cheek bloody to keep from responding.

I'd been worried about the ramifications of shutting down the Hope House, but the community had more than answered the call for help. Like-minded support groups and agencies in the area had provided housing and services to the women who'd been displaced yet again. It was much needed but seemed like a bandage to a big problem. And that's where Arianna Pemburton stepped in.

She'd been cleared of all wrong-doing and knowledge of what her pet project had really been up to. Horrified, she'd decided to take a more active role in a new initiative and funded turning her property into a new women's center. She was happy at her posh retirement community, so her family home might as well go to a good cause. Something Lissette would approve of.

The foundation was due to be fully operational any day now. Arianna had called me several times over the past months, and I'd had Macy field every call, certain that she had a few choice words for me destroying the Hope House. I'd been wrong. When she finally tracked me down, she'd thanked me for all I'd done. Then she invited me—begged me, really—to come to the grand opening of *Lissette's Legacy.*

I was relieved that she was filling a much-needed gap in support services, but I'd had to decline. I would never willingly set foot on that property again. I still had the occasional nightmare about playing Evie's sick *run for your life* game. After several weeks of insomnia, Danny had gently suggested that I see the departmental therapist. When I'd readily agreed, I'd nearly had to use smelling salts on him. The man's knees had actually buckled a bit.

Rude.

Danny gave up the battle of being polite and sailed around another driver. A few seconds later, I could feel his quizzical glance on my face. Probably because I didn't have anything to say about his replication of Frogger on an actual highway.

"Everything okay over there?" he finally asked.

"Yep. I can only assume that Tide is sponsoring you for this lap around the city."

"Haven't had an accident yet." His mouth quirked. "And those are bold words from someone who had to have my Charger towed back to the depot in two pieces."

"Tossing the bumper in the backseat before they put it on the lift does not qualify as *in two pieces*," I insisted.

"Test crash dummy says what?"

I laughed even as I hit his arm. "Shut up."

He sent me one of those special little smiles of his reserved just for me. "You're safe in my hands, Rainstorm. Always. Precious cargo doesn't even begin to cover it."

Urgh.

"I wish you'd leave my heart alone," I complained. "It's a freaking holiday, for fuck's sake."

He just smiled…right before braking so hard that I briefly gripped the *oh shit* bar, appropriately named for everything that came out of my mouth when I needed it. I heard something shift in the backseat and glanced back just in time to see my dessert slide forward. I gasped as I reached back and resettled it deeper into the seat.

I gave Danny a pointed look that just made him laugh. "Keep your pants on, Christiansen. I'll get you and your precious custard there safely."

Surely the romance was truly dead when your husband told you to keep your pants *on*. "We'll see about that," I said with a huff. "Also, no custard for you."

"And the day just gets better," he murmured.

Thanksgiving was supposed to be a time of sharing and togetherness. Friendship. Not for being a judgmental bastard with no taste in sides and no appreciation for the person who took the time and effort to put it together. Apparently, no one told that to Kevin, this year's candidate voted most likely to get pushed, face-first, into a dish of custard.

He gave my dish a little shake. "Isn't it supposed to have a little...give?"

"It's supposed to look like that," I said defensively. "I followed the recipe exactly."

"Hmm," he said.

"I saw some woman make it on Food Network," I added, hoping to bolster my dish's credibility as being edible. "Her family practically licked the bowl clean."

I got another skeptical *hmm* as he gave it another shake. I willed it to move—just a little jiggle would do. I even pushed the table unobtrusively with my hip. The surface of the custard remained placid and still as a lake on a windless summer day.

"I bet this would pass the Blizzard test at Dairy Queen," Kevin marveled. "You know, when they stick a spoon in it and turn it upside down?"

"Do it and you'll be wearing it," I informed him tartly. "Carole is the one who told me to bring a dessert. I brought a dessert."

His wife Carole had been the only hiccup regarding our group holiday. She and Paula had argued for days about who would do the honors and host the gathering. Why someone would fight over such a thing was beyond me, but I stayed out of it. So did everyone else.

In the end, they'd come to a compromise. Paula would host and handle the décor, but Carole would do the majority of the cooking. They'd both gone all out trying to outdo and in turn complement the other's efforts. The result? It looked like fall had thrown up all over the dining room—tastefully, of course—and the table was groaning with delicious smelling food in warming dishes that we weren't allowed to touch yet. Something about waiting until everyone was here and yadda yadda yadda. I'd posted up at the table anyway, hoping someone would say *fuck it, let's eat*. If they waited too long, that person might be me.

"Carole mixed up your email with Tab's. You were supposed to bring drinks. *Only*. Not this...whatever this is." Kevin shook his head. "Didn't you think it was odd that someone was asking you to bring food that actual humans had to consume? Between this and what Nick brought, I'm thinking about paying one of my kids to 'stumble' into the dessert table."

"Hey," I complained. "Nick's dish is *much* worse."

Nick had claimed his yams were going to taste like Boston Market goodness. I wasn't so sure about that. He'd run out of regular marshmallows halfway through and supplemented them with some he'd picked out of a box of cereal. Or at least, that's what he told me when I inquired why the yams were covered with hearts, stars, horseshoes, clovers, and blue moons.

"I dunno," Kevin said doubtfully. "Right now, it's starting to look like a two-way, 'Dear God what is that' tie."

I gave him a sweet smile. "You know, Carole is very passionate about food waste. Where do you think the leftovers are going to go?"

His eyes widened. "She wouldn't. Even she wouldn't bring home a custard you have to cut like lasagna."

"Wouldn't she?" I gave him a moment to remember our last cookout, when Carole had taken a container of my potato salad with potatoes that managed to be both slightly under and overcooked. "If I were you, I'd sell my custard to these good folks like it's the best thing you've ever tasted. If it helps, I brought raspberries to put on top."

His face took on a determined cast as he marched off, and I nodded in satisfaction. That really ought to do it.

Left alone for the first time since I'd walked through the door, I looked around, taking in the sounds of the holiday. I was pretty sure Paula's dining room—and home—had never been quite this lively. And *loud* with the sounds of friends and family. Most of the noise was due to Kevin and Carole's kids. All five of 'em. They were growing like weeds and making a mockery of the phrase, "use your inside voices." I wasn't too much for congregating in the name of holiday cheer, but this was...nice. Mostly because it had a definitive start and stop time. But nice, nonetheless.

My phone vibrated, and I didn't even pull it out of my pocket. I might not know *who* it was, but I damn sure knew *what* it was. At the moment, everyone I loved was pretty much under one roof—or close to it—so it had to be work. Probably Saunders. The topic? The two dead bodies I'd found entombed in the drywall of a frat house, Sigma *Ya'll Are in Deep Shit Now*, courtesy of a ghost named Brett.

Normally, I'd be chomping at the bit to see what Saunders had found. But today was not that day and right now was not the time. It was turkey time. *Godspeed to buttons and zippers* time. *Damn, I shouldn't have eaten all that but hey, is that pie* time.

My sister's serving platter landed in front of me with a thump. *Jesus.*

I recoiled as the brown turkey-shaped lump jiggled threateningly. It hadn't been that color when she'd come through the door. It had been white as can be, looking like the ghost of turkeys past. I'd tried to block her entry, but she stepped on my foot and muscled her way in, proclaiming that she needed a quiet place to baste it. When I guessed her basting recipe—equal parts liquid smoke, Worcestershire sauce, and despair—she stepped on my foot again.

"You'll eat it, and you'll like it," she said without looking my way as she arranged more parsley around the legs. They had white paper around the ends like weird-ass shoes. In my humble opinion, the dish didn't need parsley. It needed warning stickers labeled with skulls and crossbones.

"It's a holiday," I complained. "No one wants to die on a holiday. Save that shit for early Monday. Before work or during a meeting."

"I'm taking a double scoop of your custard," she said pointedly. "Even though it has the consistency of a brick. I support you as my brother...despite your culinary crimes."

Well, she had me there. "I was kidnapped by a serial killer," I reminded her, and not for the first time.

She hummed. "And that will be the highlight of your year if you don't partake in my turkey," she said sweetly.

"Fine," I groused. "I'll take a slice."

"You'll take a leg."

A whole leg? My stomach grumbled uneasily at the deal I was striking on its behalf. "When the time comes," I agreed swiftly. "Not a moment before."

She beamed and bustled off.

My phone buzzed again, and my fingers itched to check.

As only workaholics can, the PTU had made a pact that we wouldn't interrupt the holiday with work. Since we were all spending it together, it would be easy to keep each other honest. And in the spirit of honesty, we'd started breaking the pact almost before we made it.

Danny used the addendum, "as long as it's nothing that can't wait." And I'd said, "Or if my results come back early for the Olson case." By the time Nick added his caveat, Tab accused us all of having a problem. So we went back to not interrupting the holiday, no exceptions.

We'd see how long that pact held up.

Hour two and still no food.

I glanced up when someone plopped onto the chair to my right. Expecting to see Danny, I was surprised to find Dakota. One would think he'd shelve his usual uniform of khakis and t-shirts with science-related puns for a holiday. One would be wrong. Paula had looked him up and down and tutted more than once.

He'd brought a date, a quiet mountain of a man named Mitchell, and a rhubarb pie. I wasn't too sure about making a pie out of something that looked like red celery, but he swore it was delicious. Because Dakota excelled at just about everything he did, I was planning to try a slice. Or two. Just to be supportive.

He slouched in his chair, manspreading enough to bump my leg. "Granted, I haven't been to many of these things, but they do plan to feed us at some point, right?"

I huffed out a laugh. "I assume so, yes."

"Who're we still waiting for?"

"Danny. His mother sent him to pick up his Uncle Charlie from the retirement home."

Actually, what she'd said was, "I wonder if Uncle Charlie caught his shuttle on time," and Danny volunteered to go get him. Any excuse to drive the Hellcat was better than none, I supposed. Before I could suggest making a call to the retirement home, he was already in his car. My lips twitched just remembering how wide Paula's eyes had gotten when the souped-up engine roared to life.

"Gracious," she said, rushing over to smooth down a fluttering doily on the table.

"Gracious is one word for it," I agreed.

"I'm not sure I'm loving this Hellhound thing you got for him, dear," she said with a disapproving frown. "Maybe I can talk him into getting something a little more...sensible."

"Hellcat," I'd corrected, biting the inside of my cheek to keep from smiling. "And good luck with that."

Clearly of the same mind, Dakota snorted. "Sunnyvale is about a half-hour drive, so that should take him about six nanoseconds. Who else?"

"My parents. A couple cousins of Paula's." I ticked the errant members of our party off on my fingers. "Oh, and her lonely neighbor that she invited over and promptly sent to go get ice."

Dakota beamed. "Oh, I chatted with him before he left. It's so wonderful that Paula has found love, isn't it?"

"Shhh!" I waved at him as I looked around anxiously. "Danny doesn't know yet."

He gave me a doubtful look. "How can he not? It's pretty obvious."

Yeah, when it wasn't your mom, I'm sure it was. I'd feel bad, but she really should've expected this. Half her Thanksgiving guest list ferreted out secrets for a living. I winced at all the yelling in our future when Danny found out.

My phone vibrated again, and I could no longer resist the pull. I fished it out of my pocket and gave it a cursory glance. *Harper.*

I sucked in breath. I wasn't sure why our social worker would be calling on a holiday, but whatever it was, it was important enough that she'd called three times. Back-to-back.

It probably wasn't about paperwork.

I barely remembered to excuse myself from a curious Dakota. "I gotta take this. Sorry."

"No work!" he called after me.

As I crossed through the living room, headed for the back porch, there was a knock at the front door. I backtracked a few steps and opened it, fully expecting Danny and Uncle Charlie. Instead, I found my parents standing on the front stoop. I let them in on a gust of fresh air and happy hellos.

They'd dressed for the occasion—or at least their version of fancy. My father was wearing long pants and a shirt with palm trees on it, his long ponytail caught neatly at his nape in a rubber band. Things were getting wispier and wispier on top of his dome, but I knew better than to mention it. Or look at it. He had a dish in his hands and a jug of murky liquid under his arm. Probably an offering of kombucha tea, if I had to guess.

My mother was dressed in autumn colors, a version of her usual long skirt and peasant blouse, her long blond hair in a braid and intertwined with...I squinted. Leaves, maybe? Long, dangly earrings in the shape of cornucopias hung from her earlobes.

My mother hugged the stuffing out of me...as if she didn't live next door to me and hadn't popped by twice when we were getting dressed with Watson-related questions. He'd ridden over with them, and they'd dressed him in a shirt that declared him *Most Likely Not to Give a Pluck*. And here I thought I'd only have Danny to help me mess up our future children.

How shortsighted of me.

I stepped back to let them in. Watson greeted me like I hadn't seen him in fifteen years before dashing through the house with a loud bark that made Paula exclaim, "Gracious" yet again.

I had a feeling she'd be saying that a lot today with this crowd.

"How did we leave at the same time and arrive a half hour apart?"

I wanted to know as I closed the door behind them.

"We stop for traffic lights, kiddo," my father said with a grin. "Danny lost us at the first yellow."

I supposed it didn't help when we went supersonic on the highway. I bit my cheek not to agree, but only out of loyalty.

My mother kissed my cheek. "Does Paula need any help in the kitchen?"

"No, the theme this year is food with taste and flavor," I said, netting one smack to the back of the head. "*Ow.*"

She chuckled. "We brought a dessert, per Paula's email. Or your father did, rather."

"Er...what did he make?"

"It's just brownies," he said with an airy wave.

I sighed, pressing two fingers to the bridge of my nose. "The kind of brownies that we cover with a scoop of ice cream and a drizzle of fudge? Or the kind that will have us talking to a potted plant for an hour?"

He gave me a mutinous look. "Well, it's not like you have to do one or the other, you know—" He squawked as I snagged the tray out of his unsuspecting hands. He made a quick grab for it and, anticipating the move, I held it above my head. "Search and seizure. And my own son at that!"

"I can't think of anything less appropriate to serve to a room full of cops," I said. "What's your encore, a salad with ketamine croutons?"

"You're not going to put them in the trash, are you?" he asked anxiously. "I put toffee bits in there! It's my best batch yet."

"It's not so much the toffee I'm worried about as the pot," I said dryly. "I'll give these back when you leave."

"Where are you going?" My mother called after me as I headed for the back porch.

"I gotta make a call."

"You're not working, are you?"

"No," I said truthfully. "I have a feeling it's a little more important than that."

31

My seating arrangements were driving me to drink. I wasn't really a wine drinker, but the glass of merlot Carole had given me—guiltily, by the way, and for good reason—wasn't half bad. That's probably why I got up and got a refill. Then I got another because it was a holiday. And one last one because…well, hell, I was feeling far too mellow to come up with a good ruse.

By the time I wandered back in the house, everyone had migrated to the dining room. They'd proceeded to plop their fannies in all the main chairs around Paula's beautifully appointed Georgian table. That left me sitting in the auxiliary section at a table about a foot shorter. I was pretty sure it was the game-night table underneath that tablecloth embossed with smiling turkeys.

I sighed and took another sip of wine—a long one.

The fucking kids table. I was a grown-ass man in a fold-up chair with his knees crammed near his elbows. Even as I told myself to look at the bright side, Kassi, one of my nieces, spilled her drink on the tablecloth. The red liquid immediately surged across the table toward me like a cranberry juice tsunami. I frantically grabbed the edge of the tablecloth and blotted it, but not before some dripped on my pants.

Suddenly my wardrobe choice of a black cashmere sweater and black trousers seemed less uninspired and more like the move of a genius.

Kassi's eyes were wide as they met mine. "Oops."

I sighed as I blotted the rest with a stack of napkins. "Aren't you supposed to be one of the few people at this table that *doesn't* need a sippy cup?"

She sent me a sheepish grin. "I'll get some more napkins."

She bolted up from the table, sending it shaking and my hand shot out to steady Becca's paper cup before I got splashed again. I cast a glare at my fellow tablemates. They paid me no mind, occupied doing…whatever it is that kids do.

Tabitha's date, Neil, had brought his little girl, Becca, and she was busily playing a game on his phone. Kevin's five rugrats were in various stages of picking on one another, per usual. Well, four. His littlest was in a highchair next to Carole, screaming for no reason I could discern. As I watched, Kevin shook out a handful of Cheerios on her highchair table and she subsided immediately, plucking up an O with careful fingers.

Well. At least I knew what I was thankful for this year. Intact eardrums. And a special shoutout to Cheerios.

I listened with a half-smile as the kids all chattered away like the world would fall out of axis if they didn't. Well, all of them except Kari, my other niece. Apparently, she and Kassi had been told there was a chance they could sit with the adults.

When Sky checked in to see if they were okay, Kari gave her a resentful look. "You promised."

She didn't need to clarify further than that. Apparently, it had been a hot topic of debate since last Thanksgiving. Sky gave her daughter's bony little shoulder a squeeze. "Sorry darling, it's a space thing, not an age thing. Next year, ok?"

Kari huffed. "You said that about this year."

"And now I mean it even more."

My sister's tone was gentle, but there was a steely edge there. Clearly, I wasn't the only one who heard it because Kari subsided quickly. My sister might be a new age, gentle hippie, but she knew how to keep her kids in line. Mostly.

"One of your spawn spilled juice on me," I informed her.

"Rain. Good to see you're at the correct table this year." She tried to ruffle my hair as she passed, and I ducked away just in time. She stuck out her tongue and pointedly took a seat at the big-people table.

I huffed. I don't know what Kari was complaining about anyway. I was the only one at the table with freaking facial hair.

I watched Becca poke at her phone and make a sound of dismay as her game screen went to an ad. She held it up to me to "fix," in that instinctive way that kids do with the only adult nearby. I pressed "skip ad" and put it back in her grabby hands. Then I took another broody sip of wine—a long one—as I secretly plotted how to get a refill without seeming like *that relative* at the family gatherings.

"Okay, everyone, we'll be eating soon," Carole said as she bustled into the dining room carrying a huge basket. Among the plaid folds of the napkin nestled rolls that looked piping hot. "I just saw headlights in the driveway. That should be Danny and Uncle Charles, so we can get started."

I looked longingly at the adult table as the rolls landed in the center of the feast, a yeasty, piping hot guest of honor. Nick caught my eye and smirked. I promised retribution with my eyes. The where and when were still up for grabs, but I already had ideas. Before a plan could fully crystalize, a shadow appeared over my shoulder.

I looked up to find Danny standing there, cheeks pink from rushing, a perplexed look on his face. He looked all kinds of handsome in dark trousers and a dark-blue button-down shirt that matched his eyes perfectly. I'd suggested he pair it with a black vest I'd bought for him a couple months prior, and he just shrugged and put it on. He never fought me much on clothes I swore he'd look delicious in. Maybe that was because I was always so eager to peel him out of them. It was win-win, really.

I beamed as I patted the folding chair next to me because apparently misery *does* love company. "Saved you a seat."

He shook his head wryly as he sank down next to me. He was even more crammed than I was, his knees damn near level with the tabletop. "I'm not even asking how this happened."

I leaned over and dropped a kiss on his mouth. "Hi."

"Hi." His eyes crinkled with amusement. "Have you been drinking?"

"It's a holiday, 5-0," I said breezily. "So feel free to hop off my back."

He chuckled. "I don't know how it's possible to be both a happy and hostile drunk, but I swear to God you always manage it."

I grinned. "I missed you."

"I've only been gone forty-five minutes."

"I missed you," I said again, because that had nothing to do with what I'd just said.

He didn't say anything, but his cheeks got a little dusky. I felt his hand squeeze my knee a moment later. I let out a soft laugh because it was cute when I embarrassed him with how very much I loved him. I did it often—not for that reason, but damned if I wasn't enough of a shit to find it a perk.

Carole clapped her hands. "Maybe we should go around the room and say what we're all thankful for."

And maybe I'd buy her book, *How to Become the Least Liked Person In The Room In One Easy Step*. Kevin spoke loudly over all the groans and boos. "What a great idea, honey."

Clearly, someone was starting his campaign for holiday sex a touch early.

"Kiss-ass," I whispered as little Maggie threw her plastic keys on the floor. I reached over and tweaked one of her blond curls and she giggled at me.

Danny smothered a laugh as he leaned over and picked up the keys. He dropped them back in her pudgy little hands. "Language. Also, I think it's too early to disparage her father to her face."

"Well, let me know when," I said. "I have plenty to say. I'm compiling an Excel doc, so I won't forget a fuc—"

"Rain," he said quickly.

"Freaking thing," I declared.

"I'll go first," Paula said with a smile. She was elegant/casual in a soft taupe sweater, white, slim-fit pants, and ballet flats. She'd pinned a gold turkey to her lapel to match her gold, understated studs, and all of it glinted under the chandelier. "I'm so grateful to have a house full of love and laughter and friends and family alike this year. My—our—family has expanded so much and I'm so very grateful."

"Hear, hear, Paula," Carole said with a smile.

Paula turned to her neighbor, the handsome Mr. Reed, and patted his hand. "What about you, William?"

"I'm grateful that I get to spend this holiday with friends." He smiled and blushed a little. "Both old and new."

They shared a look that was a little too long. As if she remembered herself, Paula looked away and smoothed a hand over her hair. I sank down in my chair and looked anywhere but at Danny. Out of the corner of my eye, I saw his eyebrow quirk. Like he was trying to puzzle something out.

By the time he turned my way, I was already nose deep in my glass of wine. "You don't think—"

"I don't think on holidays," I informed him.

"And that's different from other days how, exactly?"

He reached for my wine glass, and I moved it away, sloshing just a bit on the tablecloth. *Oops.* "Who's next?" I asked a touch too loudly. "Nick?"

"Well, since you so graciously shouted...." He pretended to think. "Firstly and most importantly, I'm thankful everyone at my table is over twelve. And that, if necessary, I could currently pass a sobriety test."

At the snickers, I was tempted to throw a roll. Luckily for everyone, my buzz was making me nice and mellow. My table was awesome, and Nick was just jealous. I took another long sip of wine. I should've started imbibing the moment I stepped foot over the threshold. The hell had I been thinking, trying to get through a holiday stone-cold sober?

"Let's have a real one, if you please," Carole insisted even as her eyes danced. "Go again, Nick."

"Fine, fine. I'm grateful for my family. My girl. And of course, I'm grateful for these guys. My team." He looked a little pink and annoyed as we continued to look his way. "What do you want, blood? That's it."

Danny grinned. "You're sure? You don't want us to hug it out, or—"

"Shut it, McKenna." Nick laughed. "Just giving credit where credit is—"

"Due," I sang as I hit the table and made a game-show noise. "Next!"

Danny smothered a grin as he discreetly took my wine glass and replaced it with his water glass. I tried to take it back and he polished it off, giving me a cheeky smile. Bastard. "Clearly, I'm driving us home."

"Or I could just strap a jetpack to my balls and get there five minutes after you."

"Whatever you prefer," he said kindly, and yelped when I pinched his thigh.

Kevin was up next and said some appropriately sappy stuff about his wife, which she returned. The thankful procession continued around the table. Health and friendship came up a lot. So did "having another blessed year" and hopes for another.

Despite my normal state of pessimism—it is what it is—I couldn't help but get caught up in the good vibes. Doing what we did, I couldn't help but reflect on the fact that a lot of people hadn't made it this year. A lot of people hadn't made it to celebrating another year with the people they loved, sometimes through no fault of their own. I had almost been one of them.

People like Ryan deserved more time. Not a day went by that I didn't think about her or the time we'd spent together. Or her sister Regan, who'd barely had a chance at life. And Zach? That was a tough one. I knew I shouldn't care…if not for what he'd done to me, then for what he'd done to other people over the years. I hadn't known him long and I'd been jealous of him most of that time. But I was only human.

His death had hit Danny hard. We didn't talk about it much, and that was okay. Especially since I knew he'd quietly utilized the departmental therapist himself. He didn't have to talk about it with me, so long as he talked about it with *someone*.

Before long, the thankful conga line was at our table. The kids were thankful for things in the moment, as children usually were.

I'm grateful I got to wear my favorite skirt!

I'm grateful Momma made apple pie. Can we have some now, please?

I'm grateful for my best friend Penny. She shares her lunch with me, and she always brings Oreos.

I listened to them with my chin propped on my hand and a crooked smile on my face. And Danny?

"You're not weaseling out of it," Kevin said before he could even open his mouth to say *pass*. He'd gotten away with a pass last year, and apparently, that boon would not be repeated. "What're you thankful for, McKenna?"

Danny's mouth quirked as he sighed. Those blue eyes landed on me, both resigned and fond. Yeah, public declarations weren't really his thing. "I'm looking at him."

But he was so damn good at 'em.

I didn't even need to verify my blush, which only intensified when I said quietly, "Ditto."

I expected the sigh of happiness from Paula and my mother. And the indulgent smile from my father. The boos and teasing from our team, yeah, that was expected, too. It didn't last long. Everyone was pretty ravenous. We were done with the thanks part of the evening and ready for the "loosen the top button on these restrictive pants" part of the evening.

"Let's eat!" Kevin said, clapping his hands.

"Yesss," I said with a groan as my stomach contracted. "I'm starving. Bring on the fuc—"

"Rain," Danny said quickly, reminding me that no one at our table was tall enough to ride a roller coaster.

"Er, frickin' turkey."

I spent much of the next hour supervising a table of seven and making sure more food got in their mouths than on the floor. I wasn't sure we were entirely successful with that. I did, however, ace stuffing my face with reckless abandon. There was dessert and after-dinner coffee and another round of dessert. But eventually, things wound down and we were the only ones left in the house besides Uncle Charlie and Paula.

Danny insisted his mom sit and visit with her brother while we took care of the cleanup. Begrudgingly, she agreed. I got the feeling she couldn't wait until her house was empty so she could re-clean everything we were cleaning.

I was glad when the door finally swung shut so I could stop pretending to be an affable son-in-law who cheerfully volunteered—*volunteered*—to clean.

"Haven't these people ever heard of aluminum foil pans?" I grumbled as I attacked a roasting pan with vigor.

"You had a good time," Danny said, bumping my hip, presenting facts not in evidence. "And if not, you certainly ate enough for five people."

"Shut it."

He grinned. "My point—"

"And there needs to be one—"

"Is that you enjoyed the fruits of their labor. It won't kill you to bust some suds."

"We don't *know* that." I briefly wondered if I could get away with tossing the hardest pans in the man-made water feature behind the house. I'd be long gone when her blue Lapiz set finally emerged from the deep. "Maybe we could—"

"We're not throwing her heirloom dishes in the lake," he said without missing a beat as he rinsed off a platter.

Damn. The man really did know me too well.

I smiled as I came upon a familiar dish and squirted dish liquid into it. "Look at this bowl. Not a bit of food left," I crowed. "Did you see how many people ate my custard?"

"Mostly out of support," he agreed. "But yes, I did."

I shrugged. All I knew was I was taking home an empty serving dish.

The quiet was companionable as we washed dishes, working in harmony from years of practice. It had already been a great day, but I was holding on to information that I was pretty sure would make it a *tad* bit better. I just...wasn't sure how to say the words.

I mulled over that for a few more dishes before I finally gave up on clever and meaningful and just said it outright. "I got a call from Harper earlier," I blurted.

That certainly got his full attention. He stood stock still for a moment, and we had a wordless conversation with our eyes. A slow grin came over his face. "Yeah?"

"Yup," I confirmed.

He eased the roasting pan from my hands and let it drop in the soapy water. I didn't get a chance to dry my dripping hands before he turned me around in his arms. And suddenly we were sharing the same air. Just a moment before our mouths connected, he paused. "And she's absolutely sure?"

"A hundred percent," I reassured him.

His lips met mine in a kiss that went on and on...and on.

Best holiday ever.

EPILOGUE

I played with my straw with nervous fingers.

My stomach was confused. Usually going to McDonald's was a delight and no, I didn't care that I was supposed to turn my nose up at such food. It wasn't an everyday kind of thing, but there were times when only a Big Mac and some of those salty sticks of goodness they called fries would do. But I couldn't eat right now if someone paid me.

I looked across the table, only to find Danny actually enjoying his milkshake. Like he wasn't nervous at all. The man had a cast iron stomach, so I guess that didn't mean much. He could go straight from a bloody crime scene to Denny's for a late night/early morning pancake breakfast. So maybe the nerves were mine alone, and maybe they weren't.

Last Halloween had been a misery with the bags of body parts landing in my lap. But this one might be even scarier. Now that I'd gotten over my hesitation, I was all in as only Rain Christiansen can be. It was pretty much all I wanted. And of course—also in vintage Rain Christiansen fashion—I'd realized there was another side to that coin. What if she didn't like us? What if she didn't want to join our family at all?

"Are you okay?"

God, what was I even thinking! I didn't know anything about raising a kid—a girl, no less. And she was six. Six! Six-year-olds were definitely weird. Now that I really thought about it, so were seven-year-olds. And eight-year-olds. Thinking back on that phase when my nieces would only eat orange things, I amended that rule to include age nine as well. I squinted as I remembered last Saturday, when Kevin and Carole had strongarmed us into babysitting their brood. They were lobbying hard for a dog as a group—their parents didn't stand a chance—and had been pulling around a stuffed dog on a leash all night.

"Biscuit, would you like another cookie?" Katie cooed as she gently offered the stuffed animal a bite. Biscuit's glassy eyes seemed to bore holes in me as I stared at the crumbled bits of cookie that fell to the floor. "Good dog!"

Okay, I could officially conclude that kids from the ages of six to twelve were also weird. Who knew beyond that, but the data I had access to wasn't looking good.

"Baby." I blinked to find Danny looking at me, his brow creased in concern. He reached over and squeezed my hand. "It's going to be okay."

"I might be a touch nervous."

"Really? I couldn't tell," he said dryly, glancing at the shredded snowdrift of paper napkins I'd made. And a couple paper straws I'd folded into nifty little accordions.

I blew out a breath. "How did I go from not wanting this to wanting it more than anything?"

He sent me a fond look. "I'd say that's more than a step in the right direction. You know, actually *wanting* the kid we're adopting?" At the narrow-eyed look I gave him, he stifled a laugh. "This is just the first visit. Relax, Moonbeam."

"Our kid needs to know my name is *not* Moonbeam," I fussed.

It might be our first visit, but we'd already observed her at a distance. We'd visited the group home and watched her do her thing in a natural setting. She'd been free to approach us—or any of the other three adults present—but she hadn't taken the opportunity.

"Not unusual," Harper told us. "Some of the kids are shy. Some of them are a little angry with the whole process...like they're puppies up for adoption."

"We understand," Danny said softly. "Let's not force anything."

So we'd watched her play. She wasn't all that social with the other kids, but that didn't mean much. She'd been uprooted from a bad environment only a year prior, voluntarily turned over to the State from her drug-addicted mother. Her father had landed in prison for the third time and considering he'd added an attempted murder charge to his rap sheet for trying to strangle his cellmate, it looked like this time was going to stick. If her history mirrored Danny's any more than it did, they'd be fucking twins. It was part of the reason Harper thought of us in the first place.

"It was strange," she said. "I was just going through my files and yours blew off the file cabinet and landed on my desk. I put it back and it blew right back off again!"

Quinn. *I held in an exasperated sigh as I tried to look trustworthy.* "Well, whatever the reason, we're glad you called."

Our second visit was much like the first. She hadn't approached but we'd watched her play make-believe with another little girl. I wasn't sure what the rules of the game had been, but it seemed to involve a lot of twirling and being loud for no reason at all. Nova didn't smile a lot, but when she did, it transformed her entire persona from serious little person to happy kid.

I was stunned to realize I wanted a part in bringing out that smile as much as possible.

Our third visit, the die was pretty much cast. I started to get to know little things about her—obsessed about them, really. She liked the outdoors and climbing on things. And animals! Pandas were her favorite. The swings were her favorite, too. And according to the house mother, we were going to have a devil of a time getting her to eat anything other than chicken nuggets.

Danny noticed that she talked to herself quite a bit, and Harper hurriedly assured us that she was just "imaginative and creative." As if even the hint of something unusual would send us running for the hills. Frankly, if talking to yourself was a crime, I would've been locked up for life a long time ago.

As things got less abstract and more concrete, we talked terms. Nova's mother wanted an open adoption. She was in no position mentally to raise a child—she was the first person to admit that. But she loved Nova and claimed she was the purest, most wonderful thing she'd ever been part of creating. When we talked to her, I'd felt her sincerity, but I still hadn't been sure about that "open adoption" business.

Danny had been completely on board. "You need to know where you come from," he told me. "And that won't make her any less ours."

Well, I supposed he would know.

I *already* thought of her as ours. And I wasn't the only one. When I went in the spare room to find our errant Roomba, I found it had trapped itself between three paint cans and a bag of painting supplies. Two of the smaller cans of paint were black and white. I wasted no time informing Danny that he was many things, but artistic was not one of them. He only smiled and told me that he was sure my mother could knock out a few pandas on the wall.

"You know...the artist?" he added with a brow that was arched at the *no-duh* level.

Smug bastard.

"That would probably be the way to go," I agreed with a sniff.

And look at us now. We had a room decorated like a jungle and two happy panda families on our bloody walls. Paula had shown up with furniture—not baby furniture this time, but the right size. She briefly lamented that we weren't going the pink and frilly route. Then she shooed us out and made the room into a masterpiece with her decorating touch.

Just more proof that Nova was *ours*.

So what if it didn't go well?

I was tired of thinking this shit all by myself while that well-adjusted bastard enjoyed a McFlurry. So I took a page from his book—the one he'd been trying to hit me over the head with our entire marriage—and shared my fears. I might've talked so fast that his eyes widened comically.

After he tried to interrupt my word diarrhea twice and failed, he stuck a spoonful of ice cream in my busy mouth. Like I was an animal, and it was a tranquilizer dart.

I enjoyed the creamy goodness for a moment, highly insulted but thoroughly satisfied. He waited, hand poised above his cup. Like a veterinarian trying to see if the first dose was enough.

It wasn't.

"Another," I said when I finally swallowed.

"I thought that might work," he said as he complied with a grin.

The way I was feeling, he was going to need to back up the car and let them fill the trunk with soft serve. "What if we lose her?" I demanded.

His jaw tightened. "Then it wasn't meant to be."

"You make it sound so easy."

"It's not, but we have each other. We already have the life I want, Rainstorm." He gave me a smile that was just a bit embarrassed. "This is just the icing on the cake."

Yeah. I couldn't agree more. I blew out a breath. "I fucking love you, you know?"

"I love you, too." He looked amused. "But you're going to have to clean up that potty mouth, sweetheart."

We both knew that was bloody well impossible. I glared across the table at my troublemaking husband. Fuck, I missed being the guy who was on the fence about little people. "You did this to me," I accused.

His eyes danced. "Aren't you supposed to be pregnant when you say some shit like that?"

I threw one of my accordion straws at his laughing face. And of course, that's the moment when a shadow darkened our table. I glanced up and did a double take to see Harper looking at us.

She wasn't alone.

"Rain? Danny?" Harper gave us a soft smile. She tried to usher her charge forward, but she refused to budge. "I'd like you to meet someone."

There was a moment when I swore my heart stopped. And then it started beating again. Because there she was, standing next to our table in jean shorts and a pink shirt with scribble hearts printed on it. She was shorter up close. Smaller, too. But the long, dark curly hair was the same. And those big cornflower blue eyes were trained on my face.

She was holding on to Harper's hand for dear life but still managed a whispered, "Hi."

There was a whole host of things I could've told her right then. Promises that she'd probably heard before from the two families before us. They hadn't worked out. For reasons. I could tell her that those reasons wouldn't apply with us, and we'd never send her back. Not ever. I could tell her that I already knew this was right and in time, I hope she would, too. And that Danny was going to be the best dad she could ask for. I already knew that like I knew my own name—even if he appeared to be stunned into silence. Guess the shoe was now on the other anxious foot.

I could tell her...well, a lot more than that.

My parents are going to love the bones off you. And sorry, but my nieces have already claimed you as theirs. They have grand plans to do very girly things with you, and I'm sorry in advance if you don't like nail polish. I didn't have the heart to tell them that you don't seem interested in those things. Besides, I wanted to leave room for you to change your mind. But they're really cool kids and they'll probably enjoy your favorite outdoor activity...which seems to be digging in the mud and pretending you're a panda.

Not that I'm judging you or anything.

Anyway. There's also a whole team of cops already arguing about who's going to babysit you first. And don't worry, we're not leaving you with Uncle Nick. He's clutch in a bad situation, but I don't think you're ready to stay with someone who thinks action movies are educational and buffalo wings are a food group. Your Uncle Kevin, though, he can't wait for you to play with his kids. And he's already pouting about not being named godparent yet. He's getting the job but we like making him sweat. There's also this woman named Paula, and dear God...she's going to spoil you rotten. We told her that we were meeting you today, and if you listen closely, you can hear her squeals of delight even though she's clear across town.

But there would be time for all that. In the end, I said the only thing that needed to be said.

"Hi."

She peeped up at me from behind Harper's arm.

And smiled.

In hindsight, I really should've expected Quinn to stop by and admire her handiwork.

We'd taken Nova to the park across the street after lunch, and she'd finally gotten comfortable enough to have a little fun. Slightly beyond the swings, I stood shoulder to shoulder with Quinn, hands tucked in my pockets. I watched as Danny pushed her on the swings, a slight smile on my lips. She was laughing like I'd never heard her laugh before, and her main wish seemed to be *higher. Higher, higher, higher!* Danny's face was flushed with exertion and happiness as he complied.

I chuckled. "He's already so much better at this than I am."

On the last swing, he came near the front to watch, letting the swing come naturally to a stop. Or at least, that was the plan. Instead, Nova leaped off into his arms, giggling like mad. Even though he was startled, Danny caught her with ease. We exchanged a wide-eyed look and then a bemused laugh. Yep. Pure trouble.

She already knew he wouldn't let her fall.

I knew the feeling. I loved my family to bits and pieces, but I was pretty sure I'd never felt safety—the absolute certainty that someone had me no matter what—until I met Danny. He was my person. As simple as that. It made it a little easier to share him with someone else.

Quinn smiled. "She's going to need you more."

I snorted. "And how exactly do you know that?"

"You'll just have to trust me on that."

They made their way over to me, Nova practically skipping to keep up with Danny's longer stride. She kept looking up at him shyly, like she wanted to believe he was hers. She'd been disappointed enough over the years to not quite go that far. Not yet. I watched their approach, marveling at how much they looked alike. How they looked like they belonged together already. My heart, quite simply put, was full.

Quinn sneezed.

"God bless you," Nova said without looking her way.

Quinn smiled. "Thank you, dear."

"Welcome!" She skipped over to me, exchanging Danny's hand for mine. "I think I'm hungry."

I was pretty sure my eyes had never been wider as I looked between Nova and Quinn. Nova and Quinn. And then Quinn again. She sent me a little mischievous wink. "*Now* we're even."

"But you," I spluttered. "She...I can't possibly—"

"You're welcome," she said proudly. "When Regan told me about the new star, I just *knew* she was the one for you two. Like kismet, you know? All those other families sent her back because they thought she was too troubled, talking to herself and pretending she could see things that weren't there. But we know better, don't we?"

I couldn't have looked more shocked if she'd handed me a live grenade and offhandedly asked me to find the pulled pin. I sucked in a breath as she disappeared, probably for good. "Oh boy."

When I glanced over at Danny, his eyes were closed, and he was pinching the bridge of his nose. "Tell me I'm wrong," he said without bothering to open them.

"She may look like you, but it seems as though she takes after me," I said weakly. His muttered response made me tsk as I ushered Nova back across the street to the restaurant. "Now, now. That's a lot of money you owe the swear jar."

The time had passed quickly. Too quickly. Before I knew it, it was time to say goodbye. I watched Harper drive away with Nova in the backseat. She turned around a few times, trying to catch a glimpse of us, and we waved each time.

I didn't know how we'd ended up here. What our future would look like. Or how I, a person who struggled with change, would deal with so much of it so quickly. But I knew she was ours, deep down inside, where muscle met bone. The rest would fall into place. This was happening and it was happening now.

We had a little girl, and her name was Nova Christiansen McKenna.

I celebrated that knowledge as only Rainstorm Christiansen McKenna could. "Crap," I muttered. "Crappity crap crap."

Danny sent me an arch look. "You want to borrow some vowels and consonants for that, Rainstorm?"

I sure as hell did. "The last person I fell in love with this quickly was you," I accused. "And look how that turned out."

"Yes. Look how that turned out," he said, his eyes filled with a mix of fondness and exasperation.

I blew out a breath. "I'm going to mess up."

He nodded. "Yeah, so am I. Most people do in one way or another."

"That's not comforting."

"It wasn't meant to be." He gave me a crooked smile. "Hey, we can't do any worse than my parents. Look at what they did, and I think I came out okay."

I squeezed his hand. "I'd say you came out a little more than okay, Irish."

"We're going to stumble and fall. But maybe that's okay as long as we take turns catching one another."

"Always." I peered up at him a bit mischievously. "And you're sure that you're ready for life to get a little spookier?"

He grinned and dropped a kiss on my lips before parroting back my words. "Always."

AFTERWORD

Book 5? Already? How's that possible?

I'm still wondering how a standalone turned into my favorite series to write. The story it was going to be feels nothing like the story it turned out to be, and I'm so glad. And, er, you should be glad, too. Rain was going to be a mage and he had powers. Stop looking at me like that. Just know that deep down in my dead files, there's a first draft of book one where fire comes out of his fingertips…which is what happens when you watch one too many episodes of Avatar, the Last Airbender.

But I digress.

I hope you enjoyed hanging out with Rain and Danny for a little while. I certainly did…well, I always do. But there's more to the longevity of a series than loving your own characters. I couldn't have continued to write their adventures if you hadn't been willing to come on the ride. So for everyone who boarded that spooky bus again and again, thank you. Some of you were rowdy, some of you were quiet, some of you demanded I stop the bus or you'd call the police...something about kidnapping or whatever. Anyhoo, it means more than you know.

If you're interested in reading more by me, make sure you follow me on Amazon, or Bookbub, so you'll be notified of new releases. You can also join my reader group on Facebook, Harmon's Hideaway. It's a great place to get news, ask questions, and participate in giveaways. You can also sign up for my newsletter here to know what's next in my fictional world.

See you next time.

S.E. Harmon

ACKNOWLEDGMENTS

As always, thank you to everyone who was instrumental in making this book happen. That includes Leslie Copeland, my beta reader. She's a brave canary in the coal mine, and I thank her for it. I can't forget about Valerie, my alpha reader. Thank you for always finding those pesky errors that are dying to be in my final copy. Thank you to Dianne Thies, my editor, for doing that thing she does oh so well. Any errors that remain in the text are mine.

Most of all, I'd like to extend a special thank you to all the readers who took Rain and Danny into their hearts. This one is for you.

ABOUT THE AUTHOR

S.E. Harmon has had a lifelong love affair with writing. It's been both wonderful and rocky (they've divorced several times), but they always manage to come back together. She's a native Floridian with a Bachelor of Arts and a Masters in Fine Arts, and now splits her days between voraciously reading romance novels and squirreling away someplace to write them. Her current beta reader is a nosy American Eskimo who begrudgingly accepts payment in the form of dog biscuits.

Website: https://seharmon.weebly.com/

Email: silkguitar2011@comcast.net

ALSO BY S.E. HARMON

Stay With Me

So Into You

The Blueprint

A Deeper Blue

Blitzed

P.S. I Spook You

Principles of Spookology

Spooky Business

The Spooky Life

Coddiwomple

Chrysalis

Cross

Love Is

Addicted to Ellis D.

The First and Last Adventure of Kit Sawyer

Printed in Great Britain
by Amazon